I.D. RUSSELL

Political Suicide: River City Hell
Book 3

For Jeremy Dangerfield

Prologue

"Her?" The frozen and zoomed-in image on screen showed a young woman standing in the late Arthur Fritz's boardroom deep below the MTS Centre in River City Manitoba. "Can she be older than twenty?" Approximately five foot four, somewhere in the neighbourhood of a hundred and thirty pounds, dark hair and pale skin with a prominent mole above her eyebrow. Dressed in black, she looked nothing like the level of threat she'd proven to be. "She looks so—"

"Exactly," the voice on the other end of the phone said. "She *looks* like just any other girl. And yet she's been responsible for considerable damage to the authority's operations, the deaths of both Simon Karlsson and Arthur Fritz, two facility relocations, and the temporary release of multiple converted subjects on the River City Jets and beyond."

"And with her?"

He scrolled the frozen image to see her companions: one, a stocky, bearded man in flannel holding a hockey stick, the other, a longhaired man, muscled and tall, with the kind of face that looked like it belonged on posters.

"Igor Illyanovich and Rick Hansen, two members of the Jets she managed to get to before Fritz could."

"So the three of them are top priority?"

"Even more important than that."

"What's higher than the top?"

The voice on the other end of the line betrayed nothing. "Observe." The image played again and another woman entered the boardroom. Wearing a leather jacket, with dark hair pulled back in a ponytail, he watched her talking to the trio until she turned around and the image froze on her face.

"That's—"

"Detective Tockett of the RCPD. The fourth member of the group."

"Walking free?"

"A problem, for what should be obvious reasons."

"Is the force under authority control?"

"Some."

"And I have the freedom to—"

"Do whatever is necessary to make sure none of them can expose our true goal."

"Conversion?" he asked.

"Preferred. But for these cases, total elimination will be accepted."

He watched the security camera footage play out, the conversation muted between the four who were now of the utmost interest to him. The cop would be the hardest, she looked like she could handle herself.

"The released members of the Jets will be tricky if they're already suspicious."

"You are now the top-ranking member of the authority placed in River City. You have full access to whatever you need, and all the technological progress made by your predecessors. There can be no mistakes or failures, only the will of the authority."

"Understood," he said.

"Until the day of the ultimate reveal," the voice answered.

"Until the day of the ultimate reveal," he repeated.

He watched the image in silence a moment longer, committing the faces of his enemies to memory, considering the best ways to dispatch each one. So many possibilities.

"And Kirby." The voice jerked him out of his daydream, reminding him that he'd not hung up yet.

"Yes, sir?"

"There's no telling who they've told. Widen the net as you see fit. Time is of the essence. There can be no more setbacks."

"I will not fail the authority."

Dan Kirby hung up the private line and slid off his chair to his feet. He grabbed his sport coat from the rack near his office door and put it on. He checked himself in the full-length mirror hanging on the wall and flashed his best camera-ready smile.

"They won't know what hit them," he said as he buttoned his coat.

His focus turned to the door as he heard a sharp knock. He pulled it open to see his secretary, the dark-haired Miss Smythe holding an iPad. She looked impatiently at the time on her watch.

"I'm coming," he said.

"Here are your speaking notes, sir." She handed him a stack of paper lined with bullet points. "You're scheduled to talk for twenty minutes."

"Then we shouldn't let the public wait any longer," he said as she handed him his jacket and gloves.

3

Chapter 1

"Picture this, Jake 'the Snake' Roberts sitting in a seedy bar, full of *Mad Max* rejects all shouting 'Spin the Wheel, Make the Deal!' Then Sting walks in, in full make-up, mind you, with his pink and black jacket and tights and they both start going off on each other, but the whole thing is edited so weirdly that it's hard to tell if they were even in the same room at the same time. And oh God, don't get me started about the one-eyed dwarf. For some reason WCW was obsessed with having these mini-movies with dwarves and—"

"Mini-movies in wrestling?" Erin asked, cutting off Marlon mid-story.

"Oh yeah. There was the White Castle of Fear, the Dungeon of Doom, the—"

"And this was from when?" Avital asked.

"Early nineties," Marlon replied.

"And you were watching it why?"

"Because it's so terrible… but also awesome!" He grinned and raised his fist up in the air. "Spin the wheel, make the deal, spin the wheel, make the deal!"

Sam looked to Erin, sitting beside her on the candy-striped futon in the basement of River City University. She just shook her head and squeezed Sam's hand.

"Dude," Everett said, "you really need a girlfriend."

Marlon shot Everett a hurt look. They were old friends, but Everett with the million-dollar smile and carefully coiffed blond hair was definitely the more socially adept. While Marlon, overweight and obsessed with the intricacies of pro-wrestling and video games, sat uncomfortably, Everett lay on the futon at total ease like he always did. He treated every seat like it was the most comfortable one in the world. The guy was a total player, slept with anything that moved. The amount of women Sam had seen him one night stand in the two short years she'd known him was staggering. He shot her and Erin a wink, noticing their hand holding, or maybe just proud that he'd scored one on Marlon and further interrupted his story.

"I'll have you know that I've been chatting with someone in a pro-wrestling forum who insists she's a real human female who loves wrestling. We've been talking about making plans to go to a show. As soon as PCW re-opens. Which rumour has it will be soon."

"Wait." Avital sat upright on the other couch. "An actual real human female who likes pro-wrestling? Marlon, are you sure you're not being catfished?"

"Is it so hard to believe that a woman could like wrestling?"

"Yes!"

"In the old days, just as many women went to shows as men. You should hear the screams for the Rock 'N' Roll Express on the old tapes and—"

"Until we have actual physical evidence of this real human female who likes wrestling, nobody's going to buy your story, man," Everett chimed in.

"Then it's a bet."

Here they were, sitting together at university, laughing and talking like nothing had changed. Samantha Abraham and her best friends. Marlon, perpetually dressed in wrestling shirts, permanently nervous, who carried a torch for almost any woman who'd speak to him. He'd confided in Sam that he'd had crushes on both Avital and Erin and she'd been told by Avital that he'd had a crush on her, too. But the guy was a victim of his own neurosis, too terrified of saying anything, forever watching. It seemed like he'd finally managed to forgive Sam for what had happened with Erin.

Across from him was Avital, model calibre looks, a dark-haired, Jewish princess with a slightly pronounced nose, and near-perfect figure. She could have any guy she wanted, often had a few on leashes, and always made Sam feel underdressed and inadequate. A Cosmo cover come to life, Avital was so practically flawless, it was maddening.

Spread out on his own couch was her counterpart, Everett, scrolling through his phone with his legs draped over the armrest, only half paying attention to what was going on. But it was the person next to Sam who was the most important of them all.

Erin. Her roommate in a low-range apartment close to school, but also her girlfriend. Sam still didn't know if their relationship had begun while under the influence of mind control or if the effects had simply freed her to act on something she'd always wanted, but the whole thing, however it started, was exactly what she'd needed after so many bad experiences with guys. Experimental phase or not, she resolved to ride it out and see what happened. Erin, with her overly loud voice, a symptom of being slightly hard

6

of hearing in one ear, was special. She was maybe the first person in Sam's life who'd cared as much about what was best for her as she did herself. Everyone else had brought drama and danger: Joshua, with his golem state and eventual deconstruction; Rick, with his vindictive on-again off-again girlfriend, Debbie; Scott from Factor 5ive, puppet of the shadowy group called The Authority. Erin was simple. All she wanted to do was be with Sam, do things together, and share not just an apartment, but a bed. Even if it was the result of tainted alcohol, subliminal messaging, or complex mind-control techniques, Sam had broken free and made it her own.

"Okay, so when Marlon loses this bet," Everett said, "how many votes for him taking us all out for steak dinners?"

Avital raised her hand. Erin did, too. She nudged Sam in the ribs to follow suit. She meekly lifted her hand.

"All of you against me?"

"We promise it won't be an expensive steak restaurant," Erin said.

"Yeah, I'll just order cheese toast," Sam added.

"What'll you do for me if I win?" he said, crossing his arms over his chest in defiance.

"Dude, if you manage to get a date with this totally real human female who likes wrestling," Everett said, "we'll pay for the two of you to go to the nicest steak restaurant in town."

"Then it's a deal," Marlon said. "Now back to Jake 'the Snake' Roberts and Sting."

"God, Marlon, can't we talk about something from this millennium for once? I'm sure nineteen ninety-two pro-wrestling is really interesting to talk about on forums, but what about, I dunno, Katy Perry's new video, the new Spiderman movie, *Canada's Got Talent,* a cooking show? Heck, I'd even talk about last night's National if it got us away from pro-wrestling," Avital said.

"You really don't want to hear more about the spin the wheel, make the deal match?"

"No!"

"Sounds like the ladies have spoken," Everett said.

These were her best friends, the people who'd accepted her into their circle so readily. High school had left Sam thinking she was alone—Duckie and Joshua dead, Rick never wanting to speak to her again—but Everett, Avital, Erin, and Marlon had changed all of that. They were the most important people in her life, and she was going to make sure nothing happened to them. She didn't know what the remnants of the organization that Simon Karlsson and Arthur Fritz worked for might do now that she'd stopped two of their operations, but she had to be ready. She couldn't live with herself if any of them were hurt.

She squeezed Erin's hand again. Erin nestled up closer on the futon.

"Well," Marlon said, "could I instead talk about the new WWE video game? I ranked up last night. I'm sitting in the top fifty in Canada now."

"How about we just drop wrestling as a topic completely?" Avital said.

"Yeah," Erin agreed. "I think I'd rather talk about almost anything else."

"What about hockey?" Everett asked. "Hansen scored a hat trick last night. He's been playing like a man possessed ever since that Jaxxon guy OD'd."

Erin looked to Sam with a raised eyebrow. She was the

only one of them who knew the truth. She'd been there when Sam had rescued Rick from Fritz's lab, heard the story of the golems and the transformations, learned all about the necromancers, Joshua, Duckie, and the horrors of the world outside her safe bubble.

"You finally given up on trying to hook up with him again, Sam?" Everett asked.

"Everett," Avital said.

"What? The dude was Sam's ex! It wasn't that long ago that we were all going to the club trying to get his attention and—"

"That's over now," Sam said curtly.

Erin smiled again, glad to have put that drama behind her. Sam hadn't told her yet that she was still meeting with Rick. They were working on trying to uncover more of the Authority's plans. It was better that she thought the case was closed.

"Good," Avital said. "He might be a total dreamboat, but you're lucky to have someone better."

Now Erin squeezed her hand.

"Yeah," Sam said.

Erin leaned in and kissed her.

"Awww," Avital said. "You guys are so cute together."

"Wait," Everett said. "Do that again, but let me get it on camera."

Avital threw his leg off the armrest of the futon. "You're such a pig."

"What? They couldn't stop sucking face at all of the Jets games, why not now?"

A wave of embarrassment washed over Sam, remembering seeing the minor internet celebrity they'd both earned from

9

repeated exposure on the Kiss Cam at the Jets games. That had all happened during the blur of time she'd lost while under the control of Fritz's multifaceted hypnosis. She only had vague recollections of it at all, but there'd been a handful of YouTube videos talking about them, a few articles, even a fan club. Thankfully that seemed to have died down in the weeks since they'd gone to a game. Even if Erin wanted to go to another one, Sam wasn't sure they should.

"Because we don't know what you'd do with that video," Erin said.

"Do with it? You really think I need a video of that when I see it all the time live?"

"You have to make everything gross, don't you?" Avital said.

"They're the ones going full-on PDA. We used to just hang out as friends, now it's all sapphic around here."

"I think Sam's bi," Marlon interjected. "She dated guys, too."

"Ohmygod, could we not be talking about my sexual identity like I'm not here?" Sam said.

"Did I get it wrong?" Marlon asked. "That means you're gay."

"Marlon!" Sam and Erin both said in unison.

It was clear to Sam that even though he'd been acting like he'd gotten over she and Erin dating, he was still holding a grudge deep down. Or maybe Everett's needling had just made him lash out at another target. Either way, she was getting pissed off.

"Do we have a problem here?" Sam asked him coldly. She moved to stand up, but Erin held her by the shoulder. Marlon suddenly blanched, realizing his mistake. He'd seen what Sam could do back in the Big Shiny Tunes recording studio when she'd had to fight the five members of Factor 5ive.

"Sorry," he said. "Maybe I have been watching too much nineties wrestling. I'm acting like an ECW fan."

"Well, I have no idea what that's supposed to mean, but I'll take it as an apology."

They sat in awkward silence for a few moments. Everett on his phone, Avital checking her makeup in a small mirror, Marlon avoiding eye contact and Erin linking her arm through Sam's.

"Excuse me, guys?"

Someone approached their futon group, a man in a dark red dress shirt and tie, with black tailored pants. Wavy brown hair parted to the left complemented his almost amber eyes. He held a stack of papers in hand. Avital looked up and quickly put away her compact, adjusting herself in her seat like she wanted to hit the best pose.

He held out a small paper. Sam reached for one and looked it over. As she read, Avital took another and did the same.

"Graham Maddox, students' association, head of Students for a Just World."

"SJW?" Everett said condescendingly.

"While I think everyone should be for social justice and equality, the acronyms are a coincidence. Students for a Just World has been on campus since nineteen sixty-three."

The paper was a small poster, listing a series of demands the group was presenting to University Administration regarding a myriad of subjects, everything from Canada's climate policy to tuition fees, the university's stance on Palestine to access to birth control in bathrooms.

"I just wanted to let you know that we're organizing the student body with a scheduled march down to the legislature at the end of the month. There's been some really distressing revelations lately about donors, legacy fraternities, official administrative positions stated and unstated."

"How do you know what the unstated ones are?" Marlon asked.

Graham was unfazed. "We're looking to send a message, as loudly as possible, so I hope you'll come join our day of walkout and protest march. All the information is right there."

Sam noticed that Avital was barely paying attention to the paper, she was enraptured by Graham. She'd never seen her like his—the girl was usually the one hooking men. Sam took another look at this Graham and began to see what might have caught Avital's attention. Slender, smooth-skinned, but with an undeniable openness and charisma, the guy seemed like a natural speaker, totally at ease. Judging by his interests, Sam had no doubt he was studying Political Science and would probably go on to a career in politics later. She could smell the idealism on him.

"So you want us to walk out of class?" Everett asked. "What if I have a test that day?"

"The freedom of peaceful protest is enshrined in the charter of rights and freedoms. Putting all of our voices as one can really send a strong message."

"Yeah, okay," Everett said, tossing his paper to the small table in front of his futon.

"Hope to see you there." Graham lingered a moment on Avital. Shockingly, Sam saw her blush.

He turned and walked away to the next group of people on futons.

"What a dork," Everett said. "As if he's going to get people to—"

"I'm going," Avital said.

"I think we should all go," Erin added.

"Marching?" Marlon protested. "Seriously?"

There was definitely something intriguing about this Graham, even Sam felt it. She looked over the paper again, then back to Avital, whose eyes had never left the man as he spoke to the next group.

"Maybe you're right, Av."

"He was pretty hot," Erin said.

"I'd totally wreck him," Avital said softly.

Erin squealed in laughter. "Yowza!"

Avital blushed, suddenly realizing she'd been too loud and they'd all heard her confession.

Chapter 2

Rick Hansen launched a slap shot at Igor from the blue line. The puck rebounded off his left pad right to the waiting stick of Patrick Linseman, who flicked it over the sprawling goaltender right as the buzzer sounded to end the scrimmage.

Coach Chapman blew his whistle and everyone skated over. The man leaned on the open door of the home team bench and watched them, dripping with sweat, ending their afternoon practice with a collective sigh.

"Okay, boys," he said in his gruff voice. "That's enough for today. Hit the showers, hit the sauna, hit the massage tables, hit the weights, hit the bars, hit the casino, you're off the ice for two whole days. But I catch wind of anyone skipping the Goals for Kids photo shoot tomorrow, I'll have you all back here faster than you can say your own wife's name."

A few murmurs passed among the players. Jonesy spoke up. "Nobody's going to miss a charity event coach."

"I know. None of you would dream of it, but every year someone's alarm doesn't go off or their car breaks down or their wife needs to be driven to the airport and I'm the one who has to tell some poor kid his favourite player had something come up and he couldn't be there to sign his hat.

So take it serious. This is just a part of being a player in the national hockey league and it's as important as any game."

"We'll be there."

"Good. And guys, it's for the Children's Hospital, so try to remember to shave and wear a pressed suit. Be here at noon and we'll put a little joy into some poor sick kids' lives."

Players began filing off the ice, hopping up into the bench and marching down the hall towards the dressing room. As Rick got in line, Coach Chapman tugged on his jersey. "Hansen, you've got an interview request from TSN. Might as well meet the press looking like you work hard around here."

"Coach?"

"You scored a hat trick last night. You're closing in on forty goals this season. Don't tell me you haven't been paying attention."

Rick watched the rest of the team moving past him. A few sported still-healing scars on their necks from where they'd had control stones implanted at the base of their hairlines, which he'd been told was what allowed Arthur Fritz to control their actions with his own heartstone. It had been the device he'd used to make the team attack Rick, Sam and Igor deep in the lab below the arena. Sam had destroyed it and freed them. Ever since, Rick had been watching them like a hawk for any signs they weren't back to normal. He'd made sure to shower with his stick, waiting until most of the guys had left, even avoiding being alone with anyone but Igor. The guys just thought he was succumbing to his own superstitions about his point streak, but little did they know, he still wasn't sure if he could trust them yet.

Who knew how many more were out there? He found

himself trying to check everyone's necks for signs of the change. Even if they were clear, that didn't mean he could trust them. Sam, Igor, and that cop, Detective Tockett. They were the only ones who knew the truth. But what could they do with that information?

"They asked for me? Again? Shouldn't I let someone else get a chance to be on TV?"

"Some guys would love the attention," Coach Chapman said.

"I know it's just because I'm the only rookie left and I'm having a decent season but—"

"You're having a great season, Hansen. There's no denying it. You stepped up after Downie's passing. I know the brass is picked pink."

"I think it's tickled, Coach."

"Whatever. Ownership is happy. Fanbase is happy. The guys are happy. I'm happy. You should be, too."

"I am, Coach, it's just been a lot this year. Rookie season, hometown, Jaxxon dying, change in ownership, and—"

"Change in ownership? What the hell are you talking about?"

"Arthur Fritz? He's dead, right? You were—"

"Who the hell is Arthur Fritz? Julian Gerber owns the Jets. Haven't you been paying attention to who's been signing the checks?"

"Julian Gerber? But Arthur Fritz was—"

"Hansen, you sure you're not partaking of the same shit that did in Jaxxon?"

The coach was looking at him as if he was genuinely confused as to what Rick was talking about. But how could that be? Arthur Fritz, the River City Jets owner, had been the one who handed him the jersey at the draft. He'd met him in the boardroom offices of the team; the man had even suggested a real estate agent to use when he and Debbie were shopping for a downtown condo. Rick hadn't seen any news about Fritz's death, but he just assumed that the Authority had buried the story. Coach had been there in the weird lab, he'd seen the facilities, why didn't he know about Fritz? And who was this Julian Gerber?

"Of course not, I don't touch whatever it was he was into. But surely you remember Arthur Fritz and the lab under the arena with the—"

"You must be touching something else then. Julian Gerber has always been the owner of the Jets, Hansen. I signed my contract with him and went to a party he threw at the Crystal Ballroom for the other owners. I even used his guy down at the Lexus dealership. You sure you don't have dyslexia or something?"

"So you've never heard of Arthur Fritz?"

"Nope."

"And you don't remember the weird lab under the arena with the people in white coats and the—"

"Under the arena? You mean the training centre? The place we all go three times a week? Kid, that's been there for years. There's nothing weird about it. The lunchroom coffee maker is the only machine I trust to make my—"

"Excuse me, Coach Chapman, can we start?"

The coach lost his train of thought and turned to look at some people in the hallway beyond. A cameraman and a blonde woman in a tight red dress approached. It was the Jets reporter for TSN, Dawn Wilson. She always seemed to want to interview him.

Something was definitely wrong with Chapman. He had no memory of what had gone on. Did that mean he was changed again? With the Coach's head turned, Rick reached up and pulled on his collar, seeing only a mostly healed scar.

"Hansen? What the hell?" Coach Chapman said, spinning around.

"Your tag was showing," Rick said.

"Oh, uh, thanks."

He and Igor had managed to cut out stones from everyone the Fritz team had changed. Passing it off as removing a latched-on tick, the two of them had then crushed all of the small marble-sized stones they'd extracted. That should have cured them all. But maybe it hadn't.

The reporter beamed at Rick as she came to a stop near him. "Hello, Rick, nice to see you again."

"Oh, hi, Dawn."

Rick pulled off his helmet and ran his hand through his long hair, trying to look presentable for the camera.

"You look great," she said. "All set, Bart?"

"Yup," the cameraman said. "Ready when you are, Dawn."

She steadied herself and gripped the microphone in hand. "I'll do the intro and just ask a few questions about your streak, then there's a surprise—it'll only take a few minutes, I promise."

Rick just nodded.

"Dawn Wilson for TSN Jets Hockey, here with centre Rick Hansen after an intense practice. Rick, Coach Chapman has really been working the team hard to get you ready for the playoff stretch. You've been on a points streak lately, do you think these workouts are contributing to your improved play?"

Rick barely heard anything she asked him. He gave the standard answers he always gave about hustle and drive and playing three periods of hockey. She hung on his every word like it was Shakespeare, but it was nothing more than the same thing everyone said in these moments. It was a part of the game, a part he'd always taken in stride, but now, after the incident with Fritz and hearing the plans the Authority had, he wondered where moments like this fit in, if they did at all.

Finally, after not even remembering a thing she'd said, Dawn finished with her questions and gently touched his arm. She waved to her cameraman, who dropped down to pick up a small plaque.

"And now, Rick, I get to be the bearer of good news. You've been selected as the TSN player of the month. All of our panelists agreed that you've had the best overall four weeks of anyone in the league. Here's an award for you to put up on your wall at home."

She passed it along to him. He saw his own reflection in the shining surface and felt like he was looking at a stranger. Something like this felt empty.

"Uh, thanks, Dawn, this is a real honour. I'm just proud to be contributing to the team's success and looking forward to the playoffs and making a run for the cup. The people of River City deserve it."

"You've got the whole city behind you, too," she said, turning from him to face the camera. "This has been Dawn Wilson for TSN Jets hockey."

The red light on the camera shut off and Bart packed it up. Dawn smiled and touched his arm again. "That's going to look great in your trophy room."

"Yeah, I guess."

"You know, I have a degree in interior design if you wanted a professional's opinion on where that might hang best."

"Maybe," he said, brushing her off. "But I—" He was all set to tell her about Debbie at home when she turned to look at Bart and he froze. There was a faint glimpse of skin as her hair swayed, and he saw it: at the base of her neck, a thin scar, dark red, healing, but obviously somewhat fresh.

She turned back around. "You're focusing on the season, I get it. But I'm taking a raincheck on that, Rick."

She brushed her hair over her ear.

Had he really just seen that? It had only been a flash, so maybe he was imagining it. He needed to know for sure.

"Interior design? That's a weird way to get into the media."

"It's my fallback. This kind of job tends to be age specific," she said.

"No, it's—"

"I'm young, blonde, and photogenic, but I'm not an idiot. Those three traits are at the top of the list for people they hire here. Eventually, the first one's going to change. Then what?"

"Interior design."

"Exactly. Now, I'm serious. I can come by and help you put your place in order. I'll bet it's a mess with you being away so much. Or do you hire cleaners? Hmmm." She playfully held her own chin. "You seem like someone who'd feel guilty about that, am I right?"

"Well, I, uh…" he stammered. He needed to get a look at the back of her neck. But how?

"I knew I had you pegged. How about I give you my number?" She dug out her phone. "I'm assuming you don't have a pen on you, so I'll just text you."

"Uh, yeah, sure," he said and gave her his cellphone number.

She tapped away and he heard a faint swoosh of a sent text. "There, you'll see it when you're showered and changed." She grinned. "I'll look forward to hearing from you."

She turned and headed down the hall with her crewman. He tried to watch her neck but with the hair obscuring it, he couldn't help himself from eyeing her hips swaying in her tight dress.

"Shit," he muttered and stayed on the bench, alone, until he was sure she'd be gone.

"Did I see it? Or did I just want to? And how the hell am I going to explain having her phone number to Debbie?"

When he walked into the locker room, he found it empty. The rest of the guys were gone, having changed, showered, and left to wherever it was they were going. Rick dropped into his spot and leaned back, sighing heavily.

"Fuck," he said.

It had been like walking on broken glass ever since that night he and Sam had learned the truth about what went on in the bowels of the arena. The plot of the Authority to transform Jets players, use tainted beer, subliminal tones in the music; all to control people with their eventual plan to spread out to the whole world through all professional sports. They both knew it was far from over, but had no idea how to fight back. He was an NHL player. He had to go to work, but he kept his eyes open for the signs of golem transformations: vacant stares, personality changes, the implantation scars. So far, nothing. But he knew that could change at any time.

"Mr. Rick," a voice called to him from the entrance to the showers.

He looked up to see a stocky, bearded man with dark hair wearing nothing but a way-too-small towel around his waist. It was Igor, the only other player who knew what Rick did.

"Iggy, why are you still here?"

"I prefer to shower alone now."

"Yeah, I know what you mean."

"I also prefer to watch out for my teammate."

"You see anything weird?"

"Only something growing on one of my testicles. Perhaps you are knowing what it is?"

He made like he was going to pull open his towel but on Rick's horrified expression, he burst out laughing. "I kid, I kid. You are still so young, Mr. Rick. So innocent."

"And you're the first guy I'd think would want me to examine a growth on his nuts."

"It's good to know I can turn to you should the need arise."

Igor sat down and started to dry off and dress. Rick slowly stripped himself out of his pads and hung them on the hooks for the staff to clean. He showered and emerged, feeling less exhausted. Igor sat waiting for him, scrolling on his phone. The man was a great guy to have as backup. He'd been the surprise that had saved them both when Fritz had thought them trapped.

"Knock knock."

Rick and Igor both looked up to the locker room door to see a black security guard waving.

"Sorry to interrupt, guys. I'm just about finished my rounds and was wondering if I could lock this place up."

"Sure thing, uh, Isaiah," Rick said.

The man grinned, glad to know that Rick remembered his name.

"Just wanted to say goodbye, too," Isaiah said. "Today's my last day."

"Really?"

"Yup. Transferred to a new gig."

"Better than working the arena?"

Isaiah looked behind him at the hall and stepped inside, lowering his voice. "No offence, Mr. Hansen, but there's too much weird shit going on around here. I need something quieter. I'm this close to graduating and don't need more drama."

"You are going to the theatre?"

"No, Igor, he means he's seen things here, am I right?"

"You are not right," Isaiah said. "I haven't seen anything and that's what I tell anyone who asks."

Chapter 3

The flashing red lights, the reflective yellow tape, the haphazardly parked cars, the officers holding court with steaming coffee and half-eaten donuts... Detective Veronica Tockett knew right away what kind of crime scene she was walking in to.

She stopped the cruiser at the edge of a gravel lot on the banks of the Red River. Her partner, Carlos Murphy, flipped through his phone and slid it into his pocket. He looked up and saw the location: the un-gentrified part of the waterfront district. Only a few blocks away from a condo-filled, hipster neighbourhood with nice walking and bike paths, restaurants in converted pump houses, and a hotel made of a giant cube of illuminated blue glass, this was the land that time forget. A mostly abandoned, crime-riddled eyesore. Overgrown parking lots, collapsing old warehouses, and crumbling streets doing what they did best, tossing out victims.

"Looks like we're the last ones here," Carlos said.

His deeply tanned skin and slicked down black hair only made his gleaming white teeth stand out more. He was her new partner while Jimmy was rehabbing his knee. They'd been together a few months now and seemed to be meshing well, but she missed Jimmy. He, at least, kept the conversations clear of—

"Almost as bad as being the last one at an orgy, eh, Tockett?"

"I wouldn't know, Carlos."

"What? Just 'cause you're a mom don't mean you can't still get a little freaky. That's what weekends are for."

"I spend my weekends with my kids."

"And Hooper."

Word was out now that she and Jimmy were an item. They couldn't keep it a secret once he moved in with her while rehabbing his knee. No amount of protesting that she was only helping him as a platonic friend because his family lived up north would work. HR, and everyone else, quickly found out the truth. That would mean they wouldn't be allowed to be partners once he was back on the force. Thankfully, the brass had at least bought the lie that they'd only started dating because of the injury; that kept the more uncomfortable questions at bay.

"Yeah," she said. "And Jimmy."

"He's a real Sally homemaker now, eh?"

"He's doing all right."

"For a one-legged man, you mean."

"He's improving week by week."

Carlos just shrugged. "He's still missing out on the good stuff."

He got out of the cruiser and started walking towards the crime scene. Veronica quickly followed suit. Carlos lifted the police tape and walked over to where the coroner and his crew were working. Veronica scanned the scene, seeing men and women in white coats searching through the dirt and weeds.

The officer in charge spotted them and waved them over. "Detectives. Got another one here, and this one sure don't look right."

"That's because it's a left arm," Jacob, the coroner, said. The thin, bespectacled man with blond hair pulled back into a ponytail lifted up a plastic wrapped limb, severed at the shoulder with blood crusted at the torn edge. The sick looking skin had greyed, with stitch marks criss-crossing the muscles at seemingly random angles.

"Another one?" Veronica said.

"No, this is the first leftie we've found," Jacob added.

"What is it with coroners that they all think they should be comedians?"

"I dunno, Tockett," Carlos said, "that was pretty funny."

"I was told you guys were used to a little flippancy on the job," Jacob said, carrying the arm over. "Morty told me it was his schtick."

"Yeah, and he's long gone. You don't have to keep it up."

"Guys?" Jacob said, looking to Carlos and the others. "Does it bother you?"

"Don't mind her," Carlos said. "She's just pissed because her boyfriend's a one-legged man."

"I'm gonna make you a no-legged man if you don't shut up, Carlos."

He was beginning to needle her and she was angry at herself for letting his remarks get through. Carlos was like that, it was a part of his deal. Everyone called him Carlos the Jackass. She'd been warned before the assignment that the man could get under your skin, and it was proving true.

"Relax," Carlos said. Another officer passed nearby carrying a box of donuts. Carlos blocked his path, lifted the lid and grabbed a crueller. Stuffing it in his mouth, he tossed her another one. "Heads up."

She almost flubbed the catch, but saved it from hitting the dirt.

"Coffee?" he asked now.

She mumbled affirmatively as she took a bite. Carlos followed the officer to a cardboard dispenser and started filling up cups. She turned back to Jacob and the others.

"This is all you found?" she asked.

"So far. But we're combing the shoreline."

"Seems to be an epidemic of people losing parts around here, don't you think, Detective Tockett?" Jacob asked, examining the shoulder sinew with great interest.

"That's the third arm so far. And they all have those strange markings. The working theory is that there's some kind of gang war going on. Like the one between The Cold Bloodz and The Peg Town Boyz a few years back."

"I remember. I was training with Morty then." Jacob wrapped the limb in another plastic bag, this one black, and placed the combined package in a steel container for transport back to the station. "But those guys had tattoos and scars. I don't know what kind of gang marks themselves up like this. It's almost surgical."

"Some new kind of scarification, maybe," Veronica said.

"I don't know anything about that stuff," Jacob said. "I hate needles."

"Could they have been done with a blade?"

"The others appeared so. As crazy as it sounds, I'd almost say the markings were from someone trying to sew up the limbs like a quilt."

Carlos came back and handed Veronica a steaming coffee.

"Who's sewing what now?" he asked.

"Jacob, that's crazy. You're sounding like my... ex-partner's ex-partner."

Jacob counted on his fingers, trying to make sense of the math. "Wait, who?"

"Frank Malone."

"Oh shit, I met him a few times. In fact, it was on that gang case and—"

"Hey, Jacob," an officer called from one of the parked cruisers. "They're calling for you down by the water." He pointed over to the embankment where some floodlights were set up and men combed the dirt.

"Never a dull moment," Jacob said and walked away.

Carlos finished his donut and flicked crumbs off his hand. "So? What do you think, Tockett?"

"I think we need to look around and try to get a sense of what happened here."

"After you, detective." He waved for her to pass.

Despite what she'd seen under the MTS centre, and despite what she'd been meeting with Rick, Igor, and Samantha about, her job didn't wait. She couldn't devote her life to digging deeper into tales of human cloning, mind control, and sinister corporations. That had to be her side gig. Especially since it seemed like the force was at least under some influence of said corporation. Every time she'd tried to find out what had happened with the crew of ex-pro-wrestlers she and Jimmy had busted attacking the hapkido dojang, she'd been told that it had never happened. Somebody had pulled strings, and she had the impression that continuing to dig into who it was might be a bad idea. So, she had to do it quietly.

But it was slow going. Every stone she overturned seemed

to have been scrubbed clean. She felt the trail going colder by the day. Now, they were finding body parts. If there was another serial killer on the loose in River City, she had a feeling that this case was soon going to monopolize all of her time.

They moved closer to the cordoned off area by the river. The floodlights illuminated much of the embankment. She and Carlos used flashlights for the rest.

"Here we go," she said, crouching low. "Clear signs of a struggle, ground was turned over, multiple footprints going off in all directions."

"The weeds are all pulled out, too."

"We found a bent metal pipe," one of the other officers chimed in.

"Looks like someone definitely scrapped here," Carlos said.

The scene was a little too perfect. Or were they looking at two separate events?

"You guys get markings on those prints?" she asked the officer.

"They're working on it," the man said. "There's so much mud around here, we might not get anything usable."

"I sure hope we do," Veronica said. "This is the fourth scene like this we've found."

"I smell a serial killer." Carlos rubbed his hands together. "And that means unlimited overtime. Hello, new Escalade."

"It'll only be a matter of time before the press gets wind of this. Then we'll have to deal with a hundred articles saying the River City PD are nothing but a bunch of keystone cops."

The officer snorted. "Those bloodhounds wouldn't know how to do our job if they watched all seven Police Academy movies. They're just looking to stir up trouble."

"Every time something big happens in this town, it's the same," Carlos said. "We do the dirty work, they talk shit."

Veronica crouched down and examined one of the footprints in the mud. It looked like it was from a sneaker. There was nothing unique about the treads, but from the looks of them, whoever had been here had moved quick. The prints were everywhere, like a dancer's pattern. Shining her flashlight into the grooves, she saw blood staining the dirt in little droplets all around the perimeter. If she had to guess, she'd say the fight was short and brutal, and in this case left someone short one clapping hand.

"So, what do you think, partner?" Carlos asked, sipping more of his coffee.

Veronica stood up and sighed, seeing a full team working around them, knowing that there would be a whole lot of paperwork to read over soon, then her own report to prepare. She turned and looked back to the city, the lights of the huge downtown buildings off in the distance, the faint sound of traffic drifting on the air, the feeling of a heart beating below it all. "I think there's someone out there responsible for all of this and we need to find them fast."

"Duh, that's our job."

"Let's go see what Jacob found upriver." She started walking towards the shoreline and grabbed another donut on the way.

None of this seemed to make sense yet. The story was there, it just hadn't revealed itself. Sometimes there were no easy answers, but other times it just took the right person to find them.

Chapter 4

The new facilities weren't what he was used to, but he would make do. The complete location transfer had been more sudden than anyone had anticipated. He still wasn't clear on all the reasons for the move, those were above his pay grade, but his team had come together in these makeshift surroundings and would do their best with what they had access to.

"Okay," he said. "We're just about ready to attempt the operation. Send in the donor."

"Right away, doctor."

The woman in the pale blue scrubs, face obscured by a mask, left the operating theatre. The others checked the readouts on the machines that were keeping the new body alive, despite the fact that it was missing certain key components. The technology they were working with was going to change the world. Everyone on the team understood that when the test phase was complete, and whichever company they were secretly working for went public with the findings, it would fundamentally alter the relationship between life and death on earth.

"Holding vitals?" he asked one of his assistants.

"Everything's green."

He ran his hand along the hugely muscled torso, examining the impossibly fine work that had gone into creating the sleeve. Whichever team was behind this deserved a raise. Maybe he'd ask to be put into something like this as part of his bonus at the end of his contract. Then maybe he'd get women.

The doors to the theatre were pushed open by a stretcher with a body laying under a white sheet. The woman carefully threaded the path between the machines and placed it next to the larger form in the centre of the room. One dead, one alive. Roles soon to be reversed.

"Okay, people. This is it, the big one. I don't want any mistakes. Success will determine if we all get a pizza lunch on Friday."

Nobody laughed.

"Doctor, I was under the impression we were due for a substantial bonus cheque if—"

"Sorry if pizza isn't enough for you, nurse," he said, again to no laughter. "Yes, yes, there's a big fat bag of cash waiting for us if we do this. But you should be more concerned with the major leap forward it could mean for all of man, er... humankind."

"Sir?"

"Think of it. Complete consciousness transference, the end of disease and aging. We can simply use designer bodies to—"

"Sir, the replacement's in place. If you're done with your speech, we should continue with the operation."

"Oh, sorry nobody seems to realize just what it is we're about to attempt here. What it could mean for..."

He quickly realized that all the faces behind masks were looking at him like he was a different species. Clearly they weren't interested in the philosophical potentialities here.

"Alright, alright. Let's proceed."

The woman pulled the sheet away from the body on the gurney. An old man, with shaved white hair, leathery skin, the signs of wiry muscles beneath the aged physique. Asleep.

"Vitals of the donor?"

"Steady."

"Nurse, hand me the blade."

She handed him the surgical saw. He spun it once in his hand. "Okay, let's make the future."

He slowly lowered the blade towards the old man's shaved scalp.

Chapter 5

"Uncle Jimmy, you're not using your cane," Olivia blurted from the kitchen table.

"It's only a few steps, Olivia, I can manage."

Gingerly hopping on his good leg, Jimmy grasped the refrigerator door and braced himself. He swung it open to face the chaos inside. Veronica never put anything back in the right place. Egg carton on a shelf, cheese in the egg compartment, milk jug hidden behind a bag of spinach, take out container of Chinese food in the crisper—a total organizational disaster. He pulled out the four-litre jug of milk and shut the door, spinning in place. He gauged the distance between where he stood holding the milk and the table with two waiting kids and cereal bowls full of dry Frosted Flakes.

"Didn't think that through, did you, Jimmy?" Veronica stood smirking at the entrance to the kitchen with her arms crossed over her chest.

"Of course I did."

He hopped on his good leg, his socked feet sliding on the grey tiled kitchen floor. He wasn't supposed to be putting full weight on his repaired knee just yet, hence the cane, but he was growing impatient at the healing process, feeling hemmed in by his new life.

"You fall and you're on your own," Veronica said.

"What makes you think I'm going to fall?"

She watched him with that look, the one that said she was right ninety-nine percent of the time. Well, he was going to show her.

He hopped again, nearly dropped the milk, lost his balance, started to topple.

God damn her.

He was all set to toss the milk when she sprang into action and slid her arm through his, helping him stay upright. He hopped again, putting the milk down in front of Carter.

"Don't even say it," he said.

"I don't have to." She grabbed his cane and forced it into his hand.

He stepped over to his waiting chair and fell down in front of his bowl of cream of wheat.

Domesticity. How did it happen? How did Jimmy Hooper, unmarried man at age thirty, who up until a few months ago had been living in a bachelor apartment downtown and not bothering to put on pants unless someone was coming over, spending wild nights at his girlfriend's place but still free to spend others alone in his own bed, end up here, play-acting as a dad to someone else's kids?

He plopped a spoon into his cream of wheat and saw her still smirking at him.

"Uncle Jimmy," Carter said. "You forgot to pour the milk!"

"Mommy's got it." Veronica slid in to help.

He'd been rehabbing his knee for a few months now, trying to recover after that brutal beating by those 'roided up monsters who'd attacked a martial arts academy for reasons he still didn't understand. The supposed kidnapping of Jets star Rick Hansen, the potential stalker Samantha Abraham, missing pro-wrestlers, then a cover-up that made it all seem like it had never happened in the first place. It was the kind of case he was chomping at the bit to dig into, but instead, he'd slipped into someone else's life.

"Uncle Jimmy," Olivia said, pointing to his cream of wheat. "That looks like barf."

"Tastes like it, too," he said. "Unless you add my secret ingredient." He spooned out some brown sugar from a glass jar, then dropped in a dollop of milk, creating a tan slurry.

"Now it looks like poop!" Carter said and burst out laughing.

"Yeah, but poop that tastes like candy." He took a mouthful.

Veronica ruffled Carter's hair and went to pour herself a cup of coffee.

From a one-bedroom apartment in the middle of River City's downtown, surrounded by office towers and the engines of the capitol of Manitoba, to a modest bungalow on a quiet, almost rural street. Instead of a long, carpeted hallway outside his door, he had a few skeletal trees and a gravel driveway leading from an unpaved road to a double garage. Through the big kitchen window, he saw the driveway shovelled to a flat line. Not his handiwork. It would have been his job, had he been able.

Veronica had been left the house in the divorce settlement and while it wasn't a mansion, compared to his old place, it was huge. Built in the seventies, only renovated once, it was as nondescript as the neighbourhood. The distance from the moving parts of the city was only a few minutes, but felt like decades.

"Mommy, you poured too much," Olivia complained. "Now my cereal is all soggy."

"It's supposed to be, Olivia," Veronica said. "That's what milk does to it."

"You want mine instead?" Jimmy asked.

"Ewww!"

His mornings used to be his, now they were organized chaos as everyone sat down to eat breakfast before Veronica had to leave. He had no clue how she'd managed as a single mom. Even with him helping, it was frantic trying to keep the two kids—Carter, age eight, and Olivia, age six—from hitting each other and getting food all over their clothes before they'd even started the day.

Jimmy took another mouthful of cream of wheat. As he savoured the brown sugar, he caught his reflection in the spoon. Upside down and blurry, he could still tell that he looked like hell. World-weary lines traced his tanned skin, bags encircled his eyes; it was the accident, it had aged him. His usually shaved head had grown out, his hair was brushed back away from a day's growth of beard. He felt as tired as he looked. The sleep he was constantly denied by the demands of the kids at all times of the night was starting to catch up to him. Staying over before this had felt exotic, now it was wearying.

"We're questioning some tattoo artists today," Veronica said, taking her coffee mug from under the machine's spout. She took the empty chair next to his. "Maybe there's something to the weird scars we've been finding."

"That your idea or Carlos's?"

"It's just a first step. It might not lead anywhere."

"You want me to call around?"

"No, I want you to let us deal with this."

"But I—"

"Uncle Jimmy, Carter says I smell."

Uncle Jimmy. He guessed it was better than Dad. He wasn't sure how he'd feel to hear that one. This relationship had all started so innocently. He'd been put with Veronica after his old partner, Frank, had been retired. He'd never expected to develop feelings for her, that was a big no-no, but they'd meshed so well together that he couldn't help it. She'd obviously felt the same way. One night, they'd been out drinking and she'd made a move. They'd ended up in his bed and continued from there.

"Your sister doesn't smell, Carter," Veronica said.

"Does, too," Carter insisted.

"Do not."

"Do, too."

"Do not."

"Do, too!"

"Kids, kids, kids. Enough. Mommy hasn't had her coffee yet."

"How about if I just call tattoo parlours in the south end? That would at least save you two some driving."

"Jimmy. You're the babysitter, not a cop. At least, not right now. Focus on the exercises and keeping them from destroying the house."

She chugged the remnants of the coffee and rose from her seat. She headed down the short stairs to a small landing that led to the garage, where she took a police badge from a hook and clipped it to her pants pocket, then reached for car keys hanging from another hook.

Jimmy rose and trailed her.

"If I'm the babysitter, where's my pay?"

"I'll pay you later. Trust me, you'll love it."

He felt a stirring inside as he pictured them going at it after the kids were in bed. She knew how to distract him, and he felt like a goon for how easily it worked.

"How exactly?" he asked playfully.

She leaned in and planted a kiss right on his lips, with more tongue than he'd expected. Her other hand brushed his crotch.

Fuck.

"Just make sure you're ready to go when I get home."

She slid on her shoes and was all set to leave when she realized she'd forgotten something and walked back to give the kids each a hug.

"Mommy's off to work, guys, so it's just you and Uncle Jimmy. Remember, he can't run too fast right now, so take it easy on him. There's KD in the pantry and plenty of ketchup for lunch."

"Yay!"

"Have a great day," she said. "Mommy will see you when I get home."

"Bye, Mom," the kids said. "Catch the bad guys, okay?"

"I will, sweeties."

She took the two steps down to the garage door. He hopped after her. She turned and pulled him in close for another kiss, moving from his lips to his neck, around towards the back, as if she was looking for something on the other side of his skull. But his temperature rose as she went to work. Then, as suddenly as she started, she pulled away.

"What was that for?" he asked.

"Just checking to see if you are the same guy you were last

night."

She pushed through the door and got into the filthy Toyota Matrix she'd been driving for years, backing it down the driveway. He waved and hit the automatic close button, then returned to the table.

"All done, kids?" he said, noticing that Carter and Olivia had devoured their Frosted Flakes.

"Uh huh!"

"Okay, then go brush your teeth and you can play for a bit. I'll clean up then we can all watch something on TV."

"Yay, TV!"

The two kids pushed themselves away from the table and disappeared down the hall.

He sighed, finally alone. He took out his cellphone and swiped it open, tapping on the photos folder. As he spooned the rest of the now-cold cream of wheat, he moved through a series of blurred photos, a few of newspapers, some of elderly people in rest home, then one of two men talking, taken from behind a door.

"Just what in the hell were you on to in that place, Frank?" he said.

They'd been too late to save his partner from a sad end at the Shady Acres Retirement home, but Veronica had rescued the cellphone he'd let the old man borrow. They'd found a mass of pictures he'd taken that he'd insisted were supposed to expose a plot behind the scenes of the old folks' home. But without the old man to explain what they were, Jimmy was left bewildered.

"Who is that guy?"

He stopped on the last picture of the two men and zoomed in as best he could. The face wasn't familiar, but the man wore a suit, looked important. Jimmy opened the LinkedIn app and continued his search through the faces of River City's business class. Maybe today would be the day he got lucky and found the match.

Chapter 6

Horns, whistles, pounding drums, the repeated chants of thousands of voices combined into one:

"What do we want?"

"Lower tuition costs."

"What do we want?"

"Equal access to education!"

"What do we want?"

"Higher corporate taxes!"

"What do we want?"

"Sound environmental policy!"

"What do we want?"

"Better healthcare!"

At the head of the marching line of students, one voice shouted into the megaphone while throughout the crowd, signs were held up to cue the followers to the desired response. As the huge snake of people moved through the streets of downtown River City, curious people peered out of office windows, others stopped on the sidewalks, some held up phones recording the spectacle. Cars honked, either in solidarity or annoyance at having to wait for the giant parade of protestors to clear the major intersections.

Even if she hadn't wanted to come, the campus had cleared

out completely. Everyone was here, so the teachers hadn't even bothered to show up. Sam, arm in arm with Erin and Avital, marched near the head of the line. She watched Graham leading the movement, the 'call' part of the call and response game being played.

"What do we want?"

"Lower tuition costs!"

Over and over again, cycling through a list of progressive policy demands, only some of which were directly linked to their status as students at River City University, he worked the crowd. Erin shouted out the slogans energetically, Avital too. Sam simply scanned the route and people alongside it.

Police were everywhere, watching the crowd for troublemakers. They weren't hard to find. There were guys with dreadlocks openly smoking weed, some drunks, others vaping, many carrying open bottles of alcohol. Joints were handed out like candy and clouds of foul-smelling smoke seemed to emerge above them like a massive exhalation. She'd probably be getting a full contact high if she weren't near the head of the line. Every time someone tried to give her a hit, she waved her head in refusal.

"What do we want?"

"Equal access to education!"

"Why are we doing this again?" she shouted to Erin.

Erin pointed to Avital, who was eye locked on Graham. He turned and marched backwards, shouting again. "What do we want?"

When he saw Avital, he motioned for her to step in line with him. She eagerly leapt forward like a waiting puppy. He slid his arm around her and shouted again.

"And that's the last we're going to see of her today," Sam

43

said.

"What?" Erin asked.

Their lives had flipped over the past week and a half. Avital suddenly had political ideals that only the Students for a Just World platform could live up to. She'd started attending meetings, would talk excitedly about what Graham was up to the next day as they all sat and ate lunch in the futon room.

"He's so well-informed." She beamed. "He's teaching me a lot."

"We teach you a lot, too," Marlon said.

"Nobody has asked to be an expert in Bret 'The Hitman' Hart matches," Everett said.

"Hey, I know other things."

"Like what?"

"Like Miracle Violence Connection matches and—"

"Av, are there lots of chicks at these meetings?" Everett interrupted.

"A few," she'd said. "But it's not a social club."

"A few, eh? They hot?"

"Everett, these are all people intensely interested in working towards a more equitable future where everyone—"

"I'll take that as a no."

"That doesn't mean you guys shouldn't come," Avital had said. "You'd learn so much. Graham is really passionate."

"Oh yeah, passionate," Everett had said. "Oh Graham, teach me more of your passion."

They'd all burst out laughing, but Avital had only scowled. "You're not taking this seriously. This is the world we're going to be walking into in a few years. Don't you want to have a society where everyone is equal? Where the rich pay their fair share? Where nobody is being exploited?"

"Wow, Graham can cure the ills that have plagued civilization since the beginning of time?" Sam had said more flippantly than she'd intended.

Avital had scowled harder at her. "After the way you made us all go chasing after shitty bands and your jock exes, I'd have thought you'd be more willing to come and support me in something I want to do."

Feeling like she'd rammed her foot down her own mouth, Sam had clammed up.

"She's right," Erin had said. "Remember that sketchy biker bar? Does this group meet anywhere that skeezy?"

"No, they meet on the third floor of the L building. Then off campus at this old warehouse Graham rents. That's sort of like a base camp for the whole movement really. He's got this crazy library of radical literature there, stuff he rescued from a vegan cafe that closed and—"

"Vegan?" Everett said. "I'm out."

She'd looked to Marlon. "Yeah, sorry, but RAW, Smackdown, and I, uh, am going through the Smokey Mountain Wrestling tapes with Peta like every night for the next... uh, fifty years, I hope."

"Dude, are you sure this girl is real?"

"Definitely," Marlon said.

"So when can we meet this totally real girl?"

"Uh, when I'm sure you won't be an asshole to her."

"Me?" Everett said in shock. "I'm the perfect gentlemen."

"What about you, Sam, Erin?" Avital had asked. "Won't you come to the meetings?"

"I'm working at the bakery. We've got a wedding coming up and have to make pastries for two hundred."

Avital turned to Sam. She hadn't had an excuse other than

just not wanting to go.

"I, uh, have hapkido and then I have to meet some people after."

"I'll go," Everett had said. "But only to judge these politically motivated chicks for myself. Who knows? Maybe I could interest them in my own personal platform, if you catch my meaning."

"You won't be able to seduce these women," Avital had said. "They've all got too many brain cells."

"Challenge accepted."

Faced with the fact three of her friends weren't going to be supporting her, Avital had grown more distant, even skipping lunch a few days. But then, the day before the rally, she'd appeared with the poster, reminding them all to come.

"It's super important to all of our futures," she'd said.

So now, here they were, in the midst of a massive student walk-out, making their voices heard, planning to stop at the steps of the provincial legislature for an opportunity to let the elected officials of government hear their demands.

Walking arm in arm with Graham, Avital seemed in her element. Further down the line, Sam spotted Everett with a girl in a red toque linked through his arm. He was seemingly shouting as loud and as enthusiastically as anyone else. She saw the girl pass him a joint and he took a puff before handing it down the line.

"Can you believe that Everett is toking?" Sam said to Erin, motioning to the scene.

When she turned, she saw Erin tentatively taking a few puffs of her own joint.

"What?"

"Erin, you too?"

She shrugged.

Sam saw two uniformed police officers watching them intently. Maybe a little too intently, but then, just as she caught their eyes, they turned to scan more of the crowd.

"When in Rome, I guess," Erin said. "It's pretty good actually."

"You never—"

"Seems like the time."

She handed Sam the joint. Sam had only smoked pot once, at a party in high school, deep in Tommy's basement as part of a circle. A girl named Gwen had kissed her, but for weeks she'd never been sure if that had happened or been a weed-induced hallucination. Either way, the tingly head and spatial disorientation hadn't appealed to her enough to ever want to try it again. Even marijuana's legalization hadn't been coercion enough. But now, it was Erin that was offering it to her.

She stared at the smoking cigarette, considering the idea.

"It's no big deal, Sam. It's kind of relaxing."

She felt a vibration in her pocket. Her phone notifying her of a text.

"Oh shit, hold this." She passed the joint back to Erin, who took another puff.

Digging out her phone, she saw a message from Rick. "Need to meet."

She tapped a response "Where and when?"

"ASAP. Leaving on road trip tomorrow."

"Okay. Usual place?"

"1pm?"

The time on her phone said half past twelve. She'd have to duck out of the march to make it. That wasn't a big deal. She didn't really think this was her scene anyway.

"C U there."

"Hey, Erin." She looked up, only to realize that she'd fallen behind in the crowd. People passed her by. She could barely see the head of the line anymore. A pair of cops were watching her again. She started moving through the mass, looking for Erin, but it seemed like no matter how many people she pushed past, her place in the line never changed.

"What do we want?"

"Better healthcare!"

It was like swimming upstream. She couldn't catch up to the leaders. Everyone was moving faster than her, so that she was being slowly slid out the rear of the snaking line. Then, as if an invisible force was desperately trying to expel her like an exhaled breath, she was alone, watching the parade moving up Memorial Boulevard towards the distant marble of the Provincial Legislature. The golden boy sparkled in the sunshine. The snowy path of the street was trampled flat, brown from the dirt and sand.

She wanted to follow, but her feet were locked in place. Her head swam. Maybe she'd gotten a contact high after all.

HONK.

A car horn jerked her into reality. She stood in the middle of an intersection. Police moved barricades for traffic to flow again.

"Get out of the road, hippie," someone shouted.

"Oh, shit."

"Move along, ma'am," a cop said.

She was unable to control her legs. There was some kind of interference between her brain's signals and their reactions. Then, when he started to walk towards her, something clicked into place, and she staggered awkwardly off to the meridian. She stood waiting for the light to change to get back on the path to the coffee shop and Rick.

"What just happened?" she muttered as time seemed to snap back into its normal momentum. She braced herself on a lamppost as she felt faint. Her head swimming, she took a deep breath and tried to orient herself. She picked up her phone to text Erin, saw that it was now somehow a minute to one and instead sent Rick a note, "Almost there."

Chapter 7

"Just hear me out. What if we won?" Rick said. "What if this authority decided that since you'd stopped two of its agents, that maybe River City wasn't the place it wanted to work out of. Then they packed up and moved on somewhere else?"

"That's the big crisis you wanted to meet me over?" Sam asked. She sipped from her latte while Rick stirred his and worked through his thoughts. He looked up, saw Sam staring at him intently, with that look that told him she wasn't buying his theory.

"It's just that the four of us have been looking over our shoulders for weeks now, checking everyone we meet for the mark and—"

He suddenly realized that Sam hadn't seen the back of his neck, so he tilted his head to prove to her he was still normal.

"It's okay, I saw as I came in." She pulled up her hair and showed him her neck as well. "Just in case you forgot."

"There's been nothing. Nobody's come after us, no assassins, the police have left you alone—"

"Only because you managed to get the charges dropped."

"Which, if they were a part of the Authority, they probably wouldn't have wanted to do, right? Wouldn't they have just arrested you, handed you over to the bad guys, had you converted, then cackled madly from their evil lair?"

She took a sip, seemingly ready to listen now.

"The four of us were convinced there were more of them out there, watching, ready to pounce on us for knowing the truth, but where are they? My team is back to normal, you're at school, Detective Tockett's busy with other stuff. We're seemingly doing fine. So maybe the Authority just said that it was too much trouble to stay here and fucked off to wherever they're from."

"Or are working behind the scenes in another city. Rick, that might be even worse. We're the ones who know about them. The rest of the world is in the dark."

"There are people better equipped to deal with stuff like this."

"Like who?"

"I dunno, CSIS, the CIA, MI5, James Bond, The Rock, some dictator who doesn't want them horning in on his racket. Professionals. Guys with guns and teams of—"

"What if they've already infiltrated all of those places and people? What if we're literally the only ones on earth who—"

"Sam, that's main character syndrome stuff. There's what, six billion humans and—"

"And how many of them are wearing masks?"

Rick sighed heavily, knowing now that Sam wasn't going to buy it, especially because he didn't even fully believe what he was saying. Better to just admit the truth. "Look, I can't do this anymore."

"Do what?"

"Live in a constant state of paranoia. Look over my shoulder all the time, jump at shadows, feel like I'm a target of something that might not even exist."

"You heard Fritz. There's something bigger at play. They've got massive plans for the world and—"

"And maybe you set them back years. Maybe he was bullshitting, maybe—"

"Maybe leaves us vulnerable, Rick. There's the four of us and—"

"And I need to be a hockey player. That's all I am. It's what I've worked my whole life for. Now we're closing in on the playoffs and I need total focus."

She said Fritz, not Julian Gerber. *Ignore that.*

"People are counting on me to be a star, to score, to lead. The city, the fans, the ownership, Coach Chapman, Igor, everyone."

She put her hand on his and looked him in the eyes. Her touch was soft and her gaze sincere. "Rick, what if the world is counting on us?"

* * * *

The sounds of Bruce Springsteen blared over the sound system as Rick watched the time on the clock. There was a minute left in the period. They were down by one against the Devils. If they could just get a goal, they could force overtime and guarantee themselves a point in the standings.

"Hansen, you're on as soon as Iggy's off."

"Okay, Coach."

"Blocker side high."

Rick nodded. The puck was dropped, Jonesy won the face-off, moving the puck to the defence. Butterflies danced in his stomach as he waited for the guys to get out of their zone and up the ice. Igor made his tentative steps out of the crease, following the play. The crowd in New Jersey rose in excitement, cheering, anticipating a photo finish.

"Go, go, go!"

Igor was a few feet away. Rick slid over the bench, joining the play as the trailer.

"The world is counting on us." Sam's words echoed in his skull, but he dismissed them. *The team is counting on me to score.*

The clock showed thirty seconds. The puck went to Linseman, then to Jonesy. Rick arched over the hashmarks, splitting to the open side. He knew the play, point shot, look for rebound. He didn't even look back. He heard the clap of the blast from the defence, knew instinctively where the shot would be aimed, low pad, forcing the rebound to him. He had his stick exactly where it needed to be. The puck seemed to come to him as if by elastic. He flicked it up and over the sprawling goalie, right into the net. The red light flashed to life, the crowd moaned in disappointment. He raised his hand to celebrate but turned just in time to see one of the New Jersey players lining him up for a hit. The elbow hit him high, knocked him hard backwards. He crashed to his shoulder, felt something click out of place. His head hit the ice, the helmet cracking down so hard his ears rang. He heard whistles blow, the crowd cheering, Jonesy shouting.

"Motherfucker!"

His vision swam in circles. He saw the guy who hit him turn to brace himself to handle a Jet charging at him. Blood. There was a bloody gash on the man's neck. Or was there? He couldn't focus, couldn't get up. He rolled over, tried to push up to a standing position, but his balance left him. He fell face first to the ice. The helmet clinked again, vibrating his skull. He wondered what it might have felt like had he not been wearing it.

A brawl erupted. Both teams cleared the bench. Someone crouched low over his prone body. He saw Igor's bearded face under his helmet, looking down at him, the arena lights high overhead strobing. The man's voice was distant, hard to make out.

"Mr. Rick, you okay?"

"Igor?"

"You lay still, I'm going to crosscheck a motherfucker."

Rick's head rolled. He saw Igor diving into a melee, gloves flying, sticks all over the ice. The fans chanted for blood, thundering their hands on the glass, their voices a thunderous call for more violence. Someone else started to lift him up. His legs were nearly useless. His arms draped over two shoulders, he was dragged off the ice as the rest of the teams fought. He didn't remember the walk down the hall to the bench, or being put in the ambulance, but images of lights and doctors flooded his head, along with Sam's warning: "The world is counting on us."

Medical jargon, frantic nurses, the team doctors looking at him. Time phased in and out. A concussion? Something worse? He didn't know, he just knew it was bad. He realized now that he'd been deliberately taken out of commission. He understood that they'd waited until he dropped his guard and then they'd struck. He needed to warn Sam. To tell her she was right. But he couldn't stay awake. He kept repeating that it was now down to three.

"He's delirious," someone said.

"Get him some—"

The words garbled in his ear. He couldn't focus. An attack. He'd been deliberately attacked by someone who'd been changed. On another team. The Devils. They'd moved beyond just the Jets. It looked like things were heating up.

"Phone…" he moaned. "Need to…"

"Increase the dose."

Warmth flowed through him. Relaxation washed over. He fought it for a moment. He needed to stay awake, had to. But it was too powerful. He finally fell asleep. The last repeating thought cascading through his clouded mind was wondering who they could turn to for help.

Chapter 8

"It's alive!"

"Yeah, and? We've been doing this for, like, two years."

"I still like to say it."

"You are such a dork."

"A dork who's going on coffee break."

"What about the stiff?"

"He'll be there a while, we've got time."

"Wait up!"

The voices seemed to fade as the darkness that consumed him was chased off by a tiny point of light above. Eyelids fluttering, vision cleared. A head moving like molasses, stiff joints, muscles tense, like they had never been used before.

A white room, machinery beeping with tiny red lights. Alone, cold, and confused. Leaning up from a flat plank bed. Small suction cup sensors attached to the body.

A man's body.

Large hands pulled the sensors off easily. The machines whined in protest. The sound pierced his skull. He swung out a great fist, smashing the unknown technology to the ground, where it shattered into a thousand pieces.

Strength.

Eyes examined the massive right hand and arm. Powerful,

thick with muscle. The steel machine had been crushed from a single blow.

A thin sheet covered the rest of the heavy body. Tingling sensations ran through limbs waking to life in sequence. He tossed the blanket aside and stepped to the cold floor. He stretched. He could feel a powerful vitality in his muscles. He flexed, feeling the potential rippling through his body. Legs like tree trunks, arms sculpted from the Greek masters themselves. His bare skin rose in goose pimples from the cold air.

He tried to move, but his feet dragged like concrete slabs and he toppled forward. He put his hands out to catch himself, knocking over the gurney. The ground seemed to reach up and smack him in the face, knocking him dizzy. He shook his head to clear the cobwebs, vision swimming, threatening to return to the darkness.

He pushed himself up to his feet, his lagging body fighting every step of the way. Finally upright, knees locking in place, he saw a small stainless steel sink and counter, with bloody surgical instruments laid out on a cloth.

He tried to pick one up, but his fingers refused to cooperate. He tried turning the knob of the faucet, pulling it off instead, crushing the metal in his hands like tissue paper. Water poured out angrily. He gingerly touched it.

Hot or cold?

The water felt like nothing. It flowed over his hands, but there was no sensation. Was there something wrong with his skin? A blurred reflection of his face in the stainless steel stared back at him, but the metal made it impossible to make out any details.

Voices returning. Footsteps approaching.

"So then I said to her, look, honey, just because we're locked away here is no reason to lock up our— shit!"

"Lock up our shit? Are you into kink?"

He saw two men in lab coats with surgical masks dangling at their necks, holding coffees in hand. Frozen in place at the sight of him.

"Hey, he's up. That's fast."

The man put his coffee down on the tray next to the bloody scalpels and moved towards him.

"Look at the mess he made."

"How are you feeling?" the first man asked as he removed a pen-sized light. He blinked it on and shone the beam into his eyes.

Pain. Burning. He batted his hands at the beam, only missing by inches.

"Visual acuity still adjusting."

"He destroyed the tap," the other said.

"He's still figuring out how strong he is."

"But not that he needs to put on pants."

"You don't have to stare at his Johnson."

"I can't help it! It's right there."

The man with the light picked up the blanket and started wrapping it around the new body. He recoiled from the touch of the cloth.

"Relax, this'll make Vern a little less insecure in his own masculinity."

"Insecure! Do you see the size of that thing?"

"You're supposed to be a scientist."

The man finished wrapping the blanket and tied the top at the shoulder. "There you go. All ready for the toga party."

"Oh shit, is that this week? I thought it was next—"

"Vern, just help me with him. He's got to be disorientated enough without you staring at his cock and talking about partying."

They lifted up the gurney, righted it, then the two of them gently took his arms and helped him to sit back down on the middle.

The first man patted his shoulder. "You must be quite confused right now, wondering where you are, who you are. Am I right?"

He understood the words. His head bobbed up and down, feeling like it weighed a hundred pounds.

"I assure you that is normal, all a part of the process. The fog will clear in time. You'll have a task to—"

"Does he really understand anything you're saying?"

"We think so," the first man said.

"Could it be an unconscious reaction?"

"It's hard to tell at this stage. It's like being born again, I assume. We'll let him get acclimatized then take him to the education centre."

The second man ran his hands over the bare arm. He could feel the gentle touch of fingers along his muscles. The sensations were slowly coming back to him.

"Shit, look at the size of the guy. Almost makes you want to go through with the process yourself, eh?"

"It's not a day surgery, Vern. This thing isn't permanent. Yeah, he might seem like a Schwarzenegger now, but in about eighteen months, he's going to look like Charles Atlas."

"He was still pretty buff."

"I mean because he's dead, Vern. Decomposed, worm food, sheesh. I swear sometimes you're so dense."

The man kept inspecting his body. "Still, think of the

59

chicks you could score with in those eighteen months, though. Especially with a dick like he's packing."

"Fucking hell, Vern, get your mind out of the gutter. Grab a clipboard. We've got some tests to run on the big guy before he's ready for his mission."

He sat silently, watching the second man take a pen and begin writing lines onto a form in a clipboard. The motion was familiar. Faint memories of the past just out of reach.

"Okay," the first man said. "Subject SA-232 dash B. Revival time…"

Chapter 9

"I've been worried sick." Debbie plunged forward and wrapped her arms around Rick. Hugging him too tightly, she sent shooting pain down his arm despite the morphine drip. She'd clearly been crying, since her mascara had run.

"Easy, easy, they just finished setting my collar bone."

She recoiled in horror. "Oh my God, I—"

"Relax, it's not like you can put me out of action any longer, right?" He tried to laugh, but judging by her reaction, she didn't feel much like joking.

A vase filled with flowers rested on the small end table next to the bed, with cards displayed all around, from the players, the team staff, family and friends. A banner from school children was pasted to the wall, and more notes were piled on one of the empty chairs in his quiet, private room at the downtown River City Hospital. The whole response to his injury seemed a little excessive, but then River City had always been a hockey town.

"This is the first time they've let me come in," she said. "I've been trying for days."

"I've been high as a fucking kite since the injury, so I'm not sure I'd have known anyway."

"Assault," Debbie said. "You were assaulted. Everyone saw it."

"I didn't."

She tenderly brushed aside some hair from his head. "Nobody expected it, so how could you? He just whacked you in the head and—"

"After I tied the game. I still don't know if we won."

Debbie showed concern and went quiet.

"It's okay if we didn't. I got us to overtime at least. That's still a point and—"

"Do you really not remember what happened?"

"Of course I do. We were down one goal. We pulled the goalie. I was the sixth man. There was a rebound, I banked it high, game tied. I turn around and WHAM, get clocked by an elbow. I'm groggy and there's a big brawl. Someone helped me off the ice. I'm guessing Jonesy. He's too old to fight now and—"

Debbie looked at his morphine drip and jiggled the bag nervously. "They said the concussion could cause memory loss."

"Huh?"

"That's not at all what happened."

"Debbie, I might not remember the past few days, but I remember that. I—"

"It wasn't someone from the Devils that hit you. That's what makes this all so terrible."

Rick's heart sank into his chest. He felt his pulse racing.

"You were skating on the ice. You hopped over the boards a few steps early. Then out of nowhere, he clocked you in the head. With his stick."

He had no idea what she was talking about. He clearly

remembered scoring. He remembered the boos and—

"Igor. Who would have thought? He just lost it."

"Igor? What the hell are you talking about?"

"They said he found out you used to date his girlfriend."

Rick sat up. Too fast. His head started spinning and his neck ached. The machine began beeping. His bed alarm chimed.

"Rick, no." Debbie helped him back down to the bed slowly. "You're not ready yet."

"Debbie, what are you saying happened?"

"I'm saying Igor blindsided you. You never had a chance. You were out on your feet, then you landed hard. He leapt on top and just started punching. The game, the team, everyone froze. People leapt to help eventually, but he'd bloodied you badly. They carted him off. The police were involved. There's a criminal charge pending and he's been fired from the team. Blackballed from the league. Deported."

"Deported? All in two days?"

"I know this is going to come as a shock, but it's true. Igor had apparently falsified some visa documents years ago, or the New Jersey Devils had, nobody's all that sure. Either way, he's about to be put on a plane back home to Chechnya."

"Jesus Christ." Rick fell back into the bed, weakened. None of this made sense—he had such clear memories of the game up until the elbow.

Debbie pulled her phone out. She opened up a video file and pressed play, then sat up near his head and tilted the phone. He watched silently as the video played out. It was footage from New Jersey. There were the Jets, down a goal, a minute left.

"There they go, goalie out. Looks like rookie Hansen is

going to be the sixth man. He's hopping the board and— oh my God, Illyanovich just hit him. He's out. He's attacking him. The refs are blowing the whistle, the bench is cleared, everyone's on him. Hansen is seriously hurt. What in the world could have—"

"This is shades of the infamous Bertuzzi hit, Paul. Just disgusting and—"

"That was against the other team, Mike! This was his own man. Oh God, blood on the ice. Get some medical attention to poor Hansen and—"

She shut the video down and tucked the phone back into her purse.

Rick felt like he was living in a movie and he was going to faint. Everything she'd told him was right there. It had happened. Then why didn't he have any recollection of it?

"I know this has got to be hard for you," she said, patting him gently. "I told you she was bad news."

"She? You said Igor did it."

"Didn't you hear what I said? He did it out of a jealous rage. Because of one of your exes. An ex he's been seeing. Understand?"

"What are you getting at?"

"Samantha Abraham. She must have put him up to it."

"Sam? There's no way she—"

"He refused to name her, but we both know it was her. She was at our party with him."

Rick blanched. As far as he knew Debbie hadn't seen Sam there. She'd snuck past and—

"I've told the police her name. I'm sure they'll want to speak to her about all of this."

"But Sam and Igor weren't—"

He trailed off. He couldn't tell her any more without revealing all that he'd done with Sam.

"She tried to kidnap you once already. She was at our house. She attacked me with scissors. I should never have let you convince me to not press charges even though she cut me. I've got a scar and—"

"Debbie, I—"

She stared daggers at him. "Against my better judgment because I love you and I trust you implicitly. But you can't keep covering for her, no matter how much pity you might have over how shitty her life turned out. You and I are the present and the future. You have to face up to the fact that Samantha Abraham is bad news. And bad news belongs in the past."

Chapter 10

The elevator door opened. Two orderlies waited with a man on a stretcher hooked up to an IV.

Sam stepped around them and out into the hospital hallway. She looked for the direction of Rick's room. A nurse at the nurses' station eyed her with interest for only a moment until a buzzer sounded from one of the rooms and pulled her focus away.

"Room four-three-seven," she said softly, looking for the numbers on the doors.

An old man sat in a wheelchair, his head drooping down to his chest. An elderly woman lay on a gurney in the hall, hooked up to an IV, moaning softly. Another patient slowly shuffled towards the vending machine, dragging her machines behind her. It was a typical scene at River City's downtown hospital; crowded, frantic, smelling of disinfectant, a cacophony of noises and screams.

"Four-two-five, four-two-seven..."

Down the hall a blonde woman emerged from one of the rooms. Sam knew right away who it was. She slid into room 429 and pushed herself up against the wall out of sight.

"Fucking Debbie."

Of course she'd be here. She and Rick lived together, were

already famous in town for being an 'in' couple. Since high school, Debbie had tormented Sam, but Rick had assured her that the woman had mellowed when her university scholarship fell apart after a career-ending knee injury. But Debbie had been implanted. Sam had found a stone in her neck. She'd removed it, forcibly, but who knew if that was enough to truly change her? Rick had promised that Debbie was back to normal, but was normal a good thing in this case? Normal had been hate, violence, torment.

"Why do you have to stay with her at all?" she'd asked Rick during one of their clandestine meet-ups.

"The two of you never got along. You don't see how similar you really are."

"Similar? Fuck that. I'm nothing like her."

"You were way nicer to people in high school sure, but you're both driven, fight for what you want, uh, are women."

"Wow, we're just like clones or something."

He'd tried to convince her that Debbie wasn't a threat anymore, but Sam knew better than to ever let herself trust that bitch. She only wished Rick had the same sense. But then Debbie was almost impossibly good-looking. In Sam's experience, even the smartest guy lost IQ points in the presence of someone that beautiful.

She peered through the crack in the door, waiting for Debbie to walk past the room.

"Nurse?" a woman asked from behind her. "Nurse, I need to go to the bathroom."

"Huh?" Sam turned to see a woman in her sixties laying on a bed in a blue gown. She was missing a leg, while the other one was nightmarishly purple, with toes as big as farmer's sausages. She must have had surgery recently.

67

"Nurse, I have to go. Please take me."

"Oh, I'm not the nurse," Sam said, "I'm just—"

"I have to go. Now. Please. Help me."

"I—"

The woman was distressed, trying to slide herself off the bed into a wheelchair parked nearby. She wasn't going to be able to manage. Sam turned and saw Debbie pass the door. She rushed over to the woman, just as she landed with her bad leg to the floor.

"Hey, wait. Easy now."

She gripped Sam's arm so hard that she lost feeling in her fingers. The woman was much heavier than she looked. Sam almost couldn't hold her.

"Slow down," she said, straining. The woman's gown dangled loose. Scars criss-crossed a back that was painted with big purple blotches; her skin was sagged and discoloured, the colour of spoiled beef jerky. She smelled like excrement and sweat. She wore an adult diaper that seemed soiled. A catheter tube hung below. A bandage dangled from an open wound on her lower back. Mucus-like pus oozed out of a gaping hole. The combined aroma was enough to nearly make Sam retch.

The woman landed hard in the chair.

"Take me to the bathroom."

"I'm not the nurse, I keep telling you," Sam said.

"I have to go. I have to go." She gripped her again.

Sam spotted the call button and slammed it. An alarm sounded both in the room and down the hall at the nurses' station. The woman screamed and let go, covering her ears. Sam backed away and went to the door.

"The nurse is on her way."

"Wait," the woman said, "I have to go to the bathroom, you have to help me."

"Sorry, I have to help someone else first."

Sam peered out into the hallway. There was no sign of Debbie. She darted out towards Rick's room, stepped inside, and slid the door shut. Rick lay propped up in bed, watching television. He looked horrible, as if he'd aged a decade. Pale, with his head wrapped in a bandage, and eyes encircled by darkness. A morphine drip slowly descended a tube into his vein. He seemed slightly disoriented, maybe even spaced out.

"Rick," she said and stepped up to the bed.

"Sam?" he said slowly. "I was dreaming that you were here. Is this still the dream?"

"It's not. I came as soon as I could. Once we were able to find out where you were."

"Where I was? I'm in the hospital. Isn't that obvious?" He waved his hands over his gown like a spokesmodel.

"They're not exactly making what room you're in public knowledge. Detective Tockett had to do a little digging to figure it out. Then I had to wait until the coast was clear."

"The coast? Aren't we in River City?"

"No, we are, I just meant…"

His cloudy eyes showed her that he was probably a step behind from the drugs. She sat next to him on the edge of the bed. She ran her hand over his cheek, checked his forehead. He was cold. "Oh, Rick, what the hell happened to you. Sportscentre said it's a concussion and—"

"Broken collar bone, too."

"Ouch… how?"

"I remember scoring a goal then being hit by a Devils player, but Debbie told me Igor did it."

"Igor? That's crazy. Why would he attack you? He's on your side."

Rick tried to shrug, but pain wracked his shoulder and he winced. She held him down gently.

"Debbie showed me the footage," he said. "I didn't believe it until I saw it either. I mean, it was his old team, but he was traded to us two years ago."

"She showed you? But that's impossible. Nobody's seen the footage. The live feed had blacked out. CBC and TSN said it was too violent to show the highlights on TV. Anyone who had cellphone footage that's tried to upload it to YouTube or Twitter is getting insta-banned. The league has been copyright striking everything. Even Reddit posts are getting deleted. Nobody knows exactly what went on except for the people who were there. But you're telling me Igor attacked you?"

"I know it doesn't make any sense."

"Wait," Sam said, suddenly realizing the obvious. "How the hell did Debbie have the footage when nobody else does? Was she in New Jersey with you?"

"No, she never comes on road trips. Maybe the team gave it to her?"

"What did it look like?"

"Like it was shot from someone's phone. High up in the stands. But it had commentary."

"Would one of the other player's... girls have given it to her?"

"They don't usually come on road trips either. Unless they live in the city we're playing in already."

"Does anyone on the team live in New Jersey?"

Rick laughed. "No. Who'd want to?"

"So we're no closer to figuring out how Debbie had it then."

Rick was looking at her oddly as she talked, like he was trying to figure something out about her in his head.

"She told me something else, Sam."

"Yeah? What was it? Maybe it's important."

"She said you put Igor up to it. Or at least that he did it because of you."

"Because of me? Why the hell would he attack you because of me?"

"Jealous rage over our past. She said that's what all the news was reporting."

"Are they?"

Sam pulled out her phone and opened up CBC Sports in one tab and TSN in another. On both, the story was the top headline. "More details emerge in Jets assault." She read over the text quickly, her eyes showing disbelief. "This is all insane," she said. "Igor has a thing for me, but he knew I was dating Erin. He kept asking for a threesome. If he was going to be jealous of anyone, it would be her, not you. And besides, he never shut up about you. He loves you."

"Maybe he snapped."

"Did he seem like the kind who would?"

"I don't know what to think anymore."

The more Sam read, the more she wished she'd not been so busy the past day and a half working on an English paper. She'd barely paid attention to the news after the initial report of Rick's injury and then the conversation with Detective Tockett about how to find him. Had she seen any of this before, she might have been able to focus her thoughts better. It was all too insane. Then she spotted the time stamp on the news stories. They were both from only ten minutes ago.

"Hey, wait, this stuff is brand new. How the heck did Debbie know any of this before it was posted?"

"I don't understand," Rick said.

"Maybe…" Sam started to wonder just how much a part of all this Debbie actually was, whether taking the stone from her neck had broken their control at all. She read more about the assault. "Igor's being deported? His visa paperwork has proven to be false? There's way more going on here than meets the eye, Rick. Igor might be weird, but I don't think he's capable of an attack like this. Or forging his visa. Not on his own, even in a rage. There's only two explanations I can think of right now."

"Which are?"

"One, he was under the control of a heartstone. Did you happen to notice his neck the day of the game?"

"I don't remember really."

"Okay, so unless we can somehow get access to him to check before he's deported, which according to the reports, is set to be…" She scanned deeper into the story until she found what she was after. "Wait, he's currently locked up… oh shit, Detective Tockett. Maybe she could get to him in time." Sam started texting her a note as her brain fired in a million directions at once.

"You said two theories?"

She barely heard him as she finished her text, then looked up at him, not even sure he'd spoken in the first place. "Huh?"

"You said you had two theories."

"Right. The second is that all of this is an elaborate lie. That your memory is right and Igor didn't hit you. But someone wants the world to think he did. That would explain why all the footage is MIA and—"

"That's an awful lot of trouble to go to. Why would someone do that?"

"Not some*one*. The Authority. And isn't it obvious? To split us up. This takes Igor out of the picture. Puts you in traction, leaves just..."

Rick ran his hand over his neck as he listened. He scratched at a spot near the base of his skull. Sam blanched. The bandage around his head... was it obscuring the wound from an implanted heartstone?

"Leaves just? You trailed off there for a minute."

She suddenly felt like the room wasn't safe. She started looking through the cards, lifting the floral arrangements, peering behind the poster, for any sign of a recording device.

"What are you doing now?"

"Just checking for any bugs."

"Bugs? Jesus, Sam, this isn't James Bond."

"No, but I want to make sure no one's listening in. I have to do something, Rick."

She stepped back over to him, scanning the machinery for some sign of scissors, a pen, a scalpel, anything sharp to cut the stitches that would be over the wound that she was sure was hidden by the bandages. Of course there was nothing like that around. Then it hit her. The IV needle. She could pull it out and use that. She had no experience removing a needle, but how hard could it be?

"I need you to trust me. I just have to..."

She grabbed his wrist and held it gently.

"Sam, what—"

She moved to grab the tube and pull it out. "I can't promise this won't hurt but—"

"Sam, stop. You're freaking me out here, you're—"

"That's the morphine talking. I'm not going to let them get you. I just need to—"

She was all set to pull the tube out when Rick squirmed. She held tight. Had he not been weak, he'd have easily been able to fight her off, but he was in bad shape, almost like a baby in her hands.

"Sam, don't. You're—"

"Trying to save you, Rick."

She jerked the tube out in a quick pull. He cried out in pain. She saw blood seeping into the bandage at his wrist. The end of the needle dripped liquid and blood in a clear melange of medicine and gore. She reached for Rick's head, tried to gently turn him to look away from her.

"You're hurting me."

"Please, don't squirm, I just need to—"

She reached for the bandage at the back of his skull. He tried to swat at her, but she pressed his head flat against the pillow.

"Help," he cried meekly.

"You'll thank me later, I promise…"

With the needle ready, she tried to pull at the wrapping.

"Hold still, I—"

"What the hell are you doing?"

Sam turned to see a nurse standing at the door, mouth agape, watching her pinning Rick down and seemingly about to stab him.

"Uh, the cord came out," Sam said. "I don't know how to put it back in and—"

"You don't do that." The nurse ran over, snatching the tube and needle. "That's our job. You call us."

She looked over Rick, who moaned in pain, then checked

the IV and began to replace the needle and tube with new ones. "How the hell did this happen?" she asked. "And who the hell are you?"

"It was an accident really," Sam said. "I'm a friend but I was just leaving."

"Wait, ma'am. I want to talk to you a minute."

"Sorry, gotta go. I'll see you later, Rick."

"Ma'am..."

Sam ignored her and ran out of the room, moved with speed to the elevator and pressed the down button.

"Hey, you, stop!" the nurse called out from the door to the room.

The elevator pinged, the doors opened. Sam stepped inside. She rode it to the main floor, never looking back. She didn't feel safe until she was in the car on the way back to the apartment. Checking her rearview mirrors the whole way back, she realized then that there was a strong chance Rick was no longer one of them. She wondered how she'd be able to save him now.

Chapter 11

"And look at this one, the same scarification, but the limb is obviously from a much older man, I'd say nearly eighty. He must have been a veteran."

"Why would you say that?" Veronica asked.

Jacob examined a severed limb through a magnifying lens attached to a headband. He pointed out details with a pen as he spoke.

"Look, these are healed bullet wounds. Or the best thing to a facsimile I've ever seen."

"You think this old dude had them put on?" Carlos asked incredulously. "For what purpose?"

"To look tougher?" Jacob's assistant chimed in from the other side of the lab.

"We spoke to virtually every tattoo parlour in town," Veronica said. "This kind of stuff is illegal and—"

"And nobody would cop to doing it, of course," Carlos said.

"Right. And short of raiding them all to find out who's lying, we have to assume that any scarification is happening underground. If that's the case, there's no reason not to suspect that they might be doing things like this."

Carlos came over and looked at the limb. "Shit, they look real to me. Whoever did them is good."

"Hence my original theory," Jacob said, "that they are real, seems more plausible."

"So the man was a veteran of almost eighty, who'd been shot at some point in his life and recently had his arm cut off. What about the fingerprints?" Veronica asked.

"Burned off." Jacob turned the arm to show them the mangled skin of the fingers. The pads seemed to have been melted by acid.

"There's something oddly familiar about that hand," she said. She tried to think of all the old people she'd known who were male and nearly eighty. She was coming up empty. The only old man she'd seen recently was dead.

"You can ID it?" Carlos asked.

"No," she said. This couldn't be Frank's arm. She'd seen him laying on a stretcher, covered in a sheet, all in one piece. And eighty? There was no way he was that old, he'd only retired from the police force a few years ago. "I don't think I can. It was just a thought that went nowhere."

"This case is going nowhere," Carlos said. "We've almost got enough loose parts to make a new person and still no leads."

"That person would have to be made of only arms and legs," Jacob said. He rubbed his chin, distracted. "Now there's an idea. A human made only of limbs…"

"We've missed something," Veronica said, sitting back in her chair. The soft whir of Jacob's computer monitor, the chill in the room, the dim lights—the oppressive atmosphere wasn't helping her think. She needed to go out in the cruiser, let her mind wander, hope something clicked.

"Yeah, lunch," Carlos said. "How about I go and pick up some subs from the guy down the block?"

"Oh, I'll have a smoked meat one," the lab assistant said from the other end of the room.

"Egg salad," Jacob said.

"Turkey," Veronica added.

"Shit, four subs," Carlos said. "Sides? It's soup, chips or cookies."

"Just surprise us," Veronica said.

"But I wanted soup," the assistant said softly.

"Okay, four subs, assorted sides, what about drinks? It's combos so that's four cans of… oh hell, how am I going to carry all that?"

"I could give you a hand," Jacob said, brandishing the severed limb.

* * * *

With her feet on the desk, Veronica tried to piece together the events since the incident at the arena. The four of them, Rick, Igor, Sam, and her, had been meeting in a coffee shop, comparing notes, but none of them had seen a thing. The lab had up and vanished, the creature that the others had claimed to see hadn't reappeared, if they'd ever existed in the first place, and there'd been no signs of hypnosis or brainwashing effects. It looked more and more like their fears were unfounded, or that maybe, she'd somehow been played for a fool. That avenue seemed unlikely—there'd been too much going on down there that she couldn't explain at the time—but maybe whatever it was, was over. Maybe they were in the clear now. Maybe—

Her phone buzzed. A call from Samantha.

"Sam?"

"Detective Tockett, I just texted you, but this couldn't wait. Are you at work?"

"Where else would I be?"

"Can you get to Igor?"

"Igor, what are you talking about?"

"You mean you don't know?"

"Know what? I've been knee deep in something big and—"

Sam filled her in about Igor's arrest, his awaiting deportation, and the need to find out the truth from him about what had happened before it was too late.

She tapped away on her computer as Sam talked, verifying the story, finding out that Igor was indeed in custody.

"That's one hell of a story, Samantha, but there's just one problem. Igor's not here."

"He's not?"

"There're twelve precincts in River City. If he was brought in from New Jersey, then he'd have been taken by the RCMP at the airport. He'd be held in one of—"

"Can you get to him?"

"RCPD and RCMP have a bit of what's called a professional rivalry. I'd have to put in a few requests and hope for—"

"There's no time for bureaucracy. Who knows what's going to happen to him once he's out of sight? You have to try, right away."

Veronica sighed heavily. She was staring at her notes on the severed limbs, listening to her stomach grumble, and trying to decide if Samantha should be listened to at all.

"I found you Rick's room number, this is—"

"I think the Authority is taking us out one by one. Rick's in the hospital, Igor's about to be deported, this could be a part of their retaliation."

"NHL players get hurt all the time—"

"Not like this. I'm sure Rick had the mark. We need to know about Igor."

"I'll see what I can do. Just sit tight and don't do anything crazy. Leave this for the professionals, okay?"

"Text me as soon as you know something."

"I will."

She hung up and rose to her feet, just as Carlos came and plopped down a brown wrapped submarine sandwich on her desk.

"We'll have to eat it on the road, Carlos, I've got a lead."

She gathered up the food and her car keys and waved him forward. "Oh, and you're driving," she said. "I'm fucking starving."

* * * *

"We just need ten minutes with the guy. He's a suspect in something we're working on and—"

"I don't give a shit if he's a confessed serial killer," the RCMP officer at the desk said. "No authorization, no access. That's two no's, cops."

"Hey," she protested, "we're all on the same side here, right? Serve and protect? Keep the peace? I'm not asking for you to remand him into our custody, just to let us talk to him for ten, or how about five minutes? It's of vital importance to a huge—"

"This guy is not some fucking purse snatcher, lady," the man said in disdain.

"Detective Tockett," she said sternly, flashing her badge again.

"My orders came right from the top."

"Three minutes."

The man just shook his head.

Stymied, Veronica leaned her head back in frustration. The RCMP detachment at the airport was small, a dark brown cube of a room with a front desk and heavy grey door to the back area. There was never much going on here; the occasional arrest for smuggling, intoxication, someone with a falsified passport. The lock-up only had room for a few people at a time and there were only two officers on duty. She could probably take them if it came to that, but fighting an RCMP officer was career suicide. How would she justify that to the chief? Oh, sorry, boss, I needed to talk to their prisoner to find out if some kind of alien creature made him attack his centre? No, she had to do this by the book. She had to make them understand. But she was not only facing jurisdictional differences, but seemingly sexism as well.

"Look," Carlos chimed in. "Nobody's trying to horn in here, we just need to see Illyanovich, okay?"

The man turned to Carlos and shook his head again.

Carlos swung his phone around and showed them a betting app. "You play?"

"Sure. I had twelve bucks on the game the other night."

"What was that payoff?"

"Twelve hundred."

"Damn, well, I had fifty on it. And that asshole goalie blew it. If I'd won that bet, it was five Gs. You could say I'm a little pissed off at him."

What in the hell was Carlos doing? He was taking this in the completely wrong direction. But for some reason, the asshole mountie was listening.

"So what I'm proposing is this. You let my partner have her ten minutes, then you let me kick that fucking traitor in the balls as hard as I can. I figure that's payback for my lost five Gs."

"You want to beat the guy up?"

"No, just kick him in the balls. You said it yourself, he cost you money, too. And that kid Hansen was having a hell of a season. We were primed for a good playoff run. He's fucked the team and the two of us. Shit, he's fucked the city, all of Manitoba, maybe even all of Canada. The Jets could have been the first Canadian team to hoist Stanley since ninety-three. Think of that."

"Hmmm," the man said, considering the words.

She couldn't believe it. The fucker was actually thinking of going along with Carlos. Instead of her, who had an actual legitimately sound reason beyond testicle pain.

"Hey, Illyanovich is a disgrace. My partner here thinks he might also be a criminal. Give her the ten minutes, let me kick him in the balls, then we leave and you can pretend he just tripped on his handcuffs or something. Send him back to Chechnya with swollen nuts and an appreciation for what Canadians think of Joseph Willcocks."

"I don't know who that is, but I see your point. You can have five minutes with him on one condition," the man said.

"Name it," Veronica added, suddenly perking up.

"I get to kick him in the balls."

* * * *

Igor looked dehydrated. He wore only blue long johns. His hair was disheveled, beard unkempt, eyes wide with lack of sleep. Veronica stepped into the room. He looked over, barely registering her presence. Then, as if he suddenly recognized her, he sat up.

"Detective? Have you come to free me?"

"I'm sorry, Igor, no. Samantha sent me."

"Ahh, babushka. I am knowing she does not forget me."

"We need to know what happened at the game. The news is saying you attacked Rick."

"Me? This is not true. I came to his aid and—"

"Are you sure?"

She walked over and sat beside him, trying to see his neck for any signs of the implants Sam said to check for. His hair blocked the skin.

"Am I sure? What is this not believing? Watch the Sportscentre and you will see. I am not understanding."

"The footage is being suppressed. Nobody who wasn't there has seen it."

"Why?"

"That's what I'm trying to learn. Here, bend over for a second." She pushed his head. He didn't resist. She saw that his neck was clear—hairy, but clear of any scars.

"Why are you doing this?"

"To make sure you were telling the truth."

"Of course I am. I say, just watch the footage, it will prove my story."

"Igor, you don't understand. We can't get it. If anyone recorded it, they can't post it online. The story is you did it out of jealous rage over Rick having once dated Sam. They say you forged your visa documents. They're sending you back."

"Is all bullshit. Mr. Rick also dated babushka?" Igor said

haltingly.

"In high school apparently."

Igor smiled. "The man has very good taste, yes? But detective, I am not wanting to go back to Chechnya. It is a shit hole. I love Canada. Please don't let them do this."

"I'd need the footage to prove your innocence."

"Simple. Call my wife."

"Wait, your wife?"

"Yes, she is always filming all of my games. She makes what you call highlight reels."

"Igor, you're married?"

"Yes."

"But I thought you were dating babushka… errr, Samantha?"

"Yes," he said happily

"I don't understand."

"Is open marriage. She stayed in New Jersey when I was traded to the Jets two years ago. She comes to all the games I appear. She loves to film in person. Is much better than taping from online."

"Shit, Igor, give me her phone number."

"Of course!"

She handed him her phone and he tapped in the contact for 'Illyana Illyanovich,' complete with digits and a note saying 'number two babushka.'

There was a knock on the door. The five minutes were up. Veronica stood up and he handed her back the phone.

"Okay, thanks, Igor. I'll do my best to help you."

"Please. I am not wanting to have to return to Chechnya. My Czech wife lives there."

"Are you still married to her, too?"

"Yes, but she is a terrible cook."

Veronica opened the camera app, bent Igor's head forward and snapped the shot of his neck, then squeezed his shoulder. "Stay strong. We're all on this."

The door pushed open. "Time's up, meter maid."

"Okay, okay, I'm going." She stepped to the door, then realized she'd forgotten something important. "Igor, one last thing."

"Yes?"

"You have to let this guy kick you in the balls."

Chapter 12

A photo came through via text. Sam, sitting in the empty futon room, opened it up to see a harshly lit shot of the back of a man's hairy neck.

"What is this supposed to be?"

Then, a line from Detective Tockett. "Igor clear. New angle to work on."

"What new angle?" Sam texted back. "What did he say? Should we meet?"

The three lines of text showed 'delivered.' Sam waited, watching for any response. The futon room was eerily deserted. It seemed like there was nobody around campus at all. She'd come early, wanting to catch up with her friends after a few days of being holed up working on a term paper. She'd overslept and missed Erin in the morning. They didn't always sleep in the same bed due to conflicting schedules. Erin often had early morning bakery shifts and didn't want to disturb Sam when she had later classes. On those nights they almost always kept to their own rooms.

Still not seeing anything coming from Detective Tockett, Sam sent a message to Erin. "Hey. What's up? Workin'?" She added a few heart emojis for good measure.

Despite their relationship starting under confused circumstances, it was probably the only sane thing in her life right now. Being with Erin helped her forget, even if only for brief moments, the Authority, Factor 5ive, Radiant Cyanide, golems, mind control, Debbie, her parents splitting up, or having burnt through way too much of her savings the past year and a half. Their time together just felt… right.

But Erin wasn't answering either.

"Maybe she's with Avital?"

She sent her a message. Then one to Everett and Marlon and another apology to Rick just in case. Nobody was getting back to her.

"What the hell?"

Sam shoved her phone into her purse and leaned back on the candy-striped futon. It was so impossibly quiet. At this time of day the place should be hopping, jam-packed with people eating and chatting. Sometimes they'd even have to wait for a free futon. And yet, it was a ghost town.

"Where is everyone? Is this a stat that I missed?"

She checked her calendar. "Nope, ordinary day. So, what gives?"

At the end of the room, a single elevator descended from the upper level. The column was clear glass, but the compartment itself was dark metallic green. She watched the gears and hydraulics working their magic, happy that someone else was finally coming. She felt so alone and exposed.

The cab stopped. The doors slowly opened.

Marlon stepped out. She relaxed. He wore a fedora, a RAW is WAR T-shirt and tan pants, and carried a bag over his shoulder. He'd shaved and looked cleaner than she'd ever seen him. His clothes fit right, too.

"Marlon." She waved.

He made no indication at having seen her. He simply stepped out to stand away from the elevator. A second person followed and Sam's jaw dropped.

It was the woman who'd chased her at the Geld Conference Centre and Resort. The jacked bodybuilder with the two-coloured hair: half red, half black. She wore a red floral dress under an open parka. She was covered in tattoos and looked like she could probably bend a crowbar with her thick arms.

Sam stood up as the hair on the back of her neck rose with the sign of danger.

"Marlon?"

The two of them, seeming oblivious to her words, marched towards her in unison.

"Marlon, that's…"

There was something wrong with their eyes. They were dead, unfocused, as if they were staring off into space. The duo moved rigidly, stiff-legged, like they were—

"Oh no." They were acting like they were under the control of a heartstone, like they were golems.

But she had to make sure.

"Who is this? Is this your message board girl?"

Silence. They were only a few meters away. Two on one. She could probably take them on, her hapkido training being almost second nature at this point. But how could she hurt Marlon? He was a friend under someone's power. She had to figure out a way to stop him gently. Then she could deal with the girl more indiscriminately. With her out of the way, maybe she could free Marlon from whoever was in control. But how to incapacitate the big man?

The backpack.

Maybe she could use the straps to latch him onto something.

"Marlon, wake up. Snap out of it."

She backed away, hands held up in surrender, wondering if campus security was around, or if they'd see this on security cameras. Would calling for help be a good idea? No, they'd have way too many questions, might even arrest Marlon. How the hell would she convince them he wasn't acting of his own free will? Doing this here, in the open, might attract attention. She'd have to lead them away. There was a series of tunnels that connected the buildings on campus, leading to out-of-the-way locker areas that few people passed even in peak times. That could work.

"Marlon, I know what's going on. This girl, she's using you to get to me."

No response. Not that she thought there would be.

Looking over her shoulder, she saw the door to the underground tunnels. She bolted, pulled it open and stepped through. The two of them just kept walking, like robots. Brightly coloured piping lined the walls, signs at branches pointed to the different buildings on campus. The low hum of air conditioning and movement within the pipes was the only sound here below the city streets.

"Still no one around, eh?" Sam said, half jogging, half backwards walking, making sure Marlon and the woman weren't gaining on her, but were still following.

The building C junction lay ahead. There was a series of locker hallways here, rarely used. Covered in graffiti, the doors were painted in red and blue. There wouldn't be any locks on them. Sam figured she could use them to her advantage in the coming fight.

"Come on, almost there."

Another closed door. The window inset showed the hallway beyond as empty as ever. Sam stepped through.

"Okay, let's do this."

She stopped, took a deep breath and waited, visualizing what she was going to have to do. The muscled woman came first. She reached out for Sam's neck. Sam grabbed a locker door and swung it out, then stepped gingerly to the right and pushed the reaching woman as hard as she could inside the locker. She was too broad in the shoulders to go in straight, so Sam shoulder-checked her. The woman's head clanged on the metal backing. Sam tried to push her in, but a hand closed on her shoulder.

Marlon.

He pulled her back and she stepped under his grip, twisting out and putting him in line with the woman pushing herself out of the locker.

His blank expression was unassuming. His eyes were vacant. He barely seemed to be breathing at all. She charged right at him, thinking to slam him up against the woman and sandwich her inside the locker, but she'd completely misjudged how heavy Marlon actually was. She rammed into a wall.

"Oh shit."

Before she could react, he slugged her in the gut and knocked the wind out of her. Struggling for breath, Sam bent over, nearly dropping to her knees. A hand grabbed her hair and swung her head into the wall with a huge crash, knocking her loopy. Stars filled her vision as she collapsed to the ground.

"What the fuck, Marlon?" She coughed.

She struggled to her hands and knees, realizing now that

she'd been too careless. She'd gotten cocky after taking out the guys from the bands, let her high rank in hapkido go to her head. She had to step up or she was in real trouble.

A boot crashed into her ribs, one of the woman's heavy black laced heels. Sam rolled with the kick, away from her, into the middle of the hall.

"You guys aren't messing around," she groaned. "Now I'm not either."

The woman stepped forward first. Sam rolled, reached out and pressed her hand against the woman's knee above the cap, pulled at the ankle with her other hand and threw the creature off balance. She stepped up, holding the foot, and kicked out the girl's other leg, sending her to the ground in a heap, head striking the side of a locker with a loud bang. Before it could recover, Sam grabbed the heel, twisted hard, snapping the joint. With a sick pop of tendon and cartilage, she let go. The woman's foot was turned the wrong way, at an impossible angle. It was now a one-legged monster, trying to get to its feet, toppling over on the mangled foot, unable to stay upright.

"That'll keep you out of my hair for a—"

Marlon wrapped his arms around her body, pinning hers tight against her sides. He hoisted her up and she kicked at the air. He began squeezing. She felt her arms losing circulation, ribs giving way; the guy was way stronger than she'd expected.

"Marlon, let go, you're crushing me."

He wouldn't understand, not if he was under the control of a heartstone. She had to stop him on her own.

Hooking her foot behind his, she used every last bit of strength to slide her elbows up, ducking under his grip. He tried to wrap his hands around her neck, but she snaked out, got behind him and pushed him again. This time his balance was off, and he was flung forward. She tripped him, sending him flying on top of the woman struggling to rise.

He landed hard on her. This was her shot. Sam pounced, pushing him down, sitting on his back. She lifted his right leg, looped it through the other arm of his backpack. The man tried to straighten out his leg, only serving to tighten the bond. He struggled like a flopping fish, arm and opposite leg fighting each other, tied down with the straps of his backpack.

It wasn't going to hold him forever, but it was enough for now.

Sam brushed herself off and casually walked up to the one-legged woman bodybuilder. She grabbed her by the hair and took a locker door in her other hand. She slammed it against its head. Three, four times, each blow crashing loudly in the empty hall. The woman just pawed at her.

Sam grabbed one of her wrists and twisted fast in a jerking motion, snapping the creature's limb instantly. Its dangling hand slapped her like cold meat.

"Jesus, you don't quit."

Sam let the woman pull herself up slowly with the edge of the locker. Then she rammed her again, wedging her upper torso in awkwardly. She pulled the girl's good leg and the woman fell down, dangling half in and half out of the locker. Sam grabbed the flailing feet, yanked out the laces of the high boots and tied the woman's ankles together, then tied her hands behind her back.

The incapacitated thing squirmed, but was out of commission at last.

She turned to Marlon, watching the man thwarted by his

own backpack, and grabbed his hair, pushing his head down to see a bandage. She tore it off and her fears were confirmed. Stitches, from a recent implantation.

"They got you."

She let go of his head and dug into her purse. She pulled out her keychain.

"I'm really sorry, Marlon, this is not sanitary at all."

She held his head and dug the keys into his skin, tearing at the thin stitches, bloodying his shirt, the floor, her hands. Crimson gore seeped out in spurts. He fought it, but she picked away at the flaky red scab and reopened the wound. She jammed her fingers inside and felt around for the tiny stone. The flaps of skin billowed out, thick clear goo washing over her. Moist dampness, a thick slab of meat, her fingers sliding around inside the wound. Then, she found the stone. It was about the size of a marble. She shoved her fingers deeper, trying to clasp around the circumference. This would be so painful if he weren't under hypnosis. Then, wrapping around the tiny ball, she pulled hard and had the stone out with a slick sound of suction.

Her whole hand and most of her forearm was glistening red. A circle of blood slowly formed around the man's body. He fell limp.

"Have to stop the bleeding."

She yanked off her sock and pressed it down against the back of Marlon's neck. It was quickly soaked through. It wasn't going to be enough.

There was a bathroom down the hall. She ran inside and took out a paper towel roll from the dispenser and returned to the sound of Marlon moaning. She unrolled a huge wad and pressed it against his neck.

"Easy," she said, helping him roll over.

"Sam?" he said. Then he saw the blood all over her. "What the fuck?"

He squirmed away, seeing her hand holding a bloody paper towel wad.

"You need to keep something on that cut," she said, handing him more. "And you're going to want to get a band-aid, some peroxide, probably stitches."

"What the motherfucking hell did you do?"

"I saved you," Sam said. "They'd changed you."

"I don't know what the hell you're talking about."

Then he noticed the woman with the two-toned hair, hogtied, half stuck in a locker, with one of her feet turned the wrong way.

"Peta!" Marlon screamed and shuffled over to her. "What the hell happened to her?"

"Self-defence. The two of you attacked me and—"

"Attacked you? I don't know what—" He looked around his surroundings, as if he was suddenly realizing where he was. "Wait, how did we get here? The last thing I remember I was in the encampment and—"

"The encampment?"

"School? We're at school? That makes no sense. We were in a tent and—"

"Marlon, you're rambling. What are you talking about, tents and encampments? Were the two of you out camping or something? In the middle of winter?"

"No, we were at the encampment at the legislative grounds. You know, the Students for a Just World walk-out. Occupy Again? Occupy 2.0. Fight the power. The new general strike. How did you not hear about this?"

"I saw some headlines, but I didn't read the articles. I was working on a term paper. What the hell is this walk-out?"

"Graham called it. A total student strike. Everyone's put up tents. There's a whole village at the legislative grounds. And it's not just River City University either. The University of Manitoba, Brandon, hell, they're doing it all across the country. The world, probably. I don't know if it started here or just came here, but it's big. I *was* there, but now I'm here. How?" he said, trailing off and trying to think, then he remembered he was wounded. "Shit, you fucking cut me!"

"You don't remember coming here? With her? Attacking me?"

"Sam, are you on something?"

"Look, Marlon. What's been going on with this girl?"

"Uh, dating."

"Wait, what?"

"She's loves wrestling and… she's the one I met online and… Sam, you fucking hurt her. Look at her foot. They're not supposed to bend that way."

Marlon started to untie her legs and then pulled her out of the locker. His neck wound bled down onto his shirt, but he didn't seem to notice or care. He rolled Peta over. The thing's eyes were glazed over, and she'd gone slack like she was unconscious. The control had stopped.

"Jesus, look at her."

Peta's face was bloody. One wrist was broken, one leg mangled. She looked like a prize fighter who'd gone five rounds and lost.

"I'm sorry, but it was her or me and—"

"Her or you? You are fucking nuts."

"Listen to me. At some point they implanted a stone into

95

your neck." Sam showed him the bloody marble in her crimson palm. "She probably has one, too. Unless she was created in a lab, then I'm not so sure. Let me check and if there's one, I can cut it out. It'll cure her." Holding the bloody keys, she reached for Peta, but Marlon shielded her.

"Get the fuck away from her. You're not touching her again."

"Marlon, she could be a golem. I need to—"

"She's my girlfriend."

"They sent her to get to me, through you, and—"

"Wow, main character syndrome. It's so impossible that someone was interested in me and—"

"She approached you through a pro-wrestling forum, right?"

"So what? She's a pro-wrestler herself, or was, and—"

"And she tried to kill me."

"The only thing I see is the two of us bloody and beaten up and you covered in our blood. So who tried to kill who?"

"Just let me get the stone out then—"

Marlon pushed her away. "I'm taking her to a hospital. You've done enough."

"She's a golem. You were a golem, too. I cured you, let me cure her."

"I don't fucking care what she is. You are not curing anyone."

"Whoever sent her will just turn you again and—"

"If that's the only way to be with a woman like this, then golem me up, man. Look at her. She's the best-looking thing I'm ever going to get with. I had sex with her, Sam. Real human sex. It was amazing. I saw and touched tits. Hers. She let me. Just like that. Took off her shirt and let me touch her tits. Then we had sex. More than once even. I don't care if she's the bride of Frankenstein herself, she's mine and I'm not letting you ruin this."

"Marlon, this is about free will, mind control, the Authority's plans and—"

"I'm getting her medical attention." He hoisted her up and wrapped her arm over his shoulder. "And getting her away from you." He started to walk away, down the hall.

"They'll try again. Nothing will be resolved unless I get the stone out of her."

"Just be glad I'm not calling the cops on you. That's your one freebie for sending me that video with you and Erin."

"What vid—"

"Even though it was probably to rub it all in my face."

"You don't understand. I didn't send—"

"Doesn't matter. After this, if you ever come near either one of us again, all bets are off."

"This was an attack on me."

"Fuck you. I finally get something good in my life, and you make it all about yourself. First Erin, now this. We're done, Sam. For good."

"Please, I—"

He ignored her, carrying Peta down the hall and through the doors.

Sam fell backwards against a locker with a loud clang. Everything was spiralling out of control. Rick was pissed at her and probably compromised, Igor was about to be deported, her friends had gone AWOL, and now Marlon was willingly letting himself be a pawn just to get laid.

It had been some kind of miracle that no one had been here to witness the fight. But she had a problem. The floor was

97

a mess of blood. She couldn't leave it here, someone would spot it, call the cops, all kinds of strange questions would arise. She had to clean it up. The rest of the paper towel roll lay nearby. She got to work.

"Rick, Igor, Avital, Everett, Erin, Marlon…"

She was being cut off from everyone. No friends, no compatriots in the coffee group… who was left for her to turn to now?

Chapter 13

"Do you know who I am?" the old man asked him. Grey hair, sharp eyes, strongly defined features; he radiated power and authority. The man held a small blue gemstone in his hand as he talked.

His gaze was locked on the stone however. Within the facets, he thought he could see the swirling tides of the ocean. The sensation seemed to bleed through to his other senses. He could practically smell the salt breeze and feel the sand below his feet.

"I am your father, so to speak," the man said. "You have been created to fulfill a singular purpose. You are going to do my bidding which is, in turn, the work of the Authority."

Shifting in place, the ocean gave way to his current surroundings. A small blank room. He wore black pants and a black shirt, a heavy jacket and gloves. The leather of the gloves felt tight against his palms, and he flexed his fingers, straining against the material.

"You will go out into the world and await my call."

Eyes locked on the blue of the stone, the words penetrated the fog of his mind. He suddenly knew what he was to do. He turned from the old man and left, exiting through a door into a white hallway. He'd never seen this place before. He had no idea where it was, and yet knew where to go anyway. He walked along the long, white, walled corridor to an elevator. He pushed the down button, the doors slowly opening with a ping. He climbed inside, pushed the G button and waited. A soft tune played over a hidden speaker. He recognized the song, from somewhere in the distant past. A memory struggled to make itself clear. A beach. A boardwalk. A house on a hill. Then it was gone in a flash of flame.

The elevator stopped. The doors swung open. He walked right past a man sitting at a desk in front of a series of monitors showing more empty rooms and halls. Another memory. An echo of the past. A feeling of déjà vu. Did he know that man? Did he know the uniform?

He stepped outside. It was cold and drab, a bitter wind blowing from the north. People wandered the sidewalks keeping their collars turned up, coats pulled tight, eyes down. *Where?*

Somehow, he knew. He walked down the street. Something about this was too familiar. As if he'd been doing it forever. And yet, he couldn't remember anything before waking up to that blue stone. A siren wailed in the distance. A police car screamed down the street.

Police.

A smell wafted into his nostrils, from an open door to his right. He couldn't read the sign. Why not? He pushed open the door and saw people sitting in chairs, drinking coffee, talking amongst themselves. Somehow he knew he'd been here before, too.

A dark-haired woman and tan-skinned man approached, carrying a box and two coffees.

"—so he says, hey, I'm trying to eat lunch here!" They

100

laughed as they passed him.

A display case caught his attention. Under the glass were colours and flavours, chocolate, powdered sugar, crueller. The names and tastes were back on his tongue in a flash of remembrance.

"You want some donuts, buddy?" the man behind the counter asked.

Buddy? Was that his name? It didn't sound right. His hands went into his pockets instinctively, but came up empty. What was he looking for?

"No bread, no pastries, man, this ain't a charity."

A throbbing pain wracked his head. He stumbled through the door and out into the street, nearly slipping on an icy patch of sidewalk.

"Watch it, brother, ain't you learned how to walk on ice?"

Gripping a lamppost, he steadied his feet to stop the pain. Then he walked away, towards a great big blue glass building. He saw a face reflected back. It was that of a man with long dark hair, dark eyes, strong features and a thickly muscled body.

Is that me?

It didn't seem right; the image was of a stranger. But something behind him rang an inner bell. A man and a cart, next to the arena. How did he know it was the arena? The man sat in a patio chair with a tiny space heater at his feet while people passed by. The words on the cart were clear now. He could read them again. 'Hot Dogs.'

He walked across the street. Tires screeched, a car honked, someone shouted.

"Watch the fuck where you're going, asshole."

He ignored the voice and kept going, stopping as the aroma

of barbecued hot dogs filled his nostrils. The smell was intoxicating, washing away the last vestiges of the salt air that clung to his senses. It triggered something deep inside him, a memory from...

Onions. Mustard. Sauerkraut.

The man sitting down saw him standing at the cart and perked up. He rose to his feet with a smile.

"Finally! Hello, friend, you looking for a nice hotdog? I got the best in town. Although right now, I got the only ones in town. Ain't nobody stupid enough to try to sell in winter in River City.

'Cept me, of course. This spot used to be a gold mine. I only stayed in business in winter 'cause this place was so good to me. Wanna know why? Cops. One, in particular—nice old guy, Frankie something or other. He was here all the time. He ate so many he practically put my kids through college. Until they all walked out at least. Had a funny way of telling stories, too. But hell, the guy loved his wieners. He could pound 'em back like no one else I seen. Sometimes, I wonder what happened to him. It's been a dog's age. Things are slow without him, ahhh, I should probably pack it in. Wife wants me to, at least. But I keep hoping he'll come back. I'm saving up to get a trailer, retire on the coast. Pipe dream though. I'm just sitting most of the time now. I sure could use another whale like that cop to buy some of my frankfurters... shit, I'm standing here talking your ear off. You can tell I've been too long without a customer. What do you want?"

He licked his lips, imagining the taste of one of those delicious wieners. He loved them covered in onions, mustard, sauerkraut. Or did he?

He reached into his pockets, came up empty, showed the

man at the cart his palms.

"No money? Ah hell, I'll give you one on the house today. But only 'cause it's been so long since anyone stopped here, and you did an old man a solid by listening to him ramble."

He went to work getting a bun from the warmer and filling it with a wiener, then putting them into a paper sleeve and handing it over.

"Here ya go. Free sample. Just make sure you come back with money next time. And tell all your friends. If they got money, that is. Hell, maybe ask around for that old cop Frankie whatsisname. See if he's still in town. I could use the business."

He took the hotdog. The man lifted the lids to the toppings and waved at them proudly. Chopped onions, sauerkraut, banana peppers... he loaded them all on, sprayed a covering of mustard on top.

"Damn buddy, that's a load. You sure know how you like 'em. Say, there's a coincidence. That's just how I remember old Frankie liked 'em. More toppings than wiener half the time. Shit, I'll bet his farts stunk."

The man laughed and sat back down, sticking his hands close to the space heater.

Holding the piled hotdog, watching the steam rise from the cooked wiener, he walked to the edge of the arena and up the narrow side street. He stopped and took a bite. Chewing, feeling the crunch of the onions, the slippery mustard, the chewy beef and heat of the peppers brought more memories back. Eating this very thing in this very spot. But with very different hands.

"Hey, man, you looking to score?" a hunched over man dressed in a long coat and toque said, waving to him from the alley that went behind the arena. The guy's eyes shifted as he moved from one foot to the other like he had something in his boots.

He didn't reply, wasn't sure he knew how. He just took another bite. The man mistook his presence for interest and continued.

"Mary Jane, E, salts, a little oil? What you want, I got. Girls? Yeah, you look like you want girls. No? Maybe a dude, a big hairy bear for you? An otter? What age? What sex? What kink? Come on, man, don't just stand there looking all confused, tell me what you want or get the fuck out of my place of business."

As the meat descended into his stomach and the odour of the onions cleared his sinuses, the fog in his head was starting to dissipate. He remembered more with every passing second.

"Fuck you, man, get out of here. I got no time for no crazies, you gonna draw attention to me. You want the cops on my ass? Shit." He reached into his pocket and pulled out a little handle, flicking it once and clicking it. A tiny blade shot out, glistening in the daylight. "Take a hike before I stick you."

He just stared at him and took another bite. The last one of his lunch. It was clear now. Gino's dogs. Donuts. The city streets. And now... a criminal.

The man's eyes squinted as he came to a sudden realization at the same time. "You a cop?"

A cop.

That's exactly who he was.

He was a cop who'd had his lunch.

He was a cop who'd had his lunch and this man was a criminal.

There was only one thing to do with scum like him.

He wiped his hands on his jacket, then reached out and grabbed the man's wrist, the one holding the blade. He squeezed and the sick sound of bones crunching filled his ears. His grip was much stronger than he remembered. The man screamed in pain and dropped to his knees. He let him go.

"My hand, man, my hand. You done fucked up my hand!" He held up a wrist that had been compressed into licorice, with fingers flayed out like dying flowers from a bouquet of gore and crunched bones.

His tongue and throat tried to form words. The action seemed almost foreign. A slurring moan escaped out and the man looked at him, confused.

"Huh? You not speak English, brochacho?"

"Nnnnnnnnnnnn—ooooooooooo—wwwwwww..."

"Now? Now what?" the man asked. "You got some kind of mental deficiency, motherfucker? You short bus material? What you trying to say?"

"N-o-w... y—o—uuuu need t-t-t-t-ooooo..."

"Now I need to what? Huh? Now I need to what? Shit, I can't stand here all day. I need medical attention on my hand, man!"

"Now you need to under-s-s-s-s-stand..."

"Understand? Shit, I can't understand you worth fuck!"

Then it clicked. His tongue, his voice, they were back.

"Now you need to understand," he said and grabbed the man by the collar. His voice was deeper than he remembered. Stronger, booming. He liked it. It had authority.

"That I'm your worst nightmare, punk, and it's time you took your poison the hell off my streets."

"Your streets?" The man looked at him with terrified eyes, holding his useless hand, dripping snot from his nose.

"That's right. I'm not sure where I've been, but I'm back home. And home is where the heart is. And where the heart beats, the city sleeps. Safely knowing that a doctor is watching out. A doctor with a degree in protection. Fifty years of the best medical school there is, doing surgery on every sidewalk, alley, and back lane in this place I call home. Home, which is where I'm back, by the way. Back for good."

Holding the man aloft, far too easily with one hand, he bent over and picked up the knife, closing it up and stuffing it in his jacket pocket.

"Now let me put you where you belong."

He walked over to a dumpster, lifted the lid, and brutally threw the man in head-first. He slammed the lid down.

"One more criminal off the streets."

The mind, the body, the fog faded; everything was clear. He knew who he was now, even if the mirror had lied. The features were all wrong, but he was Detective Inspector Sergeant Frank Malone. He had no idea where he'd been, but he was going to clean up this town all over again. He turned to look back out at his city, at the cars driving past, the people walking down the sidewalks. The smells, the sounds, the cold air. It was as if he'd never left. Sure, he couldn't remember exactly where he'd been, but that didn't matter when he knew his purpose.

"River City, Frank's home."

Chapter 14

"Yoù've been acting funny all day, Tockett," Carlos said as he drove the cruiser down the slushy roads of downtown River City. "Is it because it's my turn to drive?"

"It's not that, Carlos." Veronica clutched a tiny square USB drive in her hand, thinking about the implications of the video she'd transferred on to it. Jerky cellphone footage of a brawl at the New Jersey Devils / River City Jets game, showing a New Jersey player hitting Rick Hansen with an elbow, then Igor and the rest of the team coming to his defence with the crowd in a frenzy and the player's equipment scattered everywhere. And yet, the official story was totally different.

"You as pissed as everyone else about those fucking students taking over the legislative grounds?"

"I hadn't really noticed that."

"And you call yourself a detective?"

"Been a little distracted."

"Your time of the month?"

"None of your business, jerk, but no to that, too."

Nobody from the Jets or Devils had contradicted the Igor attack story in interviews. The press in both cities, heck, even

Igor's other wife had all said that the situation had gone on like they were reporting.

"Why do you want footage of Igor losing his mind?" the wife had asked her when she'd called her.

"I, uh, need it to help his case," she'd said.

"Are you another of his wives?"

"No, I'm, uh, his lawyer."

"Bah, I was going to delete it anyway. I'm no longer making videos of him after finding out he has a girlfriend in River City."

"But you knew about his other wives?"

"Of course. At least they are making honest man out of him. This slut... ptooie," she'd spat.

That had ended the call but moments later, the video had appeared. Thinking that she was all set to receive nothing more than a clip making Sam and Igor look insane, Veronica had been surprised to see that the video, in fact, showed exactly what Igor had said had happened.

"It doesn't make any sense," she muttered, wondering why Igor's wife had lied. Or had she only seen what she'd been told she'd seen?

"Look, Ronnie," Carlos said, snapping her out of her reverie, "TJ Hooker makes no sense. Five seasons of Shatner as a cop? Who the fuck green-lit that? This case is simple gang warfare."

Burton Cummings blared from her phone. It was Jimmy calling her, probably wondering when she was coming home. She was tired. It had been a long day, and she was looking forward to taking a hot shower, heating up whatever he'd made for dinner, plopping down on the couch and falling asleep to another season of whatever the heck show they'd been watching.

Carlos pulled up to a red light and came to a slow stop. "You gonna answer that?"

She hit the 'busy right now' automatic reply and shoved the phone back into her pocket. "I'll call him when we're done."

"Jeez, the guy's turning into a real ball and chain, eh?"

"He's probably just desperate for adult conversation after being with two kids all day."

"Desperate for something, maybe."

"I'm ignoring that."

"Probably ignoring him, too, judging by how bitchy you've been lately."

"Bitchy? I'm just wracking my brain trying to figure out why we keep finding body parts and no bodies. Body parts that don't even match up to make a whole body. The hospitals aren't filling up with limbless people complaining of not being able to check their watches anymore, or of suddenly becoming the perfect partners for the three-legged race."

Carlos snorted. "You should try out for the funniest person with a day job contest they run down at Rumours comedy club. Lines like that, you'd be a shoe-in."

"It wasn't a joke. We've got the chief on our asses wanting to know why we've got no leads, and now some shithead went and leaked the story to the papers. Someone's calling this a Chicago Phil copycat case, wondering if there's some sicko cannibal on the loose again."

"Didn't Hooper work that case?"

"He did. With Malone."

"So?"

"So we're not going to repeat what they did. They just rebuilt that part of the University of Manitoba campus."

"Nobody bought the gas leak story, you know," Carlos

said. "There was a pool going that Malone blew the place up himself. But nobody ever collected. The reports they filed were all by the book."

"Jimmy didn't elaborate much. Just said it was a wild scene."

"Well, what did he say? Maybe someone can still collect."

"That's not important. What is important right now is catching this new killer. Your gangland contacts have given us bupkis. This killer, or arm-and-leg bandit, as the press are calling him—"

"Or her."

"We both know the stats on serial killers."

"Hey, I'm just trying to be PC."

"For the first fucking time in your life."

Moving again, Veronica turned to watch the streets going by in the passenger window. Her phone pinged with a text. Jimmy probably. She'd look later. She didn't want to lose her train of thought. She needed to work this out loud, bounce ideas off her partner.

"The MO isn't even the same for each part. Jacob says some of the limbs all seem to have just fallen off. The breaks aren't clean, like from a knife or blade, no sign of tearing either."

"Yeah, I know what he says, but come on. He's got to be wrong. Limbs falling off? Jesus, what are these guys, dolls or something?" He snorted again.

"Wait a minute," Veronica said, looking back to him. "You know what, Jimmy told me something else, early on when we were dating. I don't know why I didn't remember any of this until now. I guess I thought it was just a story but—"

"You mean when you were still busy fucking like rabbits?"

"Carlos, shut up and listen. Jimmy told me about the last case he and Frank worked on. It took years before they closed it off. It ended up with Frank shooting a high school student."

"I heard Malone shot a lot of people, never under eighteen though."

"The kid was a real head case, Jimmy said. There were body parts in this house he was squatting in. Some had been stitched together, some had fallen apart. Apparently, he was trying to create monsters."

"Fuck, he was a regular Doctor Frankenstein."

"Exactly. That's the connection."

"You think this kid is back from the grave?"

"What? No. I think that whatever that kid was into must not have been as limited to his fucked-up brain as it seemed."

"He had help?"

"Or someone else is using the same processes."

Carlos stopped at another red light and shot her a skeptical frown. "Tockett, you're the one turning into a head case here."

She didn't know if she could really trust him. Every day, she made sure to look at his neck and every day he was clean. But to just tell him all about the lab under the MTS centre, the wild story Samantha and Rick had related, to expose the existence of the Authority. What if Carlos was one of those inhuman… things, or if he was secretly working for them? No, better not to tell him too much.

"I'm just saying, maybe what Frank thought he ended, wasn't as buried as the rest of us all assumed."

"You've got something you're not telling me."

"Green light." She pointed.

Carlos continued forward, looking at her expectantly every few moments, clearly waiting for her to elaborate. It was obvious he wasn't going to let this slide. She had to feed him something until she knew for sure if he could be trusted.

Better check him again first.

"You've got something on your neck." She pointed.

He rubbed his hand over his neck. "I get it?"

"No, let me do it." She leaned over and brushed the imaginary dirt, seeing that he didn't have the telltale scar of heartstone implantation. Was that enough to fill him in?

Before she could decide either way, she spotted shadows dancing on the walls of an alleyway. A fight.

"Whoa, stop the car," she shouted.

Carlos slammed on his brakes and skidded the car over a lane to the side. It took ten feet before it came to a full stop.

She was out the door with her gun ready before he could even ask her what was going on. She ran back towards the alley, heard a crash, and saw the shadow of a body flying through the air.

"Tockett, wait up."

She slid to a stop at the edge, took a deep breath, readied her gun, and turned the corner.

"Stop, police. Put your hands up and no one has to take a bullet."

Silence.

The alley was empty. A light from above the back door of the building to her left was the only illumination. The shadows of the dumpsters stretched away from her, trash blowing in the breeze.

"What the hell?" Carlos said, catching up, panting.

"I was sure I'd seen something going on."

Was she so tired that her eyes were playing tricks on her now?

Then, a moan. She pointed her gun towards the sound.

"Someone there?" Carlos called out.

112

Veronica shuffled her feet, inch by inch, to the edge of a dumpster. She heard the moan again. She leapt out, aimed where she figured the noise was coming from.

"Stop where you... lay?"

A man in a leather jacket, half-conscious, sat in the fetal position, wrapped up with a steel stop sign pole bent around his body.

Carlos crouched down to check the man's pulse.

"He's still alive, for now."

Veronica saw what looked like handprints buried in the gunmetal steel.

"Jesus Christ," she said. "Did someone do this with his bare hands? Who could do that?"

The man moaned again in obvious pain.

"Arnold fucking Schwarzenegger, that's who," Carlos said. "Or maybe one of those punk students high on something serious."

"I don't know."

Veronica rose up and scanned in both directions of the alley, but saw no sign of anyone. Somehow they'd missed them. How? They'd been so close.

"I guess we'll just have to ask him then. If he wakes up."

She looked down at the man trapped in steel and rubbed her chin. The bigger question was how they were going to get him loose. "We'd better go get the jaws of life."

Chapter 15

"I can't take much more of this," Sam said, struggling for breath.

"You're almost done." Jan handed her a water bottle. "You're doing great."

Sam took the bottle and drained it, but it still wasn't enough to make her feel like she could remain upright for much longer. "Then why do I feel like dying?"

"Because this is a black belt test. It's supposed to push you to your limits."

"I think Master Park is secretly a sadist and likes to see us suffer."

Three hours into the most gruelling physical experience of her life, Sam was ready to just surrender. She'd been so distracted lately that the test date had snuck up on her. They'd been practicing hard, but with everything that had happened to Igor and Rick, it hadn't seemed as important. Then she'd walked into what she thought was her usual class to see a desk set up, an audience sitting in the pews, and the rest of the class already stretching.

"Nice to see you could make it, Miss Abraham," Master Park had said with his stoic, emotionless Korean glare.

From there, it had been a blur of activity. Patterns, kicking, flipping and rolling, staff work, then a demonstration of each and every self-defence maneuver, joint lock, judo throw, knife defence, and attack deflection she knew. At this point, so many came naturally that her unpreparedness had forced her to use muscle memory. But Park had been relentless, nonetheless. He'd seemingly revelled in pushing her as far as he could.

Sweat poured down her face, down her back, soaked her dobuk. Her hair was a mess, and she knew there were going to be bruises all over her body from where she'd taken shots during the attacking phase. Her knees were quivering. She'd nearly fainted a few times, but she was still alive. She took deep breaths, and watched through the window that separated the blue padded training room from the rest of the gym. Another group was going through their two-on-one combat demonstration. Park and a visiting Grandmaster from the Korean Hapkido Federation watched in their dark suits, taking notes, not showing a fraction of emotion. It was hard to know what to think. The cries of attack, the thuds of bodies, the over-reacting screaming and pounding on the mat; it all looked fine to her. But if you looked at Master Park's face, you'd think he was doing his best to hold in a fart.

"You feel up for sparring?" Jan asked.

The thick, blond-haired Jan, almost a foot taller than Sam, had been one of her most consistent training partners. He was always paired with her for demonstrations, for what Sam assumed were the optics of a much smaller woman tossing around a larger attacker. That always drew the ooohs from the crowds. And yet, for as long as she'd been coming here, almost six years, he'd just been a training partner. He'd harboured an obvious crush on her and she'd gently let him

115

down twice. Now, watching him pulling on his pads, she was glad for that. He'd have been caught up in the same hell she was. Instead, he got to live an oblivious life.

"I don't have a choice, do I?"

She slid on her shin guards, elbow pads, helmet, chest protector and gloves. They all had the aroma of old sweat permeating their every fibre. Each battle was written in rips and tears on the fabric, divots in the helmet, scuff marks on the cracked logo. Her name, written in Sharpie, had long since smeared and faded, the Velcro straps barely clung together anymore, but it was all moot at this point. The time for worry was over. She just had to go out there and spar, show them she wasn't about to quit or fail.

She looked out at the audience, the families and friends of those she trained with, all here to watch their loved ones aim for a new rank. There was no one there for her. She hadn't expected her mother to come; they'd barely spoken since Sam had chosen to live with her dad after the split. Her father wasn't in town, or so he'd said. But she knew, back before all the madness had started, that she'd told Avital, Erin, and the others about it. Just because Sam had let it slip her mind was no reason for them to have, too. None of them were here either. Marlon might never speak to her again, the others had all gone silent. They hadn't responded to texts in days. Sam hadn't seen Erin in that long either, but with the student walk-out, she'd not seen anyone at all. Two days at home, wondering what to do, texting with Detective Tockett, being told to stay put and wait for her to find more evidence. Hapkido class was her only escape.

But there was no escaping what was coming.

Master Park's wife, Joanie, opened the door to the blue

padded training room. Large, welcoming eyes and hair pulled back in a ponytail, the woman was the polar opposite of her husband. "Okay, Samantha, you're up next. Sparring. Give it all you've got. This is the last part of the test."

Sam swallowed hard. She took another deep breath and slammed her hands together to psyche herself up.

"You got this, Sam," Jan said, patting her on the back.

Joanie held the door and Sam stepped out on to the mats. The eyes of fifty onlookers turned to follow her in dead silence as she took her place in the centre and Jan took his opposite her. Then Master Park waved to another student. The huge, bald, brick wall of a man, Andy, stood up in his full pads and moved beside Jan.

"Two on one. Ready, Miss Abraham?"

"Sir, yes, sir," she shouted, refusing to show him any shock or fear. Two on one. Full contact sparring with two men both taller, heavier, and stronger than her. She shouldn't have a chance. They weren't supposed to go easy on her. And she wasn't about to go easy on them. She waited for the call, planning out her attack, knowing she had this.

"Then begin."

She cried out and charged.

* * * *

Master Park held Sam's new black belt in both hands. The thick dark fabric was folded over so she could see the golden letters of her name in both English and Hangul stitched on the side. She'd taken her red belt off and stood at attention, waiting.

His face was a mask of Korean blankness. He stood staring

at her for a long time before speaking. "Miss Abraham, what is the purpose of the martial arts?"

"To be able to defend yourself?" she replied, confused. She wasn't expecting a verbal component to the test.

"Are you asking me?"

She shook her head.

"You're partly right. Martial arts can take someone who maybe can't even stand properly and help them gain confidence for everything they do, to become a better person. That might entail defending themselves, or it might not. You've been coming here a long time now. You walked in a different person, just a girl really, barely able to kick properly. And now look at you. Grown up, proving yourself in class and outside of it."

Some of the guys here knew what he was referring to: the battle in the dojung against the Authority's attackers. Sam had shown a lot that day.

"I would say you've learned a great deal. Very few students ever get to this point, or are ever required to use what they learn in a real situation. Few get to apply the teachings properly and effectively. You impressed me."

He almost never gave out compliments. She was in shock.

"The formal test, the patterns, the movements, etcetera, that was all fine. Sloppy in a few places, but you have showed a true command of your skills with unwilling participants, a far more reliable proof that you have truly begun to grasp hapkido."

He leaned forward and wrapped the belt around her waist, tying it at the front. Then he stepped back and actually cracked a smile.

"Congratulations, Miss Abraham," he said.

She paused, looking down at the fabric, realizing that it was the culmination of all her efforts to change from the mousy picked-on freshman in high school, to what she was today. That it represented growth and change in a concrete way, showed she could accomplish anything with dedication and effort, and felt pride, for maybe the first time in her life. She fought off tears that threatened to overwhelm her.

"I just… don't know what to say."

He let his smile grow and began to clap. The rest of the class followed suit, the audience, too. The others slapped her on the back, gave her hugs, cheered. Now she did cry. Her emotions overwhelmed her. It was real, she'd done it, she was a black belt. After so many years of being treated like she was worthless or that she couldn't do anything right. Being made to feel she wasn't important enough to be heard, pretty enough, rich enough, smart enough, just enough… she'd proved everyone wrong. It might only be a black fabric belt around her sweat-stained dobuk, but it meant the world to her.

"You could start by promising to bring Rick Hansen back to the academy," he said quietly to her as he and the audience applauded. "The publicity from him training here would do wonders for enrolment."

"I'll, uh, see what I can do."

"Now, remember," Master Park said loudly, waving his hands to quiet the adulation. "A black belt is not an end, it's a beginning. It's like graduating high school. You know a lot, but you're still young, with so much more to learn. Some people stop here, others go on to university to continue studying. Well, at least people did before they all walked out." A few chuckles rippled through the audience. "But seriously,

119

I'm looking forward to many more years of training with you, Miss Abraham. Now you can really start to learn hapkido."

* * * *

Jan threw his arm around her shoulder. "Congratulations, Sam!" He held up his beer.

There was a group of them here at O'Shannon's, a faux Irish pub in a strip mall a few blocks from the Tae Ryong Park Academy. Screens above the bar showed the Jets game and rock radio blared from speakers. The walls were covered in shamrocks, Irish flags, beer labels, and black and white photos of famous Irish celebrities like Bono, Sinead O'Connor, Van Morrison, and others Sam didn't recognize. Everyone was celebrating their new belts, slapping her on the shoulder, joking about how she was now a registered weapon. It was almost too much. It felt somehow unreal. She'd almost not come, but the guys had insisted.

"That belt looks really good on you," Jan said. He was a little drunk, letting his crush show again.

"Thanks."

"Do we have to call you Miss Abraham now?" the elder of the two Browns asked.

"Come on, guys, it's still me."

"Oh shit, you're going to teach now. Don't make me do push-ups," Andy said, grinning.

"As long as you don't show up late," Sam said and sipped from her beer.

The bar was packed. Just on the outskirts of downtown, it was full of what looked like university students. Sam figured everyone must be out partying because classes were on hold with the walk-out. She saw groups of guys and girls chatting, eating pub chips, pounding back beers, watching the game, and generally enjoying their now stress-free lives. There were so many women here, she knew Everett would be having a field day. She quickly texted him that it was "babe central over here."

The last few texts about the post black belt test party still didn't show 'read.' Neither did those she'd sent to Avital and Erin. She was beginning to wonder if they were ghosting her deliberately, or if she should start being worried.

"What the hell is up with the hair?" Steven asked, motioning to two girls with dreadlocks walking past. "They auditioning for a Predator reboot?"

The elder Brown, his hair greying, his skin tanned and lined, took a sip of his beer. "When I was your age the only people that had hair like that were reggae singers and drug dealers," he said.

"I think its all wannabe hippies and white people who think they're being alternative now," the younger Brown said. He was just as tanned as his dad, but looked about sixteen. His dark hair was brushed back from his face, and he held the glass of beer in front of him like it was his first. Maybe it was.

"Wouldn't they be hot? Or weigh you down?" Steven said to no one.

"Hey, boys, you ready for another round?" a pixie-voiced waitress asked the group. The waitresses all wore tiny green plaid skirts and white button-up shirts, an outfit so cliched it had to be the owner's fetish. It only served to further remind everyone here how far from Ireland this really was.

"Bring more beer," the table replied almost in unison.

"More beer it is." She left before Sam could chime in.

"Damn it, I wanted nachos," she said. "Jan, I'm going to the bathroom, order me some nachos when she comes back."

"Yes, ma'am!" he said.

One of the rules in her school's hapkido class was that black belts were to be called sir or ma'am. She'd never given it a second thought before, but now that she was a part of it, it felt hokey. "Please don't call me that anywhere but class..."

"Yes, ma... errr, Sam!" he said again.

Sam rolled her eyes, got up and headed to the washroom. The crowd in the bar was thick, and she had to push through a congealed mass to get to the faux wood-panelled walls of the ladies' room. The inside was covered in posters and advertisements, with names and phone numbers scratched into the finish. A few women did their make-up at the mirrors. All of the stalls were occupied. Sam stood against the wall, waiting for her turn, looking at a framed ad next to the hand dryer for taxis, condoms, and casinos. *That's one hell of a night*, she thought to herself.

The women at the sink left. Sam slid into place. She stared at herself in the mirror, watching the reflection of the feet in the stalls for her chance. She looked exhausted, flushed, sweaty, in need of a shower and a good night's sleep. She ran her hands through her still-matted hair. She wished she'd had a chance to clean up before coming here, although if she'd gone back to the apartment, she may have just passed out in bed and missed the whole thing. She tried to smooth out her hair. Her mole was on full display, but she didn't care.

Both toilets flushed simultaneously. The reflection of the two stalls showed their occupants standing in unison. As one, the doors opened, and Sam gasped. Standing framed by the doors, staring blankly ahead, hair in dreadlocks, were Avital and Erin.

She spun around.

"Holy shit, guys, what are you doing here?"

They walked right past her, to the sinks, and started washing their hands.

"Whoa, hey, you can't just ignore me. I'm here. You're here. Let's talk."

The two of them just scrubbed their hands, lathering soap and rinsing with robotic motions.

Sam put her hand on Erin's shoulder.

"Hey, come on."

Erin didn't even react. But it was her, the same olive-skinned, slightly large-nosed Erin; the only change was that instead of her smooth dark hair, it had been matted into heavy dreadlocks. Why?

Sam stepped next to her, staring into her eyes. The woman was spaced out.

"You're freaking me out, guys. Av?"

She was just as oblivious.

Their hands clean, they both moved to the hand dryers. Had they been implanted? Were they under a spell? She moved behind them, tried to grab a handful of their hair and lift it to expose their necks, but they slipped away and began to walk out.

"Are you ignoring me? Are you just…"

Alone. They'd never even acknowledged her presence.

"Whoa! Hang on, you're not getting away that easily."

She darted after them right into a huge crowd cheering outside the bathroom. The Jets had scored, everyone was shouting and holding their beers up to the television. Sam looked over their heads, past shoulders for the two dreadlocked girls. Spotting them at the far side of the room, she pushed her way through bodies, past the hapkido guys' table.

"Hey, Sam, what's wrong?" Jan asked.

"Sorry, can't talk."

"But I ordered you nachos!"

She didn't have time to answer. Avital and Erin were already out the front door. Sam ran through the throng of people and pushed into the parking lot, scanning for them. They were already across the street.

"Avital, Erin, where are you going?"

She ran across the street. They'd cut through a park and were shrouded by night. Only their silhouettes remained visible. Sam took off in their direction, but they were always ahead, somehow putting more distance between them, no matter how fast she ran. She spotted the golden boy gleaming in the night at the top of the legislative building and knew where they were headed.

She could hear the noise long before she actually saw the tent city. Drums, a techno beat, horns. She saw signs, flags, campfires, but not the two girls. They'd merged with the student walk-out Occupy Again movement. A makeshift village stretched all the way across the vast legislative grounds, thousands of people had taken up residence, and now, somewhere inside, were her two best friends. And something was wrong with them.

It was clear now what she had to do if she wanted to figure out how to help them. Sam had to join the movement.

Chapter 16

"They can't expect me to be able to do much," Rick said, as Debbie parked in the underground lot of the MTS Centre. She was driving, while he was still sporting a head wrap with his arm in a sling.

"I'm sure it will just be some mild physiotherapy exercises, maybe a massage, I don't know," she said, stepping out. "All I know is that you're due and it's my job as your girlfriend to get you there."

"You didn't have to drive." He gingerly put a hand on the roof of the flashy red sports car to brace himself as he got out. "They could have sent someone to—"

"With all those vagrants crawling around downtown? No way. I'm not letting you out of my sight again."

He smirked. "So, what, you're going to lace up some skates and protect me on the ice?"

"I'm going to make sure Dave and the others know what's going to happen to them if they don't step up and keep you safe."

Rick chuckled. Debbie was going a little overboard with the overprotective vengeful girlfriend act, but then he could only imagine how worried she must have been to hear that he'd been seriously hurt. That part of the game never affected him. He just played and let things come as they may, but a part of him knew there was always a risk. One crooked knee hit and he could be Cam Neely'd out of a promising career.

"Come on, they're waiting," she said.

He followed her through the employee scan card entrance and into an elevator. She pressed the button for B3, and the doors slowly closed. Soft muzak played over hidden speakers.

"You don't have to come all the way down with me, too," he said. "I'm not helpless."

"I'm your ride. I'll wait for you."

"But it could be hours before—"

She put her finger on his lips, stopping him mid-sentence. "I'll wait for you."

The elevator reached the bottom and the doors opened up to a stark white hallway. They stepped out and Rick was suddenly confused.

"Wait, where are we? I don't recognize this place. No, I think I do, I—"

"You must still have some lingering effects from the concussion. We'd better tell the trainers, so they don't push you too hard."

She looped her arm through his and led him down the hall to an open door. Inside was a small theatre, with a white projection screen showing game footage. Coach Chapman stood at the side of the flashing images. Rows of chairs in front were filled up by the rest of the team.

"Hansen," Coach Chapman said. "Glad to see you up and on your feet again."

All heads turned to look at him, the blank faces of his teammates taking him in silently as the muted game highlights danced across the screen.

"Uh, hi, guys."

"We're going to need you back, Hansen, it's almost playoff time. So let's get to work."

"Yeah, of course, Coach."

All heads snapped back to the front and ignored him. Rick watched the footage for a moment, seeing the familiar ninety-nine of Wayne Gretzky in an Edmonton Oilers jersey.

"Why are you watching that?" he started to ask, but Debbie pulled him away.

"Not yet, Rick," she said. "You're due in the lab."

She led him down the hall to another room, this one full of weight benches and machines, dumbbells, rowing and stationary bikes, stairmasters, and kettlebells. A table was set up in the middle of the room. A man in white stood waiting for them.

"Here we are, Mr. Hansen," the man said.

"Uh, yeah, I'm here. But where's Tim?" he asked, confused as to why the usual team physiotherapist wasn't here.

"Tim?" the man said, furrowing his brow. "I'm afraid I'm not sure who you're talking about." He looked to Debbie with concern.

"Tim, the usual guy who—"

"I've been with the team for seven years," the man said. "I've worked on you before. It's me, Tomas. Surely you remember."

"Rick was hit on the head. He's still having concussion symptoms," Debbie interjected.

"Ah, I see. I was prepared for this. We're going to do a very easy assessment today. Simply to determine the best course of rehab before we start getting you back to game shape. Just relax on the bed and let me go to work."

"But I was sure that Tim—"

"Rick, you've told me about Tomas before. You're just getting names mixed up."

"Maybe you're right," he said, unsure.

"I know I'm right. So just lay down and let him get to work."

She helped Rick onto the massage table. He put his face through the headrest opening and saw Debbie's feet standing near the table.

"Now I'm just going to do some simple manipulating here," Tomas said. "You tell me if you feel any pain, okay?"

Hands began to slowly lift his legs, then his arms. Rick relaxed. Then, something jabbed into his shoulder and he tried to flinch, but was held down by a pair of strong hands.

"Hey, what was that?"

"Rick," Debbie said. "He's the professional. Just let him do his thing."

A warmth rapidly flowed through his veins. He began to feel light-headed. "Hey... wh—a—t..."

* * * *

"—waking up."

"—sedative was supposed to last for five hours—"

"—must be—"

Voices. A brilliant light above him. His eyes opened to see a curved dome ceiling and machines all around him. Faces obscured by surgical masks. Two dozen eyes watching him.

He turned his head to see another gurney with a body resting on top. More doctors cutting and digging inside. One pulled out some kind of crimson mass. He looked higher and froze when he saw the pale face of Igor laying on the stretcher. They were pulling out his...

He fought to rise. But he was tied down tightly. He pulled against his bonds, thrashing in a panic.

"Get another dose. Hurry."

"No, stop," Rick said.

A needle brandished in the hand of a woman, closer, closer, then a poke into his shoulder. He felt the fluid numbing him. His eyelids became heavy. Darkness overtook him.

* * * *

He jerked up again with a start. The rushed intake of air felt as if he was just finally breathing again. He was in a hospital bed. All around him were cards and posters and flowers.

"Where...?"

"Rick." He turned to see Debbie sitting in a chair next to the bed.

"Debbie?"

"You're awake. That's great. You just got out of surgery. You've been asleep for hours."

"Surgery? Wasn't I already out of the hospital and..."

Images of being taken somewhere danced outside his thoughts, then fell through his fingers like sand. Home. The arena. His own bed. The car. A white room. Ethereal flashes, all of them. All he could remember clearly was being struck on the ice. But waking up. It was there, too. Hadn't he already woken up once?

"Oh, Rick, they had to do a shoulder reset. It turned out there was more damage than they thought. But there's good news. You're set to recover fast. The team has got the best people working on you. They said you should be okay for the playoffs. Isn't that great!"

"Playoffs. Team? Igor. I saw Igor. What—"

"He won't be bothering you anymore. He's gone."

"Gone?" A flash of seeing Igor asleep assaulted his mind, but it was so blurry that he couldn't be sure. The team bus. The basement. A rowing machine. A massage table. Faces and masks.

"Deported," Debbie said, cutting off the images. "Don't you remember? He hit you. Samantha Abraham put him up to it. But you should be free of them both now."

"Free of them? Both?"

An itch at his neck made him reach up and try to scratch. He found a fresh bandage at the base of his hairline. Why?

"Careful," she said, reaching out for his hand. "You have a few stitches from where the stick hit you. You don't want to pull them out and reopen the wound, do you?"

"Wound? Oh, uh, no. I—"

"Oh, Rick, don't worry about a thing. You're almost all better now. The team has had it all fixed for you. This hospital is the top authority on these kinds of surgeries in all of Western Canada. Trust me. You're in the best hands. And I'm here for you, no matter what."

She draped herself over his chest and hugged him. He patted her head gently as his thoughts fled away from his mind like receding waters. An attack. Igor. Sam. The playoffs. The team. The Stanley Cup. His mind kept diverting away from blurred memory to a vision of holding that glorious trophy. *Your childhood dream.*

The more he wanted to remember, the more the cup pushed out his thoughts. *Lord Stanley. The ultimate prize. You can win it.*

He would be better soon. He'd get back on the ice. That

was good news.

The first Canadian team in decades. The pride of an entire nation. You.

"Me?" It was as if someone else was speaking his thoughts in his mind. *You.* They must be his true thoughts. *The team. The cup. The game. That's all that matters.* He understood that now.

Chapter 17

"I don't have much time," Detective Tockett said. "My partner thinks I just ran in here for some Danishes."

Sam stood against the wall of the coffee shop, hands on a chair she'd pulled out to sit down. "I've got somewhere important to go, too."

"I thought travel wasn't part of the plan."

"I'm not going far."

"I might need to contact you and—"

Sam motioned to her neck and lifted her hair, turning her head to show her. Detective Tockett followed suit. Seeing no sign of any surgical marks, Sam relaxed.

"Okay, now can you tell me?"

"The student walk-out tent city," Sam said. "I'm going there."

"Don't do that. That place is full of drugs and—"

"My friends are there."

"—I have a feeling the government won't tolerate the disturbance forever. They're bound to raid the place and—"

"I'm not so sure they're there of their own free will."

"—it'll be a giant mess. Arrests, hauling people off to the drunk tank, and—"

"The whole thing might be another part of what's going

on."

"You're not listening to me," Veronica said. "That place is bad news."

"Did *you* hear what I said? My friends are there. My girlfriend, too. And I don't think willingly."

Now, finally, Veronica seemed to understand. "Shit."

"Call it a feeling. I have to infiltrate the place to figure out what's going on. And to learn what's happened to them."

"The news said it was some kind of political protest. Spreading everywhere. Or it spread here from somewhere. I haven't had much time to pay attention."

"That's what they say, but none of my friends have even voted, let alone cared about politics. Why would they suddenly decide to join in and get dreadlocks?"

"White girls?"

Sam nodded.

Veronica scrunched up her face. "Those never look good. But maybe you're overthinking. Maybe they just wanted to join in the party and cut class."

"And change their entire appearances?"

"Okay, the hair thing I can't explain."

"Me either. Which is why I need to find them."

"Okay, at least I'll know where you are. But be careful. Don't let yourself get caught up in any drug-fuelled orgies."

"I can handle myself," Sam said flatly.

"If you need me, text. But more importantly, stay available. I'm closing in on something big. I don't want to tell you too much right now, I'm still putting the pieces together, but I have proof Igor is innocent."

"You do?"

"And maybe even proof that will expose a conspiracy. Or

at least a lead on some. A few more days tops, Sam. Then we can go public and clear Igor's name."

"If you have the video, just leak it now."

"No good," she said, shaking her head. "It would just be suppressed. We need more than that. Something they can't bury."

Sam sighed. "You think Igor's back in Chechnya by now?"

"Probably. When I saw him in lock-up, he was still his same old self, but had no idea what was going on."

"I don't know how much he knew was going on before honestly. He was strange, but sort of lovable in a weird uncle kind of way."

"He also had multiple wives in different cities."

Sam's jaw dropped. "What?"

"Long story. Not important right now. What is important is that I've got leads. Some of the pieces, just not enough. Have you talked to Rick?"

"I tried, but it didn't go well. I couldn't find out if he was clean. But in his condition, I don't know if he'd stay that way for long anyway."

"Let's hope he does."

"He blamed me."

"He bought the Igor story?"

"We might have to presume he's compromised," Sam said stoically.

"You're just going to write him off? I thought you cared about each other."

"We only dated in high school for a few months."

"There was clearly something between the two of you, even if you were both too busy to notice."

"If he's been implanted, then he's our enemy."

"You just can't throw him to the wolves. You need to help… shit," she said, noticing a tanned man coming into the coffee shop, scanning the crowd. "There's Carlos, I better go. Just sit tight for a few days and I'll be in touch." She turned and walked over to the door, talking to the other cop. The man looked over her shoulder at Sam. She dropped into her chair and looked at her phone, pretending to not notice. She didn't know what they were saying, but eventually, Veronica managed to convince him to go and the two of them left.

Sam let five minutes pass before grabbing her backpack and sleeping bag roll from under the table. She slung them over her shoulder and headed outside.

She followed the sounds of the drums down a few blocks, before turning on Broadway. From there, she could see the fires and lights of the tent city. A few police cars were parked in an empty lot across the street. Officers sat on the roofs of their cruisers drinking coffee. They didn't pay any attention to another person going to join the protest.

Carrying her bags, Sam crossed the street. With the golden boy quietly watching from the top of the legislative building's domed roof, the huge tent city sprawled all over the grounds. Barricades had been erected on the perimeter, cordoning off the village. Banners and crude cardboard signs hung on every square inch of fence space.

"STUDENTS FOR A JUST WORLD."

"MAKE LOVE NOT WAR."

"EQUALITY FOR ALL."

"Doug's Discount hotdogs."

There were concert handbills, advertisements, Playboy centrefolds, pages of the communist manifesto, graffiti art; the entire makeshift wall was a living, breathing surface of text and images. A trellis, perhaps stolen from someone's garden, made an arched entrance inside. Two women, dressed in flannel, sat in lawn chairs, handing out handbills to anyone passing through.

Sam approached. Cars whizzed by on Memorial Drive.

"Greetings, fellow autonomous individual," one of the women said to Sam. The other passed her a yellow paper.

She looked it over. "STUDENTS FOR A JUST WORLD CURRENT LIST OF DEMANDS" was printed on top. Underneath was a myriad of issues, everything from something called Bill C-82, to the public education act, the repeal of the Freedom of Employment Act, the rollback of the retirement age increase, defunding the police, reducing military spending, immigrant amnesty, lowering tuition costs, universal basic income, safe injection sites, reinstatement of the Katimavik program; dozens of diverse requests, many spanning multiple layers of government.

"Somebody needed to listen more in civics," she snorted.

"Are you coming to join our collective movement?" the other woman asked.

Sam held up her bags. "If you'll have me."

"Of course. Solidarity will bring our greatest reward."

They waved Sam through and she stepped off the sidewalk into another world.

Chapter 18

With the cold night air blowing through his hippie hair, Frank walked the streets of the city he'd called home for so many years on unfamiliar legs. River City hadn't changed a bit, even if he seemingly had. For the better, depending on how you looked at it. He couldn't help but admire his reflection in every window and mirror he passed.

"I've either been reading too many Harlequins and hallucinating, or I've been reincarnated into Fabio's younger brother's body." He rubbed his chin at the reflection of the mysterious face on the other side of the spring display in the window of the Hudson's Bay department store downtown.

"Maybe this is how I've always looked, and the forty years of aging was just a dream?"

Debating the relative merits of which reality he was going to accept, Frank walked.

And walked and walked and walked.

He lost track of how long he paraded up and down the streets and alleyways of River City. His feet moved his body as if they were reciting their own private symphony. Muscle memory. The subconscious knowledge of a thousand other days like these, going through a repeated route on an endless loop.

His new (or old?) body was an amazing machine, never tiring, never needing food or water, never even needing to stop for a piss. At least, if it did, it hadn't told him. He just walked and let his newer, more symmetrical nose find crime.

It was always there, you just had to know where to look. His old nose, despite having been broken a few times and sprouting one too many grey hairs in the nostrils, knew what to sniff out. The new one was still learning. So far, he'd only found a purse snatcher, a car jacker, and somebody dropping a deuce in an alley.

"This is a shit-free zone, buddy," he'd told the man mid squeeze.

"Buzz off, I'm busy," the man had said.

So Frank had squeezed him. More than just a few sausage lengths of turd shot out of his un-puckered asshole—the more Frank pressed, the more coils of bloody intestine seemed to spew out between the man's legs alongside the crap. It was like spraying string cheese on toast, only with a lot more blood. In the end, the man had been voided of more than just the contents of his bowels, the bowels themselves, and most of what connected them. The stinky mass lay in a pile next to a dumpster and a faded poster of The Guess Who.

Staring at the deflated skin sleeve, Frank knew something was wrong with the picture. A man breaking the law, left smeared amidst the trash of an alley. "Criminal," he muttered, trying to unravel the mystery of what he'd done.

"I'm supposed to..."

His head throbbed. His brain felt like it was expanding outward, pressing against the inside of his skull. He fell to his knees and gritted his teeth, shut his eyes, and tried to pound the pain through his ears.

"Hey buddy, you okay?" someone asked.

"Just keep walking, Bert, the guy's clearly on something."

The voices seemed to hover and fade around him. The night sky disappeared on the other side of his eyelids.

"Argh." He grunted, ready for his head to explode.

Go. Kill. Her.

"Who's there?" he called out.

No one responded. The pain faded. He opened his eyes, found he was kneeling in yellow snow. He stood up and leaned on a telephone pole. The picture was clearer now. He looked to his right, saw an apartment building, with a front door walk-up, lights on in the suites that faced the street. He climbed the steps, pulled on the door. The lock ripped clean off its hinges. The door went flying behind him. He climbed the dark green carpeted stairs to the second floor. He turned down the hall. Stopping, not knowing why, he faced a wooden door with an old brass knocker hanging in the centre. He gently knocked twice. Nobody answered.

Go. Kill. Her.

"Who said that?"

His hand turned the knob. Locked. He turned it until it bent into a crunched mangled mess in his hand. The door swung open to an empty apartment. Nothing looked familiar. "This isn't mine, is it?"

Couch, IKEA bookshelf, television. On the refrigerator a photo of a River City Jet player next to a calendar with dates circled and hearts drawn on. He moved into the hallway. Three doors. One, a bathroom. The two others, bedrooms. Messy sheets, clothes piled inside the closets, open dresser drawers, but no people.

139

"Why am I here?"

He bent low to examine the mess. His cop's brain deduced that the people had left in a hurry. They'd only taken a few things. He checked the bathroom, found no signs of deodorant or toothbrushes, yet all other toiletries were still there. Feminine products told him that one, maybe two women lived here.

And yet, they weren't here.

He sat on the couch and waited in the darkness. A remote control lay on the coffee table. He reached over and turned on the television. He clicked a few times until he found something he remembered.

"Jeopardy..."

Images of a hospital bed, of old people shouting out questions, of a mailman losing all his money, of a dozen couches and countless times seeing this same thing. His brain throbbed again, cycling a thousand kaleidoscopic repetitions of the man with the grey hair and the cue cards.

"What is... What is..."

He couldn't find the question.

Or the answer.

It was on the tip of his tongue, but his tongue was someone else's.

He sat in the flickering glow of a television bathed in darkness and waited.

Chapter 19

A paint-smeared, naked man wearing a bandana with a patchy beard held a burning torch high above his head. He ran down a path between tents and up the stairs of the legislative building. When he reached the top, just in front of the four-meter-high security fence erected to block access to the seat of the Provincial Government, he screamed primordially and waved the flaming torch back and forth.

A throbbing EDM beat drifted on the wind. A rave sprawled around the park. There were thousands more like the nude man, as far as Sam could see. Bodies crammed together, bouncing, hands waving, lost to a light show from the base of a DJ's console. The show was being powered by portable generators. Sam wondered who'd fitted the bill.

Beneath the shining golden statue at the top of the legislative building dome, Students for a Just World had convinced a mob to congregate and build a new community right under the nose of those in charge. The tents were densely packed in rows and columns that seemed to spiral outward from the rave clearing. Small paths wound their way through the maze. A hundred bonfires raged. The tiny white fireflies of light from cellphones and dangling camping lanterns illuminated the night sky.

There was canvas everywhere, with people dressed in thrift store finery socializing. The intermingling smell of sweat, weed, and patchouli was overpowering.

Sam moved through the weaving aisle between tents, looking for any sign of Everett, Erin or Avital. It seemed like hundreds of people had dreadlocked their hair now, almost as if it was some kind of uniform. This was going to be harder than she thought.

Maybe the rave...

Everyone moved together with glow sticks held aloft as techno music filled the air. A sense of unity flowed through the crowd. The smells of a thousand people who hadn't bathed in days assaulted her. She walked the perimeter of the maelstrom, trying to look into the mass of bodies glistening with sweat from dancing. She spotted joints and pipes being passed around, pills being downed, bottles sucked dry. This wasn't some big protest, it was just another party, but with a stench enough to turn off any sober person.

She wasn't about to push her way into that, not still carrying her backpack and sleeping bag, so she kept moving through the spiralling aisles of tents.

"What do we want?"

"Free access to high-speed internet!"

A megaphone-amplified voice carried from the river side of the building. She put more distance from the sounds of the rave and headed towards the call and response group.

"What do we want?"

"Nuclear disarmament!"

A long-haired, bearded man wearing a bright orange prison-style jumpsuit and goggles held a white megaphone in front of a massed crowd standing near the Louis Riel monument. Hanging with one hand from the statue's outstretched arm that clutched bronzed papers, he shouted distorted slogans. "What else do we want?"

"Legalized drugs!"

"What else do we want?"

"Equal opportunities!"

"What else do we want?"

"Affordable housing!"

The statue of the famous Manitoban watched the group impassively. This seemed like it might be where the more politically minded people were. Would Avital and Erin be a part of this?

"Who elected that guy as representative of the collective?" someone said behind her.

"I think he's there as a free and autonomous individual," a girl responded.

"Who brought his own megaphone," the other said.

"That's right." A man in a Castro hat turned around. "A free and autonomous individual representing the collective voice of the oppressed with a megaphone."

"Wow," the girl said in awe. "I never knew a megaphone could be used for that."

"What, to amplify your voice?" Sam asked, incredulous at the girl, who seemed to be either high or just dense.

"No, to, like, lead a crowd but not, you know, *be* their leader?"

"Does anyone know who the leader is around here?" Sam asked.

"What do we want?" the man on the steps shouted again.

"Quality jobs!"

"Anyone? Anyone know who's calling the shots here?"

"Maybe someone in the voting tent would know," the girl said, eyes never leaving the megaphone.

"Where's that?" Sam asked.

"It's the big tent near the Nellie McClung statue."

Sam took another look through the group listening to the megaphone man. Seeing no sign of Erin or Avital, she headed towards the other side of the grounds, where she remembered the statue of the 'Famous Five' and their table had been erected.

The snowfall covering the grounds had been completely trampled, mostly melted away from the fires and body heat. The entire tent city was at least ten degrees warmer, the chilly late winter air kept at bay by the sheer force of numbers and raging fires. The north wind was silent. Sam wondered how many people would've come had this walk-out been done in the depths of January. Something like this would have been an easier sell in Vancouver. Was their makeshift village similar?

She passed a television hooked up to another generator. It vibrated loudly behind a tent decorated with River City Jets banners and pennants. A group of people in team jerseys sat huddled together on lawn chairs watching the Jets game on Hockey Night in Canada.

"Come on, shoot the puck!"

"—really need Hansen back."

"—need a goalie, too. Illyanovich was having a career year."

"—he's in the gulag now probably."

"Dude, I don't think they still have those."

Sam wondered if the entire team had been changed by now. If Rick had, too. Most likely, they'd probably all lost their humanity. What would these people say if they found out they were being manipulated through the watching of golems skating around, subliminal advertising and subconscious implantation? That they'd been put under the spell of creatures from who knew where?

"The whole thing is a giant sham," she muttered.

Music, sports, high school and beyond. Was there anything the Authority wasn't trying to get their claws into? Was this mass walk-out and the thousands of people taking up a cause, just another part of it? Rippling outward from River City, or maybe from some other central spoke. She didn't know. But she did know that Avital and Erin hadn't been themselves that night at the pub. And everyone she passed could be another victim, or a part of the conspiracy. She had to find her friends and find out the truth.

There were signs at the edge of the tent rows, with names painted on them like street markers. Evergreen Lane, Clearwater, Hot Springs, Goddess Grove, Earth Way. They might be useful to remember.

The voting tent was adjacent to the 'Famous Five' statues, lit up with Christmas lights dangling from the iron women and all around the large teepee. A blinking VOTING sign bathed those entering and exiting the structure in green.

"Hey, you there, dark hair," someone called out to her.

She tensed up, expecting trouble.

"Yeah?"

"You wanna sign my petition against the farming of geneti-cally modified soy beans?"

He was dressed entirely in wool from head to toe and looked like he'd made the outfit himself.

"Sure," she said and scribbled a false name on his smudged

145

paper. "Say, what goes on in there?" she asked, pointing to the voting tent.

"Only the nucleus of the whole freaking operation. Non-stop debate. Free-forming and free thinking. Ideas. You know, change? Demands. The ever-evolving nature of the beast. The intellectual hydra brought to life. How we're going to change the country and the world."

"Uh, okay. Can anyone just go in?"

"Of course. All free-thinking autonomous individuals can participate. It's true democracy, babe."

"Huh."

"Hey, you want to go back to my tent, drop acid, and fuck until we see Jupiter ascending?"

"Excuse me?"

He held out a couple of small white square tablets in his palm. "I haven't used my ration yet, lady, and hey, this shit is sublime. No sense wasting it. Oh, unless you already consented to someone else. I'm not trying to put undue pressure on you or anything."

"How about a rain check on that one?" Sam said to the hairy man. She realized now that he wasn't wearing any underwear under his wool bodysuit and that most of his penis showed through the gaps in the stitching.

"Hey, right on. Tomorrow night?"

"Uh, I'll find you, okay?"

He gave her an air gun and moved along with his petition and acid, looking for more signees.

Sam stared at the glowing sign on the teepee and hesitated. Could this be where Avital and Erin were hiding?

"Only one way to find out."

She stepped inside.

146

"—as an autonomous representative speaking a consensus of thoughts offered by those in the circle for general consumption." The speaker was a man wearing a poncho with a thin moustache. His beaded hair clinked together as he spoke. "All in favour?"

A circle of people sitting around a central camping lantern erupted into motion. Their arms came together across their chests, linked at the thumbs, fingers waving like the wings of birds. Shadow puppets danced on the walls of the teepee. Sam took a place at the back of the group.

But she wasn't as invisible as she'd hoped.

"Welcome, fellow free-thinker," a bearded man wearing a sock on his head said. "What can you add to our ever-evolving platform for a new, more just society?"

Everyone in the room turned to stare at her, unblinking, waiting. Dreadlocks, bandanas, strange tribal paint, second-hand clothes, glazed-over looks; they threw her and she blanked.

"More vegan options in restaurants?" she stammered.

Immediately, every hand in the crowd swung up to its owner's chest, thumbs locked, fingers flapping like birds.

"Thank you for your contribution, valued autonomous member of the new collective," the man said. "More vegan options in restaurants is hereby added to the register."

They began hooting like owls, flapping their hands, swaying back and forth. A woman with blazing red hair standing at the focal point of the circle flapped her fingers towards them as if she was playing an invisible piano.

Sam started to sit down, but the noises stopped suddenly and they all turned to look at her and she froze again. The man with the beaded hair clasped his hands in prayer.

147

"And what about the outside world most distresses you?"

"Oh geez, I... uh. Well, there's really so many things, I guess, I just..."

"The hall of decision is the womb birthing a new concept and direction for humanity. The fermenting of thought within is like the seed sprayed forth by the male genitals, ready to impregnate our minds with the intellectual children that will lead others to a brighter future. What is your seed to implant?"

"Oh hey, I'm..."

The dead-eyed stares of the three-dozen people were chilling. She suddenly regretted walking in here. But it was clear she had to answer, or they might never stop. She looked to the doorway, wondering if she should just run away.

"Spill your seed. Spill your seed," the people chanted.

"Yes, spill it all over us, inside us, make us understand."

This is fucking weird.

"I guess I want to see a world without... uh, golems."

The chanting stopped. Everyone froze. The air suddenly became cold. The lantern light made them look pale and dead. She took a step backwards, felt the thick fabric of the teepee against her, wondered if she should just lift it and go.

"The newcomer speaks a deep wisdom," the man said. "Insightful and true. A world without golems."

"A world without golems," the others all repeated.

"Can you tell us all about golems, fellow free-thinker?"

"Uh, yeah, like... Frankenstein. The monster, not the doctor, right?"

The man nodded solemnly. "Golems. Those created by outside forces, directed by wills not their own. The society of those outside our collective. Living, consuming, following paths directed by corporations, governments, advertising agencies, the oligarchs that run the world, big oil—"

"Space aliens," Sam chimed in.

The man jerked his head to stare at her in the eyes. She wanted to look away from his piercing gaze, but he'd locked her in place.

"Aliens from space. A fitting metaphor. Those who seek to rule and corrupt the planet cannot be human. They cannot understand or feel empathy for the poor, the exploited, those left to fend for themselves in a world that refuses to change. Yes," he said softly. "Like aliens. The newcomer is wise. Please, sit and participate. I feel like you will contribute much to our new future."

It was hard to see all the faces in the room. The limited light cast by the lantern didn't stretch through the cramped grouping. Rows of logs and hay bales formed benches, where everyone sat around the centre. The first two rows were packed, but most of the third remained empty. Sam dropped onto a cold log, putting her sleeping bag and backpack down, trying to stay out of sight as she scanned the faces of those present.

Finally, the man with the beads seemed to have moved on from focusing on her and turned back to the group. "Does anyone else have grievances from the corrupt world to add to our chronicle?"

A man in a heavy lined coat lifted his hand. His shaved head and beard were poorly manicured, looking like he had recently trimmed them himself, perhaps while high.

"This whole Mars thing," he said. "If you think about it, why should we be so quick to be trying to build colonies on the red planet when we haven't even started on the grey one a lot closer to home? I mean, the moon is right there, right? I'm not the only one seeing it, right? Why don't we just go put a base and, like, get some greenhouses going? Plant some crops, work on irrigation. Then, boom, we've got totally fresh lunar lettuce up there. Free from pollutants and chemicals and pesticides."

The girl with the fire-red hair, who seemed be the leader of the group even though she hadn't spoken a word, nodded.

The beaded man saw the motion and smiled. "Excellent contribution, Echo. So, point of order, we add the establishment of moon colonies to the list of priorities for any future government to emerge from our chrysalis, with the caveat being that it must be undertaken before any further exploration of Mars. Consensus?"

All hands in the tent raised to their chests, fingers flapping like birds, voices hooting as they swayed like car dealership balloon dummies.

"Consensus reached," he said.

"Wait," a short, timid-looking girl with a buzz cut chimed in. "Shouldn't we specify that the colony be vegan only? The logistics of transporting livestock to the moon would be costly and we don't want to pollute the fresh lunar air with methane."

"Gale is right," a woman said from the other side of the tent. "Moon cows would be a bad enough idea, but we shouldn't perpetuate Terra's oppressive animal murder culture in space, too."

Sam slid a few spots around the back of the circle, looking at more faces for any sign of her friends. Everyone here was a stranger though.

"Wait," a man said, raising his hand. "Can we add an

addendum? That future moon colonies also be gluten free?"

A few more spots around the circle and Sam saw a blond man, enraptured in the proceedings. He sat tightly packed in, between two women, with his arms around them both. Each had her hand on his knees. The light was bad, but it looked like—

"Everett?" she whispered and patted him on the shoulder.

"So, updated point of order then. All future moon colonies will be one hundred percent vegan, gluten free, gender neutral—"

"Everett," she whispered and tugged his parka.

One of the women turned to look at her, checking her out for a moment, but then went back to ignoring her.

"—all before any further exploration of Mars for either commercial or scientific means."

All hands rose up to flutter away, and the group hooted and swayed. Sam finally got a good look at the man. It was Everett, lost in the proceedings, oblivious to her presence.

"Everett," she tried again.

The meeting continued. Stymied, Sam snuck back around to her sleeping bag and backpack. She grabbed them and watched Everett from the other side of the room. He didn't speak or even move much, just stayed locked to the two women. He only showed life when he joined in with the hand waving. He was in a trance, and yet, she hadn't seen any sign of scarring on his neck.

She had no idea how long this meeting was going to last, but needed to find a way to get through to Everett. Eventually, the flame-haired woman walked over to the small table holding the lantern and opened a drawer. She pulled out a bag and began passing around pills and rolled cigarettes.

151

"Partake and receive the peace of joining," she said.

"We open ourselves to a brighter world," the others repeated.

"Our minds are free from the corruption of the outside," she said.

"We create the future for all humankind."

"Each breath fills us with hope."

"Each breath shares love with others."

People began lighting up the cigarettes. The smell was strong, and Sam knew it right away that it was marijuana, and that it was potent. Clouds emerged from mouths and hung in the air. Suddenly Sam remembered the march. She'd seen joints passed around then and had seen her friends take puffs. Could that be it? Were the joints another catalyst for control? Had the Authority gotten involved here, too? It wasn't too far a stretch to move from corrupted beer to corrupted—

A joint passed to her. Then a pill. The air was quickly filling with smoke, slowly drifting up to the top of the teepee. A face turned to her. Blank, waiting. Taking a puff, about to blow out.

No!

Sam darted back, falling over the log. She landed hard on the ground. The smoke. She had to avoid it. She backpedalled, crawled frantically on her hands and knees to the side of the teepee. She lifted the flap and rolled out into the snow.

Looking up, she saw the smoke emerging from the peak of the teepee, spreading out into the shape of a misty orb. It seemed to form into a hand, elongating into fingers, reaching out over the grounds as it snaked through the air. She backed away and watched the phantom smoke limb head over towards the tent communities before gradually fading away on the night air. Had that been all her imagination or was the smoke alive? She examined the joint, still clutched in her palm. It didn't look out of the ordinary, but that smoke...

Before she could decide what she'd seen, the front of the teepee opened. They left in pairs and spread out back into the crowd. She watched for Everett. He and one of the women came next, holding hands. They walked through the arch into the grounds. They turned towards the tent city, following the path of the spectral hand. Sam stuffed the drugs in her pocket and, clutching her sleeping bag and backpack, followed.

They turned up Glittermoon Lane, went past campfires until they came to a dark navy canvas tent near a huge elm tree. They both disappeared inside.

Sam crept up to the door. Pausing, she looked to see if anyone had followed her, then lifted the tent flap.

Chapter 20

"Tell us how your recovery is going, Rick?" the stunning blonde reporter asked.

"I feel like I could lace up the skates and be on the ice tomorrow, but the trainers might have other ideas."

"Do you have a timetable? I'm sure the team would love to have you back for the playoffs."

"Hustle, putting pucks in the net, a complete three periods, battling for loose…" Rick started then seemed to trail off for a moment before massaging the back of his neck and snapping back to reality. "Team effort wins games, not individual players. You know what they say, Dawn."

"What's that?"

"There's no I in team."

"That might be true, but—"

Nothing else that the man said during his interview registered. It had been only visible for a brief moment on camera, but Veronica had sworn she'd seen it. A bandage on the back of Rick's neck, exactly where an implantation scar would be.

"Carlos, look at this," she said, waving him over to her side of the two attached desks. The man rose, carrying a cup of coffee in his hand, and stood behind her.

"Yeah?"

"You see anything funny on the back of Hansen's neck? Or did I imagine it?"

She rewound the interview video on the CBC webpage and let it play again.

"—battling for loose pucks…"

She paused it at the exact moment the man reached for the back of his neck. She enlarged the video full-screen, but it was slightly pixelated and hard to make out.

"There." She tapped the white blur. "What's that?"

"A neck guard? Maybe some of that athletic tape they use?"

"A bandage?"

"Could be. So what?"

"Just wanted to make sure I wasn't seeing things."

"Tockett, you make no sense sometimes."

"Neither does a puzzle until you start to connect all the pieces."

He took a sip of his coffee slowly and loudly. "Speaking of, we're scheduled to be at the mayor's press conference in a half hour."

She leaned back in her chair and sighed. "Fucking hell. What a waste of time that is."

"We're supposed to be a part of the show. So he can calm everyone down. Convince them that despite the fact body parts are popping up and the force has bupkis, things are a-okay."

"That's not true though. We have lots of—"

"Nothing," Carlos cut her off. "And you know it."

"Maybe Jacob's got some of the test results back on the fabric found in the last hand."

"Yeah, one hundred percent cotton. What a lead that'll be."

"Let's just go ask. You never know."

155

She rose from the desk and grabbed her coat. "Besides, you said it yourself, we're due at the press conference anyway. Hell, it could be something the mayor could offer as proof we're not just sitting on bupkis."

* * * *

"Lycra," Jacob said.

"Lycra?" Veronica asked.

"Lycra." The man nodded.

"What's Lycra?" Carlos added.

"Synthetic elastic," Jacob said, reading over the email from the lab. "You know, spandex."

"You found spandex in the hand?"

"Well, technically it was Dimitri who found it, I just sent it in for testing."

"Why would the hand be holding spandex?" Veronica asked.

"That part's not in the email," Jacob said.

"Maybe the guy was into working out," Carlos offered.

"Quick," Veronica said as an idea popped into her head. "What are a pro-wrestler's tights made of?"

"Who? Hulk Hogan? Macho Man? John Cen—"

"It doesn't matter," she said curtly. "Just look it up."

"It does matter," Jacob said. "John Cena wears jean shorts and—"

"Spandex," Carlos said from her left as he scrolled through his phone. "Most tights and masks are made of spandex. You happy, Tockett? You think that arm belonged to The Rock or something?"

"Just more puzzle pieces, Carlos. Doesn't mean they add up to a picture just yet."

✳ ✳ ✳ ✳

"—so I would like to assure all the citizens of River City that there is no need to panic. There is scant evidence of an active serial killer. Nonetheless, the police have formed a task force and the detectives you see standing behind me are the best of the best the force has to offer. We've authorized unlimited overtime and have been assured the full cooperation of all three levels of government, including the RCMP, in catching this individual, who, I stress again, is not conclusively a serial killer. Until we have retrieved a complete body or can match up any of the discovered remains with reported missing persons, we cannot assume that anyone is dead yet."

Reporters began shouting questions at a mile a minute. They blended together into a cacophony of half-heard sentences.

"Sir, do you really expect the people of this city to believe—"

"—how many limbs?"

"What do the detectives say to those who—"

"—nothing to connect the victims?"

"—re-election campaign—"

"—copycat killer—"

"—Chicago Phil incident—"

Under the glare of the bright lights and the mob of questions, Veronica spaced out. She'd been in a state of shock for most of the mayor's prepared statement from the moment she'd spotted the mark on the back of his neck, just below his hairline. Unlike Rick's, this one was obvious. He had the scar.

✳ ✳ ✳ ✳

The end of a long shift. Sitting in her car in the parking lot with the key halfway to the ignition, watching two other officers moving to their vehicles. Trying to get a look at the back of their necks. One had his collar turned up, the other looked clean.

"Relax, it was only two. That doesn't mean it's spreading."

She paused with the key inserted but not turned. "The mayor is bad enough, that's political. But Rick. We have to do something about that. We can't just leave him."

She pulled out her phone and texted Samantha a message. "Think they got Rick. Need to do something fast."

An answer didn't come immediately. "Find your friends yet?" Still no reply. She slid her phone back into her jacket pocket. Reaching for the key and looking up, she cried out in surprise to see a man standing in front of her car.

"Jesus."

He wore all black, his face obscured by a mask with silver trim around the eyes and mouth. He was just standing there, staring, not budging, not touching the hood, as still as a statue.

"Hello?" she said. "What are you—"

Another one stood at the passenger side door.

"Oh, fuck."

One in the rearview, right behind the car. The hair on the back of her neck rose and she slowly looked to her left. One more, in the same outfit, a metre away. Four of them now, surrounding her.

"Excuse me, I'm trying to leave here," she said.

She honked the horn gently. Nobody moved. She turned the key and fired the car to life.

"Last warning."

She put it in reverse. The man still blocked her. "Alright,

it's your choice."

She pressed the gas and moved backwards, but the man was gone. Slamming the brakes again, she looked out both side windows, then to the front, but all of them had vanished.

"What the—"

At the edge of the parking lot, they stood in a row blocking the way out. She backed the rest of the way clear of her spot and put the car in neutral, idling, watching them watch her.

"Who the fuck are you guys?"

Nobody budged, she just waited to see what they were going to do. She reached into her pocket for her phone, slowly, and swiped it open. Bringing the screen into her line of sight, she tapped the camera icon, saw the grainy black reproduction of the camera's POV, raised it.

A tap on her side window broke her concentration.

"Tockett, you forget how to drive?"

Carlos stood leaning down, staring at her through the window. She swung her gaze back to the windshield. In the distance, the four men in masks were gone. She rolled down the window.

"Did you see where they went?" she asked him.

"Who? Murphy and Lewis? They left ten minutes ago. Probably to the bar and—"

"No, I mean the guys in the wrestling masks blocking the parking lot exit."

He looked down the aisle skeptically, then back to her. "Uh, maybe you should lay off the OT for a while."

"So you didn't see them?"

"Cut back on the coffee, too."

Looking back to the empty lot, she exhaled bitterly. "They were right there, I swear."

"Okay, okay, fine. You swear. Now how about you go home, then you can, I don't know, get laid by that cripple house-husband of yours and clear your head. Make him fuck away the hallucinations. Then get a good night's sleep and we can get back to some serious detective work tomorrow, okay, partner?"

With no sign of what she'd seen, and no photo to prove it, she rolled up her window, put the car in drive, and slowly pulled out of the parking lot.

Her mind wandering as she drove, she considered if she should bring this up to Jimmy. "Hey, I think those missing pro-wrestlers we were looking for might be turning up in pieces. Maybe the serial killer is still pissed off about the WWE being the only... oh fuck, that sounds stupid."

The streetlights passed by in the window as she moved down Portage Avenue, half aware of the trip. "You know, Jimmy, I saw these four wrestlers in the parking lot, but then they disappeared. You think they were trying to warn me away from— no, nobody else saw them. No, I have no proof. Yeah, I have been working a lot and... oh fuck. I can't go to him with this. He'll think I'm insane."

She turned up the Moray Bridge and drove through the snow-lined parkway towards home. "He's better off not knowing. Not until I have something solid at least. Besides, he'd just want to help and he's in no condition for that. He was almost killed by those guys before. I need him to watch the kids."

Pulling into her driveway, she hit the garage door opener and waited for the overhead door to rise. "Just stay oblivious, Jimmy," she said. "Be the only sane thing in my life right now. It's the only way to protect you and my family. It's what you'd do, right? What a man would do? Carry the burden alone. Of course it is. So I'll do it, too. You'll understand when the time comes. I hope."

Chapter 21

"Everett?" Sam said quietly and crawled inside the shadowed tent.

A woman sat upright, naked to the waist, except for jingling hemp necklaces and bracelets. Everett squeezed and kneaded her right breast like bread. The smell of marijuana hung in the air.

"Oh, hey," the woman said. "The more the merrier."

"Everett, who is this?"

He looked up from her breast with glazed-over eyes. Ignoring Sam, he licked the woman's nipple.

"Let me guess, you guys are stoned."

"There's more," the girl said. "You want some?"

"No, that's all right."

She pushed back against the side of the tent, wondering what to do. The woman giggled as Everett kept pawing her.

"It might help put you in the mood. That's why you're here, right?" the woman said.

"I want to talk to my friend," Sam said. "But I see he's, uh... occupied."

The woman chirped as Everett moved up her body to kiss her in rising increments. She pulled his shirt over his head, exposing his smooth chest.

This was getting to be way more than Sam wanted to witness.

"Everett, it's me, Sam. What's going on here? In the village, not the tent. I can see what you're about to do and—"

"Lighten up," the woman said. "Let go, embrace the divine energy." She waved Sam over.

"That's alright," Sam said. "I'm divine enough right now."

"Your loss." The woman shrugged. She dug her hands into Everett's pants and they quickly fell onto each other, beads clanking together, moaning and moving in harmony.

Sam averted her eyes. She knew she wasn't going to get through to him, so she crawled out of the tent. The sick sounds of their drug-addled sex were muffled, but clearer than she ever wanted them to be.

"What now?"

Looking down both directions of the curved lane of tents, she tried to figure out her next move. Everett was either ignoring her, or completely out of it. Were Erin and Avital in another tent of their own? There had to be thousands. How would she find them? Just look in every one?

She sent another text to Erin, but the last fifty were all unreplied to. There was an almost equal number sent to Avital. Tucking her phone into her bag, she felt defeated.

"I will not cry. I can find them. If they're still in here, I will find them."

It was getting late. She had a sleeping bag, but could or should she find a place to crash here? Was it safe? That ghostly hand gave her pause. The smoke had dissipated over the whole area. She dug out the joint she'd held on to from her pocket. Maybe she could get Detective Tockett to run some kind of test on it.

She tapped out a text to her and tucked the evidence away again.

Smoke gently wafted out of dozens of tents all around her. A cloud hung over the entire area. It hovered on the wind, seeming to drift towards her.

"Nope. Not staying here."

She slung the backpack over her shoulder and picked up her sleeping bag. "I'll stay in my own bed, thank you very much." Turning to leave the tent village, she froze. At the end of the aisle was Erin. Walking towards her.

Sam's heart rose. Erin looked different with her hair in dreadlocks, but it was still her. The olive skin, slightly small chin, dark eyes. Looking at her made her feel warm inside.

"Hey." She waved as the woman came closer. Sam was ready to sweep her up in an embrace, but Erin's eyes weren't focused on her. She hadn't acknowledged her presence at all. She simply walked right past.

"Erin?"

Sam grabbed her things and followed down the row, angling towards the centre of the spiralling street. Around a corner and Erin was gone. Sam slid to a stop.

"Did she go into one of these tents?"

But when she looked behind her, there was Erin heading the other way.

"Hey, wait."

Sam ran after her, but again, after turning a corner, she'd vanished.

"Please."

Behind her again. Sam ran. Erin stopped at a tent, looked back, then crawled inside. Sam stopped at the door.

"Erin?"

She lifted the flap, ducked low and went inside. As soon as she was in, she was pressed back, against the side of the tent. The fabric collapsed. Sam was knocked to the ground. The blue canvas pressed down on her face as hands moved over her body.

"Wait, stop."

She let go of the sleeping bag and tried to force the weight off her. She rolled and Erin fell to the ground, the tent popping back into place. Sam slid back. Erin's eyes were glazed over.

"I've been looking everywhere for you."

Faster than she'd anticipated, Erin pounced. She pinned her down and rammed her lips onto hers. She smelled like weed, and as if she hadn't bathed in a while. Sam managed to get her hands between them and pushed Erin back. She slid out from under her, but the girl was relentless. She flashbacked to when the Radiant Cyanide song had turned Avital and Erin into crazed animals. Here it was again. Or was Erin just incredibly happy to see her?

"Erin, I…"

Sam was happy to see her. She caught the scent of smoke, and images of them in the apartment, in the shower and under the covers, flashed through her mind. Warmth. Rightness. Satisfying.

Something shut off in Sam's mind. She relaxed her arms and let Erin mount on top of her. The smoke moved through her nose and into her lungs. She let their lips meet, allowed Erin's hands to explore under her jacket and—

No. This isn't right.

But it feels so good.

No.

165

Yes.

Wasn't this how it all started? Hypnotized by the Authority. What about you? Are you under their control?

Unzipping the jacket, sliding it off her shoulders as the smoke descended inside her.

No.

Yes.

No. She's not in her right mind. She's being influenced.

But so are you. You found each other. She's good for you.

No. This time I'm free. This time wouldn't be—

Jacket thrown aside, hands now moving to her shirt. The dreadlocks tickled her face. She felt a tingle in her lungs.

Just give in. You want to. You need to.

No. No. NO!

She exhaled sharply and felt the smoke blow clear. She pried Erin's hands back, then held her at bay by the wrists. The desperation, the longing in her look almost broke her. It had been a while since she'd felt anything good. Just the two of them, here alone, it would feel—

"No. Not like this."

An unrolled sleeping bag on the floor of the tent. Was it Erin's? Sam slid back, took the end of the zipper and tried to tug as she held Erin at bay. It wasn't going to work.

"Shit."

She let go, then grabbed the zipper and undid it. Immediately Erin's hands were over her shoulders as her lips kissed her neck. The perfect spot. She knew exactly where to—

"No."

Sam ducked out of the grip, yanked on the open sleeping bag, spun and wrapped it around Erin. She forced her down, pushed her hands in tight and pinned her. She began yanking on the zipper, trapping Erin inside the fabric bag. She wrapped it all the way to the neck. Erin squirmed like a worm and thrashed to free herself. Sam mounted her and held her down, looking into the lost eyes of her girlfriend.

"Erin, you have to listen to me."

She moved her head to the right and saw no signs of implantation. Erin tried to kiss her hand.

"I'm going to have to hold you down all night, aren't I?"

Pinning her to the floor of the tent, looking into Erin's glassy eyes, Sam began to understand just how insidious the Authority's manipulations truly were. Whether it was unleashing inner desires, canceling inhibitions, or just making people do things they might not have been prepared to do without the prompting, it was much more than just controlling a person's actions, it was about controlling their desires and behaviours. Sam had never questioned her sexuality before. She'd had crushes on boy bands, dated Rick and Joshua. And yet, out of her own mind, she'd fallen into bed with Erin and found something totally different. Everyone told her how perfect they were for each other and being with her had been a short break of happiness during these insane times. But there was a part of her that never faced the fact that the initial hooking up had taken place while under the Authority's mental manipulations. Did that make it less real? Less true? She'd avoided the subject completely. She tried to see if this newfound identity was who she'd always been but hadn't been aware of, or if it was just what they had wanted her to do. Looking at her friend, rolled up in a sleeping bag and trying to attack her with forced affections, she still didn't know.

Erin kept struggling, but was trapped. Sam reached for her

discarded jacket and pulled it back on. She zipped it up. She fanned the air and closed the tent flap. She shifted position to the side of the sleeping bag and wrapped her arms around Erin, holding her in an embrace, trying to will her free of the control that had been exerted over her. Her phone vibrated with a message, but she didn't dare check in case Erin got loose again.

"Don't listen to the voices," she whispered to her. "Find your own. It's still in there, trust me."

Erin leaned forward to kiss her. Sam let her and kissed her back once. It threatened to escalate, but she pulled back.

"Okay, that's all we get. Now go to sleep. You'll feel more like yourself in the morning. I just hope I still do." She pulled her shirt over her mouth and nose and waited.

Chapter 22

J immy lay propped upright against his pillow on the soft, queen-sized bed, looking out the window at Veronica's expansive, unkempt backyard. Skeletal trees, a vast field of snow, and a wire fence slept quietly under the huge white moon. He left the Venetian blinds open and scrolled through his phone. Veronica finished brushing her teeth in the attached bathroom.

"There's something here on the CBC about the student protests," he said. "Apparently the Red MP Dan Kirby is going to meet with the leaders for some kind of de-escalation talks."

"Huh?" She peered through the open door in mid-brush, toothpaste leaking out of her mouth, dripping down onto the floor.

"Hey, I just cleaned that this afternoon."

She turned and spat into the sink, but didn't rinse. "You're so domestic now," she said.

"Someone's got to clean up. We can't keep relying on your mom to... oh, God help me, I'm sounding like my parents here."

Exiting the bathroom, wearing an overlong T-shirt, she padded over to the dresser and reached up to put her phone on the charger. He caught a glimpse of her exposed underwear and rounded rear and felt a stirring in his groin. It didn't take much these days.

"Maybe you should consider a long-term leave of absence and be a stay-at-home stepdad. You could open a daycare and maid service."

"That's not funny. Also, are you proposing?"

She turned back around and stretched, showing him more of her underwear. "Oh geez, that's a big step. I'm still reeling over my divorce and—"

"Ha ha ha," he said sarcastically. "I know, don't talk about long-term things, it cramps your style."

She slid under the covers, saw his pitched tent and smirked as she sat down next to him. "I've told you, this is great. This is exactly what me and the kids have needed. You're the best thing that's happened to me since... well, since they were born really, but you and me, this is still on a trial run. Who wants to rush into another ceremony only to find out that—"

"I wouldn't run out on you, Ronnie."

"Sure, you say that now, but so did my ex-husband. And look where he is."

"He was a piece of—"

"Shit, I know."

"I'm not—"

"At all like him, I know that, too. But don't mess this up by worrying about the future. Let's just focus on the present, okay?" She reached under the covers and grabbed him through his boxers. "Like this present situation we've got here."

"Hey." He flinched. "That's sexual harassment!"

"No, this is." She tackled him, knocking his phone from his

170

hands as they made a mess of the bed.

Later, when he was catching his breath and she was trying to fix her pillow, Jimmy watched her in the moonlight and was thankful he'd met her. She was, however, still refusing to face the reality of what they had and kept trying to change the subject when he brought up anything outside of the house.

"Ronnie," he started.

She turned over and looked at him. "Don't tell me you want to go again?"

"I need a few more minutes," he said.

"Okay, give me the heads up…" She burst out laughing. "Get it?"

"Yeah, I do. But that wasn't what I was getting at."

"It wasn't? I thought I was good?"

"Could we not get distracted with sex for a minute?"

"Why not?"

"Because I just wanted to talk. It seems like, and I can't believe that I'm talking like this… but that you've been, I don't know, preoccupied lately. That when you come home, it's all go-go-go, then you just want to fuck and go to sleep."

"Wait, a man complaining his woman just wants to fuck and go to sleep? Jimmy, am I hearing you right?"

"Complaining, no. Shit, that does sound weird. I was just wondering why you don't want to tell me what's going on at work anymore, how Carlos is as your partner, what's been going on with the chief or—"

"Jimmy, I told you, this case is fucked up. It's still hush hush and—"

"And I'm a cop, too. I can help."

"Not unless you're on the task force. Sorry."

"Is it messing with your head? Are you just trying to fuck

away the—"

"Don't psychoanalyze me, Hooper," she said curtly. "I just… I have a lot on my mind. I'm working on a lot of things. A lot of angles. I just need to push all that aside when I get home. The overtime is bad enough and, quite frankly, it is getting to me. But to show I'm not dismissing you, Carlos is a dick, those missing wrestlers may be connected to the killer, and the chief is the same as he always is. So that's work. Here, at home, I just want to be a mom, rest, and maybe get railed every now and again."

"In that order?" he said, raising an eyebrow.

"Depends on the day. But seriously." She reached out and cupped his cheek. "I don't know how I'd be handling things without you. You're doing an amazing job at being Mr. Mom."

He snorted.

"Cooking, cleaning, looking after the kids, you're a regular catch, Jimmy. I appreciate you."

"Thanks. That's just what I've always wanted."

"You don't have to be a prick about it."

"That wasn't how I meant it."

She started to roll over in anger. He reached out and held her shoulder to stop her. "Hey, I'm sorry. I'm trying here, too. It's hard to go from being a cop to being a domestic sex slave."

Now she snorted and allowed herself to be rolled back over to look at him in the moonlight. Her eyes sparkled. He realized then how much he really loved her, loved her kids, loved this whole set up. Despite being partially crippled and suffering from feelings of inadequacy, he didn't want to mess it up, scare her away, or blow it. But he was no good at communicating any of that. He wasn't equipped for emotional honesty.

"Not that I'm complaining about the sex, mind you."

"Good."

"What I mean is… I just want to be open, okay?"

"About what?"

"Well, the first thing you do when you get home is go to the basement. Why?"

"Really? That's what you want to be open about?"

He struggled to go deeper. He'd just let the first thought exit his mouth, realizing now how stupid it was. "Sure. It's just… you never used to do that before so, uh, why?"

"Oh God, Jimmy, laundry. That's no trade secret."

She'd made him feel like an idiot.

"Right. Laundry. Okay, that makes sense. Maybe I'm not getting it all done during the day and—"

She reached out and stroked his face again with her fingers, lightly brushing them along his stubble. "Maybe you are going stir crazy. I get it. It's not normal for a guy like you. Shit, you were living in your own filth when I met you and now you're admonishing me for dripping toothpaste on the bathroom floor. You've gone through a lot. But the hard part is going to be over soon and then we'll have a whole new paradigm to deal with. Enjoy the time off, not being shot at, not having to look at decomposing body parts all day, or listening to a sexist fuckwit making inappropriate jokes."

"Those missing wrestlers, eh? Like the one who walked out of the hospital when—"

She put her finger over his mouth and stopped him mid-sentence. "That's work. We've got it. Here at home, just us. Please. I need it to be just us."

"Okay. Separation between lives, I get it. I just feel so out of the loop. So… useless."

173

"You're not useless," she said, reaching between his legs. "Not while this thing still works."

"Goddamn it. Now look what you've done."

"I think I will."

She slid under the covers, worked her magic, then came back up to kiss him hard on the lips. "You ready again?"

"I guess so."

She kissed his neck, moving around to the ears and paused to look at something on the back of his head. Finding whatever it was she was looking for, she came back to kiss him on the lips before they made another mess of the bed.

Chapter 23

He didn't know how long he had been sitting on this couch. Time seemed to have passed without him noticing. The television was on. He'd been watching a channel that showed nothing but reruns of shows he remembered from decades ago. The faces were more familiar than his.

Alice. Tom. Kotter. Ralph Malph. Maude. Larry. Nick. Jesse. Rellic. The Littlest Hobo himself. They were all there, doing the things he'd seen them do over and over again. Their words were echoes in his mind, their lives playing out in comforting déjà vu.

The sun rose. The day passed. He stayed in the spot on the couch, remembering a different room, a different chair, a different body. But still the same things on the screen.

Go.

He stood up. An urging at the back of his skull told him that it was time to go. Whatever the reason for being here, it wasn't just to sit and watch comforting figments of a past life. He was supposed to find someone, but that person wasn't here.

Go.

Leaving the television on, he moved to the door, opened

it and walked back into the hallway. Not even bothering to close it behind him, he descended the apartment stairs back to the street.

Go.

He had no idea what time it was. He remembered that he used to like feeling the sun on his face as he walked the streets. He found comfort in the cars blowing by, the sounds of birds, the noise of movement and commerce. But those were distant half sounds. The throbbing compulsion to move was all that he could hear.

Go.

Go where?

Go.

His body seemed to understand. He trusted the process. The legs moved, the blood pumped. Surroundings changed. People ignored him as he walked down busy sidewalks as if in a dream state. A panhandler hesitated asking for change, seeing something off about his gait.

Go.

There was a hierarchy in his world. Some gave orders, others followed. It was nothing new to be unaware of the reasons to do what he was told. A good soldier listened.

Go.

Turn down this street. Then down that one. It was a familiar route. Almost as if he was following footprints he'd left in this very same snow years before.

Go.

Why? Where? What was he doing? Pain pierced his temple as his brain scrambled. Television. Hot dogs. Cars and guns. A girl. A—

Drums in the distance.

176

Go.

The pounding beat sounded out instructions, almost like they were calling to him in a kind of language.

He tried to listen, but the throbbing pain was too great to focus on any of the individual words. He stopped and looked to the sky, where a strange cloud pulsated with vibrant colours to the rhythm of the tribal noise. Was that where he was supposed to go?

Chapter 24

"There's a kink I didn't know you were into," a voice said from just outside the flap of the tent.

Sam woke up as another girl climbed inside the unzipped tent. She carried a brown bag wet with grease marks, wore a red toque over her own dreadlocks, and had deeply tanned skin and brown eyes. Visible tattoos on her hands seemed to stretch up her arms under her sleeves.

Erin had finally passed out in the middle of the night and only then had Sam allowed herself to relax. She'd fallen asleep and had no idea how long they'd been out for, but the sun was shining. A chill air hung in the tent, enough to see her breath, but at least no obvious smoke.

"Who are you?" Sam asked.

"I should ask you the same thing."

"Oh, hey, Meg," Erin said groggily. Then she suddenly realized that someone was next to her and jerked upright. "What the fuck?"

"Whoa, calm down, it's just me," Sam said.

"Sam? What the hell are you doing here?"

"I was going to ask you the same thing. You don't return my texts for days then I find out you've dropped out of society, dreaded your hair and—"

"Why were you in my tent?"

Erin struggled to free herself from the sleeping bag, shifting her arms and squirming out through the top in a near panic. She pushed it down and slunk away, kicking it to the side like it was alive.

"What did you do to me?"

"You're getting the wrong idea," Sam said, holding up her hands in a calming gesture. "You brought me here then tried to—"

"Bullshit. I was at the rave with Meg. Then I wake up and find myself pinned down and you, uninvited in my autonomous personal space."

"You disappeared after we took that E," Meg said. "I was looking for you all night."

Something about this Meg rubbed Sam the wrong way. She had similar features but was like a more tanned version of her with her darker hair and—

"Wait. If you were looking for her all night, why didn't you come to the tent?"

Meg snorted. "I spent *some* of the time looking for her in someone else's tent." She chuckled and threw her arm around Erin's shoulder. "But I was thinking about her the whole time."

Erin giggled. "You alley cat."

"Hey, what can I say? Sometimes nature calls, you know."

The way they were going on was way too familiar. There was obviously more to this relationship. But she needed to hear it from Erin herself.

"What is this? What is she?"

"What is she?" Erin repeated, as if that was an idiotic question. "She's not a tourist, for one thing."

179

Meg nibbled on Erin's ear and now it was all too painfully clear.

"You're cheating on me with her. When did this start?"

"How can I cheat on someone who's never there? Who's more wrapped up in her own drama? Who's just dabbling with a lifestyle?"

"Who's dabbling?"

"Please. You're hot then cold. You run after Rick Hansen at the drop of a hat. Then there's the weird Russian goalie and—"

"Czech, actually. And—"

"Exactly. Playing with my emotions. Using me to assuage your ego after all the bad guys you keep lusting after. I didn't want to believe it, but after becoming a part of something so much bigger than just shopping, work, and school, I understand how the lies we let be told to us can control us. They manipulate us, make us believe things that we only want to be true, but aren't. Like you being more than just bi-curious."

Meg kissed Erin on the cheek and smirked at her.

"You don't know what you're talking about. We—"

"Hooked up. It was fun. But it was a lie, and you know it. Shit, the whole fucking world is a lie. If you weren't so busy looking for others to blame for all the bad stuff that keeps happening to you, you might be able to see it like everyone else here."

"You know what happened with Scott, Tommy, Factor 5ive, Rick, the Geld corporation. None of that was make believe, it—"

"She's still living in the dead world," Meg interrupted. "She hasn't had her eyes opened to the possibilities of the new future that we're build—"

"Building?" Sam said, cutting her off. "All I've seen so far are people getting stoned out of their minds, voting on nonsensical points of order, and avoiding school."

"This is so much bigger than university," Erin said. "Students for a Just World is worldwide. It's *changing* the world. Eyes are beginning to open."

"Damn." Meg kissed Erin again. "You're so hot when you're idealistic."

"This place has to be another one of Geld's plots. I don't understand why or how just yet, but there's something in the air. In the drugs, in the— everyone here is being manipulated."

"Are you sure you're not the one being manipulated?"

"No. I see it clearly. Well, mostly."

"You're looking for things that don't exist."

"They do exist. I've seen them."

"Not here. This is about making the world a better place."

"And taking E at raves?"

"And fucking like rabbits after," Meg said, pulling Erin in affectionately.

"Oh God," Sam said.

"Look," Erin said. "I'm sorry that you had to find out this way. That's what happens when someone is never around. Shit, maybe if you'd taken more interest in what Graham was saying at all those meetings you never attended. If you'd bothered to really listen to what he was—"

"Graham? That guy who passed out the flyers about the march? The one Avital was crushing over? Is he the head of all this?"

"There's no leader. This is a fully autonomous collective of

181

individuals acting for the greater good. He's just one of the ones who helped organize it."

"Where do I find him?" Sam asked. She suddenly had a thought that Graham must be working for, or was at least under the control of, the Authority. That he was another cog in their plot. Like Simon Karlsson and Arthur Fritz before him. If she stopped the guy, would everyone disperse? Would Erin come back to her?

"You want to find him?" Meg said derisively. "Why? That's not going to win her back."

"No, Meg, maybe she should meet him. It might open her eyes."

"But you said she was a lost cause. Totally blind. She's—"

"No one's a lost cause," Erin said. "Remember what Graham said. We're working to save as many people as we can. Maybe she can be made to understand."

Meg looked at Sam like a slab of beef. "I guess anything's possible."

"Wow, thanks," Sam said curtly. Whatever had happened to Erin had totally changed her. She'd drunk some serious Kool-Aid and suddenly found idealism, and an attitude.

"Room for three here if you come to your senses."

Meg licked Erin's ear, and she giggled again.

"Don't hold your breath."

"Just go find Graham," Erin said. "Open your eyes and your mind. Then maybe you'll begin to truly belong."

Chapter 25

The Guidance tent had been set up on the north side of the legislative grounds, directly in front of the lieutenant governor's residence. Government House, the Victorian-era building with a flat steep-sided Mansard roof and flag brandishing the lieutenant governor's standard, loomed over the teepee itself. A billboard out front listed the current demands of the Students for a Just World movement. Multiple pages had been tacked to its face, each one detailing increasingly strange ideas.

Sam read through a few as she scanned the area for danger. There were people sitting against trees smoking, others playing drums around an open fire, more tossing a ball to a mangy dog; all innocuous enough. Closer to the edge of the fence that encircled the protest village, were commissary tents. A great collage of smells carried on the soft breeze: marijuana, falafel, bread, noodles, curry, other spices her nose didn't even recognize. The foodservice seemed far too varied and organized to be haphazardly sourced. She wondered how much of it had been donated, stolen, or scavenged, or if someone with deep pockets had bought it all. The more time she spent here in the tent city, the more it was clear that this walk-out was far too organized to have been spur of the moment. Somebody had been planning this for a long time, and planning it well. Could it be Graham alone?

"She said he's inside," Sam muttered to herself.

She took out her phone, saw that there was an unread message and checked it. From Detective Tockett: "Think they got Rick. Need to do something fast. Find your friends yet?"

"Working on it," she wrote back.

She took a photo of the tent and sent it to Detective Tockett. She shoved the phone back inside her jacket pocket and took a deep breath.

"So they did get Rick. Time's running out. I need to figure out what's going on here."

There was nobody guarding the tent, so she just walked right in. It was like walking into a war room. A circular table in the centre of the tent was covered in papers. A map of the legislative grounds hung on the fabric of the west side wall. A desk, filing cabinet, and computer chair had been set up opposite. A laptop rested open on top of the desk, the screen projecting a swirling colour pattern screensaver. Two men stood talking across from each other at the table— the man with a beard Sam didn't know, but the other she did. The wavy brown hair, slender build, glasses; it was Graham Maddox, the idealist who'd tried to recruit them for the march. But it was who was standing to his right that shocked Sam. Her hair was dreadlocked, and she wore a thick designer coat. Despite a layer of grime, she still looked fabulous. Avital. She watched the conversation between the two men intently and didn't notice Sam at all.

On the other side of her, a man from the CBC set up a camera as if he was going to be filming soon.

"—within twenty-four hours?" the other man asked.

"I can bring that to a vote, but I don't believe it's out of the question."

"How much sway does your word hold?"

"Everyone here is a fully autonomous individual member of the collective, but they also know who's in charge."

The other man laughed and held his hand out. "Glad to hear. Now do you have a statement ready? I think our friend here is getting antsy for something for the six o'clock."

"Sure. But the light is no good in here," Graham said and shook the waiting hand.

"Outside then. I'll do mine first."

The other man wore a crisp suit under an expensive looking parka. He turned and headed to the exit with the cameraman following mutely. When the stranger passed Sam, his eyes took her in knowingly. It was only a brief glance, but it communicated that he seemingly thought she was of no importance. Then, they were both gone in a flash.

Graham turned from the table and went over to the laptop. He bent over to turn off the screensaver, checking text on the screen. He didn't acknowledge Sam in the slightest either.

"Uh, hello?" she said.

Avital straightened up the pages on the table, staying oblivious.

"Graham?" she said again.

Tapping the screen a few times, she wondered if he'd heard her. She was about to say his name louder when he leaned back and turned to look at her.

"I remember you," he said.

"You do?" she said, caught off guard.

"Sure. You were sitting in the futon room with Avital

185

here." He walked up to stand beside her. She looked at him obediently, brushing some fluff off his jacket. "You didn't seem all that impressed with what we were planning. I detected a bit of condescension."

"I don't think I said a word that day."

"You didn't have to. I could read it on your face."

He gathered up some pages and handed them to Avital, who took them silently. Was she deliberately ignoring her?

"I get it, though, I totally do. It's hard to believe in things these days. The world is so fractured and distracted. People are more worried about posting what they ate for dinner than the fact that there are so many who can't even afford to eat. You can just swipe a person away, never stopping to consider that they even *are* a person in the first place. Grab what you can while you can, and to hell with everyone else. Burning planet, who says? Not these people. Those people don't want you to know that global fish stocks are collapsing, these ones don't want you to pay taxes, those say we're being flooded with migrant criminals, these ones that your very words are killing, those that race or gender are more important than economic disparity. With so much shouting and fighting and back and forth, what's real, what's a lie, what's important, what's bullshit, how can you get behind anything really? Right? Much easier to just go out to a club, drink appletinis, forget all that negativity. Shit's hard. Life's hard. Why fight for anything if the whole planet's on a crash course to hell?"

His piercing amber eyes seemed to bore right through her as he spoke.

"You're just like the others. You can feel it. That something's off. Not just here, everywhere. The algorithms that subtly manipulate us on every social media platform. They run our lives. Sure, maybe you like seeing the dances and cat videos, or stalking old exes, but they're designed to pit us against each another, compete for likes and attention, isolate us, turn us into dopamine addicts unable to comprehend anything beyond outrage and shock in increasingly shorter bursts. The reason you and everyone else here feels broken, is because you're only seeing the reflection of a broken world. Our generation wonders if we'll ever own a home, get a decent job, let alone be able to retire. Nihilism. It's everywhere."

She wanted to say something, to break his monologue, but she found herself at a loss for words. He stared right through her, saying what he believed to be the truth, and despite herself, she found that he was making sense.

"But that's been around before. Many times in history people have thought they were living in a time of downward spiral. What makes now different? This nihilism pervades everything that we used to believe in. Inequality, misinformation, the possibility of a World War, technological revolution, AI, genetics, robotics. Doesn't it feel like we're rushing forward, changing the world without knowing the result? Stripping power from the many to the few, grounding some into powder. That's what's brought everyone here and to all the other tent cities. Our generation is questioning our place, and where we're going to end up. I feel it myself. What's my purpose in life? What's on the other side of university? Will there be a job? What will being human be like in twenty years? I know this all sounds very existential. And I'm sure a lot of people here don't think of it that way, they just feel out of sync, lost, scared."

Avital stared at him enraptured. Sam had never seen her so

187

caught up in anything, let alone what a guy was saying. She always seemed so frivolous. And yet, this place, this room, this man, was about something bigger, something more. Sam was beginning to understand.

"I don't have all the answers, Samantha. But I do know that we, as a generation, are going to have to reconceive our place in the world. Our parents and grandparents, everyone before us had some kind of connection to each other. Church, religion, some place to meet, pause, commune, maybe ponder meaning. But that's all gone. We've ditched all that and haven't replaced it. Heck, maybe we are all just a cosmic accident, but we're still human. We require something that unites us with other humans, structure, meaning. I'm not here as a religious leader. I'm not even here as a leader. I'm part of a collective of autonomous individuals. All I'm trying to do is connect with my generation. Begin to build a framework for a better world. But it takes more than one mind. That's why we're crowdsourcing ideas. We're trying to combat that growing nihilism, coming up with answers from within ourselves. It can't be from one mind. It has to be from a collective. Everyone has value, everyone can contribute. It's not wealth or connections or birth or race or gender or anything. It's about a philosophy, a reason for being here, an understanding of what is worth fighting for. We can't let these concepts, our future, be decided by other people anymore, other generations either. We have to do it ourselves. We have to make the future, a better future. That's what's going on here."

"I... uh..." She didn't know what to say. She hadn't been prepared for any of that. She'd half-expected to walk in here and find another self-absorbed clueless goof agonizing over a list of outlandish ideas without any connection to reality, but instead, here was someone itemizing things she felt but had never articulated, offering her a sense of community.

Avital wrapped her arms around him. He put his around her shoulder.

"It's time to believe in something, Sam, not just yourself. Graham, we, all of us are doing good work here. It's getting through. That guy you just saw? That was Dan Kirby. Member of Parliament. Cabinet Minister. We've reached the prime minister."

"You have?"

"They're waiting for me outside," Graham said. "I have to give a statement to the press. But stay here. We can talk more in a few minutes. Avital's told me a lot about you."

He left the teepee, and it felt like a warming presence had left with him. A heat, a vibration, leaving the room cold and dark. Avital blinked, as if she'd been asleep for a minute. She saw Sam standing in front of her and exhaled deeply.

"Isn't he something else?"

"Yeah. But I'm not sure what."

She looked through the opening in the teepee and saw Graham speaking to the cameraman, naturally, with a commanding presence. His charisma was palpable. It radiated outward, gently touching her even through the fabric of the tent. She'd never felt a tangible static charge from anyone like that before. Maybe briefly when she'd seen Scott on stage. But this wasn't some song working a hold over her, it was ideas. Good ones? Bad ones? Bullshit or truth? Her mind couldn't unravel what he was saying beyond the feelings they'd imparted. Like being wrapped up in a quilt. He hadn't affected her like that in the futon room, but seeing the look

189

on Avital's face, she wondered if he had her.

"He's a great man," Avital said. "You're beginning to understand now. I can feel it."

She didn't know what to think. She just watched.

Chapter 26

He stood staring at the shining golden boy statue that sparkled in the late afternoon sun. The legislative building was important, that much he knew, but the drumming had devolved into nothing more than a tribal pounding on the inside of his skull, like a post-bender headache.

He didn't remember drinking, didn't even remember coming here. But for some reason, this home of provincial power, surrounded by a fence and what looked like a full-on hippie commune had drawn him. It must have been for a reason. But his memories were shrouded in the fog that hung over the tent village.

"I'm either hungover or not drunk enough."

When presented with a situation like this, the best thing to do was to find a seat in a bar and ask his old buddy, Jack. Leaving the love-in, he went wandering until he found the neon sign that would lead to the answers he sought.

'Bar'. Buzzing quietly, the sign spoke in clear words, unlike those drums. He pushed open the door and walked inside.

A thick haze of smoke that hadn't gotten the message that you weren't allowed to light up inside met him. An old TV flashing images of hockey players haloed in the dying colours of a tube on the fritz, a line of people hunched over their own personal problems, a few more shooting pool… it was like his brain was on a loop. Or was it simply déjà vu. Had he been here before? Had he ever left? He was having a hard time focusing on what was real, what was a jumbled rerun, what day, year, or decade it was. Why he was in the wrong body, or even if he was.

"My head is…"

"What'll it be, buddy?"

"Scrambled eggs," he said, as a nagging sense that he wasn't supposed to be here intruded on his thoughts.

"No food. Booze. That's it. What you want?"

"Answers. Help. Something to clear my head."

"Got just the thing."

The man poured him a tall glass of something that smelled like lighter fluid. He took a sip and it went down like water. The whole glass did.

"Hey, easy. This shit'll knock you on your ass," the bartender said.

The man poured him another glass and just as quickly it was gone.

"Whoa, hold up. That's five bucks already. You pay now."

He looked up at a leathery man wearing a vest decorated with symbols and skulls. Tattoos peeked from under his white shirt. A huge flag hung on the wall shared one of the symbols. The rest of the place fit the same decor. This wasn't just some ordinary bar. There was something he should recognize about those symbols. Some importance that was trying desperately to poke through his thoughts.

"Okay, I get it. You're a fucking bum. I should have known. You're as bad as these pieces of shit here," the man said, waving his hands at the others sitting at the bar. They barely moved. Could they?

"Five bucks. Now."

Behind him, he could hear the pool players stop to watch. He stared at the bartender and at the bottle that had drawn him here. He reached out to take it, but the man swung it away.

"Oh no. Boys," he said. "This guy's come to the wrong establishment."

The couch. The sidewalk. The park. Drums and golden statues. Voices, urges. A past that refused to stay in his head. Nothing made sense. The symbol on the wall. The words below. The leather. The decor. The booze finally kicked in. He understood now where he was. And that was a place you didn't spend any time in unless you were trouble or looking for it.

Right now, though, fog cleared, he was trouble.

A hand closed on his shoulder. "Okay, guy," one of the pool players said. "Time to pay or we're going to break your legs."

"You don't fuck with the Devil's Satans. Not on our turf."

"Oh, you're gonna get it, man," one of the winos next to him at the bar said. The man was missing most of his teeth and his eyes seemed to take both the scene and the television in at the same time.

"Man, you hearing me? You speak English?"

The leather vests, the jeans with chains that rattled, the fingerless gloves, the knives hidden in their boots. He'd seen this movie before.

"Okay, boys, he's fucked. Take him out."

Frank flexed his muscles, knowing where this was going.

"You come here like this, there's gotta be consequences."

193

One of the men stubbed his cigarette out on Frank's neck. He never flinched. "This guy tweaking?"

The guy mashed the cigarette all the way to the nub, burning a black patch of flesh on Frank's neck, waiting for some reaction that never came. Finally, eyes wide in shock, he moved to pull his hand away, but Frank jerked up and grabbed him by the fingers. He squeezed once and the man's digits were spaghetti.

He screamed in pain, brandishing a useless hand. A pool cue crashed against the back of Frank's head, shattering clean in two. Three large men in leather emerged from the back carrying bats and chains. They converged on him, swinging. Frank blocked with his forearms. He felt no pain from the blows. The other biker jumped on his back and wrapped his arms around his head, squeezing.

A flash of silver and the bartender lunged with a knife, sinking it deep into Frank's gut. Frank stopped and looked down. The bartender smiled. "You're fucked now, asshole."

"Not today." Frank clapped his hands together on the bartender's ears, a blow so quick the man didn't even have time to register it before his head exploded in a shower of gore beneath the crushing double smack.

"Holy shit!" one of his attackers screamed.

The headless body spasmed, dancing awkwardly as blood sprayed out of the stump of a neck. It collapsed to the ground and pumped out waves of crimson over the grimy floor.

The knife still sticking in his gut, Frank threw the man on his back into the wall. He crashed hard, back breaking at the corner, folding the body backwards in a way it was never meant to fold. The others were pinned in place, their minds unable to comprehend what they were seeing. Frank reached out and grabbed an attacker by the hair. He yanked but only succeeded in tearing his scalp from his head. The newly bald man shrieked in primal fear, arms frantically flailing as blood poured over his face. "Oh Jesus, oh Jesus!" he cried.

"Never needed a rug before." Frank punched another man in the head, lodging the scalp deep in his mouth. Frank's fist stuck six inches inside the skull, breaking through to the drywall. The man went limp as his brain caught up.

Frank shook the body off his hand. It fell to the ground with a dusting of plaster. Red gore dripped from his fist as he turned to the remaining attackers.

"Anyone else need a little reconstructive surgery?"

Mutely struggling to process the level of violence they had just seen, they stared wide-mouthed. Frank took a step forward and they turned tail and ran.

Watching them go out the door and into the street, he felt oddly like he'd just done his civic duty. He sat back down at his seat at the bar and took hold of the bottle with the good stuff. The toothless man next to him grinned. "That stuff must be pretty great. How about sharing?"

Frank poured him a glass then refilled his own.

"Some game, huh?" the man asked.

Nobody else said a word as three quickly cooling bodies littered the bar.

"Who's winning?"

"I don't know. That TV's a piece of shit."

Frank pounded it once, but instead of fixing the problem, the whole thing imploded beneath his fists. "Oops."

The man waved his hand dismissively. "Eh, not like he cares anymore anyway."

Frank downed his glass again. The man followed suit.

195

"Refill?"

Chapter 27

She was sitting on the edge of the bathtub staring at her phone. The door was halfway open, and he could see her reflection in the mirror. She had that concerned look she got when things weren't going her way. She had that a lot lately, but she was keeping the reasons from him. He watched her for a moment, wondering what she was hiding.

"Where are you? Why aren't you replying?" she muttered to herself.

"Why isn't who replying?" he said, pushing the door the rest of the way open.

She casually put the phone down, screen side to the sink top. "Spying? What if I was peeing?"

"You left the door open."

"You're avoiding the question. You got a thing for peeing?"

"You're the one avoiding the question. Who are you waiting to reply?"

"There's nothing to be jealous about, it's just a source looking into something. Nothing serious. Certainly not another man."

"I didn't—"

"But if you were thinking it, you can stop." She gathered up the phone and stood up. She leaned in and kissed him on the cheek. "Now, I gotta go. Lots to do. Pretty sure things are heating up with this case."

Before he could say a thing, she was down the hall and into the kitchen. He hopped after her, saw her descending the stairs to the garage just as Carter threw a banana peel at Olivia. It splatted against the wall and slid greasily to the floor.

"Hey, don't—"

The garage door shut.

"Wait, Ronnie!"

He limped after her, but by the time he was at the door, she'd pulled out into the driveway and was halfway to the road. He pressed the button to shut the garage doors and returned to the kitchen.

"Uncle Jimmy, Olivia stuck her tongue out at me, and it was covered in mush."

"Did not."

"Did, too."

"Did not."

"Did, too."

Watching the car pull away down the street, Jimmy suddenly knew he couldn't just sit around anymore. He needed answers.

"Did not."

"Did, too."

"Who wants to go for a car ride?" he asked.

"Doesn't Mommy have to work?"

"I'll drive," he said cheerily.

"You can't drive," Olivia said. "You're still broken."

"I can manage just fine, I'll have you know. So do you want to go or not?"

"Why?"

"Because it's fun."

"Car rides aren't fun," Olivia said curtly.

"What if we go to McDonalds?"

"Yay, that's fun."

"Okay, get your jackets and boots on and let's go!"

* * * *

"This is boring," Carter said from the backseat.

"Yeah, bor-ing," Olivia added.

"No, it's not," Jimmy said, eyes never leaving the precinct parking lot. "It's fun. We're having lots of fun."

"We're not going anywhere. We're just sitting here."

"We will," Jimmy said. "I'm just letting the car cool down. It got too hot before."

Her car was parked in the usual spot, and he hadn't seen her leave in a squad car just yet. He hoped that meant she was still inside. If she'd already left before he got here, then he was just wasting his time and the kids' patience.

"I'll bet it's cold now," Carter said. "Why don't you try asking it?"

"I'm thirsty," Olivia said.

"Yeah, I'm thirsty, too. When are we going to McDonalds?"

"Soon, guys, soon," he said. "I just want to—"

He spotted her leaving the building. She was talking to her partner, who waved his hands around as he talked like he was making some really interesting point. He carried a coffee cup in one hand and car keys in the other. Jimmy watched them move to one of the squad cars and get in. Carlos was driving. The exhaust began puffing from the tail pipe and the car reversed out of the spot. He fired his own to life.

"Yay, we're going somewhere," Carter said.

"Where now?" Olivia asked. "McDonalds, right?"

"Not sure yet, kids," Jimmy said.

He waited until the car had turned out of the lot and down the street, giving them a wide berth before merging into a lane and following behind.

* * * *

He snapped a photo of her talking to a man dressed in leather. Her partner was in the car across the street. The man was shaking his head to her questions. She reached into her pocket and held her hand out. He slapped it and Jimmy knew right away money had just been exchanged.

"What the hell are you doing bribing someone from a known chop shop?"

"Who are you talking to, Uncle Jimmy?" Olivia asked.

"Myself. I'm talking to myself."

"Mommy said that's a sign of senility," Carter said.

"What? It is not."

"Is, too. I heard her talking to Grandma. She said she knew that Grandpa was showing signs of sen... senility because he started talking to himself out loud."

"Lots of people talk to themselves," Jimmy said. "It a way to work out things you're thinking about."

"How old are you?" Olivia asked. "Are you as old as Grandpa?"

"No, I'm—"

Veronica had returned to the squad car and they were pulling away. Jimmy checked the mirror and quickly followed. A horn blasted behind him. He waved apologetically to the guy for cutting him off.

"Are we finally going to McDonalds?" Carter asked.

"Please. I'm so hungry."

"You just had breakfast." He looked at the clock. "Two hours ago."

"Two hours. See? We're starving!"

"Okay, okay, I heard you. As soon as we find a McDonalds and we can—"

"There's one," Carter said, pointing as they passed one on the right side.

"Oops, I missed the turn," Jimmy said.

"There's another one on the other side of the street," Olivia offered.

"I don't like that one, let's find a better one." Why did there have to be so many damn McDonald's in River City?

Ahead, the car took the exit onto the Chief Peguis freeway. Jimmy quickly gunned it to get around a car blocking his route and jerked the wheel to follow.

"Whee!"

Now they were doing eighty kilometres towards the downtown again. He wondered where her next stop was going to be. Both so far were known criminal fronts: a bar and the chop shop. In each case, she was the one who did the talking. But about what?

The squad car's signal blinked. They were turning south. He got into the same lane and followed four cars back. When the light changed, someone at the head of the line hesitated. People honked. It jerked the driver to attention and he or she quickly made the turn. But the light was short, only two cars after Veronica's making the turn.

"Shit," Jimmy said.

"You said a bad word!"

Without even thinking, he pulled around the car ahead of him and ran through the red, tailing Veronica. Horns blared at him as he cut against traffic coming right at him.

He spotted them ahead. He gunned it to catch up. Behind him, a siren blared. Looking in his rearview mirror, he saw the flashing lights of another squad car.

"Fuck."

"Whoa! Major bad word!"

He slammed the wheel with his palm and pulled over to the side of the road. He could only watch in helplessness as Veronica's car disappeared into the distance.

A tapping on the window reminded him of his predicament. He rolled it down. "Hey, sorry, I was really—"

"Hooper? That you?"

He looked up, saw the familiar face of Murphy staring back. "Hey, Murph. Yeah, it's me."

"How's the rehab?"

"It's coming along."

"You rehabbing your brain, too? Cuz you ran that red pretty blatantly."

"Yeah, I know, I'm sorry. I just, uh, I've got these kids and they're really hungry for McDonalds and—"

"These Tockett's?"

"Yeah."

The man leaned in and waved. "Hi, guys, how are you doing?"

"We are so hungry! He promised us McDonalds and it's taking forever!"

"He also said two bad words."

Murphy laughed. "Okay, okay, I heard you." He looked back to Jimmy. "Look, don't pull a thing like that unless you're at work, okay? The last thing we need right now is more bad press. Off-duty cop causes four car pileup. That'll look great with this whole can't-catch-the-serial-killer bullshit."

"No problem. Say, what do you know about the case? I heard pro-wrestlers might be involved. Any other leads?"

"Not my thing, Hooper. That's task force business. Hush hush. Why don't you ask Tockett, she's the one working it?"

Jimmy was about to give him a story when the man burst out laughing.

"Oh snap, she's cock blocking you. You've got the itch and she won't let you scratch it. Oh shit, wait till the boys hear about this!"

"You said a bad word, too!"

Murphy started to walk off, but Jimmy leaned out the window. "Wait, Murphy, maybe keep this little incident on the down-low, okay? It's embarrassing enough without the guys knowing and all, and—"

Murphy pointed a finger gun at Jimmy and smirked. "Sure thing, hotshot. Now go get those kids their happy meals."

He turned and walked away. Jimmy noticed he had a bandage on the back of his neck. He was about to ask him what had happened when a shout from the back interrupted him.

"You heard the policeman, Uncle Jimmy, get us food!"

* * * *

Exhausted and massaging his knee, Jimmy sat at the dining room table as Veronica came in through the garage. She carried a file folder and disappeared downstairs without a word. A minute later, she was back upstairs, coming into the kitchen now empty-handed.

"Hey there, big guy," she said. "Kids in bed?"

He nodded silently.

"I'll just go say goodnight." She went down the hall to their bedrooms.

Something else to add to his questions now. But how to bring all of this up without alerting her to what he'd done?

Chapter 28

"Forget the past."
  "Forget the past."
  "Embrace the present."
"Embrace the present."
"Imagine the future."
"Imagine the future."

Echoes. A voice projecting. The massed crowd standing under the full moon. Eyes locked at attention. Megaphone sparkling. Light strands like blinking stars, colours floating just out of reach. The chill air faded away from the collective energy and warmth of a unity of humanity in perfect harmony.

"Feel it now."

"Feel it now."

Pills, cigarettes, flasks, all going from hand to hand, threading through the watchers in seconds. Brought to mouths. Her hands took them without realizing. Gone in a flash. Fuzz around the edges of her sight. Images splitting and vibrating. Voices in her head. Questions, answers. Then, a beat. Deep. Earthy. Lights pulsating. Strobing. An all-encompassing pounding noise.

Rave. Bodies mashing together, the smell of sweat, spices,

and natural hair. Euphoria levitating feet off the packed dirt. In the centre of the maelstrom, heat like a sauna. She jumped, twirled, floated. Her hands flowed in intricate patterns that spelled out her innermost thoughts. The moon surged outward to the beat. People all around her stripped out of their clothes. Hundreds of nude men and women began swaying and contorting to the electrical sounds dancing through them like a live current.

Cellphone lights, Coleman lanterns, strands of blinking Christmas bulbs wrapped through the trees merged into a living being. The reds and greens captivated her, twinkling in their own language. Arms up to the sky, the vastness of space flowed down into her, lost in the moment, oblivious to the outside world. "We are not bound by what has happened to us," a man's voice spoke in her mind. "We transform and become new life. Free from the past."

Carried on the wave of passionate movement and uninhibited humanity, she understood what it felt like to be truly free. "Embrace yourself. This is the future."

A hugely muscled man, stripped to the waist, chest glistening with sweat, steaming from the heat, took form in the blurred colours of life. Standing haloed by a rotating disco ball behind him, he was staring. At her. An impossible figure, a statue of perfect flesh. But an innocent face with clear blue eyes that promised mutual understanding. The shared ideals of the collective drew them together. Pulling in close, drawn by the invisible force permeating the air; they kissed and became lost in the moment of overwhelming music. An offer of strength and protection. The focus of a common goal.

Devotion. To her. She could read it in his eyes. Words were unnecessary, nor would they be heard over the music. With wide-eyed nervousness, as scared of the moment of truth as she was, he leaned his head to hers. Her hands traced his Rodin defined muscles, a body fit for worship. It told her that there were still beautiful things in this world. "Leave behind negativity, cynicism, the fear of death, and decay."

She'd almost forgotten how. The past had taken root. The present was blurred, the future impossible to see.

"Forget the past. Embrace the present. Imagine the future. Be who you are." Like a mantra, the voice spoke to her inside the music.

Another voice tried to drown it out, locked in the back of her mind. *You took something. They gave you something.*

Inner voices were made to be ignored. She let herself be absorbed into something bigger. For the first time in years, the path ahead was clear. Collective. Union. She didn't want this moment to end. Lost in the forest of bodies, hemp necklaces, dreadlocks, unshaven faces, exposed skin, she found this man. Who was he?

"Does it matter?"

They blended. Thin tendrils of light left her body, merging with sparking currents from his. A jolt through her core as the two shafts of light danced in the fractal space that separated their atomic selves. Minds as one, bodies finding commonality.

The light flared over them, wrapped them in a static field that washed out the crowd. Then, blinking, they were inside. She tossed her coat in the corner of the tent as he stood watching quietly. The sounds of the rave were all around them. Her tent diluted nothing, the music an invisible force that rained through. Her body cried out. Glowing, his eyes promised her an end to the nightmares. "Forget the past.

Embrace the present. Imagine the future."

Mr. Right Now.

She began unbuttoning her shirt.

Taking her in, he said nothing, not needing to. The radiating colours contoured his muscles. A physique that looked like he could break her in half. Like he could break a wall in half. Gentle hands reaching out in unspoken desire. Yearning for connection.

Don't do this. The pills. The pot. Don't.

Resistance gone. She grabbed him by the belt and pulled him in close. She kissed him. The tent flap hung open, wisps of smoke tentatively snaking inside. Her mind expanded outward, to feel countless others forming their own connections in tents all around her. Their minds rippling in a great sea that hovered invisibly, merging thoughts into a collective meld. Spiritual. Understanding, a way to find truth in each other. Her hands did what others did, or was she following their script? Over his chest, down to his pants, fumbling with the button.

It's happening again. It's not right. Break free.

Dozens of pants opened simultaneously. She felt everyone's actions layered on hers. She began to slide the jeans down. They still hadn't said a word. The smoke, blinking with the beat in colours from somewhere else, met the man's glowing body, pierced inside his chest, rolled like a worm finding its way through the soft upper layers of a face. Then, having burrowed in and around him, it snaked through her, slowly over her shoulder.

Passively, the movie played in front of her. Seeing a hundred other men layered on top, the faint afterimages of other hands sliding down other pants. His eyes were all colours and none at the same time. The collective will had made all of them everything and nothing at once.

The smoke had weight. Ethereal mist with corporeal form. It met her bare shoulder and plunged inside, sending a chill wave through her body. She could feel it tunnelling deeper.

Her hands moved of their own accord.

Not with him. Not here. Not like this.

Watching life from behind her own eyes, unable to stop. The thing swimming around her core. Her reactions slowed down, screaming out to change their orders. But the body wasn't listening.

Stop! Stop! Stop!

Her throat constricted. The smoke worm stopped in her abdomen, a brief respite before a stabbing pain erupted in her gut. Churning and heaving. The fog lifted just a moment. Bile rising. Choking. The thing quivering inside of her. She was going to throw up.

"No," she half said, half croaked. She pushed back from the mound of meat standing at attention for her.

"No… no."

The mist tendrils had intertwined them, held her in place. She fell hard, scrambled as the thin vapour pulled back, like a fishing line luring her in. She had to get out of here. Away from him. It was all connected. The thing inside. She had to bring it back up. She crawled frantically out of the tent, fighting against the constricting gas. Everywhere she looked were men and women cavorting, against trees, on the snow, in the middle of the rave. Some danced, some drank, some rolled around together. The smoke flowed over them all like living madness in an orgy of human flesh.

"Got—to—get—away."

Looking to the sky, she saw a cloud flowing over the tent city. It was alive. A thousand strands leaking out like tentacles, meeting the forms copulating in every conceivable place. The rippling wave moved like an endless snake. There were eyes in the fog looking at her. A mouth formed, as a newer and larger being began slithering through the air towards her. Maw opening, fangs of grey, lunging.

She felt the air being sucked out through her, pumped through the line pulling her back to the tent. She dropped to all fours, grabbed at the mist. It shouldn't have had form or substance, but the slimy surface was as real as her own skin.

"Get out!"

She pulled, felt the thing recoiling back through pathways burrowed in her skin. She gripped hand over hand, tugging away as the massive thing in the sky lumbered closer. More and more the greasy thing emerged. Her air almost gone, she pulled one more time as something tried desperately to cling to the inside of her ribcage. Then, with a pop, it was clear. A faceless slit in coloured air. It tried to push in again, but she threw it back to the tent. The man stood naked now, reaching for her as the freed head of the worm chose to burrow into him instead, the coils of smoke serpent dangling on the floor of the tent like spilled entrails.

Air returned to her lungs. She was whole again. Her stomach rumbled. The great fog serpent passed right overhead, as if it was now blinded to her presence. It slithered into other tents, then back out. In hers, naked skin waited. But the attraction was gone. Instead, she only saw the thing feeding on him.

"Hey, I know you," a voice slurred.

Two men, arms around each other, wearing only boxers,

stumbled forward. "I saw you on TV. The dyke at the Jets games. Shit. You're hot."

The massive serpent emerged from a nearby tent, summoned by the sounds of their voices.

"Get away," she said, holding her hands up to stop them. They didn't see the thing coming for them. Its great mouth opened wide.

"Come on, two for one special here," the man said, kissing his partner.

The fog wrapped around them like a vest. Up and over, the mouth fell on them like a funnel. It penetrated their skin, left them and moved on. Silently, now one, they reached for her. She ducked away, staggered backward and ran. Her stomach was rebelling.

Get away. Get away as far as you can.

The fence. Two huge men stood at the exit gate, facing inward. One had a mohawk, the other was... the same guy from her tent? Back over her shoulder she saw the two men in boxers pushing into another tent.

The men at the gate took a step towards her. She turned and ran the other way. Pushing through the crowd, head throbbing, she headed towards the river to the gate on the north side. There were two more guards there, waiting for her. She pivoted, ran to the southeast. Hard, fast, feet pumping on the packed ground. The fence was five feet high. She had to clear it. She knew she could jump it. They practiced leaps like this in hapkido class all the time. *Remember the training.* Leap up, clear the legs, roll as you land.

Not looking back, she ran faster. From out of tents came arms, reaching out for her. Forms tried to block her route. She twisted and pushed, made for the clearing. Then, she leapt, her open shirt brushing the top of the fence. Seeing the snow coming towards her face, she rolled along the side, in a tight ball. Tucking minimized the impact, the momentum taking her through to her feet. What a jump. If only Master Park could have seen it. Highlight reel stuff.

Putting distance between her and the tent village, she kept running. The river walk was in sight. She only made it ten more steps before her stomach refused to contain its contents anymore. It all came out in a wave. Torrential bile: food she'd eaten despite having no recollection of, the drugs, the booze, whatever else she'd put in her body, all heaved over the snow in a red, brown, and green slurry. A great wave that sucked out all of her air and threatened to choke her. It burned her throat, the gag reflex trying to send her innards out with the contents of her gut. Her body screamed for it to stop, begged for air. Then, like an animal leaping out of her, it was all gone. A massive puddle melted into the snow.

She fell backwards, gasping for air. Her eyes watered. She couldn't stop coughing. She felt like she was about to pass out.

Looking back at the legislative grounds, the lights from inside the tent city sparkled. The music throbbed faintly, but it was as if she was seeing it all through a blurred lens. The rest of the world was clearer now. Her memories were clearer. She saw it all: talking to Graham, Avital showing her around the village, food being passed out. Bread. A massive collection of garbage bags piled up at the edge of the camp, clean up crews hauling them away. Others were bringing back food, chairs, tents, more people. Words being said. Smoking around a fire, listening to songs played on a guitar. A pill and a beer.

Her temple throbbed in pain. She rubbed around her eyes, trying to focus on how many days of hedonism she'd lost. It was impossible to know. She had flashes of Marlon and Peta, Everett and various girls, Erin and Meg, Avital, a giant party, listening to talks, hands making the bird signs, demands being added to the list, nights in the tent. Blank faces? The man with the muscles. How many days?

"How many days?" she said again.

More came back from within her. Another torrent was unleashed, adding to the river of slime on the snow. Panting for air, completely empty at last, she knew there was nothing left inside her.

"It's the whole place," she said weakly. "The speeches, the food, the music, the drugs. It's all mind control. But whose future are they working towards? I have to tell Detective Tockett."

She patted her pocket but didn't have her phone. She didn't have her wallet, didn't even have any change. It must all still be inside her tent. She stared at the wall around the party, saw the fires and the living smoke dancing over it all. She couldn't go back inside. Not tonight at least. Not without help.

"Home," she muttered. "I'll call her from home…"

Chapter 29

The more distance she put from the sounds and lights of the tent village, the more her head cleared. Walking through the snow, without her jacket, backpack, or purse, Sam tried to piece it all together.

"Mass hypnosis," she muttered. "What catalyst? Graham? The drugs? The food?"

So intent on getting back home, she'd never considered how she was going to get inside the apartment. Reaching her modest building on the elm-lined street, she stopped at the brick facade. The cold was starting to get to her. The glass-fronted lobby taunted her with the sight of the interior stairs.

"Shit, my keys are back at the tent, too."

There were lights on in some of the other suites. Maybe she could try buzzing someone. She scanned the intercom listings, found the caretaker and pressed the call button. The phone rang twelve times before she gave up.

"Shit again."

The guy was a grump at the best of times. He was supposed to be available, but he could be busy working or just taking a break. She leaned up against the cold brick wall of the front of the apartment building. Her adrenaline had faded. She rubbed her arms for warmth.

"Why do I keep getting into these situations?" she asked softly. "Little Miss Boring, one single friend in school, then I get drawn into this fucked-up world. Golems, necromancers, evil corporations, mind control, magical gemstones, human copies, subliminal hypnosis. Does it ever end? Do I ever get to be normal?"

Her friends were gone, Rick and Igor had been taken out, Frank was dead. The only one left who could help her was Detective Tockett. But without her phone, she wasn't even sure she could remember her number. That wouldn't matter if she froze to death. She needed to get inside.

She smelled like smoke, weed, sweat, and vomit. She'd been in the same clothes for an undetermined number of days. Who knew when she'd last showered? She didn't even want to think about what she'd done or with who in that lost piece of time.

"I need a hot fucking bath."

She almost didn't register the old woman in the brown beaver coat leaving the apartment. Passing her, the woman walked down the sidewalk towards a bus stop at the other end of the street. Sam jerked to action and grabbed the glass door just before it shut. She darted inside the warm building and took the stairs to the second floor. She went down the hall to her room and paused at the door. It was ajar.

"I know I locked that."

She slowly pushed it open. The lights were off, but the television was on. The suite looked like it always did: open cupboards, clothes on chairs, dishes in the sink, humming refrigerator covered in photos, River City Jets calendar tacked to the wall.

215

"No sign of a squatter."

She crept inside and quietly closed the door behind her. She slowly slid along the floor into the kitchen and grabbed their only large knife. Taking a deep breath, brandishing the blade threateningly, she shuffled down the hall. First, she peered into the bathroom. The shower curtain was drawn back, so nobody could be in the tub. Empty.

Next was Erin's room. It had been cleaned to a spit shine with everything in its place.

That's unlike her.

Had someone broken in, watched TV and cleaned Erin's room?

It might be spotless, but it was also empty. That just left her room. The door was wide open. Her clothes were all over her dresser. The bed was unmade and the mirror covered in fingerprints. She wished she could say that someone had turned the place over, but that was exactly how she'd left it.

But at least it was empty.

"Nobody here either."

She relaxed. She began to take normal breaths and felt her heartbeat slow. She replaced the knife in the block and latched the apartment door. She turned on the lights and turned off the TV. She poured herself a glass of water and put on a pot of coffee.

She went to the telephone and dialed the non-emergency police line. A man picked up right away.

"I'm trying to get in touch with Detective Veronica Tockett," Sam said. "I have some important information for her and—"

"She's unavailable. Can I transfer you to another officer?"

"Do you know when she'll be back?"

"Would you like me to put you through to her desk so you

can leave a message for her?"

"Sure."

The line clicked, then rang a few times before Veronica's pre-recorded voice answered. "This is Detective Tockett, I'm indisposed right now, but leave a message and I'll return your call when I'm back in the office."

"Detective Tockett. It's me. The last of us, I think. Anyway, I've got something. We need to meet. At the usual place. I don't have my cellphone right now. Call me at this number." She gave her home phone then hung up.

"I guess I just wait now."

Sam went into her room and kicked off her clothes. She tossed them into what should be the "to wash" pile. She grabbed a pair of flannel pants and a T-shirt and was about to head to the bathroom when she spotted the joint she'd been passed during the meeting peeking out of her pants pocket.

"Holy shit," she said. "I forgot all about this."

Examining it in the light, it didn't look out of the ordinary. She carefully sniffed it once. It smelled just like a regular marijuana cigarette. She remembered everyone passing them around in the march, in the meeting, during the rave. The living smoke that seemed to follow her. It had to connect.

She dug into the pocket and found one of the white pills.

"Bingo."

She ran down the hall, threw her clean clothes in the bathroom and dialed the police again. "Can I be transferred to Detective Tockett again? I forgot to, uh, leave her my contact info."

She could practically hear the man roll his eyes on the other end, but one click and message later and she was back.

"Detective Tockett, it's me again. I actually have more than

217

I thought. I hope you have access to a testing lab. Please call me back."

She hung up, feeling like she finally had something to go on. But standing in sweat-logged underwear, she caught wind of the fact that she was rank.

"I really need a fucking shower."

* * * *

The city was going to sleep. The bad people were afraid now. They knew someone was out there looking for them. They were beginning to get the message, even if he was still a little confused about who was giving it.

Wandering through the streets, letting his feet dictate the path, he came to a now-familiar apartment building. Why did he keep coming back to this place? Did he used to live here? No, it was too clean. There was no graffiti on the walls, and he remembered a La-Z-Boy, not a couch.

The door gave way to his hands. He went up the stairs and down the hall. He knew this place so well. Maybe it was his home. Maybe they'd just renovated when he wasn't paying attention.

The door. He pulled, but it didn't want to give way. Something was keeping him out of his own room.

* * * *

It felt good to wash away all of the grime and stink of the tent city. The days poured free as the warm water streamed over her body. Heaven. She didn't want to leave the thick steam. She could just stand here forever in the burning heat. But she knew she'd have a killer water bill if she did. So finally, reluctantly, she shut off the tap and grabbed her towel. She was ready for sleep. She patted down her hair as a strange feeling of dread came over her, a tingling at the back of her neck. The mirror had completely fogged over. They didn't have a working bathroom fan in this old building. She wiped off the centre with the towel and there she was, Samantha Abraham, dark hair parted over one eye covering her prominent mole. But something was wrong. Her reflection wore a tight black shirt while she was naked, slowly dripping onto the bathmat parallel to the tub.

"What the hell?"

The other Sam reached out from the mirror and grabbed her around the throat. It stared her right in the eye, looking for something—fear, maybe?

"We're the same," the clone said. "What I do is what you do. Or what you want to do."

Sam couldn't speak. The hands constricted tighter and tighter. She was losing consciousness.

"If only you weren't so stubborn. Embrace who you really are. Become who you could be. What you all could be."

Water dripped down Sam's forehead into her eyes. She grabbed the wrists of the thing emerging from the mirror, trying to hit the pressure point on the back of the hand to break the grip. The warmth of the shower was fading away as she stood at the mercy of another version of her.

"It's not too late. You still—"

Sam clamped down with the last of her waning strength against the pressure point between thumb and index finger. The clone's hands lost their grip on her neck. Sam's legs gave way. She fell backwards against the mounted towel rack. It hit her right in the lower back, sending shooting pain down her legs. She collapsed awkwardly to the tiled floor.

She heard her own voice laugh and threw her hands up to block a blow that never came. Opening her eyes, she saw the mirror fogged over with no sign of anyone there. She pushed herself to her feet and gathered up her towel. A bruise was already forming at the spot on her back where she'd hit the towel rack. She tapped it gingerly and it hurt. She wrapped the towel around her body and held onto the sink as she felt another convulsion about to wrack her body. There couldn't be anything left in her stomach by this point.

It came out in a powerful, burning stream right into the sink. She turned on the tap. The foul smelling dark green mixture slowly diluted. But something white stayed as the rest flowed down the drain. It moved.

She slowly reached for it. It squirmed. She flinched. It was some kind of larva. A tiny worm moving in the sink. Keeping one eye on it, she took a pair of tweezers from the medicine cabinet and gingerly picked the thing up. It struggled in the metal grip. Two tiny black eyes turned to look at her. It was about the size of a carpet beetle, with smooth white skin, tiny appendages that almost looked like arms and legs and—

It jumped free. She recoiled as it hit her on the cheek. A burning pain stabbed her at the impact site. She leaned into the mirror, looking for the thing. The pain moved along her face. She saw it, digging into the skin, moving through it like water, chewing and leaving a trail of blood in its wake. Tunnelling towards the centre of her face, towards her eye. She grabbed the tweezers, lined them up and pinched. Missed. It came up again and she snapped. This time she had it. She yanked it out of her face. It refused to let go, clinging with surprising strength. She pulled harder, ripping off a piece of her own cheek. The thing dangled in the grip of the tweezers. She watched it chewing the dangling nugget of skin. She pressed down as hard as she could. The tiny white thing burst with a pop of yellow and red gore, like a living zit, splashing the mirror with a streak of pus that stuck like a booger.

She wiped it off with a square of toilet paper. She tried to see if anything could be salvaged, but it was just paste. She dropped it into the toilet and flushed the creature away.

* * * *

"I'm missing it," he muttered at the locked door. "I never miss it."

He yanked harder on the knob. With a snap, the wood splintered and the deadbolt tore from the fifty-year-old screws that held it in place. The frame was destroyed, bits of wood dangling from the wall.

A woman stepped around the corner of the hallway with a towel wrapped around her body and another around her hair. Her hands were raised up high, mid head pat. She froze. He caught her eyes. She looked like someone he knew. But who? And why was she in his apartment?

"Who the hell are you?" she asked. "And why are you in my apartment?"

He wanted to ask her the same thing, but his mouth wouldn't form the words. His brain flashed through it all; asking if he'd gotten off on the wrong floor, laughing, then finding out he was next door where he'd sit down and watch *The King of Kensington* in peace, have a cold—

221

Kill her.

That scenario vanished. He lunged for her.

She screamed and thew the towel in her hands at his face. It wrapped over his head, and he staggered, momentarily blind, right into a wall. He pulled the towel off, but she'd darted into the kitchen. She reached for the only knife in a wooden block, pulled it out and shouted threateningly, "Can't you leave me the fuck alone?"

He was trying to. He didn't want to reach out for her, but he did. She slashed with the knife, slicing a line along his forearm, but he didn't even feel it.

She looked at him wide-mouthed. He examined his own forearm. The cut had gone through his jacket to the skin. It dripped blood on her kitchen tiles.

Lady, get a Band-Aid.

Kill her.

She tried to stab forward into his gut. He grabbed her wrist, impossibly fast, and squeezed. She cried out and the knife fell from her grip. He could feel the bones in her arm giving way beneath his grip. It would be nothing to shatter her and—

Kill. Kill. Kill.

Kill? Her? Why? Who was she?

Kill!

The voice in his head was insistent, he couldn't shut it out. His hands squeezed the woman's wrist more as she struggled.

"Let me go," she cried out in desperation.

Kill. Kill her.

Kill? He wasn't a killer. He was a—

SMACK!

Something heavy hit him in the side of the head and he lost his grip. Stars danced in his vision as he saw her brandishing a frying pan with her other hand.

"Get back," the woman shouted.

He wanted to listen, but his feet didn't.

SMACK. Again on the side of the head. He staggered backward. His skull cried out in agony. Blood trickled down into his eyes and then SMACK, the pan hit him a third time. He fell over the couch and crashed through the coffee table in front of the television.

Images flooded his head. A small house in the north end, a stream a short walk away. Pigs. Red wagons and black boots, fish on hooks, running through painted concrete tunnels, summer on the boardwalk, ice cream cones, the voice of The Shadow, a man hitting him on the palm with a belt, a tin lunch box, a mound of dirt, stickball, marbles, pennies, Dief the Chief, a cage in the jungle, fireworks, and a nearly rusted bicycle.

He tried to crawl to his feet but SMACK, she hit him again.

He landed flat on the carpet. He looked down to see his hand covered in blood. His arm hurt. Why? How did he get here?

He glanced up at the girl holding the frying pan in both hands, ready to deliver a final killing blow.

He could see the stars through her window, twinkling with a billion points of light. He remembered camping, the woods, his best friend and a bear, climbing trees, a dog nestled against his side, comic books, frogs, the smell of marshmallows, the click clack of baseball cards in his spokes. Bacon, and—

"Mama?" he said.

The woman holding the frying pan hesitated. "What?" she asked.

"I promised I wouldn't be late for dinner, I promised!" He

223

slowly pushed himself up, needing the couch to help. He left a bloody handprint in the fabric.

"You think I'm your mother?" she said, confused.

* * * *

Sam didn't know what to think. This massive brute had barged into her apartment, tried to kill her, destroyed her coffee table, and was now sucking his thumb and trying to turn a non-existent knob on the television.

"Can I watch TV, Mommy?"

His arm was leaking a dangerous amount of blood, but he seemed like he was done trying to kill her. Maybe she'd knocked him out of his hypnotic state. The frying pan was dented from his thick skull. This was the second time she'd had to use it to save her life from a golem attack, but from the state of it now, probably the last. She put it on the counter and carefully backed towards the kitchen. She needed to get that cut closed up before he bled out.

"Can I? Huh? Watch TV?"

"Yeah, sure. You just sit there for a minute and watch it. I'm going to get something from the bathroom."

She grabbed the remote control and switched on the television. When it flared to life, he lost all interest in her. She went to the medicine cabinet and found some gauze, disinfectant and tape. Shutting the mirror, she saw her own reflection again, still wearing only the towel. The smear of goo from the worm looked more like a fingerprint now.

She returned to the living room to see the huge man happily using the remote to change channels.

"This is Peter Mansbridge coming in live from Parliament

Hill in the nation's capitol with a breaking story."

"Boring," the man said.

"The River City Jets fall four to one against the Islanders—"

"Boo." He pouted.

"—voting against the government, breaking party ranks to—"

"Where are the cartoons?"

She stood behind him as he became increasingly frustrated, pressing the channel-up button over and over again.

"Hey... uh. Mommy needs to put a Band-Aid on you, okay? You're bleeding all over our IKEA rug."

She gently grabbed his outstretched arm. It was hard as a rock. The leather of his jacket obscured much of the cut. She needed to get the thing off to be able to staunch the bleeding.

"Mommy needs you to take off your coat, okay?" she said.

"I don't want to."

"Please? You can—"

"Have ice cream?"

"Yeah, sure."

"Yay." The man slung off his jacket and flung it over his head across the room. He wore a skin-tight short sleeve shirt that revealed a chest and arms even bigger than she'd expected. The guy must be on every steroid in the book. But he was criss-crossed in cuts and scars, like he'd been slashed more than once. That was when she spotted a knife stuck in his gut.

"Jesus," she said. "You've been through something, that's for sure."

She poured some iodine on a pad and dabbed his open wound. Expecting him to flinch, scream, or slug her, she tensed up, but he didn't budge. A crimson flow erupted where

225

she touched, singeing the scabbed portions. It quickly soaked the pad in red. The slash was wider and longer than she'd guessed, nearly six inches. It would need stitches to heal properly.

She cleaned it as best as she could, then wrapped it with gauze and more pads, tightly.

"—questions surrounding his leadership now. Will he step down and—"

Click.

"In celebrity news—"

Click.

"—allowing a community of vagrants to spring up in every major city in this country harms the national fabric and—"

Click.

"Patrick, put that down!"

He stopped scrolling on SpongeBob. He sat back enraptured at the animated antics.

"What the hell am I going to do with that knife?" she muttered as she tossed the blood-soaked pad into the trash. "This thing hurt?" she asked, touching it. He didn't even notice. Gripping the handle, she slid it out, watching as dark red blood began leaking through the hole. She cleaned and dressed the wound without any complaints.

"River City's best deals in used cars and—"

"Commercial," the man said angrily. "No. No. No no no no no no no."

Click.

"—explosions on a residential street in Charleswood rocks the quiet neighbourhood after a tense armed standoff. The tragic end to the situation comes after reports were leaked that the armed terrorists had holed themselves up in a home resided in by two River City Police officers and—"

"Next," the man said and changed the channel.

It took a moment for the reporter's words to click in her head. "Wait, did she say two police officers? Could that be Detective Tockett and Hooper?"

Sam batted the huge man's hands away from the controls. "Sorry, Mommy wants to hear that story, okay?"

"No! I want cartoons."

"After, I promise." She clicked back to a scene out of a movie. Fires raged in multiple houses, firefighting crews battled the blazes, shocked neighbours huddled together. Ambulances, police cars, debris everywhere; it looked like a war zone. But it was the fleeting image of a man with a blanket around his body that made her blanch. Shaved head, a day's worth of stubble, covered in dirt and blood, being led by two first responders out of frame: Detective Hooper.

Chapter 30

Carnage all around him; houses burned, sirens wailed, reporters covering the scene spoke to their cameras with the gravitas of tragedy. Someone slung a blanket over Jimmy's shoulders. He looked for any sign of Carter or Olivia. Had they still been inside the house when it had gone up? He couldn't find them anywhere.

He flagged down a first responder as he darted past.

"Have you seen my stepkids?"

"You have to be more specific. There's bits of kids all over the place, man." The guy looked shell-shocked. He broke free of Jimmy's grip and ran off towards a screaming woman covered in blood and soot.

Jimmy frantically looked around at the people getting help, but saw no sign of the kids. Another first responder came and tried to direct him to a ready ambulance, but he pushed him away.

"Carter? Olivia?" he shouted.

The house was engulfed in flames. Everything Veronica had was being incinerated. And everything he'd brought with him. But that was all just stuff.

"Carter? Olivia?"

Had he lost everything? First Veronica, now the kids? He

dropped to his knees meekly, letting his hands sink into the snow. His knee throbbed, but he ignored the pain and cried to the heavens in a futile rage.

What the hell had just happened? Men in masks invading his house, holding the family hostage, demanding what was in Veronica's safe. But there was nothing in the safe. Or so he'd thought. He felt the backpack dangling from his arm and knew that was a lie.

"She's crooked." That's what they told him. There was payoff money they wanted a cut of. The mayor was involved. It was all too crazy to be real.

They'd been on the phone most of the day working the hostage negotiations. He'd tried to find a way out, but his knee was a hindrance he couldn't overcome. Then miraculously, she'd snuck back home. They'd worked together to stop the gang. In the backyard, up on the roof, down in the basement. But it hadn't been a Hollywood ending. She'd been shot. He'd had to watch her eyes slowly lose their light while that bastard Banner had laughed. Veronica's final breath had drifted away in the night air like a wisp. He couldn't save it either. Her last words telling him she was sorry, that she "couldn't put you at risk."

The rest had been like an action movie; losing his cool, shooting an entire clip into the man who'd shot Veronica, falling off the roof into the snow. Then the bastards had blown the bombs they'd planted on the gas lines of half the houses on the block. Massive fireballs shot up into the sky like they were under an attack. He'd found the backpack though.

Now it was the post disaster chaos, but without any end credits to fade into black. Police scattered in a panic, people screamed for help. There were bodies on fire. Firefighters pulled neighbours crushed beneath fallen sections of their own homes free. It wasn't going away. It was real. Everything seemed to finally register in his mind. The house was on fire. The whole street, too. His girlfriend and her kids were dead.

"Why?" he said to no one. "What was so important about this stuff?"

A hand fell on his shoulder. He looked up to see Carter and Olivia, untouched from the flames, looking as clean as they did after a bath.

"What's wrong, Uncle Jimmy?" Carter asked.

"Kids!" Jimmy lunged in for a hug, taking them both in his arms. "I thought I'd lost you."

"Why? We were right here?"

"Where's Mom?" Olivia asked, scanning the crowd.

The falling embers seemed to pass right through her. They glowed with life while she seemed drained of it.

"I– I don't know how to tell you this," he said, trying to find the words. He couldn't stop himself from tearing up just looking at their faces. His two stepkids, maybe now his kids. How was he going to tell them their mom was gone?

"Your mom... she..."

Suddenly another hand fell upon the kids' shoulders. He looked up, incredulous, to see the impossible.

"Hey, guys, there you are. I've been looking all over for you."

Veronica, whole again, untouched, not a bullet hole in sight. Hair combed, skin clear, and a smile on her face that radiated love.

"Mommy!"

"There you are, Mommy!"

The kids hugged her tightly.

"Let's go home," she said, grinning.

This couldn't be real. He saw her. She'd been shot. She was dead. And yet, here she was, looking completely fine. The kids turned to her and giggled.

"We can't go home, silly," Olivia said. "It blew up!"

Veronica turned to look at the ruins of her house. "So it did. Okay then, let's go to McDonalds!"

"Yay!" the kids cried.

"How?" he asked quietly.

"Don't question it," she said, winking. "Just accept it."

She reached her hand out to Jimmy. It was smooth, white, ethereal. That was when he understood the truth. He took the hand and rose to his feet. All of his pain was gone. She slunk her arm around his. She was as light as the wind. They turned to leave.

"I…" He didn't want to ruin this moment. Looking at her and the kids dressed in white, fading slowly from his mind, as if none of this had happened at all. *Just keep them in sight*, he thought. *Don't let them go*.

Panicked workers continued to try to put out the blazes, reporters narrated, a growing crowd of onlookers came to watch. The screams of the dying, the crackling of ruined lives; cries and whispers unheard. The four of them seemed to exist outside it all, alone in the eye of a hurricane.

"There are more things in heaven and earth…" Veronica said.

Jimmy held on to her, to the memory of her, and the feeling of her touch as he watched the flames and the burning house. He took one last look at her beautiful face. She smiled as she slowly began to flicker into nothingness. Reflected in her eyes, he saw himself, alone, blackened with grime, sweat soaked and bloody, with the backpack slung over his shoulder.

He steeled himself for what came next. Firefighters worked. The embers and ash fell like snowflakes, passing right through her and the kids. Fading, barely visible. Then the house was gone, and they were, too.

No. He could still feel her arm around his. He could feel the kids next to him. They weren't there but they were at the same time. How long could he sustain that? How long could he remember how they felt?

His world burned. He and his family walked away into the night.

Chapter 31

F lipping through the news channels, trying to piece together what was going on in the city, the country, seemingly the entire world, Sam handed the strange man-child another fudgesicle. He'd sucked back four already. There were only a few left in the box, but at least it kept him quiet.

"The River City Jets today announced that popular rookie, Rick Hansen, is due back in the lineup tomorrow night against the Minnesota Wild. Hansen had been on the injured list after the brutal assault by his own teammate, Igor Illyanovich, over what was purported to be an ex-girlfriend. There had been fears that Hansen had suffered a concussion and a possible broken collar bone, but today, at a press conference, Hansen downplayed those fears."

The image on screen switched to Rick. His hair was now cut short, he wore a suit, and looked none the worse for wear. He sat with four people; Debbie, a team doctor, the coach, and a man that made Sam's jaw drop.

"We have world class medical staff here on the Jets," Rick said. "The best physiotherapists, facilities, you name it. All thanks to our owner, Mr. Gerber, who's supported me one hundred percent this year."

The man he motioned to, Julian Gerber, was captioned as being the Jets team owner, but Sam knew that Arthur Fritz had been the owner and Fritz had been killed. Gerber was his spitting image. The same aquiline nose, severe chin, blond hair.

"This is all wrong." She pulled up YouTube and searched for footage of the NHL draft. She quickly found the Jets page, and the video showing Rick being drafted. She watched it on mute as the press conference continued.

"Rick has demonstrated amazing resilience," Julian Gerber said. "He's shown the team spirit and competitiveness that have made him a two-time NHL player of the week. We're all looking forward to this final push for the playoffs and fully support Rick as he tries to lead the team to a Stanley Cup."

Reporters began shouting out questions as camera flashes erupted. Julian's face. It was like a copy. But how? First Simon Karlsson, then Arthur Fritz, now Julian Gerber. Were all three of them those things under human masks?

Glancing back to the YouTube video she froze the image. Next to Rick was the same man who'd been captioned as Arthur Fritz when she'd first seen it, but was now listed as Julian Gerber.

"What the fuck."

"Mommy said a bad word," the man with the fudgesicle said.

Sam googled and found another video of the draft on the NHL's site. It, too, listed Julian Gerber as team owner. "This is not right. It said Fritz, I remember. This isn't a Mandela effect."

She pulled up The Hockey News, TSN, the CBC, they were all the same. "I know what I saw."

If only she'd been living with her dad, she could have checked one of his back issues of The Hockey News. "They might have been able to change all of the online evidence, but not print."

"Rick," a reporter asked. "Do you have any comments on your now ex-teammate Illyanovich? Have you spoken to him or—"

"I'm shocked and disappointed," Rick said, cutting off the reporter. "You play with a guy day in and day out and then he goes and does something like that? But it's clear that a toxic narcissist really messed with his head. Let's just say there's a reason I broke up with that particular individual back in high school."

A few reporters chuckled.

Next to him Debbie smirked as Rick put his arm around her. "That's why I'm so thankful to have a woman like Debbie by my side. She's been my rock through this whole ordeal. I don't know what I'd do without her. So, if you'll all indulge me for a minute."

Rick stepped out of his seat and got down on one knee. Gerber handed him a box, and he opened it to reveal a massive diamond ring.

"Deborah Peterson, you've always been there for me and I want to always be there for you. Will you do me the honour of being my wife?"

Her hand flew to her mouth in surprise. In tears, she nodded and leaned in to embrace him. The reporters burst into applause. Cameras flashed. They looked so happy Sam wanted to puke.

"What the mother fucking hell!" she said. "Rick, she's a part of this. She's fucking evil."

235

"Mommy said a lot of bad words!"

"That was quite the scene, eh, Nick?" the Sportscentre host said as the image shifted back to the desk.

"What an amazing turn of events. The Jets star player back ready to go, and now engaged? That's top shelf highlight reel stuff, Bob."

"I think we should also give a special shout out to whoever picked out that ring. Did you see the size of—"

Sam changed the channel and slumped back in her chair. Rick, engaged to that bitch. Veronica's text was right, he must have been turned. There's no way he would have done it in his right mind.

"Red member of cabinet, Dan Kirby, today announced a special meeting of the privy council to discuss the ongoing student protests that have shuttered university campuses all across the country. We see him and River City representative of the Students for a Just World—"

Sam looked up to see Graham Maddox, dressed in a green jacket and jeans, shaking hands with an MP she'd never heard of until she'd seen him in the Guidance tent. Dan Kirby, bearded, wearing a dark suit, with greying hair and a slight belly. It was like a kid and his dad. Was he another victim? She knew how dangerous Graham could be, but did Kirby?

"If he's spread his influence to government officials now…"

She changed the channel again, this time to the local news. Clean up crews were working on the street where what she presumed had been Veronica's house used to stand. The whole neighbourhood looked like a war zone. The fires were out, but smoke drifted from the remains as people searched for anything they could salvage.

"—all of my family photos, my dog, all gone," a woman said

in tears. "I just don't know what to do next."

"That makes two of us," Sam said. She clicked away to a music video channel, but they were playing an old Factor 5ive song. She turned off the TV instead.

"Hey!" the man-child protested.

Sam ignored him. She let her head fall back onto the couch and tried to focus on her situation. Her friends were all in the tent city, probably infected with whatever it was she'd coughed up. Veronica appeared to be dead, or at least not returning her calls, Igor was MIA, the government was potentially about to be compromised, and now Rick was getting married. What was she supposed to do about all of this? And alone, too.

She stared at the strange man, who'd just about finished his latest fudgesicle, and saw one more problem she wasn't equipped to deal with.

"Frank, I wish you were still alive, you'd know what to do."

The man perked up and looked quizzically at her. He probably wanted another fudgesicle. She covered her face and started crying.

Chapter 32

Jimmy pulled the cup of hot coffee from below the spout of the machine and took a sip. It instantly burned the tip of his tongue. He recoiled in pain. *I forgot how stupidly hot this shit gets.*

The precinct was surprisingly quiet. With everyone busy doing paperwork, keyboards clacked and the normal sounds of chatter were lost in a sea of complete focus. On the table beside the coffee machine, the regular donut delivery sat untouched. *That's odd*, he thought. *Usually by now the good ones are all taken*. He grabbed a chocolate glaze and went back to his desk.

He leaned his cane against the edge and steeled himself at the mountain of paperwork to go through. It seemed like Veronica had been neglecting her reports. He flipped through her notes on a break and enter from last week, others on the arm and a leg bandit, even some on the missing wrestlers.

"Ronnie, what the heck were you on to?" he whispered softly.

Shorthand chicken scratch printing on torn pages from a notebook, articles cut from newspapers, printed screenshots. She'd started a few official reports, but had barely filled anything in past the initial dates and times. She'd been so busy the past few months, yet none of that had translated to office work. It was going to take a long time to sort this out. Luckily, he had that time. Paperwork was all he was being allowed to do right now.

"Hooper, you're injured. Stay home. Come back to work when you can walk."

"With all due respect, sir," he'd told the chief when he'd shown up earlier asking to be reinstated, "my house burned down. I lost people I cared about. I don't think I can be alone with my own head right now. I need to get to work. Figure out what happened and why."

"I can get you a grief counsellor," the chief had said. "Psychiatrist referral. It's only been a few days. You don't have to—"

"I do."

The chief had relented, told him he could be in the office, but under no circumstances was he getting a squad car, partner, or any active cases. He could assess Veronica's leftover work, consult, but that was it.

So here he was, in the midafternoon, feeling the lack of sleep catching up to him. The coffee would help. He wanted a break from the recurring nightmares of Veronica dying in his arms, of the kids being burned alive, of not knowing if what the terrorists had told him about her being a crooked cop was true or not.

"It's all in the files," she'd said before leaving him.

But whatever he was supposed to find certainly didn't seem to be in what she'd left at the office. "Severed body parts," he said softly. "None matching. Coroner found no trace of fingerprints after extensive acid burns. Possible scarification. Bullet wounds. Tattoos. Aged skin. Signs of stitching."

This was real detective work. No shooting people, no car chases, kicking down doors, or going undercover. He was going to have to use his brain until his body could heal. What would Frank have said to that? He snorted audibly. Working with the old man had made it seem like this job was an endless series of madness: creatures, curses, nightmares, explosions and things he still wasn't sure could have really happened. Through it all, he'd been the one to do the mundane bits of the job. Frank wasn't a paperwork cop, or a deductive cop. He relied on instinct, was a man who acted first and broke all the rules, but somehow managed to survive and keep coming out on top for years.

But even he was gone.

It was up to Jimmy now. Alone, he would carry on, uncover the truth, and put his late partners and their families at rest. It was all he had left.

Jimmy took out his phone and scrolled through the photo library for the hundredth time. He found the series of blurry and too-dark shots that Frank had taken before his stroke. They were just as obtuse as they were before. The strange man talking with the doctor, a face he still hadn't identified. *I don't get it, Frank, what were you trying to tell me?*

He connected the phone to the USB slot in his computer and waited for it to be recognized. He opened the photo folder and copy dragged them to his desktop. When the transfer was complete, he unplugged the phone and slid it back into his pocket.

He clicked on the photo file and browsed them on his much larger monitor.

"Still doesn't help much," he mumbled. "Maybe if I enlarge them."

He opened up Photoshop and played around with the size, sharpness and contrast of a few pictures, but still couldn't get anywhere. He dug into the backpack Veronica had left him. It contained what the men had taken from the safe in their basement, the one he didn't know she'd been using. He laid out the contents on his desk.

More newspaper clippings, a ledger with detailed payment information, a small black book she'd written in, scraps of notes in an even more illegible handwriting that he recognized as Frank's, then another phone. One he'd never seen before.

"Let's see what we have here."

The battery was dead. He plugged the phone into the USB port. Once it registered the power input, it sprang to life with a soft blue light. The rebooting process took its sweet time. Jimmy tapped nervously on the desk with a pen as a status bar slowly filled. Then finally, ping, a home screen with a picture of William Shatner in his TJ Hooker uniform.

"Cute, Ronnie…"

The phone was password locked.

"Shit."

He tried her usual phone password, but got an error. He tried her birthday, another error.

"Fuck." He didn't want to lock out the phone so he put it aside and tried to think what she might have used.

"Shatner's birthday? TJ Hooker's?"

He googled them both. TJ Hooker didn't seem to have a canon birthday, Shatner's was March 22, 1931. That would be 03-22-31. He was about to tap that in when he paused.

"If she wanted me to be able to guess this and she was using Shatner's birthday, she would have used a picture of

241

him outside of a role. It has to be connected to TJ Hooker somehow."

He searched the series final episode air date and got May 28, 1986. He searched the series first episode air date and got March 13, 1982. Either 03-13-82 or 05-28-86.

"Two options. Unless I'm completely off base. But which one would she use?"

Sweating, hoping he wasn't about to lock himself out of the phone, he stopped. If he messed up, he'd have to go down to the lab to have them crack it. It was clear she'd kept this thing hidden for a reason. The fewer people who knew about it the better. He considered his options.

"She loved that show. She would have celebrated it starting before it being cancelled." He tapped in the series start date and silently prayed.

The home screen flashed to life, showing the few apps installed on the phone. It was a bare bones set up. She'd been using it as a burner phone. He looked at the saved contacts, saw only people listed as initials. There were texts from the same people, asking her to meet, for payoffs, for drugs from the evidence lock-up. They were all coded, but codes he knew from dealing with informants.

"Oh, Ronnie."

There were hundreds of photos. Of people meeting in the distance, of things she'd taken from the lock-up, of the mayor handing something out of his limo.

"So you were gathering a case."

A clearer picture was starting to emerge of her playing both sides, but ultimately ending up on the right one.

Then there were videos. They were more of the same, except for a hockey game shot from the stands. But it was a different one that caught his eye. It was from Frank's phone. Shot from the confines of the bathroom. The same image of the two men talking Jimmy had been obsessing over ever since she'd handed him the phone upon returning from finding Frank dead. She must have deleted this after sending it to her burner phone. But why?

He opened the other phone. He checked the trash bin and there it was. With only a few days left before being deleted forever. She'd forgotten to clear the trash. He restored the video to his phone and went back to the burner one.

"What's on this video that you didn't want me to see?"

He pressed play, but noticing other officers around him within earshot, he immediately paused it. He slid on a pair of headphones and plugged them in, then hit play again.

The two men stood in an empty bedroom. Their faces were clearly visible as shaky hands recorded them through the space between the wall and the door.

"I don't know why you bother, considering what's going to happen to them."

"Appearances," the other man said. "We must maintain appearances."

"Of course. But it seems like a waste for lobster swimming in an aquarium."

The first man laughed. "Lobsters are more aware of their fate."

Then they both left the room. The video shook, then was cut off. Frank must not have realized that he'd taken a video instead of a photo, or else had decided to get both. Jimmy watched the clip again, trying to decipher what the two men were talking about.

"—what's going to happen to them."

"Lobsters are more aware of their fate."

Frank was right. Something WAS going on in Shady Acres.

The old man had been telling the truth. That must mean his death hadn't been just a stroke. Had they done something to him? Why hadn't Veronica told him about this video? Why had she kept it secret?

Next in the queue was another video. It was all black, with a run time of almost forty-five minutes. Frank must have left the thing recording and not realized it. Jimmy played it. Much of the sound was muffled and hard to make out. He sat in nervous anticipation for twenty-eight minutes before anything happened. He heard machines. The beeping of what sounded like an EKG monitor. It soon slowed to a droning wail. Then footsteps entering the room, shuffling, the sound of something metal clanging to the ground, a woman's voice.

"Time of death, who gives a shit? Next of kin, nobody. Those present? No one. Last wishes? How about feed him to the pigs?"

Back to silence and another twelve minutes before the video cut off.

Jimmy's face blanched. That was it. The proof. They killed him. No, this wasn't definitive. It could be argued away as circumstantial. He had to have more. He had to go investigate Shady Acres again; talk to some of the residents, get a few statements. Maybe someone there had seen what had gone on. He only hoped they were still alive.

He copied the file to his desktop and stared a good long while at the tiny folder. There was some reason Veronica thought this had to stay secret. Was she protecting him? Protecting someone else? Was it safe here on his work computer? He put a password protection on the folder and grabbed his cane. He rose and limped over to the frosted glass door of the chief's office. He knocked three times.

"Come in."

Jimmy opened the door and stepped inside. The man was reading through a file folder with a cup of coffee in one hand.

"Hooper?"

"Chief, I know I'm supposed to be on desk duty, but I might have a lead and—"

"You are on desk duty. No exceptions. If you have something, tell it to the investigating officers and let them handle it."

Jimmy sat down in the chair and struggled for the right words. The chief closed his folder and looked at him intently.

"What would you say if I told you that I think Ver—Detective Tockett had information that she hadn't shared?"

"Hooper, I know you're still dealing with her death, and I didn't want to say anything just yet, but maybe you need to hear this before you get too deep. She was being investigated. Internally."

Jimmy clammed up.

"Irregularities. Payoffs, corruption. Drugs. Guns. This wasn't common knowledge. It stays that way. I'm actually surprised you hadn't noticed anything. You two were... close, after all."

"How do you know it wasn't her partner, Carlos?"

"Who do you think was our man investigating her?"

"But—"

"Maybe it was money. She was a single mom, divorced, under a lot of financial stress. Who knows? That's all moot now. The men that invaded your home, they were a part of it. It was a revenge play. Internal affairs are satisfied and—"

245

"I think that's bullshit, sir."

The chief leaned back and regarded Jimmy sadly. "I know it's hard to hear. I apologize for not approaching you sooner, but to be honest, you were under investigation, too."

"Me?"

"You can't sleep with a crooked cop and not get some on you."

Jimmy clenched his cane tightly. He wanted to break it over the chief's head. Instead, he stewed in silence.

"If you have something she hadn't reported, you have to hand it over. The independent investigation unit is going to want to see anything and everything."

Jimmy suddenly regretted his decision to come in here and talk to the chief. He had only wanted to get the man to understand his leaving the office, to make him see that he was still useful, but he'd opened up a can of worms and wasn't sure if they could be rammed back inside.

"It's not what you think sir," he said. "She had notes and unfinished reports that I'm still going through. I didn't mean to imply they were more than they could be. I'm still deciphering her writing and—"

The chief seemed to visibly relax. "Goddamn it, Hooper, you're going to give me an ulcer."

"I think the donuts'll be what does, sir."

The chief furrowed his brow and took a sip from his coffee.

"So was this why you came in? Just to tell me you may have found nothing at all?"

"Yeah," Jimmy said. "I guess it was. Also to say thanks. For letting me be here. It's... helping."

"Alright then. Glad to help. But don't forget what I said. Anything you find comes to me first. We need to know how far her… corruption went."

Jimmy stood up. He walked out of the office, feeling like he'd just been hit by a truck. Veronica being investigated? Did that corroborate those goons claiming she was bent? Now the chief knew he was in possession of her files. He quickly gathered them all up in the folder and shoved them in his backpack with the information from the safe. It was a mistake to bring it all here.

He slung the bag over this shoulder and started limping down the aisle. Eyes followed him as they worked. Quiet. It suddenly seemed so very odd that no one was talking, making fun of each other, shouting out questions, making plans for after work. Nobody was ever this focused on paperwork.

He didn't dare make eye-contact. He pulled open the door to the back hallway and stepped through, going straight to his car in the parking lot.

He never saw the chief pick up the phone and dial out. He didn't know who picked up on the other end. He certainly never heard the man speaking to whoever that was either, saying, "We might have a problem."

Chapter 33

"Look, I don't know what you thought, but this was just, you know, a winter fling. We both know that you're just a tourist and—"

"That's not true."

Erin lay languidly on the open sleeping bag. "I know who I am even if you don't."

"No," Sam said. "I was having a good time, I—"

"You still don't understand the Authority. Were Scott and Tommy against your so-called will? Were we? Maybe. Maybe not."

"What do you mean? I—"

The tent door opened. Door? Since when do tents have doors? Avital walked in, arm in arm with Graham. Then came Everett, with a set of dreadlocked twins wearing only hemp necklaces. Finally was Marlon, dog-collared on a leash held by the massively muscular Peta.

"You turning prude now?" Avital said. "After all you've done?"

"For the cause," Graham said.

"It's just what we do," Everett added. His fingers stretched out, wrapping around the waists of his two stoned dates like snakes.

"Bark, dog," Peta said.

"Arf," Marlon said.

"Roll cameras."

Red lights, video cameras on tripods, phones held in skeletal hands, reporters, crew chewing on tobacco. She was laying in bed with Scott leering over her. "Just between us. And the world. And—"

"Reveal who you really are," Graham said.

Erin and Meg rolled nude on a polar bear rug. Everett laughed. Avital slid out of her dress. Graham peeled off his face to reveal the skeletal carapace of another of the monsters that had been Arthur Fritz. Rick and Debbie sat at a head table, toasting glasses of champagne high as Sam lay as the centrepiece, with food all over her body. Sam tried to scream as all around her more of those hideous faces, wearing suits and expensive looking dresses, leaned in leeringly with forks and knives in hand.

"Sam, help," Erin said.

She and Avital were on another table. They all were, laying on silver serving trays. The nearest creature stuck Sam's stomach with a fork. She felt the metal pierce her skin and tried to scream, but an apple blocked her mouth. The knife came next, slicing into her abdomen. A trickle of blood poured out onto the silver plate. The creature brought the fork to its mouth, with a pink chunk of dripping skin dangling. It popped the flesh in its mouth and chewed.

"Fresh," it said.

"Sam, please," Avital screamed.

One of the things was chewing on her intestines, pulling them out of her ripped open stomach like sausage links, smearing blood all over its green tinted hard skin. At another table, Everett and Marlon moaned in agony. Marlon's stomach was torn open down the middle, while hands dug out organs and pulled strips of skin into their mouths. Two of the things chewed on Everett's severed arm like corn on the cob.

"Sam, help. Help. Sam. Help."

"I hear the eyes are the sweetest part," Debbie said, slowly bringing the fork towards Sam's face. Inches from her retina. She couldn't turn away. She—

"Fuck." Sam jerked upright, heartbeat racing, sweat pouring over her body. Her loose T-shirt was soaked through. She'd kicked off the sheets and her bare legs glistened in the moonlight.

"Fuck, fuck, fuck."

"Mommy, you said a bad word again."

The man stood watching her at the end of the bed.

"Oh, fuck." She slid back up against the headboard and grabbed the pillow, as if it could be a weapon.

"You have to chew the soap, you have to chew the soap."

"What are you doing in here?" she asked, trying to calm down, wondering how long that man had been watching her.

"I couldn't sleep."

She'd put him down in Erin's bed, telling him it was his bedtime. He'd demanded a story and she'd made one up. He'd seemed content, so she'd closed the door and gone into her own room. But now she was beginning to wonder just how smart it was letting this guy stay here.

"It's late and, uh, Mommy needs to sleep, okay? Go back to bed."

"I don't want to. I want to watch TV."

"It's not time for that," she said. "It's time for bed."

"I'm not sleepy."

"But I– uh, Mommy is."

"Can I sleep with you?"

Sam was getting a splitting headache. She'd barely slept. Her arms and legs felt like cement blocks. The faint trickle of moonlight that seeped in through the window blinds showed the man-child sucking on his thumb as he looked at her expectantly. She wasn't about to let this massive guy in her bed, even if he did act like he was six.

"You're too big for that."

"Am not."

"Am, too."

"Am not."

She rubbed her temples. At least the horrible images of her nightmare were fading away. But this was a real life one and it didn't seem like she was about to wake up from it.

"Am—"

"Please? I had a nightmare."

The look of pure innocence in his eyes made Sam's guard relax. He certainly didn't seem threatening even if he looked it.

"You, too?"

He nodded.

"Tell me about it," she said.

"I was an old man. Very old. Everything hurt but I didn't tell anyone. I just pretended that I was strong because I used to be. One of the strongest ever. I went on so many adventures. I was in a plane, even a submarine. But I got old. Then somebody locked me up and I couldn't get out. I tried. But it was like jail. And there was this huge needle and a black and white movie and the Super Mario brothers. I was so sleepy.

251

Someone was cutting me up. Then I woke up."

There was something about his story that hit her. An old man? Locked up? The Super Mario brothers?

"Just who are you?" Sam asked hesitatingly.

He rolled his eyes. "Come on, Mommy, that's easy, I'm Frankie."

"Frankie?"

"Yup. And you're Mommy."

"Frankie, what's your last name?"

"It's… it's…" He squinted, as if he was trying to remember. "It's…"

"Malone?"

"That's right." He bobbed his head excitedly.

Her mouth dropped. Frankie Malone. A dream of being an old man? But this guy was in the prime of life. He was the size of a pro-wrestler, with long blond hair and—

"Frankie, how far back can you remember?"

The man's expression darkened. His face suddenly looked much older. He sat straighter, seemingly more tightly wound. His doe-eyed innocence instantly disappeared. "Who you calling Frankie? I've got ear wax older than you."

There was something very wrong with this guy. "Who am I talking to now?" she asked.

He snorted. "Don't you read the papers? Never heard of the Order of the Raging Beaver? The Camponelli bust up—"

"Detective Inspector Sergeant Frank Malone?"

"You can read."

"So it's not Frankie I'm talking to?"

"The only one who calls me Frankie is my mom and she's been dead and buried, God rest her soul, for almost fifty years."

"You don't think I'm your mother?"

"Are you sure you haven't been hit on the head recently?" he said. "You're a third of my age."

"Look, uh, Frank." Sam slowly stood up. "I want you to come and look at your reflection in the mirror and tell me what you see, okay?"

"I can tell you what I'll see without doing that. It'll be me."

"Just humour me."

She gently took him by the hand and led him to the mirror attached to her dresser. He stood with his arms crossed impatiently. She slid the piled clothes onto the floor and put her finger on the light switch.

"I'm going to turn on the light. Get ready."

She flicked it on, expecting him to scream in shock, but he just stood there staring at his own reflection and rubbing his chin.

"Hey, I'm looking better than I thought."

"So you think you're Frank Malone and seeing that face doesn't change your mind?"

"I know it's me, I've always been me. It's you I'm starting to worry about."

"I'm going to show you a picture and I want you to tell me what you think about it, okay?"

"More weird games. But I've played worse."

Sam grabbed her phone and did a quick search for articles about the real Frank Malone. The top hits were about his arrest for the murders of Factor 5ive and Simon Karlsson, another one announcing his death. "Hero Cop Loses Mind" and "Disgraced Cop Dead."

She found his mugshot, wild white hair, deep creases in his leathery skin, piercing eyes, all indicators of a very old man.

253

She turned it so he could see.

"This is what you are supposed to look like."

The man-child stared intently at the image on screen, then back to his current reflection in the mirror, then back to the screen, and back once more to the reflection.

"So?"

"Bad lighting," he said, shrugging.

"Okay, let's presume that it is you in that body. How'd you end up in it? You were in Shady Acres, frail, old, now you're…" She looked over the massively muscled form, so totally different from what Frank was. "Conan?"

"That part's a little foggy. I remember this guy in a white coat, Jello cups, a couple of old ladies who might have been choice numbers in the fifties, then it's all been snow, walking, and reruns."

"Have you been having blackouts? Lost time incidents? Periods where you may have been under mind control or hearing voices in your head?"

"No more than usual."

"Look, I—"

But as she spoke, the man-child suddenly seemed to shrink back into himself. He looked around the room as if he didn't know where he was. The scowl was gone, replaced by a curiously big smile. "Is Daddy coming home soon?"

"Frank, are you still in there?"

He looked from side to side like he was trying to figure out who she was talking to. "Uh, where else would I be?"

It seemed like there were two personalities at war inside his head and they flipped on a dime. Could one of them actually be Frank? He rubbed his skull as he stood awkwardly in front of the mirror, seemingly amazed at his own reflection.

"How about headaches, Frankie, you have one?"

He looked at her with the eyes of someone who spoke a different language.

"Mommy, I feel fine."

Talking to the kid wasn't going to get her anywhere, she needed the other personality back. But how to trigger it?

"Do you recognize the man on the screen?" she asked.

"Sure. That's Grandpa. But he's dead."

"Can I talk to him? Mommy wants to talk to Grandpa."

He snorted. "We'd have to go to the graveyard then, Mommy. That's where he's buried."

Then it hit her. What would settle this once and for all? Sure, it was a little extreme, but it might be the only way.

"That's a great idea, Frankie," she said. "How about we go and find Grandpa in the graveyard?"

"Can we get ice cream?"

"Uh, sure. But only if you help Mommy with the digging."

Chapter 34

"I'm just trying to tie up a loose end relating to a recently deceased patient," Jimmy said to the duty nurse.

She stared at him as if she was disgusted by his very presence.

"Detective Hooper, Mr. Malone died two months ago. His room was turned over and given to another patient the next day. I don't know what you expect to find."

"I don't know, Nurse Ironhide. Maybe just closure. I wasn't here for him at the end."

"Closure isn't something most people in here are equipped to give. When the mind goes, what remains isn't always recognizable."

"I understand. I'll just speak to a few of his friends. If only to find out if he was happy in his final days. Maybe they heard stories I hadn't."

"He was full of stories, but he was also full of shit," she said. "And a troublemaker."

"How?"

"Ranting about stolen money, conspiracies, people out to get him. It was getting himself so worked up that led to the stroke, if you ask me."

"And the stroke was confirmed by Doctor—"

"Hans, yes. I can pull up the day's logs if you'd like to see them for yourself."

"Please."

She waved him to follow her into her office down the hall. It was spartan, white-walled, bereft of photos beyond her nursing degree. She sat at her desk and tapped away at her computer. When she had the file she was after, she spun the monitor to show him.

"Here: Malone found unresponsive at 2:46am. Put on temporary life support until end-of-life plans could be determined. A do not resuscitate order was found on file and life support removed at 3:56am. Patient died 4:22am."

He read over the notes as she spoke, seeing it all confirmed in writing with times and nurses present. Doctor Hans was listed as the man making the final decision.

"And then?"

"He was wheeled out and taken away by the stretcher service. At which point he was their problem."

"You didn't like him, did you?"

"No. Quite frankly, I didn't. But in this job you can only spare so much compassion for the residents. None of them are here long term. They're here because they were too problematic for a regular care home to deal with. These are the violent dementia cases, the wanderers, the thieves, the ones who can't control themselves physically or mentally. It may shock you to hear this, but much of what made them human is gone. They've degenerated into impulses. My job is to keep them as comfortable as possible but also to keep their families and the rest of society safe. I look at this as a kind of death row, detective. Just with worse food."

This woman was almost inhumanly cold. No wonder Frank

had issues with her. She was worse than any chief could ever be.

"You're right, Nurse Ironhide. That does shock me. I'd have thought you'd have more compassion in your line of work."

She turned the screen back around, tapped a few more times on the keyboard, then spun it once more to show him a new entry in the log.

"Do you see this? This was when a resident, a former pro-wrestler, snapped one evening and threw another one to the floor thinking he was in a match. The other man, in his late eighties, was killed almost instantly. Two orderlies were severely injured. Even though he was also eighty, this man had a lifetime of combat training, simulated though it might be, and that made him dangerous."

She turned the screen again and opened up a new entry, then swung it for him to see. "And this here. A man, six foot four, two hundred twenty-five pounds. Early onset Alzheimer's. Tragic. But he attacked one of our nurses. Poor Ginny. He held her down and sexually assaulted her. He'd covered her mouth to muffle the screams. It took another resident pressing the panic button to alert the orderlies. By the time they found him, he'd... let's just say Ginny requested and received stress leave."

"Okay, I get your point. But not everyone here is a rapist or murderer. Some are just old and suffering and—"

"And I pray their suffering is brief. For all of our sakes. Now if you're satisfied, I have work to do. You may speak to the other residents that were here when your friend was, but please be finished by 5:30. That's dinner time."

* * * *

"Frank? Sure I remember Frank," the heavyset man with the grey moustache said from his chair in front of the television showing The Price is Right. "He used to steal me extra pudding."

"He stole us all extra pudding," the man's taller, thinner twin said.

"Why was he stealing you guys pudding?" Jimmy asked the pair who looked uncannily like the Mario Brothers.

"Trading."

"For what?"

"Information," Gord, the shorter man, said.

"Information? Was Frank running some kind of racket?"

"No, he wanted us to keep our eyes open for anything strange," George, the taller one, said.

"What did he think was going on?"

"Not think. Know."

"Well, what did he know?"

Gord looked over to the hallway, where he saw an orderly watching them talk. The Mexican man in scrubs leaned up against the wall idly, looking more at the television than Jimmy standing balanced on his cane in front of the two brothers.

"There are things that aren't safe to talk about in public, officer."

"Detective," Jimmy said. "And you can tell me. I'm one of the good guys."

"So was Frank. And look where it got him."

* * * *

"Help," the old woman shouted. "Help."

The voice came from a room down the hall. No one seemed to be too concerned about it. Jimmy walked inside to find a grey-haired and stooped woman in a wheelchair, sitting near the window. She pressed against the glass, as if she was trying to signal someone on the outside.

"Ma'am?" Jimmy limped over. "Are you okay? Do you need—"

"Help. Help. Help."

He put his hand gently on her shoulder. "I'm here. Detective Hooper RCPD. What's the matter?"

She turned to him in wide-eyed terror, her sunken eyes bloodshot, skin pale and sallow. "Help! Help!" She began rocking in her seat, vibrating in fear.

"Whoa, hang on, ma'am. I'm just trying to—"

"Mrs. Halsey doesn't understand you," a voice from the other side of the room said.

Jimmy turned to see a bespectacled man in a white coat standing in the doorway. Short, in his fifties or so, with angular features and a nametag that read Dr. Hans.

He walked into the room and stood next to Jimmy. "She's lost in her own mind. Convinced she's under terrible distress, no matter what is going on. She no longer has the ability to say anything other than what you hear. No treatment or therapy can change that, I'm afraid."

The woman rocked uncontrollably, almost like she was suffering from a seizure of some sort. She clammed up at the sight of the doctor.

"She's not in any real danger?"

"Of course not." Dr. Hans put his hand on her shoulder. "She's perfectly safe here and a part of her knows it, even if it can't articulate it. Oftentimes dementia manifests as a regression to an almost child-like state. Memories from the distant past become clear while the present becomes a blur. Names of long-dead relatives given to others, time confusion, losing decades of experience. In her case, she's trapped in a perpetual fear state. All we can do is provide care and let nature take its course."

"I see," Jimmy said. "I heard the shouting and—"

"A most normal reaction in your line of work. But in this case, unwarranted."

"Dr. Hans to the nurses' station, please," a voice came over the intercom. "Dr. Hans to the nurses' station, please."

"If you'll excuse me. I'm needed elsewhere."

He walked out of the room. Jimmy took another look at the sad old woman in the wheelchair. Her rocking slowed down to a gentle sway. It was clear that she wasn't going to be much help, but he felt sorry for her, nonetheless.

"I hope you can find a way to feel safe in here, Mrs. Halsey."

"Help," she whispered.

"I wish I could."

He started to go but a cold hand gripped his wrist. He turned to see her staring at him.

"You were his friend," she said softly.

"Whose?"

"Frank's. You were his friend. I saw you here visiting him."

Jimmy looked back to the door, saw no one and leaned in closer. "I was his partner. Do you know what happened to him? They said it was a stroke."

She shook her head. "Lies. Always lies in here. He was another victim. Taken away."

"Taken away? By whom? For what?"

She just shook her head sadly.

"Please, Mrs. Halsey," Jimmy said. "If you know something, you have to—"

"Help!"

Her shout caught him off guard. He nearly stumbled backwards.

"Help!"

"Time for supper, Mrs. Halsey," an orderly said, walking into the room. He gripped her wheelchair. "You don't want to miss Salisbury steak, do you? All cut up nice and soft, just the way you like it."

"Help," she said again. "Help!"

Her head turned, watching Jimmy as she was wheeled out of the room.

* * * *

He almost missed it. He'd spoken to as many residents as he could and had been given conflicting stories about Frank.

"He was crazy."

"He was nice."

"He said he used to be a spy of some sort."

"No, he said he was in mergers and acquisitions."

"You're deaf. He said murders and assassinations."

"The man was on more drugs than a beatnik."

"He and Nurse Ironhide hated each other."

"Stroke? Ha, I don't believe it. It was a heart attack. Had to be."

"He told me he was going to spring us all. So much for that idea."

Nothing was definitive or proof enough to build a case on.

And so he resigned himself to a dead end, only to, as he was almost at the locked door out of the ward, notice Dr. Hans speaking with a man in the hall, having just left his office. The man's face was burned into his mind. It was the same man he'd seen in Frank's photo.

Jimmy pretended to get a phone call, took out his phone and used it to zoom in on the man's face. He snapped a few shots of him, clearer than Frank's, centred and better lit. Maybe they would prove to be more useful in matching him.

The two of them disappeared down the hall in the opposite direction. Jimmy began shuffling back after them. Maybe he could eavesdrop on their conversation.

He passed the nurses' station, turned down the hall, only to run into Nurse Ironhide.

"Detective, visiting hours are over. The residents are having dinner."

"I, uh…"

He saw the two men at the far end of the corridor move into another room. He couldn't catch up, even if this woman wasn't blocking his path.

"I needed someone to show me how to get out. I forgot the door code."

"Of course."

Hoping for another fleeting glance of the mysterious man, he resigned himself to walking with the nurse back to the locked ward exit. She tapped in the code, pulled open the glass door and held her hand for him to pass.

"I hope you found the closure you were after, detective," she said icily.

Chapter 35

"I thought you said this was going to be hard work, Mommy," the man-child said from inside the pit.

Sweating through her parka, Sam leaned back against a skeletal tree. She marvelled at how the monster had managed to clear so much of the frozen dirt with only a shovel.

"Uh, I thought it would be, Frankie."

He snorted. A pile of dirt flew out of the hole. "Maybe for a baby."

It was still winter, but spring was in view. In River City, the ground was rock hard. She'd expected that they were going to have to find heavy machinery to do this work, but the creature that thought he was Frank was digging through the earth as if it was soft mud. More flew from the pit at the base of the tombstone that had been erected for Detective Inspector Sergeant Frank Malone.

It was a simple marker, with just his name, birth and death years listed. Nothing about his work, titles, awards, or disgraced end. Probably for the best. She didn't know how often people vandalized the headstones of cops, but he didn't deserve that indignity. Digging him up was indignity enough.

"Aren't you going to help, Mommy?" He peeked his head out of the hole.

"In a minute." She wiped her brow on the back of her glove. "I'm just, uh, taking a break."

"Don't break for too long or you won't get to have any fun."

She watched clumps of dirt fly from the pit rapidly. The man was a machine. No human could be that strong. Which told her conclusively that he was a golem. But from her experience, created golems didn't usually have the ability to speak. Joshua had been the unique exception. Which meant the confused man could have possibly been transformed into a golem by the Authority. Evidence was scant for either explanation. He didn't have the telltale scar on the back of his neck from an implanted heartstone, and he drifted between personalities. Anyone she'd met who'd been altered, the guys from Radiant Cyanide and Factor 5ive, Debbie—all maintained their original personalities and were only subject to the hypnotic power of whoever held their control stone. This man-child didn't fit either of the golem types she knew. Could he be some new kind? What benefit was there in having a slave with split personalities? Or was he a mistake?

The metal of Frankie's shovel hit something hard with a dull thud. She perked up. He'd done it. He'd hit the coffin. She leaned forward over the hole and saw him chipping away at the dirt-encrusted coffin over and over again in frustration.

"Mommy, something's in here."

"Frankie, stop. That's what you've been digging for."

"Yay, ice cream time!"

"Slow down," she said. "We need to look inside first."

He pushed off some of the dirt and felt around for a way to open the casket.

265

"Whoa, Frankie, I, uh…"

She wasn't so sure she wanted to look inside the coffin. Frank had been dead a few months now. What would his corpse look like? Was she ready to see the man she knew in that state? The man-child looked at her expectantly.

"Well?"

"Okay, clear it off. Let's look inside."

It took another ten minutes to make the space to actually open the coffin. She hopped inside the hole that the creature had made and stood in the small area he'd dug around the edge with the handles. The thing reached for the lid, but she put her hand on his to stop him.

"Just give me a second to prepare for this, okay?"

"Jesus, kid, you're acting like you've never seen a dead body before."

"Frank, is that you?"

His face had changed again, the child-like smile replaced by a furrowed brow and a deep frown.

"If it isn't, I'd like to know whose underwear I'm wearing."

Despite herself, she laughed. "You might not think that if what's supposed to be inside this coffin is actually inside this coffin."

"I'd better look inside then so I can know what I think."

He grabbed the handle and she let her hand fall away. He pulled open the lid. She gasped.

An awful stench of rot emerged. Inside was a very old man in a dark suit, much older than she remembered. He'd shrunk and lay as if sleeping. The skin had parched and been stretched tight to the bone. His hair was perfectly white and remained miraculously unchanged.

The sight and smell was too much. Sam turned and threw

up all over the bottom of the casket.

"Come on, the suit's not that bad."

"Frank." She coughed. "That's your body."

He stared at the decaying corpse in silence. Was he coming to terms with the impossibility of who he thought he was?

He reached down and touched the cheek of the corpse. Sam could only watch as he looked at the chin, the ears, the hair. He examined the faint lines of scars that were melting away with flesh decay. Suddenly he grabbed the head with both hands and tore it from the neck. It came away with a crunch. Dust and debris fell from the dry wound. Sam turned and threw up again as the man-child stared at his own severed head.

"Alas poor me…" he said. "I knew me well. Over the years, really well. Shit, when I was a teenager, multiple times a day, in fact. But I wasn't the only one that knew me. Lots of women did, too. Some damn fine ones and—"

"Put that back," she said, trying not to throw up again. "For God's sake, put it back."

He looked at her like she'd just farted in church. "It's mine, isn't it? Can't I do with it what I want? I—"

The hair slid off. It was a wig. A portion of the white scalp fell to his feet. The top of the skull had been cut along its circumference. The man-child grabbed the top part and pulled it off with a pop. He looked inside the skull and tilted it to show her.

"Look, ma, no brains!"

Sam threw up again.

"Good thing this is underground because you're making one hell of a mess."

"Frank, that's your… head."

"It was my head." He tapped his own skull while holding the top of the corpse's. "I've got a new and improved one now."

She steeled herself to look into the husk that was the old man's cranium. She saw the hollowed-out pumpkin with brownish rot and a few bugs crawling around inside. She wanted to puke again, but there was nothing left in her stomach.

"The brain was removed. Do they do that when they embalm a corpse?" she asked.

"Not unless they're Egyptians."

"Wait…" Sam reached over to the creature's head. She lifted some of his hair with her hands and it felt… wrong. She pulled off his toque and the hair came with it. The creature was bald. A huge scar ran around his skull with stitch marks alongside.

"Hey, I need that." He replaced the skull top and snatched his hair back, putting it on his head crookedly.

"Oh my God," she said. "I think you are Frank. I think they… put your brain in that body and…"

"I'm a Frank N Stein."

"Oh God. Oh my God. Oh Jesus."

"You suddenly find religion, kid?"

She felt lightheaded. She fell to her knees and nearly fainted. She was face to face with the headless corpse while Frank played with his own decomposed head. The corpse. *His* body. It was here, but his brain wasn't.

There was something else wrong with the corpse. It was lopsided. She gingerly touched the shoulder and found that an arm was missing, too.

"There's no arm here. They—"

He crouched down beside her. "What else did those bastards take off me?"

He started patting the corpse down, checked the crotch then relaxed. "At least they saved what counted."

"How can you be so calm? That's your body!"

"It's just a body, kid. I've got the key parts. Well, one of 'em. What matters is I'm here. Frank Malone is back in the saddle. Riding high on the hog of justice and—"

"Okay, I get it. But how? Who did it? Why? What the hell is going on?"

He just shrugged. "Let's ask him." He held the head up and looked into the shut eyes. "Hey, old Frank, who did this? Any ideas?"

Silence.

"Sorry, kid, he's taken his secrets to the grave."

"Oh God."

In a freshly dug grave, with a coffin covered in vomit, standing on an open casket with a corpse missing parts, Frank held his own severed, decomposed head making jokes. She had to get out of here. She needed to take a shower and burn all of her clothes so she'd never have to be reminded of this stench. Then she had to save her friends before something like this happened to them, too. She scrambled up and out of the grave, nearly hyperventilating. Frank stayed inside and peeked his head out over the edge.

"So?"

"Put your body back and fill in that fucking hole. Then let's get the hell out of here before I puke again."

"Sorry, Frank," he said to the head on his hand. "But Frank N Stein's going to lock you up again. Don't worry, I'll take good care of our brain. And I'll make sure whoever has the

269

rest of us is careful, too."

She crawled over to a tree and hugged her legs tightly, letting him fill in the hole as she struggled to figure out their next move.

* * * *

The sun rose through the window in her apartment, casting long shafts of light on the carpet, revealing dust motes floating in the beams. Wearing sweatpants and a hoodie, Sam towelled her hair off. It had taken an extra long shower to get the dirt out from under her nails, wash away the stench of the grave, and finally feel clean. But now that she was out, she tried to put the image of the corpse out of her head.

The new Frank sat on the couch in his dirt-stained pants, watching a rerun of *WKRP in Cincinnati*. He held the remote tightly in his hands as he leaned forward to listen to the too-quiet set.

"Frank, any chance of you showering and changing your clothes? You, uh, smell like the old you."

"Shhhhh…" he said, holding up his finger to his mouth. "I can't hear the TV."

"You know you can turn up the volume, right?"

She walked over and pulled on the remote. At first, he didn't want to let go, but finally relented. She raised the volume a few notches and his eyes grew three sizes.

"How'd you do that?"

"I'll show you after you wash off the stench of death."

"I don't want to have a bath, Mommy."

Oh no… he's regressed again.

"Frankie, come on. Do it for… Mommy."

270

"Will you give me a bath? Please?"

Sure, his body was that of an adult, but right now, his mind wasn't. This felt all kinds of wrong.

"Uh, is Frank in there? Can we get his help for that?"

The phone rang, saving her further debate. She walked over to the kitchen and pulled it off the cradle. "Hello?"

"Hello?"

She tensed up. She didn't recognize the voice at all.

"Who's this?" she asked.

"This is Detective Jimmy Hooper. I believe you knew my late girlfriend, Detective Tockett."

"Maybe."

"I think we should meet. To talk. I've found a few things and judging by your voicemail, you might have, too."

Chapter 36

"Sir, it appears we've lost control of our most recent specimen."

He looked up from his desk to the man holding the clipboard, standing nervously in the doorway. He didn't need any interruptions right now. Not when everything was going so well.

"How could it break the control? I was told the process was sound. That this wasn't possible."

"It's not supposed to be. We only used half of the, uh, donated brain. The original source must have been particularly strong-willed to—"

"I read the notes," he said, cutting him off. "Nothing in any of the literature said that breaking control was ever observed."

The man coughed awkwardly, revealing that he knew something more than he was letting on. "Well, sir, we didn't feel it was necessary to include all possible outcomes in the report."

He pushed aside his folder and stared at the man in the lab coat with increased anger. Julian Gerber didn't like to be surprised. He made a point of knowing all of the angles before making decisions. That was why he was going to succeed while others like Karlsson and Fritz had failed. It was why the Authority had sent him in to clean up their operations in River City. To find out that he'd not been told even the slightest detail made him want to rip out someone's eyeballs.

He stood up and slammed his hands on the desk, startling the timid man. "What wasn't included? And if I feel like you're withholding even the tiniest fact, I'm going to make you wish you'd never been chosen to come in here."

"We drew straws actually. Nobody wanted—"

"Just tell me what you know."

"In the files recovered from Professor Finkelstein, he spoke of one of his specimens demonstrating, uh, more willful behaviours. Moments where the control mechanism was… slow to take hold."

"Slow?"

The man swallowed hard. "But the professor also said that the stones always worked in the end, there was just a… delay at times."

"And our current specimen is showing this delay?"

"Not exactly. Well, we can't be sure really. It's entirely possible the delay is just really, really long… like when you used to try to download porn on the internet in the nineties and—"

"How long?"

"He's been out of contact for four days."

"Four days? And you think that's only a small delay?"

"It's certainly within the realm of possibility that he reverts to his controlled state but—"

"But…"

"We're having our doubts."

"Of course you are."

He walked around the desk and rubbed his temples. He

was going to have to report this to the Authority and it was going to make him look bad. To call him unimpressed would be an understatement.

"We're still trying, sir, and we—"

"What about the other half of the donated brain? Was that used in another specimen? Do we suddenly have two creatures outside of our control roaming the streets?"

"No, no, sir. That was used in a different project entirely. Wade and his team took it for Project C and—"

"Good. Then at least the cleanup will be that much easier." He put his arm around the man's shoulder. He flinched but relaxed as Gerber smiled warmly at him.

"So then—"

"So then I'll have to clean up your incompetence," Gerber said. "It's what I'm good at. It's why they sent me here. But—"

"But?"

"Someone has to pay. And since you're the closest person…"

The man's eyes widened in terror. He tried to squirm out of Gerber's grip, but Gerber held him tight. He lunged forward and bit down on his nose. With a rending tear, he tore the appendage off and spat the bloody chunk to the floor while the poor scientist screamed. Crimson ooze leaked from the gash, filling his mouth. He coughed and spat all over the carpet.

Gerber laughed and squeezed tighter, feeling the shoulder joints pop until a jagged piece of bone erupted from the man's far arm. He only screamed louder. Gerber reached over and yanked on the protruding bone, tore outward, shredding through the flesh and muscle, cranking, peeling it away from the body until it dangled by a loose tendon at the elbow. Then he grabbed the jagged bone with his free hand and rammed it directly into the dying man's right eyeball. Clear fluid and red blood trickled down the jutting bone as the poor man moaned.

Gerber jammed the shard deeper and deeper until the man went limp. He let him fall to the floor where he twitched a few times before falling silent.

He licked the blood off his lips and hand and pressed an intercom button.

"Tell section three to implement a clean-up procedure for section four's mistake. Send their creation out to do it. It would be fitting. Oh, and I'm going to need a new carpet in here."

He depressed the button and stared at the dead man on his floor. He sucked the remnants of blood from his fingers. "Sorry you drew the short straw."

Chapter 37

"Okay, Frank, you stay here in case I need your help. This might be a set-up."

"Wouldn't it make more sense for you to stay in the alley and watch my back? I'm the one with years of experience in these things."

Sam gently put her hand on his shoulder and looked him in his mismatched eyes. "We've gone over this ten times already. Detective Hooper called me, not you. He's expecting me, a university student, a woman, not you... Arnold Schwarzenegger, a man... and a golem."

"Right, but—"

She wagged her finger at him. Even with an adult personality, she had to act like his mother. "No buts. Just be ready and stay the old you."

He walked back into the alley and made a big show of standing behind a dumpster, mostly out of sight. She'd wanted to meet in the open, but seeing how few people were actually out on the streets right now, Sam doubted that would have made much of a difference.

"I've never seen downtown so deserted," she muttered. The faint noises of the drums from the tent city travelled when there weren't that many cars on the road drowning them out. Not far from the River City University campus, there'd normally be pedestrians everywhere, going to and from cafes, restaurants, shops, the slowly dying mall, at bus stops, flagging down taxis, panhandling, asking to sign petitions, anything. But even the people that worked in the area seemed to be avoiding the streets.

Was this a bad omen?

She waited, leaning up against the wall of an old brick warehouse that had recently been converted into lofts. She watched the sidewalks for Detective Hooper. He'd said he'd be here at twelve. It was eleven fifty-five.

* * * *

Jimmy parked around the block from the meeting place. He put up his police parking pass in the window to avoid a ticket, and grabbed his cane. He didn't know why Veronica had been keeping her relationship with this woman a secret, or what they had been talking about, but it was clearly related to her investigation. The voicemail said she had information. Maybe Jimmy could use it to clear Veronica's name. Or maybe this would just confirm her corruption.

"Only one way to find out." He limped down the sidewalk.

He'd almost missed the message entirely. The blinking phone on Veronica's desk had been partially buried under a dying plant. The voice hadn't been familiar. "Detective Tockett. It's me. The last of us, I think. Anyway, I've got something. We need to meet. At the usual place. I don't have my cellphone right now. Call me at this number." The woman had left her digits then hung up. But immediately after that, there'd been another message from the same person. "Yeah,

277

Detective Tockett, it's me again. I actually have more than I thought. I hope you have access to a testing lab. Please call me back."

It was just enough to pique his curiosity, but not enough to assuage his fears. So here he was, limping along recently sanded sidewalks, going to meet someone he'd had no idea even existed. What else about his late girlfriend's life was he going to learn?

He turned the corner, saw someone leaning up against the wall of a recent condo conversion. She wore a dark parka with a toque on. She was looking the other way down the street. When he was only a few meters away, she turned and saw him.

"You!" he said when he realized who it was.

"You," she said flatly.

"And me!" another voice said happily, a figure emerging from the alley behind her waving his hands excitedly.

Jimmy froze. He lifted his cane defensively.

"Frank, back in there, not yet!"

"What is this?" Jimmy asked as the girl he knew to be Samantha Abraham tried to force a massive bodybuilder in leather back into the alley behind her.

"I'm watching her back!" the man said with child-like enthusiasm.

"No. It's okay. He's alone. You are alone, right?" she asked, looking back at Jimmy.

"Yeah. But clearly you're not."

"I didn't know if you were setting me up or not."

"How do I know you're not setting me up?"

The big man crossed his arms over his chest. "Maybe you're both setting me up, huh? Ever thought of that?"

If Jimmy didn't know any better, it almost sounded like a completely different person talking from the mouth of the behemoth.

"Let's just start over, okay?" Sam said.

Jimmy relaxed and leaned on his cane as he eyed the girl and her friend with suspicion. "Why don't you start by telling me why you left that message on Detective Tockett's line?"

"First I need to check you over," Sam said.

Jimmy held up his hands. "I'm not wearing a wire, I can promise you that."

"Not what I meant." She walked up to him and started to walk around him, but he turned to face her. "Relax, I just need to check your neck." He stopped and lifted his toque, letting her see the back of his head.

"Okay, you're clear."

"She did that, too. I caught her a few times. Just what is it that you're looking for?"

"A sign that you've been compromised," she said curtly.

"What kind of sign?"

"Not here. It's too exposed."

"Then where?"

"Hey, Frank," she asked. "You want to get a Danish?"

* * * *

Inside the coffee shop, with only one other table occupied, Sam sat nursing a latte as Frank happily devoured an entire plate of Danishes. Detective Hooper poured cream into a coffee and sat listening to her tell the whole story about what had happened after he'd been taken out: the lab, the strange creature that was Arthur Fritz, the brainwashing, Rick and

279

Igor, her friends, what she'd seen in the tent city. It was incredible. It also sounded insane.

"So, you were working with Veronica—"

"And Rick and Igor."

"The four of you were planning to, what, expose these secret… aliens? Monsters? Something out of Lovecraft? That take over people and mind fuck them?"

"At the least."

"And some kind of grand conspiracy you're still not quite clear on."

"Still working on that."

"You four thought you could do this on your own without the help of, oh, the police or CSIS, the RCMP, the army, anyone?"

"We had reason to believe the police were a part of it, too."

"That's ridiculous," Jimmy said. "I haven't seen anything that would back that up."

"You've been at home recuperating, right? That's what she told us. You weren't going to be much help."

Jimmy sighed angrily. "I wanted to help. She was being so secretive. Maybe I could have prevented what happened to her and the kids. But instead, she had to treat me like a cripple. Fuck, I'm still a cop."

"Good man," Frank said as crumbs fell from his face.

"And just how does this pro-wrestler fit in?" Jimmy asked. "You haven't explained him."

"I don't know if I can," Sam said. "Just trust that he's on our side."

Jimmy dropped his spoon to the table harshly. "If we're going to trust each other, I need the whole story. I need to know what you have that's so important. What did you want her to test?"

Sam reached into her coat and produced a baggie with a joint and a couple of pills. Jimmy took them and stared at them in the light.

"Drugs?"

"Everyone in the tent city is taking them. At the raves, around the fires, during the march. My suspicion is that there's something inside them that's a trigger for the mind-control mechanism. I was... under the influence for a while but I it threw up. There was something inside. A creature and—"

"Ethiopian food?" Frank asked. "That happened to me one time. Turns out they don't cook—"

"No, it was like a worm thing. Alive."

"Yeah, same," Frank said. "I—"

"Frank, not now. Just eat another Danish."

"Yes, Mommy."

Jimmy looked at the two of them, incredulous. "You keep calling that guy Frank. And he calls you Mommy. What the hell kind of relationship do you two have going on?"

"Get your mind out of the gutter. It's not like that at all. It's both much simpler and way more fucked up, trust me."

He shook the baggie to watch the pills and joint bounce around. They looked like any others he'd confiscated during dozens of arrests before.

"You think these are tainted."

"I was hoping you had like, you know, a lab that could test them."

"You've watched too much CSI."

"So you don't?"

"No, we do, it was just an observation. Everyone always

thinks we have these huge labs with dozens of scientists working on every sample and bit of evidence that comes in. That we can just go and ask for a test and, boom, it's done, and we have our answer and our criminal. It doesn't work that way. Half the time we have to send it away to a central lab, sometimes out of province, which is a whole different kind of pain in the ass. There's RCMP databases and RCPD ones. Their guys don't like ours and vice versa. There's some stuff we contract out and some stuff we—"

"So you can't test them?"

"No, we can. It's just not going to be as simple, or as fast as you think. It could take a while."

"I don't know how long we have. Something's going on in that tent city. I saw the leader, Graham Maddox, on the news meeting with an MP, Dan Kirby, and—"

"Hopefully to break that shit up. It's insane they haven't sent in the cops yet," Jimmy said.

"I have friends inside. I have to try to get them out before—"

"You don't even know if the drugs do what you say they do."

Sam leaned back in her chair. "I threw up and it cleared my head. Maybe that would work for them, too."

"So just ram your fingers down their throat and watch 'em spew!" Frank said.

"There has to be a better way."

"Stomach pump?" Jimmy offered.

"I don't know how to administer one of those. And can't they, like, damage the oesophagus or something?"

"When Bacon used to swallow pennies, Mommy would give him Ipecac syrup to get 'em out."

They both turned to Frank. "What?"

"You just drink a spoonful and paint the toilet green! Wait. Please don't give me that, Mommy. I don't want to throw up."

"I've never heard of that." Sam took out her phone. "Is this something you can still buy?" She tapped away and her face brightened. "Well, shit, it is. There we go. That's how I save my friends."

Jimmy tucked the drug baggie into his jacket. "If that place is so dangerous, are you sure you should be going back in there?"

"I'll bring my bodyguard." She patted the big man on the shoulder.

"I should go, too."

"No offence, detective, but you're in no condition to help. You can do more on the outside. And if we need to get out fast, be our ride."

"This sounds like a bad idea."

"My friends don't deserve whatever the Authority has planned."

"Stay in contact," he said curtly.

"I'll need a cellphone. Mine was left in my tent and—"

"I have an extra one."

"Then it's settled," Sam said. "Operation save my friends is a go."

Jimmy didn't seem as enthusiastic as she felt.

"One more thing," he said, taking out a cellphone. "I found this image on Frank's phone. Someone he saw in Shady Acres talking to Dr. Hans just before he died. I've been looking for weeks for some match, but I haven't found one. Have you seen this guy before?"

He pulled up the picture on his phone and turned it to Sam to see. She took it from his hand and swiped with her fingers to enlarge it.

"Holy shit, I have."

"You know who that guy is?"

"It's my dad."

Chapter 38

S he hadn't been back to the two-story suburban house on the tree-lined street in ages. Large enough to show that she'd grown up privileged, but not ostentatiously rich, it was solidly middle class, with a garage, landscaped backyard, flower gardens, paved driveway and wooden fence. She'd spent so much of her life inside these walls that the memories couldn't stop flooding back. They weren't all good ones. Her mother, a former model, had been relentless in her criticisms of every facet of Sam's life. She'd grown up feeling like she'd only been a disappointment.

"Are you really going out dressed like that?"

"Can't you at least try to make yourself look nice?"

"You could talk to other people besides Trevor."

"All black? Again? Really?"

"What is that garbage you're listening to?"

Her dad had been in and out of her life, away on business so much that his presence was almost ghostlike. Had she participated in any sports growing up, he'd have been the type to always miss her games, but since she'd avoided teams, balls and anything involving points to watch movies and play old kitschy boardgames with Duckie, she was spared that bit of childhood trauma.

Standing at the base of the driveway looking at the white house, she felt empty. The first opportunity she'd had to leave, she'd jumped on it. Her dad had offered her a room in his downtown condo after the separation. With his constant out of town travel, she'd seen it right away as a chance to be on her own, finally have her own life and be free from her mother. Since moving out, she'd barely spoken to her.

Now, she had a reason.

"Okay, Frank," Sam said to the big man standing near her. "I'm going to go and talk to my mom. You keep watch outside. If I need you, I'll scream."

"Stakeout duty, eh? Ten-four."

She walked up the driveway to the front door. She never wanted to come back here. As far as she was concerned, she and her mother were estranged. But with her cellphone somewhere back in the tent city, she had no access to any of her contacts. She'd never bothered memorizing numbers. Her mom was the only person that she could ask to get in touch with her dad. She had to know how he was involved with Shady Acres.

She rang the bell and turned to see Frank peering from behind a tree near the sidewalk. Inconspicuous, he wasn't.

The door opened and her mother met her, wearing her usual yoga pants and hoodie. She looked much younger than her age, extremely tanned and fit. Her blonde hair was tied back in a ponytail.

"Samantha?"

"Hi, Mom."

"Oh, Samantha." She grabbed her in a hug. Sam stood awkwardly as her mom showed her more affection than she had in the last decade. "I'm so happy you came back. What happened? Is something wrong? Are you in trouble? Are you hurt? Pregnant? Why didn't you call? Where are your gloves? Come inside before you freeze."

Sam looked back once more to Frank, before her mother dragged her inside and shut the door behind her.

"Look who's come home," her mom said.

"Hello, pumpkin," came a voice from behind her. She spun to see her dad standing next to the coat rack at the closed front door.

"Dad, I came here looking for a way to call you. But... wait, are you two are back together now?"

Her mom let go of Sam's arm and joined her dad at the door. They smiled at each other. "It's complicated," her mom said.

"Complicated is right. Dad, I have to talk to you."

"I have to talk to you, too, Samantha," he said. "I've been hearing a lot of distressing things about you lately."

Sam tensed up.

"What do you mean?"

"You're all over the television at Jets games. The kiss cam. Lipstick lesbians, I think they call you online. Then, I get a call from the police that you may have kidnapped Rick Hansen. Wasn't he the boy you dated in high school? To top that off, I get word that you're the one who got that goalie's brain all scrambled and made him attack poor Rick. This is major drama, as you kids call it."

"Whoa, Dad," she said. "I don't know where you're getting your news but—"

"Then I'm looking at some completely innocent adult videos and I find this," he said, as he dug out his phone and spun it towards her. It was opened to a blurry video. The

287

one that still haunted her, with Scott and Tommy, that she'd been brainwashed into making.

"No! That's not…"

"Oh, it is, Sam. The mole. You know the one." Her dad brandished the phone like a talisman.

"I thought we raised you better than this, Samantha," her mom said sadly. "Just giving it away like that. And not even to a rich man."

"You don't understand." She tried to look away from the phone as she backed away from them, towards the kitchen.

"No, you don't understand what it's like to have your golfing buddies show you a video of your daughter playing trained seal at the zoo with two sleazebags from a go-nowhere rock band."

"Or to have your girlfriends ask you why your daughter is sucking face at Jets games for the whole world to see," her mom added. "We never knew she was… queer, they say. Is she some kind of… whore?"

"It's not like that. But if it was, there's nothing wrong with it or—"

"Pick a lane, Sam," her dad said. "Are you a dyke or a whore?"

"Hey, you can't—"

"We're your parents. We absolutely can. We created you."

Through the hallway, into the kitchen, they kept pushing her back.

"No. You both did your best to mess me up. You were never here," she said, pointing to her dad accusingly. Then she swung her finger at her mom. "And you were a giant bitch. You both have no right to criticize any part of my life."

The stopped and looked at each other. "How could you

speak to people who care about you like that?"

She hit the kitchen island. They slowly came closer as the horrible video played on his phone. Sights that she'd tried so hard to block away, that she thought she'd finally moved past. But he'd seen them, and his friends had, too. Clients, men she could remember tousling her hair at backyard barbecues, the parents of other kids from the neighbourhood whose pools she'd swum in. They'd all seen it. It was worse than she'd thought. She wanted to crawl under a rock and die.

"I—" She shook her head as the reality of just how many people knew what had happened to her sank in.

"You've been gone too long," her mom said. "You weren't ready for that kind of responsibility. It's okay to admit you failed at being an adult. You can come home. There's always a place for you here. With us."

"We can give it another try," her dad said. Her mom nodded. "As a family. Together."

"Why now? Why did you decide to try to salvage the marriage?" Sam said.

"Maybe we both realized that we were better off being a part of something bigger than either one of us," her mom said.

Something was off with them. They were acting like different people. They'd been so sure before that the marriage was over. The trophy wife, high school sweetheart model married to the successful businessman out of town more often than not. The bored housewife spending all of her time and his money fighting off the inevitability of ageing. Her dad probably had affairs in every city. Sam could remember the screaming fights when they thought she was asleep, the tense family dinners where he'd made them all sample new menu items from his restaurant chain. She hadn't been close to either one. They had almost nothing in common. Sam could never be a girlie girl, a make-up wearing, yoga class, expensive nail treatments, flashy dresser, day drinker girl. And she didn't care about the business world. She'd spent her entire life rebelling against their lifestyles. But it was her mom's last words that caught her attention.

"Something bigger?" Sam asked. What was she talking about?

"Marriage is a sacred vow made to a higher authority, Sam," her dad said.

Authority? The Authority? Had they been changed?

"You know, Sam, I was watching your performance, and I noticed something different about you," her mom said. "Your clothes, your make-up and hair, you were finally looking like the woman I always thought you could be."

"How drunk were you to kiss in front of the whole arena?" her dad asked. "I always pictured you as the shy type."

"Our little girl grew up right under our noses," her mom said.

"I…" Had she actually turned into her mother without realizing it? Shopping with Avital and Erin, slowly draining her savings on clothes, shoes and make-up. Spending forever in front of the mirror to look nice to go to clubs and meet guys, agonizing over how to look just right for Scott. Oh God, it had happened. She'd become what her mom wanted.

"You don't have to look at your little mistake as a mistake. You could turn it around into an opportunity. I heard from Mrs. Kinsley down the street that her daughter started some kind of website where she charges people to watch. Your only mistake was doing it for free."

"Yeah, kiddo. I've got a lot of business expertise and years of experience in marketing. If you want, we could turn this little family shame into a new income stream. Hell, I'll bet a lot of the guys would pay or be more than happy to let you use them in future videos and—"

"You two are fucking sick," Sam shouted. "I'd never—"

"Don't let opportunity go to waste, Samantha," her dad said. "The guys said you showed some real talent."

Her dad turned to check out the video. Sam screamed and knocked the phone away from his hand, sending it flying across the room.

"Samantha! Your father is trying to help you."

"Sick. You're both fucking sick. Inhuman."

Just then the back door was flung open and Frank stood in the doorway.

"I heard the scream. Let's dance."

He charged for Sam's parents. They both tried to run, but he had them in his grip before they could even move. Her mom batted at him with a limp hand, and her dad kicked him in the leg, to no reaction.

"Samantha," her dad said. "Who's this?"

"One of your co-stars?" her mom said, wincing.

"What do you want me to do with them?" Frank asked.

Still reeling from having to see that video again and rocked by what her parents wanted to do with it, Sam took a deep breath. "Let me see the backs of their necks."

"What's going on?" her dad asked.

"I need to know how inhuman you really are."

"I can't believe—" her mom started but Sam roughly grabbed her ponytail and pulled her head to the side. The back of her neck was clean. Then she pushed her dad's head away to check his. Clean again.

"So you haven't been turned into golem slaves. Then I need to know if you're on the drugs."

They both looked at each other, confused. "Drugs? Sam, you're the one acting like you're on drugs."

"Frank, hold them while I give them the Ipecac."

They'd bought all the bottles of the stuff the pharmacist would give them at the drugstore on the way over. Three. She dug out a spoon from the cutlery drawer and poured some in, then forced her mom's mouth open and dumped it down. She struggled, but Sam made her swallow. Then she repeated the process with her dad.

"What are you—"

It took hold faster than she'd expected. They both began heaving. Frank held them tightly as their stomachs churned.

"Oh God, what did you give me?"

It came in a vicious torrent. Streams from each of them, all over their pants, the floor and Frank's shoes. Huge puddles of chunky green and brown vomit.

"Gross," Frank said. "I just shined those."

When it was done, they coughed and heaved and bent over weakly. Sam examined the puddles on the floor. The stench was horrible. It almost made her add her own to the pile, but she didn't spot any of the small creatures swimming around in the goo.

"Clean again? Neither one of you has been corrupted by the Authority?"

"Corrupted by the authorities? You're talking like some hippie anarchist now," her dad said.

"I saw you at Shady Acres, Dad. You were talking with Dr. Hans. About harvesting patients and—"

"Sam, that's a lucrative business opportunity. Body dona-tions, scientific research, tissues and organs and—"

"But you're in the restaurant business."

"Diversification. Shady Acres is just one contract. On the whole, working with Geld has been incredibly rewarding. They pay top dollar and—"

"They're killing people."

Her dad looked shocked. "Old people just die, dear. Trust me, it was all above board. Signed contracts. I have deals with hospitals and universities, even a few people in China who—"

"It's a part of their plot to mind control people."

"Who?"

"Geld. The Authority. The monsters under the skin."

"Come now, Sam," her dad said, wiping his mouth. "Just because they're in positions of authority doesn't make them monsters. I've been dealing with Geld for years and they always pay their invoices on time and—"

"You killed my friend Frank. The old cop in the home."

"What? I didn't do anything."

"They harvested his body. His brain—"

"Yeah. For research. To figure out why he snapped. CTE, they thought. It was sent to a lab. The one he'd broken up when he went insane, if I'm not mistaken."

"Are you trying to tell me you've been working with Geld and the Authority in a business partnership? And you have no idea what they're really into?"

"Of course I do. I've seen the labs. Those guys are on the cutting edge of medical research."

"And nobody there tried to change you or turn you into…"

She grabbed his hair and pulled his head back. She began

digging her fingers in around his neck, looking for folds of skin that could be peeled back to reveal the alien face.

"You're hurting me."

"Stop!"

Nothing. He was human. They both were.

"Jesus Christ," Sam said, staggering back over to the kitchen island. No implantation scars, no signs of those worm things, no skin mask. Her parents weren't a part of it.

"So both of you aren't working for them. You're not being controlled or hypnotized. You're just assholes?"

* * * *

It was a simple house in the suburbs: two stories, white trim, large picture windows. The lights were on in the upper floor, but the curtains were drawn. Someone was probably home.

What was so special about this place? And why was he here? There must be some reason, but he couldn't put his finger on it. He found himself walking around the back of the house, looking into the windows to see if anyone was there. He saw a dining room table set up with still-burning candles and plates of food left half touched. A bottle of wine sat in a bucket of ice.

He circled around to the side of the house and peered through another window to see the kitchen. Something had spilled all over the floor. A man and a woman talked. She held her head, shaking it back and forth. He patted her on the shoulder gently. It was the soft touch of people familiar with each other. He was probably in his fifties, with thinning greying hair. She looked younger.

Why watch them? He didn't understand the purpose of

294

being here at all, yet he couldn't look away. She motioned to the mess on the floor. The man led her out of the kitchen, into the other room of the house. Through the window, he could still see them in the hallway, turning up the stairs.

There was a back door near the attached garage. He tried the lock and found it open. He carefully pushed his way inside the house, making as little noise as possible, compelled by some urge to go after them.

His shoes creaked on the kitchen floor, and he slowed his footsteps to a cautious shuffle. Something smelled rotten, but he ignored it. Plush white carpeting, a flight of stairs leading up. He took each one at a snail's pace. Faint voices came from a room above him. The master bedroom, that's where they were. The lights inside were dim. The voices grew clearer.

Go.

Two adults. Changing out of their clothes. The woman, stripped naked, turned on a shower in the en suite. The man, paunch dangling over briefs, slowly rolled off his dress socks.

"I don't understand any of this," the woman said. "What could have come over her?"

"She's confused," the man said. "Everyone her age has gone nuts. Running off to live in those tent cities. Nobody shows up to work. I hope Kirby gets them shut down and—"

The man looked over to the door and saw him watching them.

"What is it?" the woman said. She leaned out of the bathroom door. She followed his eyes, caught sight of the presence at the door.

They both screamed as he lunged at them.

Chapter 39

"Nothing doing, Hooper. Perfectly normal street drugs. MDMA and cannabis. Not even laced with anything." The chief leaned back in his chair.

"Results so fast? Must have been slow at the lab."

"It's never fast enough when drugs are involved."

"True," Jimmy said. "But I only submitted the samples this morning. It hasn't even been eight hours."

"Get them a bouquet of flowers if you're so blown away. Otherwise, stop getting involved in things you're not authorized to."

Jimmy stood to leave.

"I'll expect a full report, including who gave you those narcotics, by the end of the day."

"Uh, sure thing."

Jimmy returned to his desk and the pile of Veronica's notes he'd been going through. He'd never expected the lab results so soon. Someone must have been doing him a favour. Sam had been so convinced that they were tainted, but turned out her theory was off.

He watched the recording from Frank's phone again, wondering what connection Sam's dad had with the care home. She hadn't texted him yet with news of what she and Frank had discovered. There had to be some logical explanation; something apart from possible alien creatures posing as human beings. He'd seen a lot of shit working with Frank, but shit that had terrestrial explanations.

He tapped out a text to Sam: 'lab results negative' and tucked the phone back inside his pocket. He had a report to write. The ramblings written on napkins about organ harvesting and mysterious deaths at Shady Acres painted a picture that he was going to have a hard time selling. He certainly wasn't going to be able to bring the bodybuilder Sam had found who claimed to be the reincarnation of Frank's brain forward as expert witness. This was going to take some creativity to explain.

He picked up his "World's Third Greatest Partner" coffee mug and found it empty. Frank had given him the thing the first Christmas they'd been teamed up. Facing the stack of inconclusive notes, he rose for a refill.

Every desk in the precinct was full of police officers on paperwork duty, typing away in quiet focus. No music played, no one engaged in idle conversation, they were locked in total concentration. Sometimes it felt like they were deliberately avoiding talking to him. Maybe they were just worried about triggering his grief.

"Hey, Adams, you see the game last night? That Hansen kid is really stepping up, eh?"

Adams mustn't have heard him, he didn't even look up.

"Gomez? You see that deke he made in period three? Pretty impressive for a guy who was supposed to be out for the rest of the season."

Gomez didn't respond either.

Everyone must be behind or something.

Shrugging away the indifference to his presence, he walked over to the snack table and grabbed a chocolate glaze from the still-full donut box. Again, Jimmy had the first pick of the bunch. Was no one else eating these things anymore? Had he missed some new diet fad? He took another and filled his mug to the stain line.

He sat back down and ate, watching everyone working diligently, typing like professionals. Clearly things had changed in the time he'd been off. The place was feeling more like an office than ever. Maybe he was the one slipping. Maybe he was in need of a tune up.

He gathered up his notes and decided to head down to the shooting range in the basement. Adjacent to the underground parking garage, there were usually at least a few officers in here working on their aim, but today it was deserted. Paper targets hung untouched at the far end of the cavernous cathedral of plain concrete walls. It was cold down here. An eerie hum of emptiness enveloped him.

He took up position in one of the booths, laying his cane down and putting on the earphones and goggles. He loaded his sidearm with target rounds, then lined up the first shot and fired. Not quite a bullseye, not quite a stopping shot either. He was rusty.

Imagining the target was one of the men responsible for Carter and Olivia's deaths, he fired again. Closer, but still off centre.

Coming here always cleared his head, the focus required drowning out any distractions that rolled around inside.

Another shot, another miss.

No tainted drugs. No word from Sam. No clear evidence in the files. What do we do now?

Another shot. Getting closer. He'd been a damn good shot before the injury. He pressed the button on the small remote that called the target down. It rolled along the track to his booth. This place had been here since the seventies when they'd built the building. He wondered how many times Frank had come down during his career.

Four shots, all off centre. He replaced the sheet of white target paper with a fresh one and sent it down the aisle.

Maybe it's the gun.

He checked it for any signs of malfunction, but knew deep down that the malfunction was inside of him. He aimed, but hesitated.

Since when do lab results come that fast? Even on drugs. I remember Frank and I sending a batch of pills in and it taking a week. Then there was that mushroom store that opened up and—

There was something off about the chief's explanation. Why'd he call him personally? Why didn't the lab guys do it? Why would the man care? One pill and one joint. It wasn't from a major bust, intercepted shipment, or even a package sent through the mail clandestinely. Come to think of it, Jimmy didn't remember ever telling the chief about it in the first place.

He fired and missed again. The bullet hole was only a few inches off centre.

Why would the chief lie to me? What would he have to gain? Could the lab guys have lied to him?

He fired one more time, finally hitting the centre.

"I'll talk to Jacob."

He had to know who was lying to him. He cleaned up and headed to the lab first, finding Jacob and the others in the middle of a chemical test.

"Jacob, got a minute?"

"Sure. It's not like this leg is going to get up and run off on us, is it?" He flashed a toothy grin as he held up a blueish leg, broken off from the knee down, in his black gloved hands.

"Still nothing on those missing body parts?"

"Not enough to make a whole person, if that's what you want to know."

"And no ID?"

"Just a lot of arms and legs."

Jimmy leaned on the desk, partly to take the weight off his throbbing knee, but also to look nonchalant.

"Got a question for you," Jimmy said. "About those drugs I dropped off for testing."

"Not the priority right now, Hooper, I'll get to them when I have time. Chief has all resources directed to this arm and a leg bandit. Got a problem with that, talk to him."

"Oh, okay. I was just looking for an ETA."

Jacob sighed and looked at the others in the lab, back to his desk, back to the clock. "Unless you want me to send them off and wait God knows how long, you'll have to be patient. I'll try to run something on them by the end of the week. Besides, I heard you weren't even back in any official capacity yet. What are you doing bringing stuff down for testing anyway?"

"Just something that came up. But thanks, Jacob. Let me know when you've got something."

So there it was, out in the open now. The chief was lying. But why?

* * * *

300

"You know the rules. Don't take anything anyone hands you, don't smoke anything anyone hands you, don't eat, drink, chew on, suck on, or swallow anything anyone hands you."

"Yes, *Mom*," Frank said petulantly.

"Look, Frank," Sam said. "I don't know if you can talk to Frankie in your head or what, but he has to understand this, too. Maybe the stuff they're lacing is only on the drugs, maybe it isn't. Maybe it only works on people, maybe not, we can't be too careful. Just keep that mouth shut and stay as close to me as you can. We don't want to get separated in there. Especially since you don't have a phone."

"Kid, I've gone into worse places than this. Remind me to tell you about the time my ex-wife went to a disco run by a vampire sometime."

Sam stared into the mismatched eyes of the massive creature that housed Frank's twin personalities and wondered if it was a good idea bringing him here at all. If he regressed at the wrong time, who knew what might happen? But then walking into the maelstrom of the tent city without backup was probably even dumber. She had to take the chance.

"Disco is dead, Frank. This place has EDM. I don't think there are vampires, but it's been a few days, so anything could have happened."

"I'd feel a lot better with a gun," he said, crossing his arms over his chest.

"Normal people don't have those. Especially university students. Especially me. Now just come and act like you're a student here to protest pretty much everything."

The drums pounded from inside the brightly lit makeshift village. Lit up from the legislative grounds' lights, strung up Christmas strands, bonfires, and hundreds of other individual sources, the place was an ever-shifting halo of reds and greens and blues.

The barricade fence was a thick wall of signs now, blocking completely any glance through at what was going on. The arch entrance, where she'd originally just walked in on her first trip, was now blocked by two huge doors that looked to have been stolen from a church. Two muscled men, wearing dark pants and no shirt, stood standing like statues at either side. Their chests were covered in paint, but they held no weapons.

Sam took Frank by the hand and led him across the street. The police cars parked on the perimeter of the encampment were still there. Officers watched her intently as she and Frank approached the locked doors.

The two guards didn't acknowledge her at all.

"Uh, hi, my friend and I hate everything about our country and want to, uh, help change the world."

They didn't move or speak.

"We heard Graham, uh, Graham Maddox talk, and we're totally with him. You know, solidarity forever, that sort of thing. Can we come in?"

They still said nothing.

"I heard there was a wicked rave going on and I just have to—"

"Look," Frank said, pushing past her. "There's drugs in there that need smoking and we're the ones to do it. We want to get so high that we're singing show tunes in sequins. I don't really care what Chairman Maddox has to say, I just want to play drums and recite beat poems. So, are you going to let us in or what?"

They still didn't move. Frank and Sam looked at each other,

unsure what to do. She was about to suggest they just jump the guys when the doors swung open to reveal the sprawling lines of tents curving towards a massive bonfire at the base of the steps of the legislative building.

"I knew you'd come back," a woman said. Her face was mostly obscured by her beaded dreadlocks. She wore furry boots and the thinnest wisp of a white shift. Her body was painted in glowing phosphorescent blues and whites. Necklaces of tinkling charms bounced around her bare breasts.

"Avital?" Sam said in shock at the change that had come over her friend.

"Come." She held out her hand. "It's time you saw the future."

She looked to Frank who just shrugged. She took Avital's outstretched hands and let her lead them towards the fire.

* * * *

"Where are you going?" Jimmy muttered as he pulled into the next lane over. He kept a full block away from the chief as he followed him in his dirty silver Audi. The stylish and expensive car stood out on the roads at this time of year. Most people didn't drive something that nice when the streets were covered in salt and sand, not unless they didn't care about the body rusting out.

The chief idled at a red light. So far, the man showed no sign of noticing Jimmy's tail. He'd been watching the guy all day from his desk, trying to understand why the man had lied to him. But no matter how much coffee the chief drank, how many phone calls he took, or how long he sat at his desk, the man never left his office, not even to go to the bathroom. He simply sat at his computer and worked. All day.

At precisely five o'clock, the moment he'd put in his day's work, the chief grabbed his coat and hat and headed to the parkade. Jimmy had zoned out and almost missed him. He'd grabbed his cane, leapt to his feet, and hobbled after the man. Down the stairs, past the firing range and lab, to the parkade. He'd leaned behind a concrete pillar, as the chief fired up his filthy Audi and pulled out of the underground parking garage. He'd hopped as fast as he could to his own car, a tan Corolla and started tailing him through the final trickles of rush hour traffic.

"Home?" Jimmy asked aloud. "Out to eat? A massage parlour?"

The light changed and the chief pulled forward. Jimmy's row was stuck behind someone waiting to turn as people crossed the street.

"Shit."

He gunned it into the next lane, cutting off a black pick-up, who honked and shook a fist at him. Jimmy waved apologetically at the driver and raced ahead to catch up to his quarry.

He nearly drove right past the man. The chief had turned off and pulled into a strip mall. Jimmy circled around at the next intersection and by the time he came to the parking lot, the chief was already out of his car.

"Where the heck are you going?"

Jimmy pulled into a parking spot in front of a bakery at the other end of the strip mall and watched as the chief went inside the constituent's office for Dan Kirby, the member of parliament for the South Centre riding of River City.

The same man who'd been all over the news lately with this student protest.

"Kirby? What's he want with him?"

* * * *

They danced around the fire, lathered in phosphorescent paint as the drums and pounding EDM flowed through the air. A thick haze of smoke trailed upwards towards the night sky. A crowd of people sat in a circle all around the dancing masses, swaying their arms in the air, wiggling their fingers as they blurted out strange noises. Everyone was nearly naked.

Sam was sweating through her coat already. She saw beads of water dripping from Frank's chin.

"Av, what's going on? What is all of this?"

She looked at her with glassed-over eyes. A man descended from the head of the stairs, naked like the others. His wiry body was painted in abstract shapes. His face paint mimicked the creatures' carapace-like skin. It was Graham Maddox. Some kind of twisting snake coiled around his waist.

"What is all of this? It's community. Shared passion. Mutual collective action. The coming together of autonomous individuals with unified intent. The future."

He raised his hands to the sky and a line of smoke billowed from behind him, down through the people, towards her.

"It's beautiful, Samantha."

"Av, this isn't what you want. This isn't—"

"Oh, it is," Graham said. "Just ask them."

"Guys, we have to—"

"Don't you understand, Sam? We're finally part of something important."

305

"He's controlling you—"

"Join us," Graham said. "We accept all who devote themselves."

Wisps of smoke seemed to envelop Avital. They caressed her naked skin, flowed around her body and into her nose. Her eyes rolled back, and she began to lurch and twist awkwardly. Her arms flew out and she kicked up dirt as she joined the circle.

"Av."

Around and around, they danced, moving in rhythm to the music. Sam examined the faces sitting en masse around the fire. Men, women, beards, dreadlocks, their painted faces done in skull-like carapace patterns, just like the creature that had been Arthur Fritz. Their white eyes glowed and they moved as if they were blades of grass in the wind.

Guttural cries and drone-like chanting assaulted her mind. The smoke slithered through the air, twisting towards her. She was frozen in place. It hit Frank first, wound around his body, then up into his nose. His head whipped back, and he looked at his surroundings anew. His face looked younger again.

Oh no. Not now.

He began pulling off his jacket. "It's so hot, Mommy," he said.

"No, Frank, don't."

He threw the leather jacket far into the night. He grabbed his shirt with both hands and shredded it in two, revealing his massively muscled chest, slick with sweat. Two face-painted women emerged from the group carrying bowls. They began drawing symbols all over his body with their fingers, strange swirls and letters she didn't recognize.

Sam could only watch as the two nude women covered Frank's chest. Then they slid off his pants and painted the rest of his body. He stood, eyes locked on the fire, meekly allowing it all to happen. It was then Sam realized who was painting him. Erin and Meg.

She wanted to say something, but her mouth was locked shut. When they were finished and Frank was a glowing phosphorescent beast, they turned to her. Erin reached out and unzipped Sam's coat. Meg began stirring the paint. Erin slowly slid off Sam's sweater, dropping it to the dirt floor. Meg ran the brush over her bare skin. It was warm and felt like thick moisturizing cream as their fingers went all over her body.

A gentle touch on her pants, then they were slid down. She couldn't stop them. As if someone else was controlling her body, she lifted her legs and each one kicked loose their bonds. More paint was applied and the warmth penetrated right through her. Alive. She felt so alive.

Erin locked eyes with her. She understood now. Graham wanted the best for all of them. The music, the voices, the chanting, they called to her. She joined the circle.

* * * *

The chief had been inside so long that Jimmy began to wonder what in the heck he was doing in there. He stepped out of the car and grabbed his cane. He casually walked towards the other side of the parking lot, looking into each window: pizza place, physiotherapist, eyeglasses, coffee, then Dan Kirby's electoral office. The big open window was plastered with signs featuring Kirby's name, the numbers of bills to support, and other community events. Inside, he could see the chief talking to Kirby, the bearded, thinning haired member of the Red Party who'd become a national celebrity recently. Jimmy barely paid attention to news, but he'd seen the guy in the papers and in online and YouTube thumbnails.

"What would he be talking to him for?"

They seemed to be very familiar with each other, laughing and going on with an easy manner. He debated going inside, but there didn't seem to be anywhere to hide if he did. He was all set to go back to his car when they both turned to look at him. The chief waved.

"Oh, shit."

Kirby waved, too. They wanted him to come inside. The jig was up. He limped forward and pushed open the door.

* * * *

Around and around, the drumming mirrored her staggered steps. The warmth of the paint made her feel like it was summer. The fire spoke to her in crackles. The chanting was clear and finally made sense.

"There is no I, only we," Graham said.

"There is no I, only we," the crowd repeated.

"The we, are they," Graham said.

"The we, are they," the crowd repeated.

"Void the self."

"Void the self."

"Void the self," Sam said.

* * * *

"Detective Hooper, glad to have you aboard," Dan Kirby said. "Your chief here has been telling me how interested you are in what we're up to."

His teeth seemed to glimmer. He had that slightly too-perfect grin of the career politician. Jimmy didn't really know much about him other than he was a cabinet minister, an important MP. He didn't look threatening: average build, short-parted hair, close-cropped beard. He wore a nice suit and had an easy confidence about him. But what was he expecting, a sinister laugh, twirling moustache, shifting eyes? He was just like any other man in a suit you'd pass on the street.

"Chief?" Jimmy asked.

"Took you long enough, Hooper. But then you are only half a cop right now, aren't you? I wondered just how much Tockett had kept you in the loop. She was quite the investigator. But when you came bearing drugs, that told us all we needed to know."

"Why did you lie about the test?"

The chief looked to Dan Kirby, who rolled his eyes. "Are you sure he's even half a cop?"

"His girlfriend might have been the brains of the operation," the chief said. "And after all those years of thinking he was the smart one next to Malone."

"Sir, I don't get it. What's going on?"

"The great awakening, Hooper," he said. "But that's way out of your pay scale. Just know that Kirby here is about to become the new prime minister. When he brings forward a caucus revolt, old Vachon will see the writing on the wall."

Kirby nodded. "He'll step aside and in a stunning party motion, I'll be chosen as the new leader. Hardly the first

309

unelected leader to be Prime Minister, but most definitely the last."

Jimmy clenched his cane tightly, wondering if he should run for it or hear the man out.

"Oh, don't worry, I won't be one of those leaders who calls for austerity, budget cuts, or program elimination. I'm not going to preach infrastructure investment or job creation. I don't care about the deficit or the environmental impact we're leaving for our kids and grandkids."

"Then—"

"Everything I do will be in service of a higher authority," he said, grinning.

* * * *

"The old ways are going to be washed away in waves, nothing will ever be the same," Graham said.

As she danced, free and unencumbered under the stars, Sam saw someone emerge from the crowd. The symbols on his naked body moved in swirls of light. It was Everett.

"It's time to become one of us, Samantha," Graham said. "It's time to submerge the self."

Everett held out a pill to her; tiny, white, the same one she'd taken at the rave.

"Go ahead, Sam," he said. "It's ecstasy."

* * * *

Kirby went to a shelf behind his desk and pulled out a small brown bottle. "You like scotch, Hooper? Of course you do, you're a cop."

He poured three glasses.

"This is a vintage blend. Usually, I save it for special occasions, but I think this meeting of minds fits the bill, don't you?"

He opened up a tin and pulled out a tiny pill. He held it up for Jimmy to see and dropped it in his glass. It started to fizz. He handed the chief a different one and then gave the still-bubbling one to Jimmy.

For some reason, he reached out and took it.

Kirby held up his glass for a toast. "To the future," he said.

He and the chief clinked glasses. "To the future," the chief repeated.

They both stared at him, holding their glasses out. He saw himself clinking it against theirs, heard his voice say, "To the future," and fought against his own body bringing the scotch to his lips.

No!

* * * *

"Go on, Sam, you'll feel great," Everett said.

She saw Erin and Meg, Marlon and Peta, all painted in glowing light. They were all watching her. She'd stopped dancing, but the crowds moved behind her in waves.

She took the tiny pill.

"A second chance for the truth," Graham said.

"Go ahead," Erin said. "Join in." She kissed Meg and ran her hands over her naked body.

"Come on, Sam," Marlon added. "There's so much more you'll understand."

"The future." Avital started to push Sam's hand to her

311

mouth.

* * * *

No. No. No. No.

Closer, closer. He could smell it. The scotch, the strange added aroma of the bubbling pill. Like baking soda. His tongue flicked out.

"Nothing beats the taste of a good scotch, Hooper," the chief said.

* * * *

"One tiny pill and you'll feel better. No more pain, no more fear, no more worries," Avital said as Sam resisted her hand.

"Think about it. No more confusion over who you are or what you are. No more laying awake at night wondering what's going to happen."

"Trust me," Everett said. "It goes down smooth."

"Self-confidence in a pill," Marlon said. "I'm glad I took it."

"Your friends are with us," Graham said. "Waiting for you."

One pill and her life would change? Sure sounded like a good idea. She raised it to her mouth.

* * * *

Thick, brown, inviting. Closer. Almost there. Just drink.

No, no. No. Sam warned you what it would do. No. No.

"Hooper, you are a member of the RCPD, and I order you to drink that. Everyone else has. You want to be a team player, don't you?"

"Soon enough, there'll be more like us than you. Don't miss out on the future, Hooper," Kirby said.

"The future?" Jimmy said haltingly. He didn't want to get left behind. He didn't—

No! Don't.

"No!" Jimmy shouted, finally breaking the spell. He threw the glass against the wall, and it shattered into a thousand shards of glass, soaking the wall with scotch that slowly slid down to the carpet like ooze.

* * * *

"Become one with the Authority. Leave your past behind."

"Void the self. Void the self."

So close. Just swallow it.

"One little drug?"

"One little drug," Avital said.

"Drugs are bad!" a child-like voice shouted. A massive hand swatted Sam's, knocking the pill away. It flew right into the fire where it exploded in a cloud of green dust.

"Frankie?" she said, snapping free of the hold over her. "You—"

"Winners don't do drugs," the naked behemoth said.

* * * *

Breathing heavily, Jimmy felt his circulation coming back. He could feel his legs again, his hands on the cane. He could move.

"I thought you said he'd go easily," Kirby said to the chief.

"Maybe I underestimated him. Maybe Malone rubbed off

on him more than I thought."

"You're done, Kirby," Jimmy said. "I know who you are, and I know what you're doing. I'm going to stop you."

"Of course you will. They always think that, don't they?" he said, looking at the chief again.

"They do."

"I was afraid something like this might happen," Kirby said. "Thankfully, I came prepared. Miss Smythe, come in please."

The door chimed behind them. Jimmy swung around to see a woman walking into the campaign office. But not just any woman, this one was—

"Veronica?"

She wore a black bodysuit and jacket. Her mouth had the same natural downturned pout. She showed no recognition as she stood blocking his exit.

"As close a facsimile as we could arrange, I'm afraid," Kirby said. "Now I make you one last offer. Join us and she can be yours."

Jimmy limped forward and gently touched her chin. She didn't move, didn't even look at him. She was like some kind of doll. Her skin was too smooth, too clear. There were no little wrinkles at the edges of her eyes or lips. The hair was oddly flat. And yet, it was as close to her as he thought he'd ever see again.

"Well?" Kirby asked. "Don't you want another chance?"

"This isn't Ronnie," he spat. "She's gone. And you're going to be, too."

"Well," Kirby said to the chief, "you can't say I didn't try. Alright, Miss Smythe, kill him. And do make it painful."

The false Veronica's hand shot out and grabbed Jimmy around the throat.

* * * *

"Frankie," Sam said, slowly regaining her faculties. "You saved me."

"Saved you from a life of regret and rehab, kid," he said in his adult self voice.

"Oh, Sam," Avital said sadly. "Why did you have to be so stubborn?"

"You never did know what you wanted," Erin said, arm locked around the naked waist of Meg.

Graham shook his head sadly. "I'm sorry, Samantha. Now you'll have to learn the hard way that when you fight the Authority, the Authority always wins."

From out of the crowd came an impossible sight. A massive misshapen thing, with two torsos fused together on one waist, two oversized arms and two heads. Bearded, long-haired, grimacing in pain. They were both—

"Igor…" Sam said. "What the hell did they do to you?"

"She's all yours," Graham said and waved his hands.

The beast that used to be Igor's two heads roared and charged.

* * * *

The clone Veronica was faster and stronger than Jimmy had anticipated. Holding him by the throat, she pushed him back into the desk, bending his spine over the edge awkwardly. She squeezed his throat. Her hands closed around him like a vise. Jimmy tried to hold her wrists, shaking with effort, but the hand closed tighter and tighter.

He reached back and grabbed the bottle of scotch and

swung it at the false Veronica's face. The bottle shattered on the side of the girl's head. The hand went slack for a brief moment. Jimmy threw his opposite elbow and hit her in the eye. The girl staggered back.

The clone spun in mid-air, foot sweeping out and hitting him square in the jaw. He was knocked back and landed across the desk. He rolled off, crashing to the floor. He pushed himself up just as the clone punched him in the face. His head flung back, and he knew right away his nose was broken. Blood poured into his mouth. He stumbled back into the wall. Clone Veronica jumped but he held his cane up and it went right into her open mouth, lodging down her throat with a sick crunch.

The thing flailed and danced around as it screamed inhumanly.

This was his chance. He had to get out of here. He leapt over the desk, hopping awkwardly, knocking the phone and papers everywhere. He pushed past Kirby and the chief right through the door and out of the constituent's office into the cold night air.

* * * *

The thing was seven feet tall, with arms as big around as Sam. It grabbed her around the waist and lifted her in the air.

"Igor, stop!"

"Bab-ush-ka…" it moaned.

"Mommy!" Frankie charged low, hitting Igor in the back, staggering him.

"Igor, let go. You don't have to listen."

"Bab-ush-ka…"

"He can't hear you, Mommy," Frankie said, trying to leap up and put the thing's left Igor head in a headlock.

"Igor, they did this to you. Them. Not me."

He shook her so hard she thought her neck was going to snap. She tried to pry his hands open, but he was too powerful.

"Igor, please."

"Bab-ush-ka."

"Fight him, Mommy!" Frank said. The other arm grabbed him by the neck and launched him across the field, bowling over dancers in a heap.

"Kill her!" Graham shouted.

"It's me, Sam… your babushka."

The grip relaxed. Igor's right head's eyes blinked. "Bab-ush-ka?"

"That's right. Your little babushka. Remember? We went to Rick's party. We had pizza and cupcakes and—"

"Babush-ka?"

"I was your… girlfriend, I think."

He let go. She dropped to the ground and coughed in agony. Her ribs felt broken.

"Babushka!" Igor's right head said.

"Kill her!" Graham repeated.

"Kill!" Igor's left head said. The left arm reached out for her. It grabbed her around the neck and began choking.

"No. Not my babushka!" Igor's right head said. The right hand clocked the left head right in the nose. The grip let go of Sam's neck and the left head snarled at the right. It then clocked the right in the face, and they began trying to swat each other.

"This is… insane…" Sam said.

317

"Watch out, Mommy!" Frank shouted. He charged head-long at Igor, holding a park bench like a battering ram. He hit the squabbling two-headed thing in the chest and knocked it backwards, right into the massive bonfire.

"Igor!"

* * * *

The swelling from his nose shutting his eyes and the pain still reeling through his head, Jimmy hopped towards the car and yanked open the door. Fumbling for his keys, he spotted the clone Veronica crashing through the door of the office in an eruption of glass and metal.

"Oh, fuck."

He turned the keys, put it in reverse and gunned it back-wards. But the other Veronica punched right through the car window, reaching in for him.

"Holy shit," Jimmy screamed and cranked the wheel. The car spun backwards in an arc, dragging the doppelganger along, as it struggled to stay attached.

* * * *

Sam watched the massive two-headed creature scream as it was set alight. It danced out of the bonfire and began wildly swatting at anyone that came too close. It knocked Graham halfway across the square into a group of revellers, toppling them over like bowling pins. The poor beast thrashed in pain, moaning as the fire consumed him. She wanted to help. It was still Igor, at least partly. But there was no water source nearby, no fire extinguisher either. The thing wailed in agony, trampling people as it stumbled around.

"Time to vamoose, kid," Frank said, grabbing her shoulder.

"We have to save him," Sam said.

"There's no saving him now." Frank hoisted her up on his shoulder. The crowd began converging on them.

"Coming through!" he shouted and charged. They scattered where they could and where they couldn't, he made them.

* * * *

The creature managed to get its upper torso in the car. It reached for Jimmy, trying to choke him. Its hands clawed at him like a zombie. Jimmy punched out, smacking the thing's face, trying to push it back.

He careened into traffic.

HONK! A massive horn blew from a semi truck. He pulled the wheel suddenly to the right and drifted back into his lane. A car next to him swerved out of the way and blasted its horn in protest. The clone's legs and lower torso dangled outside, kicking in the air. It was trying to climb all the way in. Jimmy pushed her back and gunned it, driving towards a telephone pole.

"Sorry, Veronica, wherever you are." He swung the wheel, crashing the side of the car into the pole. There was a sickening grinding sound as the doors scraped along the wood and metal. The clone's eyes bulged open, and she fell forward into the front seat. At least, half of her did. Jimmy cried out in shock to see the thing cleaved in two at the waist, blood pouring out all over his front seat.

But it wasn't dead. It pawed up at him.

319

"Shit, shit, shit, shit." He smacked the still-moving thing. The monster grabbed his collar and started tugging. Jimmy hit the window button at his side, rolling it all the way down. Cold air blew in his face as he drove along the street. He took his hands off the wheel and grabbed the torso, hoisting it over his body and pushing it out the window. The beast held on to the edges, refusing to be thrown outside. Blood pouring all over his legs, he tried to use his knees to steer. His hands sank inside the thing's torso up to the elbow; he could feel organs and bones inside. He yanked free, punched at the creature's fingers where they gripped the edge of the door. One hand fell away. The thing lost its grip. The torso flew outside to the ground, crashing and rolling on the pavement. Jimmy slammed on his brakes and skidded to a stop. He got out of the car, soaked in blood, and approached the half of his dead girlfriend as it squirmed on the pavement and snow.

* * * *

As Frank moved, Sam saw the crowd behind them slowly form up and start to follow. He turned down the tent aisles, running as fast as his naked feet could take them. Away from the flames, she was beginning to feel the chill on her bare skin.

Then a roar and the beast that was Igor began pursuing them. Still ablaze, it set tents on fire as it ran, scattering the people inside, charging as if it had gone mad.

"Frank, it's gaining."

"I can see the way out. We're almost there."

The great double doors were shut tight. There were no guards on this side of the fence. Frank set Sam down and looked for the handles.

"How do I open these things?"

She watched silently as Igor charged. His skin melted off as he moved, his tattered rags long gone. He screamed and raised a fist, as if he was going to crush her. She simply looked at him quietly.

The hand moved to descend, but then it fell limp at the side of the beast as the strength finally left it.

"I am so sorry, Igor," she said as it fell to its knees in front of her. It was so tall, she was looking at him eyes to eyes. The left side head slumped forward and dangled uselessly. The right, flesh mostly melted off, completely hairless, smiled at her.

"Bab-ush-ka," he coughed out. "I'm sorry, too."

"You didn't do anything wrong. This is all my fault."

"No. It is theirs. Promise me you'll stop them."

"I will."

"This is good. Try to help Mr. Rick. He is a good man. I know he cares for you."

Tears welled up in her eyes as she watched the head that was Igor slowly lose the life in his eyes.

"I'll save him, Igor. I will."

"This is good, too."

He coughed again. The head tried to stay upright, but swayed. His right hand came forward and gently touched her cheek. The skin was hot to the touch, crimson rare, and smelled of burnt meat.

"Did you ever love me, babushka?" he asked. "Like I loved you?"

She couldn't break his heart, not now. Not at the end. "Of course I did, Igor. I was just playing hard to get. A man

321

doesn't respect a girl who puts out too easily."

"Nyet," he said, coughing. Blood erupted from his mouth, and he started gagging. A thick ooze poured down the remnants of his chin. "You cannot lie to me," he said. "I know you too well."

"Not as well as you think."

She leaned forward and kissed him on the mangled lips. He tasted of blood and fire and as she pressed her lips against his, she felt the life leave his body. When she pulled away, she saw a huge, surprised smile plastered all over his face. He wasn't breathing. She backed away as he fell to the snow and lay still.

Her vision clouded with tears, she watched him laying there for a time that seemed to never pass. The crowd of naked revellers had stopped. They stood watching her. Nobody moved. A hand fell on her shoulder.

"Doors open."

She turned to see that Frank had pulled open the great double doors. She took one last look at Igor and followed Frank out of the burning tent city.

* * * *

Jimmy stood in the middle of the street, drenched in blood to his shoulder. His pants were soaked. He looked like he'd taken a shower in gore. He stared down at the upper torso of the Veronica clone. It had stopped moving. The fall and loss of blood had finally ended whatever twisted life was left inside. There, on the ground, was half a perfect copy of her. Same hair, same eyes, same features. How had they done it? And was any part of it her?

A growing stain soaked the snow. It *was* still a part of her, and he decided it didn't deserve to end up like this.

He looked into her dead eyes. "That's twice I couldn't save you."

He picked her up by the arms and carried her over to the trunk of the car. He threw her inside and wiped his face with a bloody hand. He looked at the carnage he'd left behind him on the street lined with blood.

"Just what the fuck is going on here?"

Chapter 40

"You've lost two phones in the tent village now?" Jimmy handed Sam a cup of hot coffee.

"It wasn't my fault," she said. "There's some kind of overpowering collective will that takes hold of you in there. I almost lost myself, but Frankie saved me."

"That's twice now, kid. I'm gonna have to start charging interest soon."

Sam sipped the coffee, trying to restore some feeling into her body. "That thing you fought was… he used to be… a friend."

"You certainly hang out with a strange crowd," Frank said. "Those nudists your friends, too?"

She massaged her neck and took a deep breath. "Yeah. The camp changed them. They were painted just like whatever Fritz was. I don't understand."

"That makes two of us," Jimmy said. "My boss and Dan Kirby sent a clone of my dead ex after me. How is that even possible?"

Sam watched him sit at the table in the motel room they'd rented. It was in the south end of town, as far away from the legislative building as possible. Jimmy had found them both, naked and freezing, stumbling through the snow near

324

Assiniboine avenue. He'd been circling the grounds looking for them and had skidded to a stop when he'd spotted them. Now they were all crammed into the two-bed suite in a motel with a beer vendor attached. It was the kind of establishment that only existed due to some arcane River City liquor sales law, a place Sam had always assumed just offered rooms for show rather than ones you could actually rent. But it had a shower, and was clean.

"Detective Tockett came too late," Sam said. "The lab under the arena that Fritz was using to turn the Jets into golems had more to it than what she knew. Different divisions, I think. I saw my own clone there. But it wasn't really me. It was like a blank slate. It didn't have any scars, or skin blemishes, nothing. If you didn't know me, you could mistake it for me, but it was more like a living doll."

"And what happened to it?"

"Dissolved into a pinkish sludge and flushed away."

"What did they do? Steal your DNA?"

She just shook her head. "I wish I knew. They cleaned the whole place out before the cops could come. Not that the cops would have been much help. Detective Tockett thought they were compromised."

"She should have told me." Jimmy pounded on the table, rattling his hotel keys. "She should have trusted me to help."

"She had her reasons, I'm sure."

Jimmy stared silently out the window, as if he was trying to compose himself.

"Detective Hooper," Sam said. "She—"

"Don't."

"There are some things words can't fix," Frank said, patting her on the shoulder. "Like a door frame. For those you need nails and—"

"What am I supposed to do about all this?" Jimmy blurted out, his voice cracking, seemingly near tears. "Three people I cared about are dead. That guy says he's my dead partner. You tell me aliens or fucking monsters are trying to mind-fuck everyone. The goddamn MP for my fucking riding just bragged about sliding into the PM spot and ruling the country. You two just bust out of the student orgy tent city, buck ass naked, mind you, ranting about two-headed freaks made of an ex-River City Jet who was supposed to have been deported for attacking another player over his love for you. The player you're telling me we now have to save before he marries the girl that picked on you in high school! Oh yeah, and the chief is—"

"Jesus, rookie, take a breath, why don't cha?" Frank said and sipped his own coffee.

They'd all had showers and cleaned off the paint. They wore thrift store clothes Jimmy had swiped from the donation bin behind the Value Village. But despite smelling and feeling better, they were just as lost as ever.

"He's right, Frank," Sam said. "This is a problem so much bigger than the three of us. We don't know how many people are involved. Veronica thought we had to keep our circle small, and it turns out she was right. We can't trust the police, we can't trust friends or family, all we have is each other."

"I'd feel a lot better with a gun," Frank said.

"But we know something else now," Sam said. "We know that they—whoever they really are—are worried. They're afraid of what we know and will go to whatever lengths they have to, to stop us."

"Again, I'd feel a lot better about that with a gun."

"Knowing is only half the battle, Sam, surely you remember that. We need a plan."

"We might not be able to get to Dan Kirby or take down the entire police force, but we can do one small thing to fuck up the Authority's plans."

"Just tell me who to shoot. And where to get a gun."

"What do you have in mind?"

She put the coffee down and picked up the newspaper that had been waiting for them in the room. The front page of the sports section had a huge photo of a smiling Rick and Debbie. Below the photo was a small blurb about the two of them getting married. It was all set to happen after the playoffs. The city hoped that the Stanley Cup would be the guest of honour, of course. But a single line in paragraph two, about them having an engagement party before the first round started, gave her an idea.

"We're going to crash Rick's engagement party."

"What's that going to accomplish?"

Sam tossed the paper back to the table. "I made a promise to Igor. But also, I really want to wipe that smug fucking smirk off Debbie Peterson's face."

"Hmmm." Frank looked at the photo of Rick and Debbie. "A woman that fine has got to have something evil about her."

"Besides," Sam said, "the new owner of the Jets will be there. I don't care what Google says, Arthur Fritz owned the team before. This Julian Gerber is his spitting image. He's got to be another clone."

"Maybe we'll get lucky, and the chief and Dan Kirby'll show up. If it's a real social event, all the movers and shakers will want to put in an appearance with the city's favourite son."

"Again, with a gun I could shoot them all," Frank offered.

"We can't hope for everyone we're after to be in the right place just because it would be easier. The paper said Kirby was on his way back to Ottawa for a big vote. We might have to settle for Rick."

"Are you sure you're thinking clearly here, Sam?" Jimmy asked.

"No. But I made a promise and that's all I have right now."

"Then let's figure out how to crash that party."

Chapter 41

"I can't believe this was the best plan we could come up with." Jimmy adjusted his white shirt, flattening the lapels down, ensuring that the folds were even as he watched the elevator lights change.

The cab slowly rose up to the ballroom level of the Fort Garry Hotel, River City's oldest and most opulent hotel. The queen had once stayed here, but now it was mostly used by tourists or for weddings.

"Listen, Jimmy, the classics never go out of style."

He still couldn't get used to the massive, armed, Arnold Schwarzenegger circa 1982 mountain of a man talking to him with the voice of his dead partner. The legs like tree trunks, the long and flowing hair, the rented tuxedo and bowtie—none of it was the leathery old man he knew, and yet both Samantha and the behemoth believed it to be true.

"Exactly how many times have you pulled a stunt like this?" Jimmy asked.

"Crashing parties was half the job in the eighties, kid."

"We're not here to pull off some crazy prank, we're just here to lace a drink with Ipecac. Nobody's mingling, we're not pulling a caper while distracting a bad guy, we're not even going to talk to anyone if we can get around it. We don't need to complicate this by turning it into a big clusterfuck."

Even though he wasn't supposed to be working, Jimmy had been calling in sick for three days. Too paranoid to go back to the precinct in case the chief had another Veronica clone waiting for him, he'd stayed in the motel room with Frank, reminiscing while watching old reruns. The more they talked, the more it became clear to him that even if the guy wasn't actually using Frank's brain, he at least had all of his memories.

"You're starting to sound like a real killjoy," Frank said.

"We get in, lace the drink, and get out with Rick," Sam said. "No more than that."

"And if it doesn't work?" Jimmy asked.

"Improvisation," Frank offered. "I'll think of something."

"We are so screwed," Jimmy said.

"No improv," Sam said. "Just follow the plan. It's going to work."

Disguised as caterers and a waiter in a tux, the three of them looked like something right out of a Three Stooges movie. It was almost too stupid to work.

"This is almost too stupid to work," Jimmy said.

"Trust me, kid, it's the stupid plans that turn out the best."

"Take this." Sam pressed a vial of Ipecac into Frank's hand. "Put it in the glass when it's time to hand out champagne for the toast. It'll do the rest. I hope."

"What exactly will it do?"

"If Rick was drugged like I was, it'll get him to spit out the worm thing; if not, then it'll just make him sick."

"And that helps us how?" Frank sniffed the open bottle before restoring the lid.

"When Rick goes to the bathroom to throw up, we grab

him and run away."

"I have to admit," Jimmy said, "it's simple and elegant. It gets him away from the group and gives us a way to get out of here without being recognized."

"Now, Frank," Sam said. "It's important that when you're out there in the crowd, you look for people with what look like scars or recently healed wounds on the backs of their necks. That means they've been altered. If Rick's got one, then we're going to have to perform a little minor surgery, too."

"You've done this before?" Jimmy asked.

The elevator doors pinged to the ballroom level. A sign directing people to the engagement reception for Rick Hansen and Debbie Peterson pointed them to the left. Another for the staff directed them to the right.

"Too many times," Sam said, walking out. "Now let's do this thing before it's too late."

* * * *

"He's going to cause quite a scene if he reverts to the little kid," Jimmy said, as Frank took a tray of hors d'oeuvres out to the floor.

"Let's just hope he stays as old Frank."

"I'm not so sure that's better." Jimmy watched as Frank shoved a plate in front of two elderly guests in fancy dress.

* * * *

"—perfect time to get into equity funds, a balanced portfolio should show meaningful growth in as little as six months."

"Look, Gramps," Frank said. "These things aren't going to eat themselves, so cram a few in and your waistline will show growth in as little as six minutes."

Frank shoved the tray towards the man who looked at him wide-eyed. He awkwardly lifted a tiny sausage roll and took a nibble.

"You, too, Edna," he said to the woman.

"Are these free range or ethically—"

"From the looks of it they used to be pigs. Trust me when I tell you it doesn't matter how free their range is, they still roll in shit all day. So just eat it before it gets cold, okay?"

She cautiously took one and put it in her mouth.

"There we go, enjoy the free food, folks, I'll be back with more later."

* * * *

Ornate wall mouldings, oil paintings, plush red carpet, the place was definitely high society. The crowd was full of some of the top people in town, including most of the River City Jets. Sam recognized faces from the team calendar she'd pinned to the wall in the apartment. She tried to see the backs of their necks through the crack in the swinging door that separated the kitchen from the ballroom, but everyone had collars on. They were showing the beginnings of playoff scruff. It was tradition to grow beards and let their hair get shaggy as the team tried to win the Stanley Cup. Some were getting a head start. The playoffs were supposed to start in two days. This was going to be the last chance for most of those guys to let loose before they had to focus hard for, potentially, weeks more hockey. But if they'd been turned already, would they even *be* able to cut loose?

"You, what are you doing?" a voice shouted at her from the kitchen behind her.

"I, uh…" Sam stammered as she turned around to see a woman in a dark suit moving through the kitchen like she ran it. "I was just—"

"I know what you were doing. Checking out the guys from the team. There's no time for fucking around, get back to work. Wait," she said, pausing. "I don't recognize you."

"First day," Sam said.

"Oh, great. This is my biggest contract of the year, and they send me a fucking noob. This is supposed to be perfect. If you knew how much of a fucking Karen the bride to be was, you wouldn't even think about standing there ogling guys. Of course, why would you care, it's not your reputation or name on the company. You're just a goddamn temp."

"Hey, wait, I—"

"If you think you're going to get any part of the tip payout, then get the fuck back to work and don't let me catch you here again. I do, and you're out the door, got it?"

This was always a part of the plan she'd anticipated. Infiltrating the chaos that surrounded a catered event wasn't tough, it was keeping out of anyone's notice, that was the challenge. One she'd just failed. She took one last look at the party and saw Rick talking to guys from his team. He seemed normal enough. She quickly moved into the kitchen and tried to find something she could do to look busy.

"I'm on it," she said.

The woman quickly lost interest and ran off shouting at someone else. "Not those. Those go out after the pâté."

* * * *

Jimmy watched Sam disappear through the kitchen doors out of sight and Frank moving through the crowd with a tray. Dressed as an usher, he tried to look like he was manning the entrance while also monitoring the crowd.

When she'd told him her plan, he'd protested trusting Frank to be the one to slip the syrup. "Why don't you do it?"

Sam had pointed to her forehead, at the large mole above her eyebrow. "Everyone in there I went to high school with would spot me in a second. And you're walking with a cane. How the hell are you going to carry trays of food or drinks?"

His part was to wait for Rick to run out to the bathroom and corner him in the men's room. He hated being on the outside, but as he watched Frank move, he had to admit that so far at least, the ruse seemed to be working.

* * * *

A photographer weaved through the crowd, taking snapshots. Frank had a new tray of hors d'oeuvres to distribute. A couple of women eyed him as he passed by. Other people picked food off the tray, hardly noticing him at all.

The room was a hustle of activity as servers kept the crowd fed. On the other side of the doors, it was worse, with an army of cooks slaving away on dozens more appetizers and desserts for later. Nobody took notice that he wasn't supposed to be there. He looked the part and, so far, was acting it perfectly.

Was there ever any doubt?

"You there"—someone waved at him—"what are those?"

He carried the tray over and held it out to the young woman

334

in a ballgown who eyed him up appreciatively. "Wieners," he said. "Good ones, too, I hear."

She raised an eyebrow. "Didn't they tell you any more than that?"

"What else could you need to know?"

She ran her hand along his arm and smiled alluringly. Dark-skinned, of Indian ancestry if he had to guess, she downed her glass of alcohol and dropped it awkwardly on his tray.

"You know who you remind me of?" she said, slurring her words. She must be drunk already. "Fabio. Remember that guy? He was like some kind of model... are you a model?"

"No, ma'am. I'm a waiter," Frank said.

"I bet you'd look so hot in a loincloth." She ran her hand along his chin.

* * * *

Not seeing any sign of the bitch from hell running the show, Sam frantically moved away from the station she'd claimed, lining up crystal glasses, and moved back to the door. She wanted to know how Frank was doing.

Scanning the crowd, she spotted him talking to a woman.

"Oh, shit," she said.

It was Nan, one of Debbie's crew from high school. She didn't know what they were saying to each other, but the woman waved over her friends. The entire Slug gang—Xiu, Emily, Lindy, and Stacey—came to join her. It was John A. MacDonald High School's original crew of *Mean Girls,* the same people that had tormented her for years. She'd expected them to be here, but seeing them in the flesh brought back mounds of painful memories.

335

"Come on, Frank, ignore them. They're bitches."

She saw Nan whisper to Emily and point at Frank. The others were hanging off him, picking food from his tray, playing with his hair.

"Shameless skanks."

She only hoped Frank could handle the attention from five young, hot, drunk girls. Looking back over her shoulder, she spotted the woman in the suit moving through the kitchen. She let the doors swing shut and ran back to her station.

* * * *

"What does a girl have to do to get a refill around here?" the blonde one asked him flirtatiously.

"Come on, Stacey, leave him alone. Can't you see he's busy letting us eat his sausage?"

Another one laughed, suggestively sticking a wiener in her mouth and biting the tip off.

"You're a big one. Do you work out?"

"Of course he works out, Emily. I'll bet he looks great with his shirt off."

"Oh, can we see? Please?"

"Now, ladies, I'm supposed to be—"

"Serving people," one said. "Doing whatever it is we ask you to do. Isn't that right, Xiu?"

The smallest one, Chinese, smirked. "Oh yeah, we're the bosses, don't you know?"

"Really?" he said, confused. "Did Mommy tell you that?"

Five girls. Old enough to be his babysitter. But which one was in charge? And where was Mommy? Frankie saw a lot of old people talking to each other, but no sign of his mom. But

336

at least he had lots of food. It looked good, too. He grabbed a few off the plate and ate.

"Oh, yeah," the dark-skinned one said. "Mommy told you to do whatever we say. You don't want to make Mommy mad, do you?"

"No way," he said and bit into one of the wieners. It popped with a spray of sauce on his coat.

"Oh no, you've got it all over you. How about we go and find somewhere to clean you up?"

"Did Mommy say it was okay?"

"She sure did." The woman took his hand and started to drag him through the crowd.

* * * *

"What the hell are you doing, Frank?" Jimmy said, seeing the girl leading the man towards the doors out of the ballroom. He looked softer, more innocent, like he was… a little kid.

"Oh, shit," Jimmy said as they both passed right by him. Four other girls, laughing together, trailed the two of them. They all seemed pretty drunk already.

Jimmy met Frank's eyes and tried to catch his attention, but the man didn't seem to know him.

They were taking him down the hall to the washrooms.

"This is not good."

* * * *

Sam put more glasses of champagne onto trays, unsure how many were too many, but arranging them in a circle.

A hand grabbed her on the shoulder.

"What? I am working!"

She turned to see Jimmy looking frantic.

"We have a problem," he said. "Frank just went to the women's washroom with five drunk girls. And I think he was, uh, little Frankie again."

"Oh, fuck." She turned away from the tray. "I'll handle this." She took two steps away from her station when the woman in the dark suit came charging around the corner.

"You again? Where the hell do you think you're going?"

"The bathroom?"

"Not until everyone out there has champagne in hand for the eight o'clock toast. Nobody leaves even if they have to piss themselves standing up."

"But I—"

"And you, unless you're in white, get the fuck out of the kitchen," she shouted to Jimmy.

"I—"

She looked like she was about to bite his head off. Jimmy turned tail and hobbled out. "Was just leaving!"

* * * *

"My, what big muscles you have," the woman said as she helped Frankie slip off his jacket.

"Gee, thanks."

"Is there anything else big you've got?"

"I have a pretty big truck in my sandbox."

She giggled. "I just love big… trucks."

"Me, too. You should come over and play sometime. I'm sure Mommy would say okay and—"

"Mommy wants to play right here," she said.

The other girls laughed as they fixed their make-up at the massive sink and mirror. "Nan, you're so bad."

"Oh no," Frankie said. "I'm not supposed to play with bad people."

"But I'm nice." Nan slid her cold hands down the front of his pants. When she grabbed his special zone, he froze in fear.

"Mommy said nobody's supposed to touch me there."

"Oh, but Mommy said it was okay this one time."

Holding him tight, she backed into the large bathroom stall. Because of the grip, he had no choice but to follow. What kind of game was this supposed to be? It made him feel uncomfortable. He wanted to call for help, but she said that Mommy told her it was okay.

She kicked the stall door shut and pulled him in for a kiss.

"Come to Momma."

* * * *

"Oh shit, oh shit, oh shit." Jimmy stood at the entrance to the two bathrooms. He had to get Frank out of there before something crazy happened.

"I have to go in."

He reached for the door, but it swung open. Four attractive women in ballgowns stepped out, blocking him.

"What are you doing?"

"I'm, uh, about to, uh, check the plumbing."

"You some kind of pervert?"

"No, staff. I heard reports there was a backed-up toilet and —"

"It's fine. Occupied. Now go before we tell your boss."

Faced with a line of four angry women, he looked at the shut door and prayed Frank was okay.

* * * *

"So hot," the woman said. "This is so hot."

"Is it summer?"

"I don't know, this is just hot."

She kept kissing him. Why was she being so gross? Yuck, yuck and double yuck. She ran her hands all over his body, around his neck, then up into his hair. She grabbed a handful and pulled him down, but his head didn't budge, just his hair. It came off in her hands. The wig dangled loose, and she looked at it, confused.

Then she looked at him, seeing his bald head, criss-crossed in scars and stitch marks. Her eyes grew wide. She screamed. Her eyes rolled back into her head, and she fell over to land seated on the toilet.

Frank reached out and picked up the wig from the floor, replacing it on his head. He waved his hand in front of her face, but the woman was out of it.

"Can't handle her liquor, I guess." He left the stall. He saw his reflection in the mirror, straightened the hair, fixed his jacket and bowtie and pushed outside.

* * * *

"Frank, is that you?"

Jimmy stood anxiously pacing on the other side of the four women who'd formed a human shield in front of the door.

"I should hope so, otherwise who the hell was that in the

mirror?"

The four women turned to look at him, surprised.

"That was fast," one said snidely.

"Tell that to your friend."

"She's still in there?"

"Sleeping like a baby."

They parted to let him by as he walked towards Jimmy.

"Did you?"

"I should hope not. I was underage."

They looked at him confused as he marched back towards the ballroom. Jimmy hobbled after him.

"What happened?"

"If those walls could talk, kid. I'll fill you in later. We have a drink to spike."

He joined the crowd and headed towards the swinging kitchen doors.

* * * *

Sam ran her hands over her head, frantically trying to work out some improvisation to save her plan. Should she just run away and crash into the bathroom? The slugs would recognize her. There'd be a fight at the least, then what? Five versus one. Jimmy wouldn't be much help. Frank had regressed again. What if someone heard the commotion? It would blow the whole thing.

Shit, shit, shit, shit.

"No other choice…" She pushed away from the champagne trays just as Frank came storming towards her.

"Frank!"

"The one and only. Now give me some booze."

She was about to hand him the tray when he pulled out his bottle of Ipecac and poured some in a glass.

"One drink spiked."

"Just make sure Rick gets that one."

"Gotcha."

"You there," the woman with the dark suit shouted to Frank. "The toast is about to happen, get those out of here."

"I'm on it," Frank said.

"And you, they need help with the desserts, go and make yourself useful."

Sam turned to Frank. "You got this."

"I got this," he said.

"Of course he's got this," the woman said. "Now go, before I fire your ass!"

Sam ran off, leaving Frank.

* * * *

Frank faced the tray which contained the glass he'd poured the Ipecac into. He tried to remember which one it was, but it had slipped his mind. Pointing at each one, he went through the mental math. Second from the left? Third?

Oh shit, was that the spiked one? Or was it that one? Maybe the other one?

He stepped back, trying to figure out which of the cups he'd dumped Ipecac in, counting them, losing track, then giving up.

"Time to improvise."

He poured his reserve bottles into as many glasses as he could, emptying out all three Sam had given him. He didn't have the chance to do every glass before other waiters started taking trays.

"Let's hope this works." He took his tray and pushed through the doors into the ballroom.

A man stood at a podium with a microphone. Waiters moved through the crowd, while more emerged from the kitchen with additional trays of champagne.

"—are passing around the glasses of champagne for a toast to the future bride and groom. Everyone, grab a glass."

A hand took one from Frank's tray. Then another. He spotted his quarry and moved through the crowd towards Rick. People took glasses, quickly depleting his supply. He came to Rick, who was empty-handed. Another waiter cut him off. Rick took a glass from him.

Frank ducked in the way and snatched it out of his hand.

"Hey!" Rick said.

"Sorry, sir, that one had a bug in it. Take this one." He was all set to give him one from his tray when he realized he was out.

"Uh, what one is that?" Rick asked.

"Gimme a second, I'll go get some more."

Frank ran back towards the kitchen. He burst through the doors to see an empty table with no more trays of champagne.

"Frank, what's wrong?" Sam said, running back to him,

"I ran out. Rick didn't get it."

"Oh, great." Sam looked through the doors. "Wait, he's got one in his hand."

He joined her at the door and saw it to be true. He examined the glass in his hand and looked back to Rick. "Let's just hope it's one of the good ones then."

* * * *

One of the girls from the bathroom clutched an unfolded piece of paper as she read into the microphone.

"—talking about how she was going to have a big wedding and wear a princess dress when she got older." The woman broke down crying. "And now, she's going to get to do that. I'm so happy for you, Debbie. To the future bride!"

"To the future bride!"

Everyone took a drink.

"Okay, that's two," Jimmy said. "When is this stuff going to start to take effect?"

A slender man with slicked hair took the microphone and tapped it.

"Julian Gerber, Rick's boss. But I'd like to say his friend. I wanted to toast the new power couple of River City. May your future wedding be the icing on the cake of the year Rick helps bring home the Stanley Cup!"

Everyone cheered and toasted again.

"Three now," Jimmy said. "Let's see some action."

* * * *

Sam peered through the door with Frank, watching Rick, waiting for some sign that he was going to be sick, but he looked completely fine.

"Come on, Rick, spew. Hurry up and spew!"

* * * *

"—two became inseparable. Through good times and bad, heartaches and people trying to split you up. You stayed true to each other and here you are. Raise a glass to Rick and

Debbie's future. It's so bright." The man reached into his jacket with his free hand and pulled out a pair of sunglasses. "That I gotta wear shades!"

Everyone chuckled and took another sip.

"Almost the whole glass now," Jimmy said. "Come on, come on, come on."

* * * *

"—kind and thoughtful and someone who always…" The man at the microphone started to cough. "Always…" He coughed again, then lurched forward. His skin started bubbling. Greenish pustules swelled out, foam poured from his face as flakes of it cracked away, revealing the carapace beneath. The flesh started melting all over his suit. The woman next to him screamed as her face began smoking and dripping away. Then another scream and another filled the room as it descended into chaos.

Watching from the doorway, Sam could only stare wide-mouthed. "What the hell did Frank do?"

Suits and ties, dresses and ballgowns, caught fire. Horrible growls of agony as every other person started to bubble and boil and dissolve away into sick green puddles.

Rick grabbed Debbie in a hug as they watched in horror. Sam saw Julian Gerber disintegrating, his skin peeling away in long strips of spaghetti, as he imploded into himself.

"Frank, get Rick." Sam pointed.

The big man ran through the sea of screaming people and deflating corpses towards Rick. He scooped him up under the waist before the man could move and ran towards the ballroom exit.

345

"Oh shit, wait for me," Sam said and followed.

"Where the fuck do you think you're going?" the woman in black shouted after her and grabbed her arm.

"Lady, I quit."

"You can't quit, you're f—" She saw the chaos through the kitchen ballroom doors and her jaw dropped.

"No way I'm cleaning up that shit." Sam broke the grip and tore after her friends.

* * * *

"Quick, in the elevator," Jimmy shouted, propping the door open.

Frank charged, the kicking form of Rick Hansen on his shoulders. Behind him, Jimmy could see the insane madness in the ballroom as the young and the old were crying out in horror or pain from turning into a pile of smouldering goo.

Sam was close behind. The two of them crashed into the elevator as he let the door close. He'd already pressed the parkade button.

"Holy fuck," Sam said, panting. "Frank, what did you do?"

"What you told me, spiked the drinks."

"You were only supposed to spike Rick's," she said.

Frank put the man down. "I improvised."

"But why the hell did people start melting?" Jimmy asked.

"Maybe that's what Ipecac does to the alien physiology?"

"Sam?" Rick said as he realized who was in the elevator with him. "What the heck are you doing here? And what the hell did you do to my engagement party?"

"You can thank me for saving you later, right now I need to see the back of your neck."

346

She spun him around before he could react and saw the scar at the base of his hairline.

"Guys, hold him for a minute, I need to cut this out of him."

"No!" Rick batted her hand away. He backed up into the wall away from them.

"No?" Sam said, confused. "Rick, they've implanted you with a stone again. I have to get it out to save you and—"

"Sam, fuck off. Did you ever stop to think I don't want you to do that?"

"That's the stone talking." She took out a steak knife she'd pilfered from the kitchen. "You'll feel better when I cut into your neck and forcibly remove the gem."

"Don't you dare. Don't even try it. I've had it with you and all of this, okay? The stone clears my head. I don't even have to think out there on the ice and I play like Wayne fucking Gretzky. Understand? I'm having an amazing season. The team is in the playoffs. We have a real shot here."

"You're under their control!"

"So? It's the Stanley Cup. Think about it. The Jets have the story of the ages here. A player who died from a tragic overdose, superstar comes back from a contract dispute, goalie attacks rookie, then rookie overcomes injury to lead the team to the cup. It's almost like it was all planned out. We can't lose."

"That is a hell of a tale," Frank said.

"Exactly, this guy gets it. Wait, who are you exactly?" Rick asked.

"Rick." Sam brandished the knife. "What about free will? What about not being a meat puppet of the Authority. What about being the best you are but also human? You saw what Fritz was and—"

347

"All of that shit is overrated. This is the Stanley Cup. The hardest trophy to win in all of pro sports."

"But Debbie is working with them."

"So? She's had my back all this time and she's a fucking smoke show. I'm the envy of every red-blooded man in the country and I'm a superstar in the national game. My life is pretty goddamn sweet."

"Again, he has a point, kid," Frank said.

"Shut the fuck up. Rick, I'm not taking no for an answer. I'm saving you from the Authority and that's that."

She moved to go after him with the knife. Jimmy stepped in the way.

"Sam, you heard him. He doesn't want you to."

"That's them talking."

She pushed Jimmy. He tripped over his cane and fell hard to the ground. She grabbed Rick's hair and yanked his head down. She tried to stab the scar with the knife when a hand grabbed her wrist. It was Frank.

"You shouldn't hurt people like that, Mommy," Frankie said. "It's not nice."

"It's okay, Frankie, Mommy is just going to cut the bad out of him."

"No. You're being bad. You should stop."

The elevator pinged. The doors slid open to reveal a family carrying suitcases. Two kids and two parents stared at them, Sam holding a knife, Frank holding her, Jimmy struggling to his feet, Rick flinching.

"We'll, uh, take the next one," the dad said.

The doors shut again, and Jimmy pressed the hold button, freezing them in place.

"Frank, let go."

"Sam, stop," Jimmy said. "You heard him. He's happy where he is."

"How can he be? He's a golem."

"You heard Fritz," Rick said. "I've been one my whole life."

"No, you haven't. You've been working for a life that you earned. Don't take the easy way out."

"Maybe I want the easy way out, huh? Maybe I'm tired of working so hard. It's the Stanley Cup, Sam. You can't understand what that means to a hockey player."

The knife shook in her hand as she struggled against Frank's grip. Finally relenting, she dropped it to the floor.

"You're right. I don't understand. I made a promise that I'd save you, but it's your life. You have the right to choose what you want to be a slave to."

Jimmy let go of the hold button. The elevator doors opened up to reveal the family still standing there.

"Uh. Still waiting for that next one."

"Come on. The police will be here soon. Leave him and let's get the hell out of here," Jimmy said.

"Yeah, Mommy," Frankie said. "I want to watch cartoons!"

Jimmy hobbled out, pulling on Sam's hand. She resisted for a minute, but then let herself be pulled out, too. Frank leapt over the doorway with a skip, smiling happily. The family stepped inside, next to Rick. The dad kicked the knife away.

"Going up?" the dad asked.

"Yeah. Ballroom please," Rick said.

The doors started to close. Sam rammed her hand inside, forcing them open again.

"Are you sure about this? Once you're one of them, that's it."

"I have everything I ever wanted, Sam. Hopefully one day

349

you will, too."

She looked at her impossibly handsome ex, with his muscled form poured into his dishevelled suit, dark hair and firm features, and was only reminded of what she'd lost. What she'd had a crush on so long ago, what she'd briefly tasted, only to toss away for another. She knew she would live to forever regret that choice. She understood now why she'd wanted so desperately to save him from the Authority, why she cared beyond reason despite claiming not to, who it had always been for her, even when she never saw it. Erin and Meg were right and wrong—she was a tourist, but not in her sexuality. She'd tried to find others, Joshua, Scott, even Erin, but nobody could measure up. Had he never told her how he felt back in high school, had she never had the chance to be with him, even for that short while, she might have been able to live never thinking they could be possible, never knowing what it was like. Her heart would always belong to Rick, but now his belonged to someone and maybe some*thing* else.

"I'm not so sure that's possible," she said and took her hand out of the door space. The elevator shut tight and took Rick away from her. Forever.

Chapter 42

"—truly a stunning turn of events—"

"—unprecedented maneuvering—"

"—Vachon forced to step aside—"

"Tonight's top story, how the member for River City South Centre, Daniel Kirby, took over the job of Prime Minister and—"

The news kept happening. The country was changing. She didn't want to leave the motel ever again. As the days went on, it kept getting grimmer.

"Later, on the National, our 'At Issue' panel discusses the remarkable cross-party unity that has brought forth the series of sweeping omnibus bills that are set to fundamentally alter the fabric of—"

Click.

"The River Jets continue their stunning playoff resurgence—"

Click.

"Hansen is showing grit, heart, and determination. He's got the entire city behind—"

Click.

The longer she stayed inside, the further down the spiral they went. She didn't care anymore. What was there to care about? She just lay on the bed, eating chips, watching terrible old TV shows with Frank.

"The King of Kensington's on," Frank said. "You'll like it. It's about this guy who—"

"It doesn't matter what it's about," she said.

Jimmy pushed open the door. He carried a brown bag of food in one arm as he limped inside.

"You two look terrible. Have either of you gone outside lately?"

"Why?" Sam asked. "We have everything we need right here."

He deposited the bag on the small table in the corner. "This place is starting to look like a dump. You two have heard of trash cans, right?" He swept empty wrappers off the table and into the bin, then slid more along the carpet in piles.

"They have maids for that stuff."

"Not here, they don't. I'm not sure this place has ever been cleaned."

"What does it matter?" Sam said matter-of-factly.

"Look," Jimmy said. "I know you're depressed. Believe me, I'd like nothing more than to just stay here and eat junk food too, but things are happening out there. Dan Kirby is the prime minister, that guy Maddox is some kind of media darling, the Jets are kicking ass in the playoffs. There's been police outside my apartment for weeks now, at yours and your parents' house, too. They're looking for us but instead of doing something about any of that, you're just hiding."

"What do you want me to do? What can we do?" Sam said.

"Give me a gun and I'll show you," Frank said.

"You can't shoot everyone, Frank. They've won. The Authority beat us. Their plan was too big. We're no team of heroes. I'm a twenty-year-old student, he's a one-legged cop, and you're half-man and half-kid."

"But that half is fifty percent more man than any of them. And even though I'm only operating at seventy-five percent right now, this body's got a good sixty percent more bang in it than my old one. Which still puts me over the red line. I'm somewhere around a hundred and forty percent man. Which should be more than enough man to deal with those things we saw at the hotel."

They both just looked at Frank in confusion.

"Wait, what?"

Frank dug into the grocery bag. He found a Mars bar and raised it above his head like a trophy. "Mine! I call firsties. Mars, mars, mars. Mine!"

Jimmy looked to Sam who just shook her head sadly. She pushed herself up from the couch and walked to the bag, digging out a package of instant noodles. She filled it with water from the bathroom tap and shoved it in the ancient microwave next to the room door. She tapped in five minutes and turned back to Jimmy.

"He's getting worse," she said quietly.

Jimmy watched Frank tearing into the candy bar, bobbing his head to some kind of invisible tune. He sat cross-legged and watched the TV with rapt attention, more than any kid now would give to the King of Kensington.

"I've noticed," Jimmy said. "He ping-pongs back and forth between personalities much faster."

"It's not just that," she said. "He's decaying. I've seen this before. My, uh, first ex, Joshua. After a while the magic or bonding agent or whatever the hell makes golems breaks down. They grow weaker, then eventually fall apart and die

353

again, I guess. It's happening to him. He's losing muscle mass. I have no idea how long he has left."

"Maybe it's better he gets to spend the time watching TV. I imagine that's what he was doing in Shady Acres. Or at least what he would have been doing if he hadn't been investigating the body-snatching conspiracy."

"It's his second chance at death," Sam said.

"Is there anything we can do?"

"Joshua begged me to smash the stone that controlled him. It released the magic bond and let him die in piece. But we have no idea where Frank's is. Who has it, anything."

"Then we look for it. At least it's better than just hiding away in here."

The microwave pinged and Sam pulled out the steaming paper cup of noodles. She dipped a plastic spoon inside and stirred them around.

"I've been fighting this for so long, Jimmy. Since high school. Even when I thought I wasn't, I was. And what did it get me? I've lost all my friends. Rick chose to walk into their arms willingly, Igor was mutilated and burned to death, my parents sold out, what's left? I've got nothing to fight for anymore."

Jimmy reached out and grabbed her elbow to stop her from sitting back down. "I've lost people too, but there's always something to fight for. There's always hope. You can't just give up."

"I already have, Jimmy. I'm sorry."

* * * *

It was peaceful down here by the river. The snow was

receding slowly as the air warmed up. The air was fresh and clean. Jimmy's feet crunched in the snow as he let his mind wander. Carter and Olivia playing in the snow, Veronica's smile, waking up next to her; days when all he had to worry about were Frank's horrible reports.

His leg was feeling stronger. He still needed the cane, but he could see the day coming when he could throw it in the trash. He was alive. So far, his paychecks hadn't stopped, and the chief hadn't sent out the force en masse. They either didn't think he was a threat or figured that eventually they'd find him and he'd be an easy catch.

Either way, that felt like an opening they could exploit.

The path alongside the river ended at a small park. Beyond was mostly bush, the backs of some towering apartment buildings with riverfront views, and a few massive old mansions that he'd never visit unless someone was murdered in one. The scene was quiet. No one else was out walking at this time of night.

The moon was up, an owl calling out in the darkness. He felt, for a moment at least, free. But he knew that this was only temporary. Eventually they'd have to leave the motel. Then what?

* * * *

Frank coughed violently. His massively muscled form hunched over as he heaved. When it was done, he stared at a patch of red on his fist. He licked it once. Blood?

"That's strange," he said. "Maybe that Mars bar disagreed with me."

He looked over to see Samantha staring at him sadly. "Why

so glum?" he asked.

"It's nothing, Frank," she said.

"Had you already called that Mars bar?"

"Yeah. Yeah, I did."

* * * *

He just kept walking. It felt good to stretch his legs, test out his endurance, get away from the depressing sight of Frank and Samantha living in their own filth. Now he had the news that Frank was dying again to deal with. Another knife in the gut. At least this time, he'd have the chance to say goodbye the right way. How does someone do that?

"Frank, I know we had our arguments but being your partner was the best training a cop could ask for. I learned so many things not to do that it made me a better officer. And I'll never forget the time you arrested yourself for murder. The guys always get a kick out of that story."

He chuckled to himself. "Nah, just keep it sweet. He won't want anything mushy or too emotional."

A pair of lights danced in the brush ahead. Flashlight beams. Someone was down by the river's edge. Probably just some people looking for a late season skate on the trail. But then it was spring. Hadn't they closed the thing?

"Shit, it's probably not safe. I'd better go break it up."

He pushed through the snow, using trees as leverage, closing in on the flashlight beams. He saw three men at the base of a clearing. They'd parked a van at the end of a cul-de-sac and were dragging some kind of bag down through the snow. A trail led all the way back up the incline. He couldn't make out the writing on the van, it was black and nearly invisible in the night, had it not been for the snow cover.

The men wore parkas, with hoods lined with fur. One was using a shovel to pound through the ice, digging down to the water level. The others were aiming their lights to help him see.

"—could help, you know. This would go much faster with another digger."

"We only brought one shovel. You want me to use my hands?"

Jimmy leaned up against a tree, watching. He took out his phone and snapped a few shots, just in case.

"There," the first man said. "I'm through. Now get the stuff."

"Finally," the second one said. "My grandma could have dug faster."

"Fuck off."

"Here's the bag. Just dump it so we can get out of here. I'm getting cold."

"Nobody told you to leave your gloves back at the lab, dipshit."

One of the men dragged a black bag towards the hole. He worked at untying the handles with bare hands slowed by the cold.

"Okay, you guys are the ones with the gloves, so go to it."

"So that's why you fucking forgot them. You clever bastard."

The man just grinned.

They were all three of them slender, pale-skinned, bland-looking guys who needed a tan. If he had to guess, he'd say they worked in an office and didn't get outside much. Maybe IT workers. But then one of them pulled something out of the bag that made his jaw drop.

The man held a severed arm and pushed it into the hole in

the ice. "See ya later, arm."

The next man came up with a leg and dangled it over the hole. "Want to see if it sinks on its own?"

"Quit screwing around," the other guy said. "Just ditch the stuff."

Jimmy snapped another picture, then pushed around the tree and hopped towards them. "Hey, you, stop. Police."

The men all turned to him and froze.

"Hands up," Jimmy said, not wanting them to know he was unarmed.

They all raised their hands. One of the men was holding an arm.

"Officer, it's not what you think," one said.

"I think you're throwing human body parts into the river."

"Okay, then it's sort of what you think."

"Those aren't human limbs?"

"Uh, not exactly?"

The three of them could have run away. He'd never catch even one of them with his bad leg, but they were so caught off guard by his sudden appearance that they just stayed put. None of them seemed like the kinds of people who had dealt with the law before.

"So that's not a human arm you're holding?" Jimmy asked the man with the extra limb in hand.

"I know it looks like one, but trust me. This is medical waste. We work in a lab and—"

"Hey, that's top secret. Remember the NDAs."

"Oh, shit, right. Okay, we work in a... uh, place that makes these things. You know, like, engineering. I can't really say more than that without getting sued and I don't want to lose the job. It pays fucking great. Bonuses, pizza parties, Chinese even. Yeah, we don't get to leave much but—"

"Dude, shut up."

"Oh, right, sorry. Forget all that. Just know that we're only dumping medical waste into the river, not like actual human body parts. Well, they are, but they're not being used. Or they were used and didn't work out. I'm not entirely sure. That's a different unit. I was in the sound triggering group that—"

One of the guys punched him hard in the shoulder to shut him up.

"Hey."

"Shut up."

"Right. Okay, sorry."

"Guys, even if I believe your story, which I don't, mind you. What the hell would make you think you can dump medical waste into the river?"

"It's easier. There's so much red tape with this stuff and we've got deadlines and—"

"What the fuck? No! That stuff washes up later. People like me, you know, cops, think it's a dead body and we spend time investigating it. Shit, haven't you guys heard of the arm and a leg bandit? We've been finding parts everywhere. There's a fucking task force on it. My partner, uh, late partner was in the thick of it. We had no leads. The media was on our asses. And you're telling me it's been you guys all along?"

"Not exclusively us," one of the men said. "It's just our turn. We thought the river was a better idea because of the whole winter thing. Maybe the others just threw theirs out of a window or something."

"For fuck's sake." Jimmy took a step towards them. "I'm confiscating those parts and I'm going to have to take the

359

three of you in."

They all looked to each other. Something silently passed between them and in a flash, they bolted up the hill.

"Hey, wait!" Jimmy said, trudging after them. The incline was too steep, he had no push off his leg. His cane slid and he fell face first in the snow.

"Stop!" he called out, but they were all in the van. They slammed the doors shut and peeled out before he could even get halfway up the hill.

"Goddamn it." He brushed himself off and walked over to the hole. There was no sign of the limbs they'd tossed in. He snapped a photo and started the long walk back to the motel.

* * * *

"—appointed special director of a new youth outreach program, inviting students of all ages to a live town hall in two weeks' time. Maddox says he has a message of hope for a bright future that he wants to present to everyone in the country. We've already had confirmation that school divisions in every major city are going to be connecting into the livestream and—"

Click.

"The new omnibus bill receives royal assent today, putting forward sweeping changes to—"

Click.

"—investing in unproven technology like this has the potential to put Canada at the forefront of a technological revolution."

Click.

"Rick Hansen celebrates his game-winning goal to advance

the Jets to the final round for the first time in team history—"

Click.

"I promise Canadians that we'll have a great unveiling of our party's plans for the next decade in the coming weeks. I've already asked for network time to—"

Click.

"Would you just pick something and watch it?" Frank asked.

"It's all shitty news," Sam said.

"Then go back to the reruns."

Click.

She froze when there on screen was Molly Ringwald sitting on a countertop as Annie Potts put on a record.

"—one more tune then it's off to enjoy a terrible relationship. Furrier next door loves this." The record starts, Annie Potts points off screen, someone bangs on the wall.

"Oh no…" She knew this movie. She knew this scene. She'd watched it a hundred times with Duckie… Trevor.

Jon Cryer slid into frame with his goofy hair and mustard jacket. He started dancing as Molly Ringwald watched in horror.

Every memory came flooding back in a torrent. Her entire childhood: nights alone with Duckie, the two of them ostracized for being different, hated by everyone, treated like dirt by Debbie and her slugs. He'd loved her, he'd never given up on her even when she'd never noticed. The twisted magic of the stones had corrupted him, jealousy ate away at his mind, but he'd cared about her. The evil had broken him, just like it had broken everyone she knew. Now it was breaking the country itself. She might be the only one who even understood what was going on. She might be the only one that could stop it. Instead, she was sitting here moping. Frank only had so much time left. Instead of letting him waste away, they could try together to do something… anything. At least it would be trying. She had to hold out hope for… hope.

She couldn't let the Authority have the future. She couldn't let them win without a fight.

The door opened. Jimmy came in sweating, with snow-soaked pants, looking like he was going to pass out.

"I did it. I solved the arm and a leg bandit case. They got away. But I know what was going on now and—"

"That's great, Jimmy," she said, rising to her feet as Jon Cryer danced. "Now tell me, how much money do you have left in your bank account?"

"Uh, enough. Why? You want to move hotels? Maybe something with a hot tub?"

"No. I want to go to Ottawa."

"Ottawa, why?"

"I've lost everyone who cared about me and everyone I cared about. The bastards think they've already won, but they're wrong. I won't lose my country, too. We're going to stop Kirby, Maddox, and anyone else they're controlling."

"How?"

Frank perked up. "A really big gun?"

She looked at him, feeling like she had hope for the first time in a long time. "If that's what it takes."

Chapter 43

"Mr. Speaker, this government has ended the scourge of partisanship. We have ended the tradition of party unity and opposition. And we have ended the petty political squabbles that made so much of the day-to-day work of running a country more inefficient than it ever needed to be. Unlike our predecessors throughout history, this party has shown that a common, unified goal brings members of all stripes together. And together, as one, we will bring forward the future that every living Canadian has long dreamed of."

The room erupted in applause, the kind of applause usually reserved for golf games. There was none of the standing and stomping of feet, no jeers, catcalls, or shouts, not even a dissenting voice. Every single person in the chamber responded in polite kindness.

"I've never seen it like this," Jimmy said.

"Where's the hatred, the mistrust, the disagreement, the antagonism... where's the life of the place gone?" Frank asked.

They sat in the upper gallery, watching as Dan Kirby spoke to parliament and the entire country. This was a speech being broadcast to everyone on every channel and live on the internet. Unless you were actively seeking to not watch it, most of the country would be tuning in, in some way or another.

"He's taken it all away. How many of these members are golems, or clones, or whatever it is they did to the students?"

"Judging by the applause, I'd say maybe all of them."

She'd never thought that the Authority's conspiracy could go this far. It had seemed so localized before, despite what Fritz had promised. A minor league rock group, a washed-up boy band on a reunion tour, NHL players... but parliament was as high as you could go. They'd gotten their man into the top spot all while she'd been busy trying to save her friends and her ex. Their true plans had been going on in the background, on levels way beyond her. There'd been nothing she could have done. Nothing any of them could have done. It was too vast.

"At least it makes our targets easy to pick out," Frank said.

"Even Vachon seems like he's one of them," she said, looking at the pockmarked and red-faced former prime minister who'd astonishingly stepped down to allow Kirby to sweep to power.

"I never liked the guy," Jimmy said, "but at least he wasn't replacing people with mind-controlled golems."

"Looks to me like he was the first one they went after," Frank said.

Vachon applauded mutely along with everyone else.

"I don't even understand what the fuck happened," Sam said. "Right under our noses."

"If we only watched CPAC," Jimmy said, "maybe there'd have been some warning."

"Kid, nobody watches that shit. They could have been

showing reruns and who'd know?"

"They used our systems against us," Sam said. "What we listened to, what we watched, what we took to get high. They changed how we thought, how we acted, who we associated with. It was all a distraction, a way to grab control of the country. But for what?"

All around them was the majesty of the seat of Canadian government, the old-world wood and green leather decor that had served its people for a hundred and fifty years. Now it seemed a mockery of everything it had stood for.

They sat watching the proceedings from the gallery, along with a few tourists. Most people who came here quickly grew bored and wandered off to look at the rest of the massive parliament building, maybe tour the library or admire the photo of Joe Clark in Centre Block, even peruse the gift shop. But the three of them stayed, watching, eyeing each and every member for clues that they were no longer normal humans.

"Mommy, this is boring," Frankie whined.

"We're almost done here," she whispered.

"Can't we get ice cream now?" He seemed on the verge of a tantrum. He'd been regressing even further back lately, and the spells seemed to last longer. The plane ride here had been an embarrassing disaster. They'd almost caused an early landing until Sam had managed to convince the cabin crew that Frank was "special."

They couldn't afford another scene like on the plane. Here, his voice would echo through the cavernous viewing area and call attention to them. That was the last thing they wanted. Not with what they were here to do.

"Mommy!"

She had to get him out of here fast. "Okay, Frankie, we'll

go get some ice cream."

"Yaayyyyyy!" He ran to the exit. A guard near the doorway looked at her with a raised eyebrow.

"Come on, Jimmy," she said. "We've learned what we needed to."

"But Kirby hasn't gotten to this great unveiling he keeps mentioning. It's got to be important, right?"

She saw the camera crews filming as the man spoke to the nation, flashes going off every few seconds. The moment was being captured a thousand ways.

"Something tells me we won't miss it."

* * * *

"So," Jimmy asked, "we really going through with this? Taking Kirby out live on CPAC? We'll be international fugitives. Where will we go? Russia?"

"I don't know if there's anywhere we can go," Sam said, scrolling through her phone in the public washroom off the main hall. No matter where she looked, the same thing was happening all over the world. On every channel, in every language, all over the internet. World leaders were giving speeches to their citizens in some kind of massive, unified message. She didn't understand what most of them were saying, but she thought it was probably the same thing Kirby was right now. She turned the phone to Jimmy to let him see what she'd seen.

"It's everywhere. All at once."

"So even if we take out Kirby, what do we accomplish?"

Frank stripped off his jacket and started ripping off the internal liner, pulling out clumps of what looked like playdough, wires, and metal inserts.

"It's all we can do," she said, watching him assemble the vest.

"You really think you can just walk up there and shoot him, Frank?" Jimmy said, turning to him. It was then he saw what Frank was taking out of his parka. What he was assembling was an explosive vest with enough power to blow the whole place up. "Whoa, what the hell is that? I thought you were just going to smuggle in a gun."

"It's the big one, kid," Frank said. "Enough boom to kill 'em all and let God sort 'em out."

"Where the hell did you get all that?" Jimmy asked. "And how the hell did you get it past the metal detectors?"

"I called in a few favours from some old friends. Hadn't spoken to them in years. Took a few tries at the old code words, but they listened. Hooked us up. And metal detectors are easy to fool with the right tech," Frank said, tapping his torn coat.

"We're just going to blow the place up? We'll be terrorists."

"You two won't be anywhere near here. I'll be the one blowing it up."

"Frank," Sam said. "That wasn't what we talked about. You were—"

"We both know I'm here for a good time, not a long time. You said it yourself. This new body's not long for this world, right?"

She looked to Jimmy—he hadn't told him, had he?

"I didn't say anything," he said.

"You didn't have to. I'm old, not deaf. Well, the mind is. Sometimes. Look, I already died once, and it sucked. It wasn't the way a man like me should go out. Drugged and chopped

367

up into pieces. A man like me needs to go out guns blazing in a hail of bullets. But since this body would probably be able to take too many, I'd rather make it quicker... and more impressive."

He slung on the vest, surrounding his body in explosives. A detonator button dangled from a handheld remote that he grabbed in his palm.

"There's got to be another way," Sam said. "We can look for the stone, I can—"

"Nah. I don't want to fall apart into my component pieces, or waste away into a twig. Let me do this and make one last statement."

"What if there are still some regular people down there?" Jimmy asked. "We don't know that they're all compromised and—"

"The tree of liberty has to be watered with the blood of patriots and tyrants, okay? I think Thomas Jefferson said that."

"You're taking the advice of an American? We can—"

"You were okay with the idea of shooting Kirby," Sam said.

"Yeah, one guy, not taking out the entire seat of Canadian government."

"You've got to cut the cancer out completely," Frank said.

At one time, the thought of incinerating the entire parliament building would have seemed insane to Sam, back when she was a normal teenage girl living her insular life in River City, believing that everything was on the level. But now, a conspiracy of epic proportions had changed her reality. Dan Kirby was seemingly the head of it all in Canada, but who knew where he fit in internationally? It would take someone else to stop this globally—all they could do was try to save

Canada. Even if it didn't work, at least they'd tried.

"You sure this is what you want?" she asked Frank.

"I'd prefer a bottle of jack and a whore. Maybe another go with Southside Annie. She knew her stuff. I ever tell you—"

"You're going full suicide bomber here," Jimmy said, cutting him off.

"Yup. And you all better vamoose before I change my mind."

He slid his jacket back on over the bomb vest. He looked at his bodybuilder physique in the mirror one last time and smiled.

"Too bad I couldn't have enjoyed this body a little while longer. I'll bet I'd have been a big hit down at the beach."

He walked out the door, leaving them alone.

"We should stop him. Innocent people are going to die here," Jimmy said.

"Innocent people already have."

* * * *

Frank held his coat closed with one hand, the other gingerly gripping the detonator control as he walked the marble halls back into the viewing area. The politicians below him were like ants sitting in their chairs as Dan Kirby spoke. God, the guy just kept going on and on and on.

"Boring," he said, rolling his eyes.

Why do old people have to talk so much, don't they have anything better to do? Couldn't he just wrap it up and go for ice cream?

"Ice cream, that's a good idea." He looked around the seating area for some place to get a cone, but it was just a boring old building.

"Mommy, I want ice cream."

His coat flopped open. He wondered why he was wearing a playdough vest. Below him, the old man was reaching a key point in his speech.

"And now," the man said, "that we are unified together under one rule, we can reveal the truth. The time for the great unveiling is at hand. Please, watch and understand. We are your leaders. But we have always been here. Your bankers, your CEOs, your champions of industry, heads of state, emperors and kings, drivers of technology, pushers, engines for the advancement of your collective growth. You are nothing without us and have always been so. But now, now you are ready to learn the truth. The great unveiling."

"I'm so hungry," Frankie said. He broke off a piece of his playdough vest, sniffed it, then took a bite. It tasted funny, not like playdough at all. *It tastes almost like...*

"Jesus," Frank gasped, stopping himself. He spat the piece out of his mouth. *What the hell was I thinking?*

Down below, Dan Kirby was fiddling with his neck, reaching into the skin as the cameras flashed and recorded it all.

"Behold your true rulers!" the man said.

He ripped off his skin mask. A woman screamed. The man's face was some kind of carapace. His deep-set eyes glowed yellow. His teeth were exposed, without lips, his nose a gash in the skull-like face. Dan Kirby wasn't human. Some in the seats began doing the same, tearing their skin free to reveal more of the creatures. A commotion broke out as a few shocked people downstairs began shouting.

Guards swarmed them and brought them down to the ground. They began shoving something in their mouths. Frank looked to his right. He saw a guard approaching him.

To his left, another one. He was next.

"Well," he sighed, "no way around it, time to go full Paul Joseph Chartier."

He stepped to the edge of the viewing area. He thought about his life, his career, the years of fighting the good fight. The women, the places he'd been, the hotdogs he'd eaten. Not even Satan himself had been able to stop him.

"Time to paint the town red," he whispered as the men closed in.

"Mommy? Mommy, where are you?" Frankie was too high, he didn't know how to get down.

"She's dead, kid, but she's waiting for you on the other side," Frank said, trying to calm the little voice inside him.

"I want to see her now!" Little Frankie protested.

"Me, too."

Frank teetered on the edge of the railing, looking down on the house. The two men were rushing towards him. It was now or never. He depressed the detonator button.

"Sic Semper Tyrannis!" Frank shouted and jumped off the platform.

Chapter 44

They were running past the Centennial Flame when they heard the explosion. The shockwave knocked them both to the ground. Sam spun on her back to see a great cloud of flame shoot two hundred feet up into the air. Smoke plumed from the gaping hole where the parliament building had once stood. Fire raged as sirens wailed in the distance, people scattered, the debris fell like rain. She pushed herself to her feet, using the carved shields of the provinces on the monument.

"Do you think he got them all?" Jimmy coughed beside her.

"I don't know." Sam brushed herself off. "I hope so."

"He got to go out with a bang like he always wanted."

Looking at her phone, Sam saw the news flooding through every channel. It had all happened live. The replay showed a man jumping from the gallery, then an explosion of white that cut off the picture.

Sirens and security swarmed to centre block. Firetrucks converged on the area, the nation's crisis team going to work. From through the wall of smoke, they watched.

"So, what happens now?" Jimmy asked.

"They revealed themselves to the world," Sam said, watching people discussing Kirby and other leaders removing their masks. "Everywhere."

* * * *

"—you see that profit margins rose in the third quarter and—"

Kylie and Darby sat in their high-backed chairs in the boardroom, looking at each other in shock. Their boss, Vernon, spoke as if nothing had changed, and yet he'd started the meeting with an important announcement where he'd somehow removed his face. Then George and Lynn had followed suit. Now, three people with monstrous, shell-like skin and glowing eyes shared space around the table with seven others frozen in shock.

Should they run away? Should they call the police? Kylie didn't know what to do. Vernon went about his usual weekly presentation the same way he always did. Darby shrugged. Jerome, Betty, and Carlton all just turned their palms up and sat intently.

Finally, Vernon finished and turned from his spreadsheet projections to the rest of the room. His strange alien eyes seemed to glow.

"Any questions?"

Kylie raised her hand.

* * * *

"This is your captain speaking. We are pulling up to the runway to prepare for departure as soon as we're cleared. It should only be a few minutes' delay."

It was so exciting to be in an airplane for the first time. Declan sat eagerly in the seat. Leaning forward and looking out the window, he saw the terminal in the distance, planes coming and going, the sun shining above. He couldn't wait to take off.

"Sit straight," his mother said, pulling him back to the seat. There was something wrong with her. She was looking nervously towards the front of the plane.

"What's wrong, Mommy?"

"Just sit tight, okay?"

Maybe it was something to do with the stewardess walking down the aisle checking everyone's seatbelts. Her face was all wrong. Like the skin had been peeled off and her skull was on the outside.

"Seatbelts on?" the thing said. Her voice was normal, she just looked like a monster. But Declan's mom couldn't stop staring.

"Mommy, it's not polite to stare."

* * * *

Isaiah Washington tapped his fingers on the counter, playing a beat he'd heard somewhere once, but had long forgotten the name of. The glass top was worn out from years of people sliding packages and coins across it. Beneath the surface he could see the various custom stamp and coin sets that this particular branch of the post office had for sale. Hockey players, famous actors, landscapes, nothing that meant anything to him. He couldn't remember the last time he'd even mailed a letter.

Today's finally the day, he thought to himself. *After all those years of courses, I've finally got my diploma.*

He'd handed his missed delivery notice card to the clerk,

shown her his ID, and waited for her to find his envelope in the back. It felt like things were finally looking up for him. After so many false starts, so many hardships, he'd achieved something.

"HR management professional," he said. "I like the sound of that."

The grey sliding door swung open and the dark-haired older woman, the post office clerk, walked back towards him. She looked like she'd seen a ghost.

She handed the manilla envelope that held his brand-new degree to him and he immediately tore open the seal and gingerly removed the paper. There it was, certification. Fancy cursive letters that told the world he was something now.

"Check this." He held it up for her to look at as she returned to the cash register computer. "This means no more security guard work, no more overnights, no more getting hit on the head, working with crazy old man murderers, no more guarding the back doors to the arena, no more freaky puck bunny stalkers, no more listening to Duane shit on me, no more being a no*body* and a whole hell of a lot more of being a *some*body."

"Congratulations," the woman said. There was something wrong with her—her fingers shook, her face had gone pale, like she was spaced out or something.

"Hey, you okay?" Isaiah asked. "You look like someone just died or something."

"Haven't you seen the news? Heard about the bomb?"

"Bomb? Hell no, I took the bus down here as soon as I found out you guys had my letter."

"They blew it up!"

"What? The bus? Shit, good thing I wasn't on it then."

"No, parliament, in Ottawa."

"So a bunch of old white dudes went up in smoke, plenty more where that came from."

"Not just that. Didn't you see? We were being ruled by... horrible creatures."

"Yeah, old white people. What else is new?"

She turned her phone to him, showing him a video of some kind of shell-faced thing giving a speech.

"What the fuck..."

Just then, a panicked woman in a bright red shirt, the uniform of the drug store that housed the local post office, came rushing to the counter. "Jolene, Jolene, we've got a situation here." She didn't even acknowledge Isaiah, which was typical with white people.

"What is it, Sandra?"

"On the news? Did you see? The bombing?"

The postal clerk nodded. "I saw. It's awful."

"Those things. The prime minister. They're everywhere," Sandra said, pointing to people walking through the aisles of the store, oblivious. One had the same face as that creature.

"What do we do? Are they dangerous?"

They both turned to Isaiah with plaintive looks.

"Oh no," he said. "I'm done with this. This HR management certification diploma means I don't have to help any more desperate white woman. I'm—"

"Could you at least talk to it? We don't have security here. At least until we can call the cops."

He looked at the shopper, minding its own business, seemingly content to stare at skin care products. He slid his diploma back in the envelope.

"I knew I should have just stayed home and waited for this goddamn letter."

Isaiah walked down the skin care aisle towards the browsing creature.

"Excuse me... uh... ma'am?"

* * * *

Another careless driver going right through the stop sign. It never failed to wait here, parked a half block away from the intersection near the community club skating rink. He'd catch at least a few every day.

"Gotta make that quota," Officer Banks said. He trudged to the stopped car on the edge of Laxdall Road, near the ditch that was filled in with all the leftover snow pushed off the road by the plows. Soon it would be completely melted. A few faint pieces of grass poked through. No matter the season, he'd be right back here waiting.

He didn't get to do much more than play traffic cop. The guys called him the highway patrolman of the suburbs. But he ignored them. It was quiet here. He didn't have to deal with anything close to what they did downtown, or in the north end. No bums, no strung-out drug addicts, no violence. Just people breaking traffic laws because they thought the cops didn't bother them here in the southwest of River City.

He had his ticket book ready to go, already knew how this was going to transpire. If it was a man, he'd argue that he stopped, if it was a woman, she'd play dumb, bat her eyelashes a few times, hope he went easy on her.

Joel Banks didn't go easy on anyone. That was why he had the highest traffic infraction caseload in the precinct. He was making over six figures a year with overtime and court appearances. It was also why he was safely ensconced in the cushiest part of the city, doing the easiest work a cop could do.

He knocked on the window. It looked like a woman. He could see the outline of long hair through the window. It whirred down with a press of the automatic button.

"Ma'am," he began but then stopped and dropped his ticket book in the snow.

"Officer, I'm so sorry, I was just a little distracted and—"

"What the fuck are you?" he said and had his gun out, aiming at the skull-faced thing sitting in the Nissan, idling on the lonely snow-covered road in the middle of the safest neighbourhood in town.

* * * *

The sound of the horn jarred him back to reality. The red light blazed, the Anaheim goalie lay dejected on the ice. The fans were on their feet, screaming. Music blared over the PA system. The other guys were skating towards him, throwing their sticks in the air. What had happened? How'd he—

Jonesy leapt on him, Patrick scooped him up, Dave and the others swarmed him.

"You fucking did it, Hansen. Way to fucking go!"

"I did?"

Elation, emotion, a screaming arena throwing their beer and popcorn in the air in a massive celebration. He looked up at the scoreboard, saw Jets 5, Ducks 4. Second overtime.

"We won?"

"No fucking shit we won, Hansen!"

He saw the Stanley Cup waiting in the aisle to come to the ice. He saw frantic jubilation and the crew setting up red carpets for the ceremony. He saw it all and had no idea how he'd gotten here.

"What a goal! What a motherfucking play!"

"I scored?"

"You did good, kid." A hand slapped him on the shoulder. He turned to see Coach Chapman grinning at him. He had no skin. His teeth were exposed, his eyes yellow lights, his face a carapace of white over black sinew.

Rick screamed along with fifteen thousand fans. It was only then that he saw just how many looked like Coach Chapman.

* * * *

My first time. What'll it be like? Is he really the one?

Pia lay anxiously in bed, under the hotel sheets, wondering what was taking Nathan so long. He'd said he was just going to freshen up in the bathroom. What did that even mean? Maybe he was putting on cologne. Maybe guys had to do something with their dicks beforehand. Who knew? She'd finally convinced him to come and do this, to sleep with her so she could stop feeling like she was the only one of her friends to still be a virgin but now her chosen date was leaving her high and dry.

"Nathan?" she called out. "You okay?"

The bathroom light shone into the hotel room hallway. He'd finally opened the door. She tensed up, nervously waiting for what she was about to see. Was it true that dicks looked like snakes? Did they move on their own? Were they gross to look at in real life?

"You ready?" Nathan said.

"Sure," she said as suggestively as she could.

Would he like her? Would he respect her after? Were her boobs right? What about—

He stepped out into the room and stood naked in front of her. Her eyes rose up from his feet, higher...

Something was off. His skin wasn't... where was his skin?

Higher, higher. Exposed bones? Sinew? What was going on? Then, the face. Yellow eyes, exposed teeth. She couldn't even scream.

"Hey babe, ready to get busy?" he asked.

* * * *

A crowd had gathered at the Centennial Flame, confused gawkers, hippies with drums, painted dancers, men and women in uniforms, parents and children. Everyone was wondering what was going on. They watched as the crews battled the fire that raged over the parliament building.

"Now what?" someone asked.

"I heard they're all dead," another responded.

"They say Pierre Vachon did it, bitter over losing his job."

"No way, it was some top-secret agency taking out that alien thing."

"I saw more of them on the way over here. They're everywhere."

"Anyone have a gun?"

Cars sped down the streets, some stacked high with suitcases and supplies.

"Looks like people are panicking," Jimmy said.

"We're in uncharted waters now. The federal government's

wiped out. Everyone's learned we're not alone. There's going to be questions, freak-outs, riots maybe."

People began stripping out of their clothes. The drumming began. Dancers moved around the fire slowly.

"Welcome to the future, I guess," Jimmy said.

Parents hugged their children, sirens blared, a baby screamed. A crowd was converging on the devastation.

"Another tent city?" Jimmy asked her.

"I don't know. We'll see, I guess."

A burning hole in the ground was all that was left. How would the country respond? And what was going on around the world? What did the Authority want next?

"Why is no one telling us anything?" someone shouted out.

"Should we say something?" Jimmy asked her.

"What would we tell them?" She stared at the fire. "All we can do is hold on and see where this ride takes us."

"Then we'd better get back to River City," Jimmy said. "I don't want to hang around here."

"Why? What's there to even go back to?"

"I still haven't finished that TJ Hooker DVD set," Jimmy said. "And besides, I have a feeling it's going to be better to be home when things start to shake out."

"I did also give post-dated rent cheques on my apartment," Sam said.

* * * *

"So that's it? The project is done?"

"You've all served your purpose. You've made great strides for the human race. But now it's time to move on. We're shuttering the research departments, effective immediately.

381

Don't worry. Your developments are going to serve the Geld corporation and the Authority for generations to come."

"What about our bonuses?"

"Taking solace in knowing that you helped enslave your entire planet and undermine the fabrics of your carefully built societies all through subtle manipulations, hypnosis, and impulse direction? That you cracked the code of the human will and allowed us to implant ourselves in every position of authority needed to begin the process of making this world over for our own ends? That you, unwittingly, were traitors to your entire species? This profound knowledge isn't enough for you?"

"I was kind of hoping for cash actually."

THIS IS NOT THE END!
MORE TO COME IN RIVER CITY HELL BOOK 4:
THEY CAME FROM WITHIN!

AFTERWARD JEREMY DANGERFIELD

When I was in University I could never manage to get into the filmmaking class. There was a strict class size limit and I was somehow always just too late to grab a spot. So I did what anyone in that position would and took classes at the local arts collective instead. The Winnipeg Film Group was a great place to learn how to make a short, experimental film but I was young and impatient and decided that instead of doing that, I would make a full narrative feature.

I'd just seen *Blood Feast* and figured that the model of a low budget gore-fest interspersed with some police procedural scenes would be doable. So, a couple of us got together and did a little brainstorming and from that, I went off and wrote the script for what became *The Killing Death*.

But a script is just a piece of paper. We logically knew that we'd need actors, props, locations, effects, etc. We trolled thrift stores, called in favours, checked out a local acting class and put up an audition notice on a few bulletin boards. I had no idea if anyone would show up, let alone anyone that would fit the parts.

Then one bright summer's day in 2006, in my parents backyard, some actors began arriving. Each one was gracious enough to read the sides I'd put out. All were talented and eager, but one man in particular blew us all away. His stage name was Jeremy Dangerfield and he was a seventy-five year old retired former crown prosecutor. He was acting just to stay busy and involved in his old age. Of course I wanted him for the role of Frank Malone, but I had no idea if he'd agree to work for free for a group of know-nothing University students.

Spoiler alert. Not only did he take the role, but he made it more than what I'd even envisioned at the time. Throw away lines became zingers, his confusion at what was going on was palpable (and probably real), and his seriousness and years of experience in court gave everything he said a gravitas beyond what was on the page.

He shared with us a lifetime of amazing stories from famous and infamous cases he'd prosecuted, was incredibly kind and generous with his time, not only to work with people who were flying by the seat of their pants, but also to come back a second time for *Cybernetic Showdown*. All for no money too!

It turned out that things were about to change for him. A few of his prior cases had turned up with irregularities and he became the unfair target of a media witch hunt. He decided to spend his final years in British Columbia, away from the hounding press.

Ambitious reporters, learning that he'd been in two of my movies started approaching me, at first feigning interest in my work, but then revealing their true motives of wanting to get in touch with Jeremy. Each and every time I shut them down. I felt, and continue to feel a huge debt to how much he helped me, but also how much he inspired me. No amount of personal press would be worth selling out the man who I credit with everything I've done since. I sincerely believe that

I wouldn't have been able to write the 40 or so odd books I've written without that initial performance he brought to THE KILLING DEATH. He's who I picture in my head every time I put to paper a new Frank Malone adventure. I imagine him acting it out, chuckle, and wish he could have had the chance to make twenty more movies with me.

Jeremy quietly passed away in late 2023 but news didn't trickle out until early 2025. He spent his final years in privacy, away from the spotlight. He was a tremendous guy and will be greatly missed.

JEREMY GEORGE DANGERFIELD (1931-2023)
RIP and thanks for everything

About the Author

Author, filmmaker, martial artist, collector, gamer, dad; Winnipeg based I.D. Russell has been crafting a shared universe of books and films for the past decade and a half. Beginning with the feature films *The Killing Death* and *Cybernetic Showdown* and continuing with the *High School Hell* and *Revengist* book series, his crazy comedy/horror/action stories have found an international audience. *Political Suicide* is the third book in the *River City Hell* Series and the latest project expanding the world of River City Police Officer Frank Malone and University student Samantha Abraham. The next four books in the series have been written, so plenty more is on the way!

Check out *The Killing Death* and *Cybernetic Showdown* now streaming on Amazon Prime, Tubi, Vimeo, and Gumroad. Visit the YouTube pages *Ringo Jones Productions* and *Jeremy Sockman Movie Reviews* for additional content or click to www.ringojones.com to stay up to date on all upcoming work!

Follow on Facebook, Twitter, Instagram, and YouTube!

You can connect with me on:

- http://ringojones.com
- https://www.facebook.com/IDRUSSELLAUTHOR
- https://www.instagram.com/idrussellauthor
- https://www.patreon.com/ringojones

Subscribe to my newsletter:

- http://ringojones.com

Also by I.D. Russell

The story of Frank and Samantha expands in:

Sudden Death: River City Hell Book 2
Killing the song wasn't enough.

Samantha Abraham thought she'd stopped the madness when she ended the pop careers of Radiant Cyanide and Factor 5ive. But little did she know that there was much more to this sinister plot than just a few hit songs. The River City Jets hockey team is the next target for the shadowy figures of The Authority and it's going to take all she has to save rookie sensation Rick Hansen from one monstrous transformation.

Waking up from a Rock 'N' Roll Nightmare, she finds herself facing...

SUDDEN DEATH!

Rock 'N' Roll Nightmare: River City Hell Book 1

High School Hell was just the beginning...

Samantha Abraham graduated, her best friend and golem boyfriend didn't. Hoping to put their deaths behind her, she's off to River City University for a fresh start. Great friends, fun parties; life in the big city was everything she'd hoped. Until she meets Scott, the mysterious, tortured lead singer of the rock band Radiant Cyanide. Their music doesn't just make the crowd go wild, it might be making them go insane...

Suddenly her dream life is turning into a ROCK 'N' ROLL NIGHTMARE

Beyond the Dark Forest

Time has no meaning in the dark places.

Rock Peak lake, deep in the heart of the Whiteshell, a pristine patch of wilderness that has stood since time immemorial. Every year people flock in for a chance to experience the rustic life. But on this weekend camping trip, it won't matter if you're a retired cop, a rock star, an influencer, or an experienced outdoorsman, no one is safe from what lurks in the trees.

Between now and then something stirs BEYOND THE DARK FOREST

Demon in the Sack

Game Over?

The streaming life isn't for everyone. Spending your time hanging out, eating pizza, and playing as many video games as your eyes can handle takes hard work and dedication. But when one third of the popular *Three Gamers* show decides to start looking for love outside of blinking screens and six button controllers, he finds out that while there might be someone for everyone, he's just become the target of a creature not-quite-human.

This one's not after his fame or money, but his SOUL!

Cursed Words
Some stories should be left unwritten…

Fifty years ago the Van Lundgren estate was the sight of unspeakable acts of evil. The truth has been long buried and forgotten. Now, the house is re-opening as a bed and breakfast and twelve souls show up for the weekend. But some crimes transcend time and when a raging thunderstorm traps them inside, the guests start dropping one by one. Soon the survivors are going to learn that some horrors can never truly be locked away.

Trapped in a nightmare, there's only one truth…

Sticks and Stones may break your bones but Cursed Words can KILL YOU!

Under Blood Lake

Somewhere in the darkness below the surface of Lake Winnipeg, the Deep Ones are waiting.

He thought it was just a simple weekend trip to put his brother's affairs in order and lay him to rest, but when River City's toughest cop shows up in the sleepy harbour town of Lakeshore, he unwittingly steps right into a community suffering under an ancient curse. Someone is pulling the strings and suddenly he's got bigger fish to fry. Off duty, without a weapon and under orders to stay on vacation, can Frank survive when he faces up to creatures more inhuman than real?

The Killing Death

He was ready to retire but then a madman started leaving victims in pieces. Can this aging cop solve one last crime before a killer finishes his deranged pizza?

When an unhinged pizzeria owner stumbles on an ancient Egyptian ritual, he begins a spree of brutal killings that leave a city in shock. It's up to veteran detective Frank Malone and his rookie partner to piece together the clues and catch the murderer. One problem, this isn't just a simple case of catch the bad guy, it could resurrect long dead spirits of evil.

With Egyptian magic, action, gore, and an insane ending you won't believe, this comedy/horror book is a wild good time!

Heart of Stone (High School Hell Book 1)

It's bad enough being the most unpopular girl in school, but when a strange new exchange student shows up, Samantha Abraham discovers she may be in love with a golem.

It was love at first sight for Sam when Joshua, the dark and mysterious foreign student from Eastern Europe, walked in to class. He's dreamy, great at hockey, and she's landed the chance to be his tutor. But the more time she spends with him, the more he seems to harbour a sinister secret. It's starting to look like he's a criminal, but he might also be a monster . . .

With the help of her over-zealous, secretly- crushing BFF Duckie, and with the popular girl bullies nipping at her heels, Sam must go up against a bunch of weird science, and a hellish high school social life, before she has a remote chance of a first kiss . . . or of surviving the Halloween dance.

Heart of Clay (High School Hell Book 2)

Samantha Abraham has the power to magically control her boyfriend's every action, but now someone wants that power—and wants him dead.

After the fallout from Heart of Stone, Sam has learned the truth: that her boyfriend, Joshua, was created in a lab by a mysterious scientist known only as The Professor. A magical ruby gives her the power to control him by thought. It seems like the perfect relationship, until a gauntlet of assassins show up in River City with murder on their minds.

On a quest for the truth that takes her to Toronto and into the den of her enemies, can Sam, Duckie, and hockey-hunk Rick save Joshua's life before it all goes to hell?

Heart of Flesh (High School Hell Book 3)

Samantha Abraham lost everything when she lost Joshua—but the fight for the ruby, and what it means, isn't over yet.

Sam is back in River City and the events of Heart of Clay have left her raw. If deranged necromancers were bad, you'd think Debbie and her slugs would be small potatoes, but Sam's life has gone straight back to hell in her senior year. Even with her high level hapkido skills, and a budding relationship with hockey hunk Rick Hansen, nothing seems to fill the gaping hole that Joshua and Duckie's disappearances have left . . .

But just as suddenly as he vanished, Joshua reappears with grave tidings, and Sam must decide what lengths she'll go to prevent her life—and her boyfriend's body—from falling apart.

Drug Wars Part 1: Lethal Dosage

Yellow Sunshine. More addictive than opium, more potent than cocaine, more dangerous than heroin. It ruins lives, destroys communities, and threatens the very country itself. It will take the River City police force everything they have to fight the scourge from street to bloody street.

Someone's dealing the worst drug the city has ever seen. THE REVENGIST is on the case with a brand new partner and a list of broken lives he's going to avenge. But to find the source of the poison, they'll have to go so far undercover that they might never make it out alive.

Drug Wars Part 2: Blood Money

MechaMountie. The secret CSIS project in cybernetics set to revolutionize the world of law enforcement. Stronger than ten gorillas with a brain faster than twenty IBM computers, the robot is laying down the law in a city under siege!

After the death of Eddie Camponelli, River City is in chaos. Rival gangs are shooting up the streets, attempting to gain control of the drug trade. The police are powerless until the government sends in their top secret weapon.

Now THE REVENGIST is in for the fight of his life to prove that no robot can do his job better than he can. He's going to show that he's still got it, even if it kills him!

Drug Wars Part 3: Iron Curtain

Ninja. The silent assassins. Using ancient martial arts techniques passed down through the secret orders of hired killers, they stalk by night and murder without a trace. Now they've come to River City and it's not to sightsee!

He might have killed the world's biggest drug supplier in Carlos Mendoza, but that only made the real bad guys mad. Now they're after him with everything they've got. In an all out battle for the future of Canada that spans the globe, THE REVENGIST is in a fight for more than just his life!

The explosive finale to the Drug Wars trilogy!

Go-Team # 1: Bitter Rivals / African Assault

The old Go-Team is gone, long live the All-New Go-Team. Led by Jessica "Doll-face" Dawes; they're sent in to infiltrate a tiny African nation in the throes of a bloody civil war. Their mission: to try to preserve the peace in the face of a brutal warlord.

But are the supreme sniper Brutal-Suzy and the kung fu assassin Hunglo enough to take on the American's better equipped, highly public, no-so-secret commando team: Uncle Sam Squad?

It's a battle between Bitter Rivals for the right to save Baangolo in an African Assault full of action, suspense, and... spring break?